Slave of Chu Kutall

Slave of Chu Kutall

Michael McCloskey

iUniverse, Inc.
New York Lincoln Shanghai

Slave of Chu Kutall

iUniverse books may be ordered through booksellers or by contacting:

iUniverse
2021 Pine Lake Road, Suite 100
Lincoln, NE 68512
www.iuniverse.com
1-800-Authors (1-800-288-4677)

Cover art by Gerald Brom

ISBN-13: 978-0-595-37854-8 (pbk)
ISBN-13: 978-0-595-82227-0 (ebk)
ISBN-10: 0-595-37854-4 (pbk)
ISBN-10: 0-595-82227-4 (ebk)

Printed in the United States of America

Dedicated to my reviewers, without whom this novel would not exist:

Kristi Allard, Derrick Barnsdale, Susan Bowers,
Ralph Halse, Charles K. James, Anna Kassulke, Ryan Morini,
Kip Mussatt, Steve Westcott, David E. Wile

CHAPTER 1

Slave of Chu Kutall

Night had fallen and the war galley of Chu Kutall rested quietly on the waves. In the inky darkness below decks, Nergal rubbed his aching arms and legs. The great brute rested on the rowing bench, having ousted his oarmate to the floor nearby. Only two days now, and already Nergal felt thinner and weaker. The hulking half-orc greatly regretted his foolishness in the city of Woldwall, which had led to his capture and enslavement on this ship.

Nergal had contemplated for many hours how he would enact his escape from this hellish prison. A single heavy manacle wrapped his left ankle, joined by a thick chain to the sturdy oak rowing bench. Nergal's oarmate, the scrawny mainlander who called himself Skaggs, had an identical manacle on his leg. Unseen in the gloom, more benches around them held other slaves the same way. The odor of their sweat filled his nostrils. He heard the steady sounds of their breathing and the creaking of their benches.

Nergal rolled over on the rowing bench, fumbling for Skaggs in the darkness. He succeeded in grasping Skaggs by the neck with one meaty, powerful hand. There was an exhalation of surprise from the annoying man, and then Nergal felt Skaggs's smaller hands lock around his forearm, attempting to break the half-orc's grip. His other huge hand slapped across Skaggs's face and opposed the force of his grip on the man's neck. A muted pop and snap told Nergal he now manned this oar station alone.

The half-orc allowed himself a moment of satisfaction, until he smelled the released urine of his victim from below his bench. Although annoying, it was not a terribly bad smell by the way Nergal reckoned things. He reached down again, this time for Skaggs's hand, which he pulled up to convenient biting distance. Placing the dead man's forefinger into his mouth, Nergal bit the member off and began to leisurely clean the flesh from the severed finger with his teeth. Having had a primitive upbringing, he did not find the taste unpleasant; in fact he savored it somewhat more than strictly necessary.

The heavily muscled half-orc had eyed the keys to his manacles on the officer's belt for the entire first day, fixating on the item of his salvation to the exclusion of all else. However, during today's rowing, Nergal had spent a great deal of time thinking about killing his overly talkative oarmate and mutilating his corpse so thoroughly that even his mother would not recognize him. During these rather limited imaginings, he had come up with a most satisfying plan. Taking the bone from his mouth, he felt the rounded ends of it in his grimy fingers. Selecting a spot below one rounded end, Nergal placed it against the outside of his manacle. He began to scrape it back and forth, putting a great deal of force onto the finger bone.

Nergal scraped the bone for a long time. Twice he stopped, thinking someone had heard the noise and come to investigate. When he heard nothing, he continued. Slowly he wore down the bone until the knob flattened into a tab like the key he had so desperately eyed the first day of his enslavement.

Nergal attempted to place the modified finger bone into the lock and turn the mechanism. Extreme displeasure struck when he found that he could not grip the other end of the bone with sufficient force to turn the bone tab. Nergal snarled and stomped on Skaggs's body in rage, breaking several more bones in the corpse. It made him feel a little better. He waited silently for a while afterwards, in case he had made too much noise. That had always been his problem with thievery: the necessity for silence. Nergal much preferred the openness of outright murder and pillage. He had experienced more success as a highwayman and brigand than as a burglar.

The half-orc clenched his teeth and forced himself to remain quiet. If only Skaggs were still alive, Nergal thought, he would make him pay for the failure of his finger bone. If only he could have taken the bone without killing the man. One of Nergal's teeth was rotting in his mouth, and it pained him greatly as his jaw muscles worked. This gave Nergal another idea, which he considered equally brilliant to his first. Taking his manacled foot up onto the bench, Nergal placed the bone firmly between his clenched teeth and tried to insert it into the keyhole.

Try as he might, Nergal could not quite reach his foot with the key in his mouth. Now at last the scream of rage escaped his lips, erupting forth through his self-control like an exploding volcano.

"Aarrrrrrghgghhhhhhhh!!!!! Skaggs is son of fairies! Arrrghghghhh!!" he screamed, spitting out the carefully fashioned bone.

Now there was a commotion amongst the oarsmen, and the light of a lantern appeared at the stairs on the end of the hold. A guard peered into the darkness several rows beyond Nergal's grisly scene of mayhem.

"Shut yer holes ye useless arses! If ye wake the capt'n it'll be yer hides!" Having delivered this warning, he walked back up the steps.

Darkness returned to the smelly, crowded hold. Nergal could barely sense the grumbles of the other slaves. They did not have the courage to curse at Nergal openly, even though they knew he bore shackles like the rest of them. Nergal considered them beneath contempt—even worse than Skaggs—because at least Nergal had been able to shut him up at last. Yes, Nergal thought, smelling the urine in the darkness, he liked Skaggs the best of them all.

If only smarts came to me easier, thought Nergal, *the key plan would have worked.* The officer demonstrated too much wisdom to ever get anywhere near Nergal with the key. The half-orc just didn't have the flexibility to reach his foot with the key in his teeth. But now, as he was forced to think again (a rare occurrence), Nergal realized he had almost been able to reach the keyhole.

Once again, the half-orc reached for Skaggs.

"My best friend, Skaggs," uttered the orc under his breath. He brought up a foot this time and began to chew hungrily on the fetid body of his erstwhile oarmate. Nergal produced a considerably longer foot bone this time, ideal for his needs. He went immediately to work on the bone, forgetting entirely to test its length before beginning his labor.

"What's that noise?"

Nergal thought he recognized the voice, that of a bald man with a sickening smile, who sat chained across from him.

"Be quiet," commanded Nergal in a growl as he continued scraping the pirated bone against the rough surface of the manacle.

"What are you doing?" asked the man after another moment.

"Be shutting up," Nergal said more loudly, and then remembered he had to be quiet as well. Nergal stopped scraping for a moment and applied the full force of his brainpower.

"I will be killing you, you not be shutting up," he explained in a painfully long sentence. Then he continued. The man whispered questions twice more, but Nergal did not waste the effort to answer; eventually the other slave gave up.

At some point much, much later, after a lot of scraping and suppressed cursing, after many hand cramps and a hurt claw, Nergal had fashioned his second bone key. He pulled his leg up onto the bench and placed the key between his teeth, and clenched them painfully. Nergal inserted the key and tried to twist it to unlock the manacle. He had to try several times in different directions at random, with pains shooting down his leg and in his rotted tooth until at last he unlocked the steel device.

Once again Nergal took a moment to enjoy his progress. *I have the smarts*, he thought. *They will not have Nergal to row for them.*

Nergal rose to his feet and walked across the hold to the oarsman who had asked about the scraping noise. Nergal felt around in the tenebrous prison until he found the man. There was a muffled grunt and a gurgle as Nergal affixed his hands around the man's soft throat.

"I told you, I be killing you," Nergal whispered, and squeezed harder. Even though the half-orc could not see well in the dimness, he knew what was there: a red, swollen face grimacing in fear and white eyeballs almost popping out of their sockets as Nergal applied his tremendous strength.

Having satisfied his immediate urges, Nergal once again returned to thought. His head began to hurt from the constant effort. Once free, he would not have to apply himself so. Nergal needed a weapon to kill the warriors of Chu Kutall who had enslaved him. That came easily enough from killing the first man. Killing was Nergal's best tool with which to fashion solutions, because he excelled at it.

Nergal made his way past the rows until he was at the front of the hold, where the guard had appeared earlier. He peered up the stairway, at last able to see a little as a feeble light came down from the outside. Nergal did not know or care if the light originated from the moon or torches above, as long as he could see. The half-orc moved up the stairs quietly and carefully examined the next deck of the great galley.

Most of the deck formed a barracks of some sort. Men were strewn about on their sleeping racks, which were built into the port and starboard walls. No one seemed aware of the half-orc's presence, and Nergal could not see the sailor that had come down to yell at his disruption. He skulked up to the first set of beds bent low so his knuckles almost scraped the ground, and squatted in front of a wooden trunk. His fingers worked with a great deal of dexterity as he gently lifted the lid and peered down into the container. Nergal briefly struggled about whether to grasp the knife or the sword he saw inside until he resolved to take them both.

His left hand held up the trunk lid while his right set the dagger on the deck and then clutched the sword by the hilt. He drew it out of the scabbard, which he left in the locker. Then Nergal took the knife as well, and stood slightly higher, regarding the weapons with near glee.

The half-orc considered the many men in the barracks. There were two, three…many men. He would have to start without waking them up, or they would be too numerous for him to handle at once. One of the few skills Nergal had mastered in his nineteen years of existence was how to kill silently. He almost snickered aloud as he considered this, but managed to stifle the noise as he remembered his priorities. It never even crossed his mind to leave them alive, as he had learned to hate them all in his short stint of enslavement.

Nergal had almost slit the throat of the third-to-last man, when a watchman blundered into the barracks. The darkness hid the wounds Nergal had inflicted. The sentry walked calmly towards the half-orc, as if to make a quiet inquiry.

Nergal turned from the sleeping man, letting his sword dangle limply by his side in the darkness. Nergal reckoned it invisible to the human's poor night vision.

"What is…Aaaahhhhh!" screamed the sentry as Nergal's sword slid into his chest.

The last three men started at the scream, but Nergal was already upon them. He slammed the dagger into the first and left it there, turning to hack at another man. The half-orc's strength proved sufficient to shear off the next man's lower leg with the strike, and once again a scream sounded in the barracks. The third warrior was scrabbling for his weapons when Nergal killed him.

Now sounds of alarm could be heard above, and Nergal made his way towards the entrance of the hold. He knew there were not many left now, but one would be the captain and another the officer on watch. Those two might well be superior swordsmen, and Nergal did not relish having to fight them without the element of surprise.

He came up onto the next deck and could hear men approaching from port. He dodged into the shadows the other way and reached the edge of the deck, where he could look out onto the waters.

There was land! The light of a waning moon allowed the half-orc to see heavily forested mountains across a modest distance of water from the ship. He needed no further encouragement. Placing the sword into his belt, he clambered through the opening and hung above the waves while grasping the ledge with his hands. He released his grip and fell into the warm tropical sea, starting immediately for shore. Nergal did not swim well, but he was sure he could make his way to freedom.

Nergal noticed two things at once: the shore was farther than he had gauged, and the sword in his belt weighed him down alarmingly. He could still hear the men on the ship, but so far none had started to search for him in the sea. Loathe to give up his only weapon, he turned onto his back to ease his swimming. He was free once again.

CHAPTER 2

An Orc In Need

"A stranger draws near!" shot a voice out of the darkness. Quickly following this another voice accosted Nergal, causing him to halt his steps on the road.

"Who goes there, dark one? Perhaps a bandit come to threaten decent people on their travels?"

The half-orc considered this and almost agreed hypnotically to the interesting suggestion. Instead he remained silent as he shambled forward, weak and hungry. He wore the loincloth of a rower slave and a leather jerkin he had taken from an abandoned farm many leagues back. Since stepping onto dry land, Nergal had wandered aimlessly, trying to discover what land he found himself in.

The light of a torch illuminated the faceplate of ornate armor. "Hold your swords! It is but a solitary traveler. My, you're a sorry-looking brute. Your outfit..."

Nergal almost panicked at this, seeing that these were smart ones who would realize he was an escaped slave. He froze at these words, fearing the worst. The richly adorned knight took notice of his fear.

"Don't worry, friend, we won't sell you to the slavers. We're champions of the people, and stand for good and righteousness. Come, share our camp and partake of our food! Tell us of your travels!"

The light of a campfire filtered dimly through the nearby trees lining the side of the road. Nergal realized that he had stumbled onto their campsite, causing them to challenge him. Could these strangers be trusted?

Nergal remained wary as he shuffled further towards the light. He was brought up short by an elf, who leaped in front of him. A trap! Nergal stepped back and clasped the hilt of his sword. But the elf had a calm look on his slender face.

"Stay your wrath, denizen of Nod! I'm not hunting orc on this day. My name is Zanithweir."

Nergal looked briefly at the others. "Elf no fight Nergal?"

The light-boned elf, clad in leather, shook his head solemnly. "We're on the road for a greater purpose. We intend to destroy the evil that has cursed this land."

Nergal had no idea what the elf spoke of. He was still uncertain as to whether he could trust such a vile creature, and wondered if the forest vermin was making fun of him. Another member of the group stepped forward to greet the traveler. Nergal saw it was a human female, also wearing metal armor.

"Well met, Nergal. I'm Dalwen, warrior-priestess of the Norngawen."

"Dal-wen," echoed Nergal poorly. He tried his best to hide his disgust at the human female, who was smooth skinned and so slender as to appear starved to the half-orc. Her metal breast accoutrements thrust forward over a childless belly. In Nergal's society, the females did not go out with the warriors, but stayed in the caves with their grublings. Most would not even dare speak to a male warrior unless they had been given permission.

"I've never met an orc before," she mentioned casually, looking Nergal over even as he examined her.

"Half-orc," corrected the elf quietly at her shoulder.

"Oh, I didn't know. There aren't many orcs…or orcish-related…people in the Kingdom." Dalwen smiled at Nergal warmly. Her mane fell from her head long and straight, as if the hair sought to root itself in the ground. Her strong, clear face showed no fear.

"Doubtless you're eager to hear more of this monster we've vowed to slay," the knight said boldly as he handed Nergal a slab of mutton.

"Hmm, yes, tell more," Nergal murmured briefly between huge bites of flesh. He didn't really care about the monster, but he wanted to distract the others while he ate.

"The Shadow Beast has ravaged the entire coast with its evil," explained Dalwen. "It's been preying on the innocent and weak. Travelers such as yourself are in grave danger, and even the trade guilds are beginning to consider abandoning these routes."

"Well, this particular creature is about to meet its end," a second knight said. "So swears Melvin of Elniboné." This second knight looked smaller and more delicate than the first. He had the straight plain nose of all humans, though Nergal could see that it was thinner than the nose on the knight with the deeper voice.

"And I, Garbor," boomed the knight who had first welcomed the half-orc. This one took off his helmet and Nergal could see his bristly red hair and a thick neck that disappeared behind a heavy breastplate. His face looked wide and powerful, matching his voice.

"We're but three days travel now from the ruins of Salthor Castle," Dalwen continued. "It is there that the curse of the Shadow Beast first arose, and we believe that is where we'll find this abomination and destroy it."

The elf looked sternly at Nergal. "What do you say, Nergal? Shall we put aside the mutual enmity of our peoples and unite against a common foe?"

"Mmm," said Nergal uneasily. He shifted briefly from foot to foot. "You have more mutton?"

"Yes, we have plenty of mutton," assured the elf. They started to walk through the trees towards the fire ahead. "But what say you to our offer?"

"I go with you," Nergal agreed readily. "Must have food, have traveled much far." The group reformed around their large fire, and Nergal grunted in satisfaction as another piece of lamb was offered to him. He decided he liked the strangers despite their dizzying words and shiny armors. Unlike Nergal, these ones had all manner of equipment arrayed about the camp. He glimpsed at bedrolls, cooking utensils, and backpacks out of the corner of his eye. So many things they had!

As Nergal ate, he peeked at the human female again. Her legs were smooth and well muscled, her stomach flat. Why was she starved when so much food was available? Perhaps she had displeased one of the males and now suffered her punishment? Yet her straw-colored hair looked healthy and well kept. Her face was fair and smooth, without a single boil or scar. Nergal shook his head and resumed his rapid consumption of the meat.

These people were the first natives he had stumbled upon since coming to shore. Although he did not know what a shadow beast was, Nergal liked the idea of joining the war party. It was clear that these adventurers were out for blood. That was something Nergal could understand.

When Nergal's hunger had diminished somewhat, he became aware of the others watching him. He tried to dispel his discomfort by reassuring his hosts of the quality of their food.

"Good food," Nergal said, nodding at the knight who had handed him the mutton. "Nergal like."

"Well, ummm, you're certainly welcome, my friend," said Melvin. Something seemed to be troubling him. He held a compact frown on his face beneath his slender nose.

"You kill many shadu beests?" asked Nergal.

"No, this is the first," Melvin told him. "It's a powerful creature, most dangerous indeed. There's certainly nothing to be ashamed of, if you're too afraid to take on such a fearsome thing."

Nergal shook his head vigorously. "No. Nergal no afraid. Nergal help you kill."

Garbor laughed. "Of course you will!" The knight turned to his companions. "He looks like a stout fellow! No doubt his sword arm is mighty." The knight had a deep voice and an unquenchable vitality to him. The tension in the others seemed to ease.

Nergal decided that he liked Garbor the best. Like the half-orc, he was thickset and strong, and he used simple words. Melvin confused Nergal with his strange language; Dalwen disturbed him with her very presence in the war party; and the elf…Nergal had killed many an elf.

The other knight who had named himself Melvin rose and clapped Nergal on the shoulder. "Well, perhaps I misjudged you. I apologize, I assure you, uhh, Nergal, that I meant no offense. You should know that it takes more than a skillful swordsman to annihilate this creature."

Nergal considered this for a moment, trying to decipher the words. Melvin must have mistook his look of confusion for disbelief, for Melvin was quick to explain further.

"We've heard many tales of this creature," he said to Nergal. The others around the campfire became quiet. "The few who have encountered it and survived say that it cannot be killed with a sword."

"Hmm," grunted Nergal. Then he realized what the knight was talking about. "Like troll?"

"Well, somewhat different than a troll," Melvin said. "It doesn't seem to exist in this world like you or me. Some say that regular swords will go right through it. Now normally I would dismiss such rumors, but the thing did destroy all of Salthor. I knew the castellan there, and he was a very capable man."

"We have also spoken to sages," Dalwen said, "and they have told us that some things do exist that cannot be hurt by a sword unless the weapon has been gifted by a mage."

"Tell me, Nergal, does your sword possess a powerful magic?" asked Garbor. His eyes looked concerned as he examined the rusted weapon that Nergal had stolen from the weapons locker.

Nergal's eyes bulged. "Magic? Nergal no shaman."

Melvin nodded. "Don't worry, my friend. We'll find you something appropriate."

Garbor nodded. "I have just—"

"We'll find you something before we get to Salthor, of course," Melvin interrupted swiftly. Garbor looked sharply at Melvin. Nergal paid them no mind, and he hoped they were done talking.

Melvin moved back from the fire slightly, preparing his bedroll.

"I believe Zanithweir has the first watch, so if you will excuse me…"

"Eh?" Nergal became confused again.

"Oh, that is to say, I'm going to sleep now. I'll see you in the morning Nergal!"

"Oh," Nergal acknowledged. He usually woke up about now. But he seemed to remember that humans always slept at night when he was about and around. Luckily Nergal had gorged to such an extent that he now felt like taking a nap.

Melvin moved back a few paces from the fire and lay down amongst his equipment. Nergal saw that the knight had a trail blanket under him and a pack to rest his head upon. He shook his head again at the strange ways of these men.

Nergal wandered away from the fire and found an old log in the dim light. He dragged the log parallel to the fire and lay down before it, using the wood to shelter his back. He rested his head on a tuft of grass, after patting it down to scare away any vermin that might be hiding in it.

He gave one last thought to his safety. He nestled close to the log and pulled the sword from his belt, leaving it in his hand. Then he fell asleep.

When Nergal awoke, he felt slightly refreshed but not stiffened as if from long sleep. Darkness covered the camp, broken only by the glowing embers of a dying fire.

He sniffed the night air. The smell of the campfire and the strangers lingered. Sitting up, he saw Garbor, Melvin, and Dalwen asleep around the fire.

Nergal looked out away from the fire. Where was the elf? Did he even now draw back an arrow aimed at Nergal's heart?

Nergal came to his feet and took a few uncertain steps away from the fire into the reassuring shadows. He couldn't see anyone else. He took one last look back at the others to make sure they still slept, then slipped into the surrounding woods.

Nergal considered leaving the humans and their elf companion. They did have food, but their ways were strange. And Nergal felt he shouldn't be around the elf anyway. They were the enemies of his people…it felt wrong to share a camp with one.

He took another uncertain step forward. A voice came to him faintly, carried on the cool air from beyond the trees. He moved towards it, watching where he placed his feet to avoid noise. His eyes had adjusted nicely to the darkness but he still found it difficult to find places to walk without breaking sticks or disturbing leaves.

At last he caught a glimpse of Zanithweir through the leaves. The elf stood facing away from Nergal, looking off into the darkness.

Who did the elf speak to? Nergal couldn't see anyone else.

"They have no suspicions," the elf said. "We're still headed for Salthor. I'm sure your Shok Nogua will take care of them once we've reached the castle. If not, I can always lend a hand."

So, the elf speaks behind their backs, too, Nergal thought. Perhaps he should do them all a favor and finish the elf now. But he knew that the scout would hear if he crept any closer. He'd have to charge up and give Zanithweir a chance to defend himself. Then the others would come…and they would never believe Nergal. They would join together and kill him.

The elf nodded once and turned away, moving off to Nergal's left. Nergal stood thinking. Perhaps he should leave them now. But what of the big one, Garbor, who had spoken kindly and given him food? Should he leave that one to the elf's treachery?

Nergal decided to go back to the fire. Whatever the elf had in mind, it would please Nergal to foil it. He stepped carefully back the way he had come, trying to be utterly silent. He almost made it back to his log before being interrupted.

"Where have you been?"

The voice of the elf. It came quietly, from nearby. Nergal peered out, finally seeing Zanithweir sitting on a stump.

"Nergal go out into woods…had to go…"

The elf didn't demand any further explanation. He nodded but Nergal saw an angry look on the elf's face. The elf didn't believe him, Nergal thought.

"Well then…. would you like to take the next watch?"

Nergal blinked. "Nergal guard?"

"Yes, stay awake and watch for danger," the elf explained.

Nergal nodded. "Yes, Nergal do." He crossed his arms and sat back against his log, trying to look alert.

"Very well," Zanithweir said. He found a spot around the fire and lay back. Nergal took a deep breath and resolved himself to the watch.

After long minutes of watching, his eyelids grew heavy. Nergal decided that nothing threatened the camp. It would be fine to take another nap. He let his chin fall onto his chest, and closed his eyes.

Many hours later, Nergal awakened to the sound of breaking wood. He groggily rolled up onto all fours, getting his bearings. Dalwen worked near the fire, and Melvin seemed to be gathering his many things. He couldn't see Garbor or Zanithweir.

"Good morning!" Dalwen said. Nergal saw that the female had gathered wood and revived the fire in the early morning light.

"Hrm…yes, good morning," mumbled Nergal.

"So tell me Nergal…do um…do people eat breakfast, where you're from?"

Nergal considered this for a moment then shrugged.

"Orcs eat when hungry," he said.

"Ah, I see. That sounds very wise. Where are you from?"

"Nod."

"Yes. I see. I suppose Zanithweir's guess was right, then. I didn't want to assume you came from Nod…it's a long ways from this land."

"I imagine that slavers may have brought him this far," Melvin said, walking up to the fire. "Is that right, Nergal?"

Nergal bit his lip and wondered how much he should say. Sometimes, if he said bad things, it got him into trouble. He ended up just nodding.

"Well, we'll do our best to make you welcome here," Dalwen said.

Zanithweir and Garbor came into the clearing from the woods and slowly walked up to the conversation, side by side. Garbor smiled widely at Nergal and nodded at him. Zanithweir gave him a withering stare.

"I see you're still here," Zanithweir said.

"Of course he's here, we haven't yet met the Shadow Beast in battle," Garbor laughed. "Have you forgotten so soon his oath to aid us?"

Zanithweir shrugged. "We shouldn't hold him to his word…he only needed food, after all."

Nergal felt anger rise. He didn't think on the truth of the words, only who spoke them.

"Nergal fight beest," he said urgently. "We be going to it now, be getting started."

Garbor nodded. "Well said! Let's get our things and get on with our journey. I'm eager to meet this menace, as well."

Melvin frowned. "Um…without breakfast? Our bodies need nourishment so that we may function at our best. We'll get to the monster, soon enough."

Nergal nodded. "Soon enough."

CHAPTER 3

Salthor Castle

Lightning flashed again, engraving the image of the entrance briefly in the orc's mind: a tall set of thick wood doors with large metal handles set into the massive stone of the main keep. The handles were formed into leering beast-faces with large noses and stubby horns.

The adventurers had just made it to Salthor as the storm broke. The portcullis of the outer wall stood open, allowing ingress to a courtyard overgrown with vegetation. On the other side of the clearing the entrance of the inner keep beckoned.

Melvin stepped forward in the light drizzle and heavy wind. The knight tried one of the doors. It swung open slowly. Nergal had not absorbed the full depth of the story that Dalwen had told him the other night. It amazed him that such a wealthy landowner would leave his castle unguarded, but surely there were guards inside at least. Nergal supposed that the lord had left on a long campaign and the caretakers had grown lax, or maybe the place had already been sacked by a war party.

No one in the group made mention of the unlocked portal; they filed into a warm, dry entrance hall and closed out the gale behind them.

Nergal's fine night sight revealed a room of six alcoves, three on either side of the high vaulted chamber. The thunder outside could still be heard, although it was subdued by the stone walls. At the end of the room, another set of large doors closed off the rest of the castle. Nergal peered into the nearest alcove and saw a hideous beast of horn and claw.

"Monsters!" he exclaimed, pointing his battered sword towards the depression in the wall.

Dalwen clasped a strong hand onto Nergal's shoulder. "Hold, Nergal," she said calmly. Nergal almost struck her by reflex, but then remembered that the others regarded her as an equal. She finished lighting a lantern and swung its hatch back to illuminate the area.

"Seems it's only a statue, my friend," she said dryly.

Nergal looked again at the thing and saw that its skin was indeed of stone, not of scales or fur. Still a menace resided in its eyes, and Nergal had never seen anything like this. A thrill of danger made his back tingle, but he said no more and simply grunted in assent to her evaluation.

The group turned back towards the doors on the far wall. Nergal's teeth ground together in irritation when he saw Zanithweir trade amused looks with the human woman. So the elf thought Nergal was stupid. Elves and orcs had fought many battles where Nergal grew up. If he had his way, this elf would not live a day longer. The half-orc resolved to find a method by which he could dispose of him.

Garbor once again looked carefully at Nergal's weapon, and now he seemed to come to a decision. Melvin gave him a pained look, but Garbor paid him no heed.

"Nergal, good friend, I will not let you fight by my side without a proper sword," he vowed. The big man reached behind his back, took out a beautiful short sword, and held it out for the half-orc. Nergal murmured in awe and accepted the weapon eagerly. He attempted to put the rusted sword into his belt, but when that didn't work because he stared at the new sword rather than his waist, he simply discarded the old weapon on the floor.

"The blade will not rust as your old one has," he told the brute. "It has a dweomer that will make it strike true. Now you can face the Shadow Beast with some hope of killing it!"

"If it can be harmed," Zanithweir muttered.

"Not yours?" asked Nergal, still examining the precious sword. In Nergal's strong grip, the weapon seemed so light that he could hardly tell he held it.

"That's my secondary weapon," Garbor told him, drawing an ornate war axe from his belt. Garbor's great double-bladed axe looked valuable as well to Nergal's eyes. He wondered how much money these two weapons would fetch in the city. Nergal forgot his goal of killing the elf and decided he had to have the weapons for himself. He would not kill Garbor, he thought, but perhaps steal away with the arms in the night.

After bestowing his gift, Garbor took the lead with Melvin staying close at his side. Zanithweir and Dalwen formed a second rank of sorts, while Nergal slunk along after them. The elf's back tempted his shiny new sword, but Nergal was wise enough to know he couldn't kill the elf so conspicuously. His head began to hurt again. Kill the elf…take the swords…so many ideas in such a short time. How could he sort it all out?

Nergal smiled in the darkness. *I have the smarts*, he thought. He would wait until the time was right.

The group moved into some sort of entry hall, which appeared to be richly decorated but covered in a layer of dust.

"Everyone gone," Nergal said.

Melvin misunderstood the orc. "Yes, amazing isn't it? To think that a castle so great could fall to a single creature."

Nergal now began to recall their mission here. Something about a beast that could not be killed with rusty swords. It was all a jumble in his memory.

"What beest look like?" asked Nergal, looking expectantly at Garbor.

"We have only two accounts of its appearance," Melvin began. Nergal winced, since he had hoped that Garbor would explain to him. Now he had to try and understand the one with the hard words.

"The menace is partially ethereal, flickering in and out of sight. It has a large body, but the descriptions there are somewhat confused. All we really know is that its primary offensive weaponry consists of tentacles with bony teeth or ridges on them. Sometimes a fluting noise is heard as a precursor to its attack," explained Melvin.

Nergal blinked. He understood a few of the words. "Teeth?" he inquired.

"Yes, there are sharp teeth on its appendages," said the knight. "The tentacles stay otherworldly until the moment of attack, when they solidify to gouge and tear the flesh of its victims. I'm theorizing that that moment is the only time the tentacles can be severed."

Nergal nodded. Actually Melvin had lost him quickly after "sharp teeth".

"Which way should we go?" asked Garbor, eager for action.

The hall had three exits other than the double doors through which they had entered. As Nergal stood with his back to the entrance, a stair went up to the next floor on his left, and passageways led off straight ahead and to his right.

"It's late and I'm tired," said Dalwen. "Yet we have at last reached the castle and I wonder if it's safe to rest."

"We can scout out a safe spot," Zanithweir assured her. "Actually it's probably safer than outside."

"I disagree," said Melvin. "Many people were slain here, remember? That's why the castle is now abandoned."

Nergal caught this part. Now he understood why the castle had no guards. The Shadow Beast caused this! Nergal gripped his sword tighter in his enormously powerful fist.

"Well, we'll keep watch, of course," the elf fired back. "Besides, didn't you say its attack was announced by a fluting noise?"

"Sometimes," conceded Melvin. "Very well. But I'm sleeping in my armor!"

"Of course!" exclaimed Garbor. "We thought nothing else!"

Nergal found the humans' armor quite silly. It would be a simple matter to just cut their heads off at the neck. What good did the heavy metal breastplates and helmets do anyway? Even more ridiculous were the large metal cups that held the breasts of Dalwen, and the metal greaves on her skinny legs, held on with thin leather straps. Nergal shook his head quietly at this.

"Nergal watch for shadu beest," he announced. "Yell real loud if beest comes."

"All right. Let's just find a safe spot to get some rest," Dalwen concluded. "Upstairs makes the most sense for that."

"Yes, the castellan's quarters would be up there somewhere," said Melvin.

Nergal marveled at the easy agreement of the knight to the suggestion by the female. Melvin acted as if he were no stronger than she and could not simply slap her into submission. It was as mystifying to Nergal as the armor.

The group moved up the aged stone stair to explore further. Melvin directed them by memory, since he had been to some parts of the castle before. They made their way cautiously to the castellan's chamber.

Nergal found the room an amazing place. Many colors met his eyes even in the meager torchlight. Then the wall sconces were lit, and the full luxury of the room became apparent. Rich tapestries lined the walls, and countless books rested in niches in the walls. They found a study or lounge in a side room, and Dalwen claimed this as her own.

"Wake me for my watch," she said, and threw her bedroll down on the floor. Once again, Nergal felt disappointed. He had been watching for days now to discern who mated with the female, but it seemed that she would not lie with either of the knights. They did not seem to claim her. Nergal couldn't understand it all.

"You will take the first watch then, Nergal?" asked Zanithweir.

"Nergal watch for shadu beest," the half-orc confirmed.

"Wake me for the second watch, then," the elf told him. Nergal watched with carefully disguised hatred as the elf made himself comfortable in a corner of the room. Garbor blew some of the wall lanterns out, and everyone but Nergal settled in for sleep.

For an interminable time, Nergal watched for the shadow beast. He remained uncertain just exactly how he would recognize it if it appeared. Nergal thought briefly about killing the elf again, but he knew that he didn't want to kill Garbor, who had been so nice to him. Slaying the puny elf and leaving the others alive would risk being caught. Nergal had been caught a lot of times, and it usually meant something bad would happen to him.

With an abrupt realization that he was hungry, Nergal forgot about the elf.

Need food, he thought. *Nergal eat now*.

The threat of the Shadow Beast gave the hulk pause. Melvin, the long-winded one, had spoken of teeth. Nergal considered the things he knew that had lots of teeth. The rock lizards of his homeland had a lot of teeth, but they were slow and stupid. He had killed one by crushing its head with a heavy rock. Nergal looked at the perfect sword he now had and decided that he could handle the thing with the teeth. It was only rusty swords, after all, that could not kill it. He would just have to be careful.

Thoughts of his companions' safety did not cross the brute's mind as he slipped from the room.

Nergal realized that to evade or kill the Shadow Beast, he must see it before it saw him. He slinked quietly down the hall, at home in the darkness. Now and then a bolt of lightning would cause dim light to penetrate into the hall from distant windows or murder holes, so that he would see if the Shadow Beast were to approach.

The half-orc reached the end of the hall, which split into several corridors. He paused, uncertain of his course.

Nergal had inherited a fine sense of smell from his orcish father. He caught a faint scent despite the proliferation of hairs hanging from the nostrils of his great pointy nose. Nergal tentatively identified the weak odor as something possibly edible.

Selecting what he discerned to be the right direction, he resumed his stealthy progress.

In the instant during a flash of lightning, Nergal became aware of a threat. Nergal saw a humanoid form immediately to his right, and started in surprise.

Nothing could have moved so quietly! Nergal brought his sword around in a flash and confronted the intruder.

Lightning flashed distantly again, and he saw a perfect facsimile of himself staring back from a plate of polished brass. It was a reflection! Nergal had seen himself in water before, but this was something entirely different. He regarded himself for a few moments in the scant flickering light: a slightly hunched, huge-shouldered creature, with beady eyes and a protruding chin. His scraggly hair grew long like a mane. The new sword in his hand looked particularly menacing. Nergal felt reassured by it.

Once again a need for food prodded Nergal into action. He turned from the plate and continued down the hallway, still moving silently.

Nergal found his way through some kind of large gathering room full of tables. The outside storm raged away, louder now because of the presence of two large fireplaces. At the opposite end of this room, Nergal came to a closed door. The smell became stronger now, and Nergal felt certain it came from just beyond the door.

The door would not open. Some sort of simple metal latch protruded from this side, but it did not move when Nergal grabbed it. Not to be dissuaded, the half-orc tensed his magnificent muscles and focused his strength on the handle. The metal bent and warped, and at last something on the inside of the door snapped. The sound was much louder than he had anticipated, and Nergal froze, wincing at the noise he had produced. After a moment he opened the door, ignoring the destroyed latch, and saw some sort of larder beyond.

His eyes adjusted to the darker interior. Soon he located the source of the scent: a haunch of salted meat hanging from the wall. Nergal joyously approached the haunch, his mouth already slavering. The age of the meat might have given others pause, but Nergal was not particular. He effortlessly cut a piece of the tough, dry flesh with his sword, and began chewing vigorously.

"Nergal?" Nergal jumped in terror at the sound of the voice. He had heard nothing!

He turned to see the elf, Zanithweir standing in the larder with him. Now Nergal remembered something about elves being able to move without noise. He cursed Zanithweir silently.

"Umm?" Nergal responded unintelligibly, swallowing a mouthful of meat.

"Why aren't you on watch? I was looking for you and heard a loud noise. Was it the Shadow Beast?"

In answer, Nergal simply held out a sliver of the dried meat. Zanithweir made a face.

"Er, no thanks. How could you—"

Without warning, Nergal attacked the elf savagely. Zanithweir reacted quickly, receiving only a shallow cut across the chest as he dodged the sword thrust. The elf reached for his sword as Nergal slashed at him. Zanithweir ducked the attack and recovered. He faced the half-orc, their swords touching between them.

"I knew we should not have trusted you, foul creature of Nod," sneered the elf. "I have slain your kind before—"

Zanithweir ended his speech abruptly as Nergal pressed the attack again. This time the elf backed off, stepping into the corner of the larder. Nergal saw his chance. With his adversary's back against a wall, it would be harder to dodge Nergal's attacks, and he could bring his superior strength to bear. The half-orc rushed again, hacking at his enemy.

The elf parried the blow, but did not anticipate Nergal's incredible strength. The block faltered and the elf's grip on his sword slipped slightly. Nergal attacked again, putting more muscle into it. The elf tried to duck away, but Nergal kicked him back into the corner and grabbed Zanithweir's sword arm in one huge beefy hand.

Nergal held the elf helpless in his iron grip with Garbor's sword at his throat. "Elves kill Nergal's father. Now Nergal kill elves."

With that final statement, Nergal slit the elf's throat, sending blood spraying out onto himself and the floor. The elf collapsed with a gurgle and died.

Nergal saw that the elf had been smart, acting as if he were not ready when in fact he had been on guard. He had been lucky to fight Zanithweir in the confines of the larder, where the elf could not make full use of his superior agility.

Slowly Nergal began to realize that the others might find out what he had done. How could he explain this to them?

Food helped Nergal think. He thought until he was full, and then an idea struck him. The sound of the rain outside had reminded him of the moat that surrounded the castle outside. Nergal had simply to throw the dead elf into the moat! Nergal could blame it all on the Shadow Beast.

I have the smarts, Nergal assured himself. *They not find out.*

CHAPTER 4

The Search for Zanithweir

"Wake up!" commanded a loud voice. "Where's Zanithweir? Who's on watch?"

Nergal stirred from sleep. He opened his eyes and saw that Dalwen stood in the middle of the room, urging the knights to wakefulness.

"I don't know," Garbor declared. "I haven't been awakened for a watch, myself."

"Nor I!" exclaimed Melvin, holding his unsheathed sword out before him. "Nergal?"

"Eh?"

"You had the first watch. What happened?"

"Nergal watch for shadu beest," the half-orc told them. Nergal's eyes shifted to the side as he continued, "Elf watch for shadu beest. Nergal sleep."

Garbor brandished his axe and carefully opened the door. The hall beyond, utterly quiet, held only gloom.

"Zanithweir!" he called out. "Zanithweir, are you there?"

There was no reply.

"Basilisk dung! What should we do?" asked Garbor.

"He might just be scouting ahead, as he sometimes does," Melvin speculated. "I hope the Shadow Beast didn't get him. Foolish to go off on his own in any case."

Nergal nodded in agreement. "Fewlish," he seconded.

"We should go looking for him," said Melvin.

The group gathered their things together rapidly and prepared to search the castle. Once again the two knights led, with Garbor holding a torch to add light to what filtered in from outside. Nergal fell in beside Dalwen and the group moved out to find their lost companion.

The group stopped at the next chamber door, and Garbor tried the latch. He opened the door carefully and held the torch forward to see what waited inside.

"Some kind of bedchamber," he noted. "Looks a lot smaller than the castellan's quarters, of course."

"Let's just keep moving and find Zanithweir," suggested Dalwen.

Garbor nodded and closed the door. The group continued on, checking three other doors down the corridor. They found two other bedchambers and a storage room of some kind, containing barrels, spare wood, and linens.

They turned back and moved down a different corridor, searching for hints of Zanithweir's whereabouts. They arrived at another door and Garbor prepared to open it.

Nergal sniffed. "Someone dead," he announced.

"What's that, Nergal?" asked Melvin.

"Someone dead," Nergal repeated. "Nergal smell dead."

Garbor braced himself and opened the door. He stepped through and held his torch high.

"Yes, I see a dead man, but it's not Zanithweir," he informed the others. The knight stepped into the room and everyone followed him.

They were in a larger living chamber of some kind with connecting rooms on both sides. Like the castellan's chambers, the room contained more decor. Nergal saw candelabras of silver and gold, ornate wooden chests and a collection of jade statuettes. The archways connecting the rooms held the likenesses of vines and flowers. Halfway between this room and the left side room, in the doorway, a desiccated corpse lay on the floor. The remains were face down, mostly covered in torn blue robes except for the head and feet.

"Poor soul," mumbled Garbor, lighting a candle that he saw next to the bed. Dalwen pointed her lantern this way and that, scanning for threats.

Garbor stepped over the corpse and entered the adjoining room on the left. Soon he had lit more candles in the side chamber, and the others moved in to investigate.

Nergal saw a room full of bookcases, with a desk of some kind in the middle of the space. Garbor lit a candelabra on the desk, which threw a meager light onto the dozens of papers on its surface. Nergal could see scribbling on the papers, but he did not know how to read.

"What is this?" Melvin said, looking at the papers on the table.

"Some kind of magical workshop," commented Dalwen. "The body kind of looks like he might have been a scribe or a mage."

"Hmmm, I think I can read this," said Melvin distractedly. He fumbled for the chair and seated himself before the workbench, absorbed in his examination.

"Well, let's look around and see if we can find any clues," suggested Dalwen. "Nergal, you search these bookcases in here, and Garbor and I will check the other rooms."

Dalwen did not wait to see if Nergal would accept her suggestion, but instead turned away with Garbor and left the room.

Nergal glanced at the knight at the table. Melvin seemed completely engrossed in the strange diagrams and symbols. The half-orc turned towards the wall next to him, which was cluttered with books and candles. Uncertain exactly what he was supposed to be doing, he stood and stared at the bookcases. He noticed a glint on one of the shelves, and saw some sort of jewelry sitting there. Glancing back at the knight to be sure he was not being observed, Nergal grasped the item, some kind of pendant with a large gem centerpiece. He pocketed it within his worn, ill-fitting jerkin.

No sooner had he accomplished this bit of thievery than Dalwen and Garbor reentered the room.

"Have you deciphered any of it?" Dalwen asked the knight.

"Yes! It's actually quite amazing!" Melvin answered. "Apparently this wizard worked for the castellan himself. These are actually the diagrams for the construction of some sort of warding device…to protect the wearer from the Shadow Beast!"

"A lot of good it did him," said Dalwen, contemplating the corpse lying flat on the floor. "He must not have completed it."

"Actually, his notes speak of success…but that's the last entry here." Melvin trailed off in thought. "We must find it! It could be an invaluable aid in destroying the beast."

"Maybe he was running for the ward when the thing got him!" exclaimed Garbor. "It could be here in the workshop! We should search the whole room for it."

"Yes! The whole castle if need be," agreed Melvin.

Garbor and Dalwen whirled into activity. Garbor started to search the corpse, examining the rags for anything of note. Dalwen began to examine the bookcases, taking books out of their places and looking behind them.

Melvin took one of the work papers from the desk and held it up.

"It looks like this, friends. Nergal, did you happen to see it when you searched the bookcases?"

Nergal peered at the detailed drawing of the warding device. He recognized it as an exact duplicate of the pendant that he had in his pocket.

"Nergal no see," said the hulk, shaking his head vigorously. "Worth money, yes?"

"Much more than that," Melvin told the half-orc. "It protects the wearer from the Shadow Beast!"

Nergal looked uncertainly at the drawing again. How could such a tiny necklace protect anyone from anything? Nergal did not understand, but he knew the nitid gem held value if he ever made it back to the city.

"Nergal look," he assured Melvin. Then, to prove his assertion, Nergal turned his head this way and that, looking at the bookcases. Melvin raised his eyebrow and started looking himself.

The group searched for long minutes. At last, Melvin gave up.

"It's not here," he said. "Perhaps he'd already delivered it to the castellan…but the rumor was that he'd been slain. If that's the case then it wasn't any good after all."

"Friends, we now have three things to search for," Garbor bellowed. "Zanithweir, the ward, and the Shadow Beast."

"Let's hope we find them in that order," said Melvin.

The party reformed into their familiar formation with the knights at the front and left the wizard's rooms. They came to another intersection, and Nergal noticed the large brass plate again. Melvin looked at it momentarily as they passed, but he did not seem to find it as fascinating as Nergal had. The group retraced his progress of the night before and came to the large room with the tables and fireplaces.

"Looks like a dining hall," Garbor assessed. "We probably won't find any of the things we seek here."

Garbor started towards the larder that Nergal had raided last night.

"Ummm, we go this way now," Nergal prompted. He shifted from foot to foot nervously. Nergal had carefully dropped Zanithweir's corpse into the castle moat, but he had neglected to clean up the blood from last night's brief fight, and feared the smart ones would see.

"But I was going to check this door," Garbor said.

Nergal stepped around Garbor and opened the door, careful to block the way. He pretended to look inside and examine the interior.

"Hmmm, nothing there," Nergal summarized. "Go this way now," he said, pointing to an exit on his right. Nergal walked toward the other egress, hoping to lead the others away.

"Are there any other doors out through there?" asked Garbor. The big knight opened the door to the larder, and Nergal hunched lower, holding his breath. Garbor held his torch into the small room, peering inside.

"Nothing. You're right, my friend," he said, nodding at Nergal. "Let's go this way as you suggest."

Nergal quietly exhaled in immense relief.

They made their way through audience chambers and an arsenal. The ravages of the Shadow Beast were apparent: they found three dead bodies rotting on the stone floors. They searched each one carefully, trying to find the magical pendant or clues of its whereabouts. Then the group headed into a guard tower at the corner of Castle Salthor.

The tower formed level after level of barracks, with dust-covered weapons racks and rotting beds. The dim light of a cloudy day filtered in through the many arrow slits. As they neared the top, Nergal detected a barely audible scampering from above. He looked upwards, but saw only dusty support beams and cobwebs above their heads. He sniffed the air, smelling the old wood and damp stones.

"What's wrong, Nergal?" Dalwen asked.

"Hrm. Is nothing," Nergal said, but his face held a frown.

They continued moving higher into the dusty tower. Nergal held his sword in a tight grip, his eyes shifting all around. The scratching sound came again. Nergal brought his sword up and checked the ceiling again. This time he looked up into the many glistening eyes of a huge spider descending upon Dalwen.

Nergal roared warning and brutally shoved Dalwen out of danger. His sword arm arced around in a powerful blow, landing squarely in the center of the spider's foresection. The strike cleaved the front half of the hairy terror in two.

The others recovered from their shock, staring at the remains of the spider. The thing had grown to the size of a large dog before meeting its demise at Nergal's sword.

"A giant arachnid!" exclaimed Melvin. "The people haven't been gone long, but already the vermin are moving into the ruin."

"Uhhh! What a hideous thing!" Dalwen spat. "Nergal…you saved my life! If it had bitten me, the others couldn't have healed me."

"And struck down in a single blow!" Garbor said in his deep, hearty way. He slapped Nergal on the back. "Bravo my friend! Did I not tell you he had a mighty sword arm?"

Nergal inflated under the praise. "Nergal kill good."

Even Melvin appeared pleased by the slaying of the large spider. It seemed at times that he distrusted the half-orc, but Nergal guessed that his doubts had been receding. Nergal hoped that now Melvin would treat him as a full-fledged member of their group.

Truth be told, Nergal had only reacted instinctually to the threat. Still, he was beginning to accept Dalwen as a companion despite her sex. Nergal found it easier to tolerate her without the elf around. He could see her as a real friend as long as she didn't walk with one of his blood enemies.

Nergal took his sword to the spider once again, hacking off its eight hairy legs. He collected them together while the others watched in confusion. The half-orc grasped a travel sack from a peg on the wall nearby and dumped the legs into it.

"What are you keeping those for?" asked Dalwen. "Are you going to sell them to a wizard?"

"Good eating," Nergal explained, patting the sack proudly. Dalwen and Melvin made strange faces and looked away, but Garbor only laughed.

"A strange fellow to be sure, but a strong sword arm," Garbor repeated.

The group made their way around the outer battlements and across to the next tower. The impressive view of the castle revealed no other inhabitants. Dalwen occasionally called Zanithweir's name, but with decreasing vigor. Nergal thought that maybe she started to despair of finding the elf. They entered the next tower warily, looking for more of the large spiders. The bodies of two guards were all that greeted them. They searched each tower in turn but they saw no more spiders or creatures of any sort.

After they had made their way completely around the castle's battlements, Melvin stopped, scratching his chin.

"We can go back through and look more thoroughly," he suggested. "But I guess we're running out of daylight."

"We searched every place that it would make sense to find the amulet," Garbor said.

"It may be in the most mundane of places," said Melvin. "There's a dungeon below the castle," he added. "We should check that out as well."

"I just wish I knew what had happened to Zanithweir," Dalwen said. "No fluting noises, no sounds of battle, and we didn't find his body. It's almost as if he just deserted us."

"The elf wouldn't do that," said Garbor, always quick to defend anyone's character. "Something or someone got him. I don't know if it was the Shadow Beast or not, but that seems a likely candidate."

Nergal remained silent on the matter.

"Tomorrow we'll check the dungeon," Melvin said.

They headed back to the castellan's chambers to take their rest. Dalwen took the first watch, so Nergal prepared for sleep. He patted the lump in his jerkin pocket and smiled to himself.

CHAPTER 5

Into the Dungeon

The night passed without incident. In the morning the adventurers talked little, absorbed with the task at hand. Dalwen took out a package of thin road cakes. She passed one of these around to everyone. Melvin unwrapped a cloth revealing a large chunk of cheese covered in wax. He cut this up with a dagger into four sections and added it to the snack. Nergal forced himself to choke down the crumbly wafer, then relished the cheese, wax and all.

After they ate the light meal, everyone packed up their gear. Melvin led them to a dungeon entrance he remembered from the days when the castle was inhabited. The knight led the way with his longsword drawn.

They became more dependent on the light of Garbor's torch and Dalwen's lantern as they descended a flight of stone steps into the darkness of Salthor's dungeon. At the bottom they found themselves in an ancient torture room, filled with rusted metal implements of pain. Nergal did not understand the function of most of the devices, but he did know that they disturbed him.

"You've been down here before?" Dalwen asked, looking with concern at the paraphernalia arrayed around them.

"Yes," Melvin said, offering no more explanation. He seemed distracted, looking carefully at the room. "The holding cells are to the right, I remember," Melvin muttered, "but I don't know what's to the left."

Melvin turned them to the left and they walked through half of the torture room, looking for anything of interest. At the far end of the room, the walls closed in to form a wide tunnel. The stone surface became irregularly shaped. A great deal of moisture coated the walls. Pools of water dotted the floor.

"This doesn't look like a man-made part of the castle," commented Dalwen.

Melvin nodded. "It appears to be some sort of natural—"

An eerie fluting noise echoed down the tunnel. The haunting, otherworldly dirge could not be mistaken for any human instrument. Everyone froze, listening to the dreadful sound.

"My harpy's left tit!" whispered Garbor. "It's down here!"

The adventurers exchanged glances and prepared themselves for battle. Melvin kissed his blade and spoke to it softly. Advancing slowly, they came to a natural cavern of some kind, empty but for a pile of bones scattered in the corner. Still the airy tones of the Shadow Beast sounded ahead. The hair rose on Nergal's back, and the thrill of danger drenched him.

Another tunnel exited from the other side of the damp, dark cave. The disturbing song of the monster grew stronger. Melvin and Garbor entered the next passage side by side, tensed for action.

There in the tunnel, they met the Shadow Beast.

The air shimmered around the twisting blackness that filled the passage ahead. A least a dozen tentacles writhed around the thing, flickering in and out of existence. One moment Nergal saw only a shadow, the next a translucent horror that hinted of knobby black flesh and too many bobbing, glassy eyes that were completely black with no apparent irises or pupils. Details were impossible to make out in the chaos of semi-transparent tentacles. The creature released a shrill collection of notes at them that sounded like four trumpets hitting random notes simultaneously.

Nergal decided to leave. The Shadow Beast was fearsome indeed, much larger than an adult rock lizard. He slipped back into the darkness, unnoticed because of the presence of the Shadow Beast. He made his way many paces back the direction they had come, when he heard Garbor's war cry. He looked over his shoulder, but he had already retreated too far to observe anything. He heard Dalwen's voice steady and sure in the background. She uttered some sort of chant or spell. Nergal had heard magic before, from the war-shaman of his tribe.

Nergal hesitated. He liked the brave human warrior named Garbor. Shouldn't the half-orc be at his side in battle?

Then a man cried out in pain.

"Garbor!" Melvin's voice rang out. "Hang on!"

Nergal realized he couldn't leave when Garbor needed his help so badly. He hadn't felt that way since going into battle with fellow orcs years ago. He sprang into action, running back the way he had come. He could not let Garbor die!

Nergal entered the wet, sickly echoing space again. Garbor lay propped against the wall. His left hand clasped a blood-covered right arm. Melvin slashed at the nebulous form of the Shadow Beast, trying to keep it at bay. The torch and Dalwen's lantern had been discarded on the floor, and their combined light was barely enough to illuminate the damp passage. As Nergal approached, a huge pillar of fire shot up from the ground, completely covering the monster and filling the area with bright light. The strange flame produced no smoke, but Nergal could feel its heat on his face as he watched.

"Argh!" Nergal exclaimed in wonderment. It seemed that the priestess Dalwen had powerful magic.

The flames died down seconds later. The thing still hovered before them, untouched. Melvin cursed and Dalwen let out a cry of denial. The Shadow Beast had retreated fully into its other-where to hide from the flames. Now its tentacles became slightly more substantial, pulsing in and out of their dimension, as it reached for Melvin.

Nergal ran up to Garbor, who watched the scene with a grim mask of pain on his face.

"Here," offered Nergal, holding out the pendant to the injured knight. "Garbor take! Take!"

"You found it!" exclaimed Garbor in a pained, wheezing voice. "My friend, you must put it on! Put it on and slay the Shadow Beast! It's our only chance!"

Nergal stared at Garbor, who looked unwell. The burly man bled from a cut on the side of his head as well as his arm. The ornate helmet he usually wore had been knocked off in the combat. He considered the knight's request. The half-orc shrugged and placed the necklace around his neck, trying to figure out the clasp.

"Nergal! Help us!" urged Dalwen.

"Loot no fit on!" Nergal exclaimed, trying to affix the warding device.

"Norngawen Alofzin!" exclaimed Dalwen as she spotted the necklace in Nergal's hands. "I'll help you!" she said, and ran up behind Nergal.

Melvin had not seen the necklace and did not understand what was going on.

"What're you doing?" demanded Melvin, desperately trying to hurt the monster. His veneer of sophistication left him as his voice lilted in terror. "Help me!"

As he pleaded for assistance, the shadowy form moved in again. Tendrils of darkness flowed forward to envelop the knight. Melvin yelled and thrust his sword at the body of the terror. There was a frenetic hooting and fluting as the creature reacted to Melvin's attack, and then tentacles solidified into existence around the knight. Most of the tentacles slid harmlessly along Melvin's breastplate, but the man cried out as one of the appendages found and tore at the flesh of his upper leg, another slashing his unprotected wrist.

At last Dalwen finished her desperate work. "You have it! Kill it Nergal! Kill it!"

Nergal needed no further urging. He could glimpse the mottled, lumpy surface of the horror that was mauling Melvin. The half-orc leaped forward with a cry of rage and lunged at the monster with his sword.

The weapon went completely through the shadowy outline, but Nergal could feel some slight resistance to his blade, like cutting the fat from a freshly killed pig. Once again a burst of alien notes sounded from the Shadow Beast, and it focused on this new attacker.

Nergal almost stumbled forward from his rush, surprised by the lack of resistance to his charge. He regained his balance and slashed savagely at the thing as it reached for him.

Nergal felt an icy rush on his skin like cold water, and then the awful tentacles began to slide into existence around him. The cold slick feeling quickly disappeared in a flush of warmth as a burst of white sparks erupted from Nergal's necklace. The occurrence stunned him. The Shadow Beast shrieked out in a burst of discordant noise.

Nergal stood stunned as the beast wailed again and moved away.

"Nergal!" Dalwen added a shriek of her own. "Chase it! Kill it!"

Nergal snapped out of his shock and closed with the horror again. His sword thrust and slashed out. The Shadow Beast moved back from the humanoid attacking it and retreated down an adjoining passageway.

The orc came after it in an instant, with Melvin staggering close behind. Water sloshed first against his feet and then rose to his knees as Nergal pursued the monster down the passage and into another open space. The thing moved off into the darkness, but Nergal could sense it just ahead, and he chased it despite his fading vision.

"Varanius almighty!" swore Melvin several paces behind him. "I need the torch!"

Nergal ignored him and slashed out into the darkness. The fluting noise sounded nearby, and he felt the cold thrill rush over his skin. White sparks flew again, and Nergal saw the hideous, many-eyed monstrosity looming before him. The thing screamed in agony, its unholy sound filling the chamber until Nergal could feel it in his bones. The Shadow Beast was completely solid now; it did not flicker or fade. Nergal slammed his sword forward at the thing, closing his eyes from the terrible sight of the monster. He felt the thing's teeth slicing into him from several places at once.

The cry of the Shadow Beast sounded again in distress. Nergal screamed back at it, hacking away as darkness consumed him. This time his strikes hit home. The sickly stench of the creature's lifeblood filled the air as the weapon sliced into the foul thing's body. His sword struck repeatedly and the half-orc fell into a mad fury of blood-lust.

When Melvin reappeared with the torch, he found Nergal standing hip deep in water, breathing heavily, with the remains of the unspeakable thing floating around him. He was covered in his own bright red blood and the monster's sticky brown fluids that mixed reluctantly with the water.

"Nergal, are you all right?" whispered Melvin, looking at the scene in awe.

"Mmmm. Nergal kill. Nergal very good," he assured the knight. Then he remembered Garbor.

"Garbor all right?"

"I—I don't know," stammered Melvin. "Dalwen is seeing to him. Let's go find out."

They staggered back to find that Garbor rested on the wet floor, breathing steadily as Dalwen worked on cleaning and binding his wounds. The knight looked up as Melvin and Nergal approached, and saw the ichor coating Nergal and his sword.

Despite his injuries, Garbor smiled, blood dripping down his face. His deep laughter boomed through the bowels of Castle Salthor.

"You did it Nergal! You killed the Shadow Beast!"

CHAPTER 6

The City of Spires

"And just what proof do you have of this deed?"

King Callowain looked expectantly at Melvin, who spoke for the group of adventurers. Nergal stood nervously with Dalwen and Garbor at the foot of the stair which led to the magnificent throne of the ruler of Raktan, City of Spires. Around them were the nobles and scribes of the court, watching as the survivors of Salthor related their tale to the king.

In answer Melvin pulled up a large and obviously heavy sack from the steps behind him. The guards watched suspiciously as Melvin opened the sack and poured out its contents: four score and three large white teeth, gathered from the pool in which Nergal had slain the Shadow Beast. The pile of teeth was all that remained of the horrible thing that had terrorized the entire region for months.

The king looked to the side at his court wizard, expecting explanation for the pile of wicked-looking teeth. The mage's eyes grew wide and he addressed his king.

"The tentacle spikes of the Shadow Beast," he said in a quiet voice. "We dug one out of Knight Brollan's back shortly before he died."

The king snapped his fingers and motioned to one of his guards. Nergal found the entire situation unbelievable, that everyone followed this fat old man's every whim. If Nergal felt more at home, he would simply step forward and slap the old man aside and take his throne. Despite his certain superiority to the old king, Nergal held back. Some instinct told him that all was not as simple as it seemed.

The soldier stepped forward and fetched him a single ragged spike from the pile on the step. The king took it and turned it over in his hands, and then looked back to the group. Nergal saw that the king had sharp eyes, even if he looked feeble in every other way.

"The reward goes to these heroes," he pronounced. The court applauded, and the king motioned them forward.

The king seemed to notice Nergal for the first time. His eyes narrowed as he looked at the half-orc with obvious doubt.

"This...he helped you kill the Shadow Beast?"

Nergal felt that the king did not like his kind. Perhaps he would be challenging the king for his throne after all.

"Yes, my lord," assured Melvin. "We would have perished without his assistance."

"Hmmm," the king grudgingly accepted this. "Then the four of you shall be rewarded. Rothgar here will see to it that you receive my gratitude." The king indicated a scribe of some kind who stepped forward with a dainty step and bowed. Nergal almost laughed aloud at the outfit worn by the king's servant. Lacy cuffs fluttered at his tiny thin wrists. Golden buttons criss-crossed his silken tunic at random. The half-orc bit his tongue and held it back. He reminded himself that these ones had strange ways just like his new friends.

"This way, if you please," the court scribe said in a high voice.

The adventurers followed the thin man out of the audience chamber and down long halls of the palace. The rich splendor of the City of Spires and the countless treasures of the palace where the monarch resided overwhelmed Nergal. Many times now his thoughts had turned to thievery, but as of yet he had not had a chance to act in the presence of his new friends.

The king's scribe brought them to a large armory, full of weapons and armor. Nergal gasped. Every breastplate and helmet gleamed. He smelled the oil on the air, every blade coated and rust-free.

"Through here," he said and led the way through the armory to a portcullis in the back. "These are the men who slew the Shadow Beast," he said to the guard, who nodded and motioned through an arrow slit. After the gate rose they made their way through it.

"There's gold, of course," the scribe told them airily, "but the king wanted to give you something special for ridding the land of that thing. These are singular items of great value. You may choose one item, each."

The room was large and L-shaped. Several sconces on the walls with lit torches provided light for the visitors. Racks of weapons and armor lined the walls. There were cabinets with wands and rings on display. Nergal's eyes bulged as he took it all in.

The scribe waved his hand in the air. "Remember, only one item each. Take your time, I will go fetch your gold." The dandy left hastily.

Melvin, Garbor, and Dalwen began examining the items in the room, murmuring in appreciation. Nergal felt that many items looked valuable, but he had not as of yet locked onto anything that kept his attention. Besides, he could hardly steal things with the others nearby. He walked twenty paces ahead so he could see around the bend in the room. At the far side he saw a collection of shields and another portcullis.

Nergal approached the shields, trying to assess their value. Unlike breastplates and helmets, he could comprehend the usefulness of a good shield. Sometimes bad weather would come while travelling, and it could be used to keep one's head dry and warm.

Nergal picked out a particularly large, heavy shield easily. He glimpsed something out of the corner of his eye, and realized that there were more items behind iron bars of the gate in the corner. Taking a look back, he saw that the others had not come around the corner to this part of the trove. Nergal walked up to the iron bars.

A small room with no other exit waited beyond the bars. Although there were no torches in the smaller room, Nergal's eyes found a large mace on the floor at the far side in the darkness. A mace was exactly Nergal's style, and this mace seemed to be somewhat oversize, sporting frills of sharp ridges on a cylindrical head.

Setting the shield against the wall, he grasped two bars in his beefy hands. Nergal applied pressure to the iron, trying first to bend the bars apart, and then attempting to smash them together. The portcullis remained solid, resisting even his considerable strength.

Nergal growled in frustration. He reached lower and grabbed a crossbar, setting his legs and lifting. Slowly the barricade rose, until Nergal stood holding the immense weight. Nergal briefly felt the satisfaction of success, until realizing that the bars would fall as soon as he released them.

The half-orc stood for a moment, holding the gate open with his awesome strength. Then he looked down at the shield resting against the wall, and realized what he must do. Straining mightily, he grunted and lifted one foot from the floor. Nergal gritted his teeth in concentration, and pushed the shield under the portcullis with his foot so that it rested against the wall under the gate. Then he set the bars down upon it.

This entire operation had taken less than thirty seconds, but now Nergal realized the necessity for speed. At any time, one of the others might get curious and walk around the corner. Nergal did not wish to be caught. He slipped under the suspended metal and loped to the mace, a bounce in his step. Grasping the weapon, he slunk back quickly and put the mace on the far side of the portal.

It took him only a moment to restore the gate to its original position, and then Nergal took up his prize with glee, admiring its heavy construction and wicked spiked ridges.

If I were you, I'd put me down.

Nergal jumped, raising the mace to smash the intruder. But Nergal could see no one.

You're probably going to get into trouble for this.

"Where you be?" demanded Nergal, narrowing his eyes and looking all around, examining ceiling and floor.

Right here. In your hand. It's me, the mace.

Nergal's enormous hairy brows came together in consternation. "Mace?" he inquired, staring at the weapon. "Uh, Nergal not feel so good."

Hey, I was just trying to warn you. It's fine with me, take me. Flaming hellions, I was getting pretty bored back there anyway. It's been a long, long time since anyone used me.

"Mace talk in Nergal's head," Nergal wondered. "Must be magic."

What are you anyway? Some kind of orc halfbreed?

"Watch mouth!" snapped Nergal, slamming the mace into the stone wall. It made a heavy clank and the shock numbed his hand.

"Nergal, is something going on?" Dalwen called out. "I've been hearing noises from back here." She peeked around the corner to investigate. "Did that gate back there come down?"

"Trying out mace," Nergal explained, showing her the weapon.

"Oh!" she said, seeing the mace. Her eyebrows were raised in surprise. "Alofzin! That must be a giant's mace." She turned back and disappeared from sight. The mace resumed their conversation.

Look friend, I'm a mace. You can't hurt me by hitting me against something.

"I hurt you," Nergal growled, bringing the mace back for another, more powerful swing against the wall.

Uhh, hey guy, I'm sorry. I didn't mean to offend. Just curious, really.

Nergal stopped and stared at the weapon. "You good mace?"

Well, I haven't had any complaints.

"Yeah, you good heavy mace," Nergal confirmed. "You be good mace for me. Give name now…. Ummmm." The half-orc descended into thought. His eyes squinted and his face pinched up under the strain.

Heh, don't hurt yourself there friend. I already have a name.

Nergal's eyes lit up. "Ah! I call you Elf Smasher!"

No No No! Listen to me please! My name is Krollon!

Nergal made a face. "Is dumb name, Crawling."

Krollon! That's my name.

"Nergal keep Crawling," the orc announced.

Nergal rejoined the group in the next room. It seemed that they, too, had selected their rewards and were ready to depart. Nergal had been so distracted by his mace that he had not pilfered anything else.

"Who were you talking to back there?" Dalwen asked with a smile on her face. "You aren't one of those guys who talks to their weapons like Melvin here, are you?" she teased.

"Uh, Nergal thinking."

"Ahh," she said, accepting his explanation as quite likely. "Sometimes I think out loud, too." Once again a smile crossed her features. Nergal did not quite understand what was going on.

She finds you amusing, Krollon told him. *But don't get your hopes up, you're kind of ugly.*

"Be shutting up!" growled Nergal.

"What?" Melvin asked.

"Er, time we shut up and get gold," Nergal covered.

"Heh, yes, all that lovely gold!" Garbor agreed, hefting a new helmet in his hand. "The Shadow Beast broke the nose guard on my old helmet. I figured I should get a new one…but that's not all. I can see in the dark with this thing!"

"Eh?"

"Melvin found an inventory of the cache," Dalwen explained. "We know what all these things do. Should we look up your mace for you, Nergal?"

"No! Er, Nergal know mace is good."

"Well, there are several maces on the list anyway," Melvin muttered, disinterested in the conversation. He seemed to be focusing on a new ring he had placed onto his left hand. Nergal saw that Dalwen had selected a silver cross with some kind of avian carved into its front.

Nergal took Garbor's short sword and scabbard and handed it back to the knight. "Nergal have new weapon now," he explained.

"Thank you. Just tell me if you have need of it again, my friend."

The effeminate scribe returned and a guard waited on the far side of the gate with a small chest of gold. The scribe made a cursory examination of the group's selection, but he didn't seem to distrust them enough to check carefully. Nergal had placed his new mace in a leather weapons belt he found, and he took the chest when Garbor motioned to him. The little chest seemed heavy for its size, and Nergal decided it must contain a lot of gold. He shook it gently, listening to the subdued clinking of the coins within.

"Rich! What we do now?" he asked.

"I know just the place!" said Garbor.

"Oh no," said Dalwen.

"Come on now, my dear. We've earned a bit of respite!"

"Respite? Is that what you call it?" she asked with a smile.

They dropped off their chest of rewards in their quarters within the palace and made their way into the commons quarter of the city. Nergal followed them blindly, dependent on the other's sense of direction in the confusing city. He felt out of place in the city. Although he had been in human settlements before, Nergal didn't have experience with this level of civilization. He hadn't seen even one other orc or part-orc since arriving.

Garbor selected a tavern for the group and they claimed a worn but solid table for themselves. Nergal inhaled deeply. The smell of ale and mead lay heavy in the air. The place was just starting to get busy with evening patrons, so no one paid them any attention as they settled in.

"A toast to our victory over the Shadow Beast!" boomed Garbor, and they drank some of the bitter liquid that the wench had brought to them. Nergal noticed that Dalwen did not drink.

"No good?" he asked of the priestess.

"My mind must be clear to act as my deity ordains," she told him. "Haven't you ever met a priest or priestess before, Nergal? For that matter, it seems that you haven't spent much time around humans at all."

Nergal shook his head. "Mother human. She bring Nergal to orcs to live. She no want orc-child."

"Ah," said Melvin, and an uneasy silence ensued.

Disgusting. These people are soft and weak. They pity you now, Krollon said in Nergal's mind. Nergal almost yelled at the mace but he bit his tongue. The others would hear him and think he was crazy. Instead Nergal fantasized about smashing the mace into a large rock.

Easy fella. I'm on your side.

"Well, we should have a wizard in our band," declared Dalwen, trying to change the subject. "I have some contacts at our temple here, and I have learned of some we should consider."

"That's fine with me," Garbor said. "I know nothing of magic, but it's always good to have a mage on your side."

It was enough for Nergal that Garbor had agreed so enthusiastically. "Yes," said Nergal. "Good."

I hate wizards, myself, Krollon commented in Nergal's head. *It was a wizard that put me in here.*

"Very well," said Melvin. "We should learn some more about them and see if we can convince them to join us. Sometimes wizards prefer to stay in their laboratories rather than journey about the land."

"Well, the first one is an elf named Rilivan," Dalwen announced.

"No! You no say wizard be elf!" spouted Nergal.

All heads turned to regard the half-orc.

"What's wrong?" asked Garbor.

Nergal stared back, aghast at his slip. He did not know what to say.

Melvin had a revelation. "Nergal…did you and Zanithweir get in a fight?"

Nergal froze, overwhelmed with dread. At his hip, Krollon recognized the reaction.

Uh oh, Krollon chimed in. *Anything you wanna tell me, fella?*

"Umm…" Nergal gurgled.

Dalwen's eyes grew wide. "You did! Zanithweir and you got in a fight, and he left. It must be because you're part orc. He probably couldn't overcome his racism towards you."

"And you must not have told us because you feared that we would blame you!" exclaimed Melvin.

Dalwen leaned forward, and gently put her hand on Nergal's arm. "Is that what happened, Nergal?"

"Umm….yes?" Nergal guessed.

Heh, trusting aren't they? commented Krollon. *Where did you find these bleeding hearts, anyway?*

"You don't have to worry, Nergal," Dalwen promised. "If the elf feels strongly against orcs, then we wouldn't want him in our group anyway."

"Absolutely," confirmed Melvin.

"You're with us no matter what," Garbor told him. "We don't like anyone who doesn't like you, Nergal."

"Okay," Nergal said woodenly.

Heh. Orcs and elves. This should be interesting, the mace chuckled in his mind.

CHAPTER 7

The Wizard Rilivan

"So you're the heroes who killed the Shadow Beast," Rilivan said, ushering the group into his workshop. The wizard was a graceful and thin elf, dressed in deep green robes that seemed to shimmer slightly in the late afternoon light.

"Yes, that's us," Melvin acknowledged. "I am Melvin of Elniboné, and these are my companions, Garbor, Dalwen, and Nergal."

The wizard looked the group over as they were introduced. If he had a negative reaction to Nergal's presence, it was not detectable. Nergal tried to submerge his own feelings about the elf. Somehow he felt the others wouldn't approve of it.

The workshop occupied the entire first floor of the mage's house. It contained a wild variety of items that Nergal could not begin to categorize. In addition to the usual array of mysterious magic books, there were jars and vials full of unrecognizable things of all shapes and colors. Nergal smelled a slightly burnt odor in the air, but he could detect no food so he didn't analyze the scents further.

"It's good fortune, then, that you've come to visit me. Another monster threatens the land. You're just the warriors to slay it."

"But we just killed the Shadow Beast!" blurted Garbor. "A creature so terrible it paralyzed the entire coast! And now you say there's another monster we must slay?"

Rilivan nodded solemnly. "Yes, it's a very dangerous flying creature of some sort that has been plaguing Halfor Bay. The docks there have been shut down, so terrible are its attacks."

"Such bad luck this region is having," Melvin murmured.

"Perhaps," Rilivan said. "It may not be bad luck. Tell me, do you still have any of the Shadow Beast's teeth that you showed the King?"

"Word travels quickly," Dalwen commented dryly, fingering a bony ridged spike hanging from a leather cord around her neck. "I kept one for myself—in fact I think we all did."

Nergal and Garbor nodded. Nergal had kept some of the teeth as trophies of his killing prowess. They were in a backpack he had purchased with some of his reward money. The satchel sat in the middle of Nergal's back, dwarfed by the broadness of his shoulders.

Dalwen took off her spike and handed it to the wizard. "Amazing, isn't it?" she asked.

"That it is," Rilivan replied, examining the tooth carefully. "But there's more to this than it seems, I'm afraid. This new threat is actually the third monster, not the second. What's worse, this latest one appeared slightly before the last one was killed."

Some crazy wizard must be making the monsters, Krollon thought to Nergal. *I hate wizards.*

"Wizard make monsters?" asked Nergal, echoing Krollon's suspicion.

Melvin and Dalwen stared at Nergal in shock. They found his sudden deductive acuity quite surprising.

"As a matter of fact, that is exactly what I believe," said Rilivan. "You have a very perceptive companion here." Nergal felt his hatred for the elf rise as the wizard's sharp eyes examined the half-orc.

I hate wizards...you hate elves...we can work together on this one, Krollon said silently.

"Uh.... Yes," Melvin said.

"May I keep the tooth for a short while? I need to use it in my research to attempt to locate what or who has been causing this. If it's another mage, I may be able to locate him by using remains of his creations."

"I'm fond of the spike, but of course your need is the greater," Dalwen said. "Please, keep it as long as you want, so we can discover the source of this evil."

"Thank you very much, priestess," said Rilivan. Apparently the mysterious wizard knew of her sect, for Dalwen had mentioned nothing of herself thus far. "Also, I must implore you: go to Halfor Bay and try to kill this thing. The natives are calling it the Night Reaver, for apparently it's exclusively nocturnal. If you can bring me back a part of this creature it may provide additional clues that we need."

"We had hoped that you would join us," Melvin said.

"No, I cannot," Rilivan told them. "I must stay and work on discovering what's going on. I've already been examining the remains of the Crawler, which was killed last year in the southern marshes. Now I have a piece of the Shadow Beast. Hopefully by the time you return I shall know some more."

As soon as they had exited the house, Dalwen turned to Nergal.

"Nergal, that was a great guess you made back there! I must admit I had thought maybe you were…well, a little slow. But I see now that it's just because your grasp of our language is limited. You're really very wise!"

Nergal nodded. "I have the smarts," he told her.

I said the thing about the wizard, complained Krollon. Nergal fidgeted but ignored the mace.

"Well, let's hope that we can slay this Night Reaver as well, and bring back another clue to Rilivan," said Melvin.

Garbor shrugged. "I've slain many creatures in my time, and my father the same before me," he announced. "These monsters are not mysteriously connected. All manner of beast have threatened man since the beginning of time, and they shall continue to do so. This is nothing new. That's why brave souls like us are needed."

No one felt the need to add to Garbor's speech. They walked back towards their inn for a while in silence. Nergal could tell that something was bothering Dalwen. She walked uncertainly and had a distant look in her eyes. At last she broke away from the group.

"I'll catch up with you at the inn, I have some things to attend to. I assume we will leave tomorrow morning for Halfor Bay?"

"I plan to," said Melvin.

"And I!" exclaimed Garbor with his usual enthusiasm. "We must follow this through to the end!"

Nergal nodded.

"Until tomorrow, then," she said and walked off.

Nergal, you must make an excuse and turn back, the mace Krollon said in the half-orc's mind.

"Mmmm?" mumbled Nergal, unwilling to speak in front of Melvin and Garbor.

Tell them you have business too.

"Uh," Nergal said, stopping. Melvin and Garbor turned to look at him. "Nergal have…"

Other matters to attend to. Other matters to attend to!

"Other matturs to attendu," he finished.

"Oh," said Melvin, somewhat surprised at Nergal's choice of words. "That's fine...will you meet us by morning for our mission?"

"Um, yes," Nergal assured him, nodding enthusiastically. Then the half-orc turned on his heels and walked back the way they had come.

Melvin and Garbor looked at each other.

"He's been acting kind of strange lately..." Melvin said.

"He's been learning some new words from you, I think," said Garbor. The knights laughed and continued on towards the inn.

Nergal walked back the way they had come, with Dalwen a dozen paces ahead of him. The half-orc evaded her detection so he could follow her unnoticed.

"What we do?" whispered Nergal.

Follow her.

"Why we follow?" Nergal asked.

Look, one of the few advantages to having your essence encased in a weapon is that you get to understand people better. That's because you spend all your time watching instead of doing, explained Krollon.

Now take Dalwen for example. It's very clear to me that she is still disturbed about Zanithweir. She thinks she can find him and convince him that you are a good orc. And the wizard just mentioned that he might be able to locate a wizard given some monster remains. So Dalwen is thinking, she can get some wizard to find Zanithweir!

Nergal couldn't understand it all.

"The elf?" Nergal said, frowning.

Exactly. We've got to follow her. What if she finds out you offed the fairy?

"How you find out?" snapped Nergal.

Heh. It was just a guess. Now I know.

"Huh?"

Never mind. My point is, she might be dangerous to us.

"Dalwen not danger," Nergal asserted.

What if she finds out about Zanithweir?

"Mmmm, dat be bad."

Exactly. We might have to kill her.

"No!" said Nergal, his eyes bulging. He reached for the mace's handle and brought it up to eye level. "Nergal beat mace against wall again."

He heard an ethereal sigh. *Ok. Wait. Let's just see where she's going first.*

Nergal nodded and returned the mace to hang by his side.

They followed Dalwen to a shop with a strange sign hanging out front that Nergal did not recognize. After watching from an alley for half an hour, the half-orc spotted Dalwen leaving, headed back towards the inn.

I've no doubt she hired him. A curse upon you wizard! spat the mace. *Nergal, he might find out. If you won't kill Dalwen, you're going to have to kill this wizard.*

"He no bother Nergal. Nergal rather kill elf wizard."

All in good time! But this one might find Zanithweir.

"Shado Beest kill him," Nergal explained slowly. "Nergal dump elf in water."

The mace lay quiescent for a moment, as if thinking.

Nergal, there is no doubt that the wizard will find out what really happened. They have the magic to do these things. If you don't kill him, Dalwen will find out, insisted the mace urgently. *Then she won't like you anymore. Garbor and Melvin will hate you, too.*

"Nergal kill wizard," Nergal said quietly.

This wizard is going to have traps set for intruders, Krollon explained, the words coming into Nergal's mind. The half-orc was still getting used to the unsettling voice in his head. *We'll have to sneak in tonight and do it.*

Nergal ignored the mace as it told him this, and made his way across the street to the wizard's shop.

Where are we going? Not into the shop!!!

The half-orc stepped into the tiny shop, stooping down slightly so that his head did not hit the top of the door frame. Nergal could see shelves of trinkets and charms in the dim interior. A short bald man stood behind a wooden counter.

What are you doing? The mace's thoughts seemed somewhat worried now.

"Can I help you?" asked the wizard, his right eyebrow raised at the sight of the hulking orc that had entered his shop.

"Mace talk too much," Nergal said, stepping up to the counter and grabbing his mace.

The wizard's other eyebrow raised as well. "Your mace talks?"

"Yes. See?" demanded Nergal, raising the mace over the counter for the mage to look at. Without hesitation, he swung the heavy weapon in a tight arc and smashed it into the side of the wizard's head. The man fell back like a sack of beans.

WHAT ARE YOU DOING!!!! What if someone hears us?

"Wizard dead now," Nergal stated with finality.

Quick! Lock the door before someone walks in!

Nergal walked back to the door and dropped the crossbar. Then he began looking around at the wizard's things. His instincts directed him to pilfer the place for anything valuable.

You did it. You don't mess around do you? I'm glad the wizard is dead, but you sure took a chance there.

"Nergal no take chance. Nergal only kill when they not ready. Nergal have the smarts."

I meant that someone else might have seen us and called the city guard. Can't we plan it a little more carefully next time? pleaded Krollon.

"Plan make Nergal bored. Looting more interesting," he said. Nergal searched through the outer room, but did not find anything that caught his eye. Moving around behind the counter, Nergal saw an iron box built into the counter. He placed his hands on the surface and snapped away part of the wood like dry bread, allowing him to get hold of the container. It resisted at first, but then slowly slid out of its snug hole.

Nergal placed the box on the floor and took up his mace again.

Hey, don't forget about the traps, Krollon warned. *Besides, someone will hear us.*

The brute realized that Krollon was right. The shopkeeper next door might know the wizard and come see what made the noise. Nergal took the iron box, heavy with coin, and put it into his backpack. Then he exited through the back of the shop and started for the inn.

Behind him, the wizard shifted on the floor and groaned faintly.

CHAPTER 8

The Terror of Halfor Bay

The adventurers prepared to leave the next morning. It seemed that none of the others were aware of Nergal's deed the night before. The iron box still rested in his backpack, as he had not yet had the chance to try and break it open in solitude.

Dalwen had purchased horses with some of her reward money so that they could get to Halfor Bay in a few days. Nergal stopped short and frowned when he saw the beasts.

I will tell you how, Krollon assured him. *Put your left foot into the stirrup.*

Nergal walked forward to a horse and then hesitated, painfully aware of Garbor watching him. The half-orc placed his foot gingerly into the metal loop and awaited the next command.

Now grab the saddle with one hand, then step up and throw your other leg over the horse.

Nergal took a good grip and lifted himself onto the horse, wavering clumsily as he placed his considerable bulk. The horse seemed a little nervous, although stout enough to carry him.

Seeing Nergal hunched over on top of the horse, Garbor thundered out a strong laugh. "Been a while since you have ridden, Nergal?"

"Nergal no ride good," explained the half-orc, clinging to his mount desperately.

"You'll get the rhythm of it," Melvin encouraged him.

I'll help you, Krollon told him. *Just think, we wouldn't have to do this at all if that elven wizard hadn't put everyone up to it.*

"Stupid fairy," Nergal mumbled under his breath.

We should really figure out how to get rid of him. But we need to make a plan ahead of time so that we don't risk getting caught. We make a good team, but if they catch you they'll take me away from you.

The half-orc grunted in assent. They would wait until the time was right.

Nergal found the next days on horseback quite unpleasant. Riding on the back of a large beast of burden felt uncomfortable to him. Yet he was loathe to give up these interesting new friends, so he stayed despite the soreness of his rear and quavering of his stomach.

They traveled into a hot, humid valley that opened onto a wide plain. Soon the bay became visible, and they found a well-traveled road leading to the city. Nergal thought that it would become cooler near the water, but instead the heat became even more intense, as if the water were boiling and its steam heated the land nearby.

They came at last to a squalid city that occupied rolling hills which descended into Halfor Bay. The streets were largely devoid of people. The soldiers seemed dismal and nervous, with lowered heads and black circles under their eyes. The adventurers made their way to the baron's keep overlooking the city and asked for audience with the leader, which was granted almost immediately.

Baron Ronvlack was a plump man with gray hair and disheveled attire. He emanated a nervousness as he met the group. The man seemed to have lost hold of his dignity somewhere along the line, and now he appeared to be a truly troubled soul. They met him in a small audience hall that seemed rather dismal after the great palace in Raktan.

"Sire, the four heroes from Raktan," announced a servant.

"Welcome to my court," said the baron. He wiped his forehead with a cloth. To either side of him servants waved large fans, fighting the oppressive heat. "We honor those who slew the Shadow Beast. You may speak freely."

"In Raktan we heard of your dire situation. We're eager to learn more of the Night Reaver and rid you of the menace," announced Melvin, speaking for the group.

"It's not called the Night Reaver any more," said the baron sullenly. "Now it's just the Reaver. It has been attacking in broad daylight."

"Really? That's fascinating," spouted Melvin. Then he reined in his enthusiasm, trying to sound concerned. "Um, and unfortunate. Pray tell us more, sire."

"As you've noticed, it's very hot in Halfor Bay. The waters are unnaturally hot due to a curse set upon the region hundreds of years ago. In addition it's a hot summer. So the dock workers always load and unload the cargo at night. A long standing tradition around here. Anyway, the beast attacked at the docks and we have been losing men rapidly. Ten men refuse to work the docks for every one man struck down by the monster."

The baron shook his head, sighed, and continued.

"We decided to switch over to working in the heat of the day. It's not possible to get as much work done, but at least we didn't have to worry about the creature, we thought. Turns out it's just as happy feeding on us in daylight as it was at night."

"But now you can use arrows?" prompted Garbor.

"We've been trying," said Ronvlack. "I moved all my archers down from the towers here at the keep to the docks. But the arrows never strike the creature, and when an arrow is loosed at the Reaver, it gets mad. It almost unerringly kills anyone who shoots arrows at it. Half my archers were killed in three days. Now all the remaining archers know that firing at the beast would mean their death. They're completely demoralized."

"Pardon me, Lord, but what did you mean when you said the arrows never strike the creature?" inquired Melvin.

The baron shook his head. "It's like the thing is protected by a spell," he told them. "The arrows fly into it, but they won't pierce its skin."

"We shall have to use other means, then," Melvin said.

"I hope you succeed. We're suffering greatly from the lack of trade coming through these days." The baron indicated a dark-skinned man with sharp black eyes. "This is the captain of the guard, Kerok. He will tell you more about the Reaver so that you may destroy it. Now I fear that I must retire, as my health is not what it once was."

After being dismissed by the baron, they followed Kerok through a set of doors to an empty meeting chamber. The tall warrior did not seem unfriendly, but he got to the point quickly.

"What do you need to know?" offered Kerok.

"What Reaver look like?" asked Nergal.

"It's disgusting. It has big scaly wings like a bat. There is no head, just a body with a mouth in the center facing down. It has four spindly limbs like spider legs, and each limb ends in a razor-sharp blade four feet long. I've personally seen the blades decapitate three men in three seconds." Kerok frowned, obviously recalling the scene in his mind.

"Does it eat the men it kills?" asked Dalwen.

"Not that we have seen. It just seems to kill for the fun of it. A bloodthirsty horror, to be sure. Did you really kill the Shadow Beast?"

"Yes, we did. Actually Nergal here delivered the killing blow, er blows," Melvin told him.

Kerok looked at Nergal's enormous musculature and nodded. "You look like a mighty warrior. But this thing has killed many like you," he warned. His hand flicked over his throat, indicating a throat slitting or perhaps decapitation.

"You are skeptical," Melvin announced. "I don't blame you. But I promise you that we will do our best to help you."

"Your help is welcome. Stay with me on my rounds and you will see the creature within the next two days, I guarantee it."

"Actually we should make a plan rather than simply await its next appearance," Melvin said.

"Yes! We could set a trap for it."

"What do you think, Nergal?" Dalwen asked.

Hire some mercenaries to work the docks under your protection until it attacks, Krollon thought.

"Er, hire soldiers. Work docks while Nergal watch. Reaver attack, then we kill," Nergal translated.

The group stared at Nergal.

"Uhm...amazing. That's an interesting idea!" sputtered Melvin. "Part of the reason the situation is so desperate here is that no one has been able to load or unload cargo safely since the monster appeared."

I'd also move some ballista down from the keep, added the mace.

Nergal nodded. "Get balleesta from keep," he said.

"Alofzin! The baron might let us do that," Dalwen replied.

Kerok nodded. "We can do that on my authority, but I don't know if the bolts will have any effect since arrows cannot harm it. The ballista are certainly more powerful though..."

"Not ballistas...catapults!" exclaimed Melvin.

"That's ridiculous. The thing flies all around, we couldn't possibly target it with a catapult," said Kerok.

"We can if we know where it's going to fly," said Melvin. "Each of us will go out on a dock in the open and shoot at it with arrows. When it comes to retaliate, we'll have catapults set up to hurl nets over it. Then when it gets netted we'll overwhelm it with numbers and kill it."

Wow. That's a better idea…if you're suicidal that is, Krollon commented.

Nergal nodded. The plan had escalated beyond his ability to understand, but everyone else seemed to like it.

"It's very dangerous. You're very brave," said Kerok. "We'll need five catapults—"

"Five? Are you going to be bait too, Kerok?" asked Dalwen.

"I cannot stand by and watch strangers risk their lives for my city without joining in," Kerok told them. "The plan is bold, but it just might work."

"Right," Melvin agreed. "Kerok and I will look over the docks and discover which ones would provide the best chances. Dalwen can oversee the transport of the weapons from the keep. Garbor and Nergal can procure the nets we will need."

"Aye, that we shall," announced Garbor, and he slapped Nergal on the back. "Let's go to it, my friend!"

CHAPTER 9

Hunting the Reaver

Nergal stood on the hot planks of the dock, which extended over fifty man-lengths out into the bay. The heat soaked through him, as if the water below were at a full boil. Once again he scanned the sky for the flying thing. Garbor had explained it all to him very carefully while they obtained the nets.

Even harder to grasp had been the operation of the bow, which Nergal now clutched in his huge hands. The thing seemed little more than a toy to the big orc, who could pull it back far enough to snap its arms. He had destroyed several bows during practice in just this way before learning how much a bow could withstand. Now Nergal could loose an arrow, although with poor accuracy.

Back where the pier met the land, the catapult crew watched Nergal at his post. The catapult had been tested early in the morning until it was certain that the weighted net would hit exactly where Nergal stood. If the net fell true over both of them, he would have a very close encounter with the Reaver indeed.

Beyond the nearest ship, other piers had been set with the same trap. Dalwen, Melvin and Garbor stood in similar spots awaiting the beast on Nergal's right as he stood looking out over the waters. The ship blocked Nergal's view of the others. Soldiers worked slowly to unload cargo from the ship in the instense heat.

The orc stood for more than an hour at his post, until the boredom was so great that he braved conversation.

"We kill Reaver today," Nergal said. The half-orc spoke in a normal voice since the distance to the catapult prevented him from being overheard.

I don't mind a few distractions, Krollon told him, *as long as we get back to the wizard soon.*

"Why you hate wizard?"

Why do you hate elves?

"Nergal ask first."

I hate all wizards. Look, I used to be just like you, before a wizard captured my soul and imprisoned it in here.

"You were orc?" demanded Nergal, sounding somewhat skeptical.

No, I mean I was a walking, talking person like you. I was human, but you wouldn't hold that against me, would you?

Nergal shrugged. He took off his small backpack and fished out the iron box.

Someone might wonder what you're doing, Krollon warned.

"No. They no pay attention. They look for Reaver," disagreed Nergal. Many of the baron's soldiers had stared at Nergal curiously, but none save Kerok dared to address him for any reason. Nergal could tell they were terrified of him.

At least put it downwind of you, urged the mace.

"Eh?"

There might be a gas trap.

"Ah," Nergal grunted in assent, and put the iron box down away from the hot wind. He looked up to scan the skies one last time. Seeing nothing, he brought the mace up to strike the box. Nergal breathed deeply and struck downwards with every ounce of his enormous strength, growling fiercely.

It was a truly tremendous blow. The iron box clanged and the board beneath it shattered, sending the box hurtling down into the water below.

"Zeck rag nok!" he cursed in orcish.

Hey, it's no big loss. At least you still have most of your reward money for the Shadow Beast.

A long screech from afar interrupted the talk. The call seemed distant and muted, as if the hot air did not carry the sound well. Nergal started scanning the skies, as did every man on the docks.

The half-orc first saw it as a speck in the sky, but the creature drew closer with startling speed. It looked like some sort of malformed bat with segmented legs hanging down from under it. The last segment of each leg curved into a scythe-like weapon.

At first it seemed to be coming straight for Nergal, who felt the hair on his neck rise. As the creature approached closer, Nergal realized that it planned to attack a ship nearby. Men stood on the deck, swords drawn as the thing approached. A few smarter ones darted for the cover of the hold.

The Reaver swooped around a mast and slashed at a man with two of its legs, knocking him off balance effortlessly. The man screamed and fell into the bay, some twenty man-lengths from Nergal's post.

The thing screeched and descended to finish its intended victim.

"Shoot! Shoot!" The soldiers manning the catapult were yelling at Nergal. He broke out of his paralysis with a start.

Nocking his arrow, Nergal brought the flimsy bow up and drew it back as far as he dared. He aimed briefly, targeting the creature as it hovered over the mercenary.

Nergal released, sending the arrow arcing towards its target. The Reaver dipped just at that moment, diving downwards to slice the helpless man. Nergal's arrow flew over the creature and stuck into the side of the ship. A short scream sounded and then the victim was dispatched, his head completely severed from his body.

Having killed its target, the Reaver gained altitude with powerful strokes of its leathery wings and arced over the ship. It sailed over and away, out of Nergal's sight. The half-orc turned and ran down the pier towards the city.

We have to stay here in case it comes back! Krollon told him.

"It come back, Nergal come back too," he said. The Reaver had headed towards Dalwen and Melvin. Dalwen was an excellent shot with her sling, and Nergal feared what would happen when she got the Reaver's full attention..

A commotion erupted from farther down the dock. Nergal saw Dalwen's catapult launch its net up ahead, but a merchant vessel blocked his view of the priestess on his left. He redoubled his speed, urgently trying to arrive on the scene before battle was joined. He could hear soldiers calling out and the screech of the Reaver. At last he cleared the intervening ship as he ran up to the catapult.

Nergal looked out onto another section of the bay. He saw the net lying on the pier where it had been cast. The creature hadn't been trapped, but Nergal could see Dalwen underneath the net, unmoving.

"Must go help!" Nergal told Krollon. He looked down the pier and saw that Melvin had witnessed the trouble and was running down his ramp towards the scene as well. Nergal arrived ahead of him since he had abandoned his post earlier.

Nergal ran past the catapult, seeing that the crew was desperately cranking it back, with a fresh net loaded into it already. He turned out on the pier and started running out onto the planking that extended out into the bay, towards Dalwen.

A screech broke the air and the half-orc saw the form of the Reaver again, gliding down towards the net and its victim.

It's too far! exclaimed Krollon.

Nergal saw Krollon spoke rightly. The creature would be upon her before he could arrive. Nergal grabbed his bow and desperately nocked another arrow.

Look, your aim is poor. You could hit her, Krollon thought.

"Nergal no miss," asserted the orc in a most determined fashion and loosed the arrow almost without thinking. It flew towards the Reaver for a long second, coming up and then down in a long arc, and struck a wing. The arrow snapped into pieces and fell into the bay without harming the Reaver.

The monster screamed in anger and changed course, heading straight for Nergal.

Now what are you going to do?

"We smash Reaver brains!" Nergal said, but his face betrayed his brave words by showing a grimace of fear. The thing dove at them, leaving no time for any decision.

One of the sharp legs slashed out at Nergal's head. The orc responded by blocking it with the huge mace. The tremendous mass of the metal cushioned him from the force of the blow, but Nergal could tell that the creature possessed impressive strength. Nergal ducked another swipe as he heard a catapult release.

Suddenly the sky fell in on Nergal and the Reaver. The expert crew had stopped cranking the catapult and loosed it at less than full tension, so its net would fall where Nergal had stopped to engage the creature. Half-orc and abomination crashed together under the unexpected burden, slamming into the wooden planking. Nergal felt the lumpy, bony thing writhe against him, and he howled out involuntarily.

Melvin ran up to the struggling mass under the net, his eyes wide with horror. His sword whipped around and he thrust it into the body of the Reaver, until its blade disappeared to the hilt. The thing released a wet scream and struggled under the net. Without skipping a beat, Melvin drew his dagger and slammed it deep into the Reaver's back.

The catapult crew ran up to help Melvin with their swords and shields in hand. The monster made a horrific sound and struggled under the net, thrashing about violently. The men hacked and slashed while Melvin attached himself to his sword hilt and tried to wrench the weapon free. The thing seemed to be growing weaker. At last he drew the blade from the creature, and a geyser of blood erupted from the wound. The Reaver wailed and became still.

"Ah, Nergal, please say something?" asked Melvin, fearing that the orc had been skewered as well.

"Um, you think Reaver good eating?"

"You're alive!" declared Melvin joyously, helping Nergal out of the net. Nergal paused to pull his huge mace out of the Reaver's mouth. Acting as one, they turned towards the end of the pier, seeing Dalwen's form lying motionless.

"Oh please…" Nergal heard Melvin mutter as they loped towards the fallen priestess.

Nergal approached the net and stepped over it until he reached Dalwen's prone body. He stuck his hands through the large weave of the rope net.

"Head still on?" mumbled Nergal, gently lifting her head under the net. "Head still on!" he told Melvin excitedly.

"Good, good! Do you see where she's hurt?" he replied his voice breaking in near panic. Melvin struggled to lift the net off the priestess. "Oh Dalwen, please don't be dead!" he wailed.

The force of Melvin's reaction surprised Nergal. Perhaps the knight held feelings for the female that Nergal had not appreciated before. The knight was practically coming undone right before him.

They disentangled her just as Garbor and Kerok ran up. The word spread quickly over the docks that the Reaver had been slain. The men were starting to cheer from the docks and the ships.

"There's no blood…" Melvin said. The group hovered over Dalwen, trying to discern any injury. Then she stirred and groaned, opening her eyes.

"Are you alright there, my friend?" boomed Garbor.

"Uh…I think so….Where's the Reaver?"

"Dead, I assure you," said Kerok.

With Melvin and Garbor's help, she sat up on the dock, rubbing the back of her head.

"The thing took a slash at me and I ducked," she told them. "It flew right by but the catapult had already released. I remember bracing for the net, but it hit my head like a rock!"

"One of the anchor weights must have grazed your head!" Melvin said. "I was sure you'd been cleaved in two or something." Melvin recovered from the panic that had gripped him.

Suddenly a new uproar came from one of the ships at dock. Kerok and Garbor looked at the ship to see the cause. Then Nergal saw it as he peered out into the bay.

"Galleys," he announced, pointing out into the harbor. "We run now," he told the others.

"How do you know they'll even attack?" asked Melvin.

"We cannot just run!" Garbor said.

"Warriors of Chu Kutall," explained Nergal. "Too many. Too strong."

"I must go warn the baron!" exclaimed Kerok, and bolted down the pier towards the dock. The catapult crew stood in shock for a moment, then started hurriedly packing the catapult.

"We should go to the baron's keep as well," suggested Garbor.

Melvin studied the force for a moment longer. "We need to get off the docks at least. Nergal is right in his assessment of their strength. There are more than enough to seize the city, I think."

They made their way back towards the monster, and Melvin slashed off one of the swordlike appendages of the beast to bring back to Rilivan.

"This is a terrible time for an invasion," Dalwen yelled as they loped up the pier. "Even Salthor castle…Alofzin!"

"Are you thinking what I'm thinking?" said Melvin.

"It's no coincidence that Salthor was emptied out by the Shadow Beast and that Halfor Bay is weak," Dalwen realized. "Chu Kutall's wizards have orchestrated this!"

The group made their way up through the panicked docks amidst the confusion. Most of the ships were being abandoned, although a few brave captains had rallied their crews to resist the initial onslaught. Nergal figured they were doomed now, as another wave of galleys had entered the bay and still more attackers would be joining those already in action.

As they made their way through the streets towards the small keep, Melvin turned and halted the group.

"This is more than a raid," he announced. "Clearly this has been planned carefully. The Chu Kutall are too many, and the baron's men have been weakened by the Reaver. We need to ride to warn the king."

"We cannot just leave these men here to die!" Garbor urged. "They need our help!"

"I know it's difficult, but Melvin's right. We must think of the greater good," said Dalwen.

"The baron will send a messenger to the king," Garbor stubbornly replied.

"You may be right, my friend. But think on this: Chu Kutall has been way ahead of us on this. They've planned carefully. Chances are they'll see to it that the messenger doesn't make it through. But I think we could make it," Melvin argued.

The Reaver could have been what they were relying on to stop the messenger, Krollon guessed. *We don't know what kind of control they had over it.*

"Maybe Reaver going to stop mess anjer," Nergal echoed for the group.

"Yes, maybe they were counting on the Reaver," Garbor said, seeing a point for his side. "But now it's dead so the messenger can get through."

"You're just guessing," Melvin said. "You saw the keep here. It won't hold against these numbers, not against a surprise attack like this."

"We're being cowards!" Garbor maintained.

"Look, right now they have Salthor open for the taking," Melvin continued. "Maybe King Callowain has moved a small force there, maybe he hasn't. If we ride quickly and warn him, the king's knights can make it to Salthor Castle before the warriors of Chu Kutall. We'll need you to help make a stand there, where we have a chance of beating them."

Garbor gave Nergal a pained look, hoping Nergal would back him up. Nergal just shook his head. "Nergal fight Chu Kutall before. Nergal lose."

"We're wasting time!" urged Dalwen. "Look, we're not being cowards. This is important! We'll fight Chu Kutall, just not today, not on their terms!"

Garbor heaved a great sigh. "Very well, then. But when the king's knights attack, I will be numbered amongst them!"

CHAPTER 10

Return to Salthor

"That is grievous news indeed," King Callowain said in a low voice, running a hand over his thick black beard. "Chu Kutall has invaded. Our chances of repelling them at the coast are completely nil. We must stop them at Salthor."

The king sat with the heroes in private chambers. Nergal found the luxurious quarters overwhelming, an alien environment of rich colors and confusing furniture. Tapestries and carpets hid the walls and floors as if the king were afraid to see the stone of his abode. Nergal tried to sit on a soft three-legged chair with no back, but as he settled his weight he heard the creak of wood. He stood back up and stepped aside to an empty spot before a giant painting of knights riding into battle. There he fidgeted while the others spoke of strategy.

Rilivan and Morkath, the leader of the legions of Raktan, had joined them at the king's command. Morkath held a grim look on his scarred face. The warrior-lord wore harsh, dark clothing and kept a sword at his hip even in the king's chambers. Rilivan wore the same shimmering green robe as he had when they last met.

"We should ride to Salthor without delay," Morkath agreed. "We can hold them until the rest of the army arrives." As the man talked, Nergal could see that the scar tissue on his face did not flex as easily as the undamaged parts. The man clearly wanted to spring into action, but he awaited the command of his king.

"Yes, that's our plan. Salthor Castle hasn't been prepared for a long siege, but the knights won't have to hold it for long. When the foot soldiers arrive they'll break any siege that has been started. After this meeting, Morkath will go and prepare the knights for immediate departure. I'll take command of the foot legions and follow in a day or less."

Garbor saw his chance to speak. "My lord, may I ride with Morkath and the knights?"

"I believe that Rilivan has something else in mind," the king said, motioning to the elven wizard. Rilivan seemed comfortable in the king's presence, and Nergal suspected that the wizard had met the king before.

"I have a spell prepared for incantation this evening," Rilivan told them. "As I hoped, you've brought me something from the Night Reaver, which will greatly enhance this particular enchantment. Within a few short hours, I will have a device which will lead us to whoever has been summoning these monsters."

"What does your spell have to do with me, wizard?" demanded Garbor.

"We must find the parties responsible and stop them," Melvin finished for Rilivan. "We'll need your help, Garbor."

This is too good, commented Krollon. *Now we're supposed to kill a wizard. We won't have to get this one in secret, Nergal. Your friends will actually help us!*

Nergal shrugged slightly.

Heh, I know, out of sight is out of mind. You're thinking more about Rilivan right now.

"Melvin is right, this will be a most dangerous task. That's why, with the king's permission, I'd accompany you as well," announced the elf.

Oh boy.

"Yes! All of you must do this thing. We're depending on you," said the king.

Garbor looked torn, but he did not dare oppose the king's order. His eyes met those of Morkath.

"We'll miss your sword, Garbor," Morkath told him kindly. "But there's no shame in this. Quite the opposite, we're depending upon you. We can defeat the warriors of Chu Kutall on the field as long as they don't have the help of this evil wizard, whoever he may be."

After encouraging Garbor, Morkath told the others, "We leave before sunset. Time is of the essence and we cannot wait for the morning."

"Go now, all of you, with my blessing," King Callowain told them and took his leave. Garbor left with Morkath, leaving Melvin locked in conversation with Rilivan.

"It would be fascinating to observe your spellcasting," Melvin said to the elf. The knight held one of the blade-like arms of the Reaver, collected for the wizard at Halfor Bay.

"That could be arranged, my friend."

Dalwen turned to Nergal. "I have to give a report to my Klandur. Would you like to see our temple?"

Nergal nodded to her, and they left Melvin and the wizard to their discussion. She led the way out through the palace grounds. The beauty of early evening in Raktan seemed subdued by the gravity of their plight. As they walked to Dalwen's temple, Nergal thought about Chu Kutall and wondered if he would become a slave again.

They arrived at a massive construct of sky blue stone, extending above the nearby buildings at the edge of the palace grounds. Dozens of steps led up to the giant columns which surrounded the square building. Dalwen gracefully ascended the steps of the beautiful temple and Nergal followed at first, but as they approached the entrance gates he fell behind.

"What's wrong Nergal? Won't you come in?"

Nergal did not meet her eyes. "Nergal done bad things…"

"Most people have. What does that have to do with it?"

"Only good ones go in temple," Nergal said.

Dalwen stood closer to Nergal and put her hand on his beefy shoulder. "Nergal, you have done a lot of good since I met you. Whatever evil you sowed before, you can overcome it. Such are the teachings of Alofzin. I have done bad things before, but I strive to correct those mistakes."

Nergal struggled to understand but only partially succeeded. "You done bad things too?"

"Yes. Whatever we have done in the past cannot be changed, but we can try to do our best with the future."

Nergal nodded. "Nergal try," he assured her.

"Good. You can wait here if it makes you more comfortable. I'll be back out within the hour."

Nergal sat down on the finely crafted steps, puzzling this over. The conversation had invoked strange emotions. When he remembered his father and how the elves had killed him, he felt anger and the need for vengeance. But when he thought of Dalwen and her kindness, he felt ashamed for the killing he had done, especially her friend Zanithweir. It was as if he had to betray his father or Dalwen, but he wanted to be loyal to both.

Krollon detected that Nergal had been troubled by Dalwen's speech.

I hope you're not buying all that Alofzin crap, Krollon told him. *That's just stuff that they tell people to keep them in line.*

"Nergal don't know," said the half-orc, shaking his head.

Just don't worry about it. We'll do just fine without any Alofzin. Killing wizards isn't bad anyway...they all do bad things like make monsters. So we're doing good by getting rid of them.

Nergal nodded but he did not answer. The half-orc wondered if Dalwen had ever killed anyone before. He waited the rest of the time in silence, just watching the people going in and out of the temple. At last Dalwen emerged and rejoined Nergal.

"We should go back to Rilivan's house and see what those two have produced," she suggested. "Sometimes I think Melvin is really a sorcerer at heart, he's so intellectually inclined. But his father, Lord of Elniboné, would never allow it."

"Nergal have father, teach Nergal to fight," Nergal said. Nergal wanted to add 'until he was killed by elves', but he held his tongue.

They caught the two waiting outside Rilivan's house. When Rilivan saw Dalwen and Nergal, he waved and motioned them over to his side.

"We've met with some measure of success," said the elf. "This wand will direct us to the party responsible for the monsters," he explained. Rilivan held a slender black rod, perfectly smooth and featureless. Nergal wondered how it could possibly direct them to anyone.

"Since the wand has indicated our target lies east, we shall ride with the knights, at least as far as Salthor," Melvin added.

The group retrieved their horses from a commons stable and went to the east gate of Raktan to await the knights. Less than an hour before the sun set, ten score knights and a like number of squires rode out of the city in a column. Garbor joined his fellow adventurers near the front, where Morkath was organizing a group of scouts to run ahead. The scouts were unarmored and traveled light on swift horses so that they could serve as the eyes and ears of the force.

Three days of hard riding seemed to blend together in Nergal's mind as the knights pushed the limits of their steeds to beat Chu Kutall to the castle. Morkath drove them forward relentlessly, even resorting to rotating horses between knights and the less heavily armored squires to get the most of their beasts of burden. It came as a shock to everyone on the third day when the scouts returned to report that the stronghold lay in enemy hands.

Morkath and the adventurers gathered to discuss the troublesome turn of events.

"This is most unexpected. Surely the force we saw at Halfor Bay could not have arrived here already," said Melvin. "Maybe some fraction of them seized mounts at Halfor and came to hold the castle for the rest."

"There was only a token garrison placed at Salthor after you killed the Shadow Beast," Morkath told them. "Somehow Chu Kutall has overcome it. We must retake it before more of their forces can arrive from Halfor Bay."

"That'll be quite difficult, considering that we left quickly with only our arms and our horses," Garbor observed. "We have no siege equipment or infantry to speak of."

"What can be done?" Dalwen asked of the group.

Rilivan stepped forward. "I am no siege expert, but I believe we're a force of some means," he stated. "We have highly skilled warriors and two of us have magical ability. Perhaps a small group could infiltrate the front gatehouse tonight, and bring down the drawbridge to allow the knights into the fortress."

"A bold plan," Morkath told the elven wizard. "I don't think it would work if they had a sizeable force in the castle, but it looks like they're undermanned. They were probably expecting the castle to be deserted and took losses in seizing it. How do you plan to get the group into the castle?"

"I'm not sure...probably using magic," Rilivan said, rubbing his chin with his long, delicate fingers. "I can get one of you into the castle, if that will help."

"Even assuming an intruder could overcome the guards silently, the winches for the drawbridge will be loud. The same goes for the portcullis, which would have to be raised before we could get in," said Morkath.

"I can help with that," said Dalwen. "I can make someone completely silent with magic, and I can silence the drawbridge as well."

"It would be very dangerous. I volunteer to go," announced Garbor.

"You're a good warrior, Garbor, but I know Salthor better than any of us," argued Melvin. "It makes sense that I go."

"If this were a task requiring cleverness and quick wits, I would concede the honor to you, my friend," said Garbor. "But, this is more a matter of brute force..."

Dalwen looked at the knights with a smirk on her face. "And who is the strongest of us? The portcullis will have to be raised quickly, but such a mechanism often requires the strength of two or more men."

She's trying to stick you with the task, Krollon warned.

"Nergal go," offered the half-orc.

Demon dung! Don't do that!

"Rilivan, can't you make one of us stronger with a spell?" demanded Garbor.

"Given time, yes. But I should save my energy for the main objective. Besides, it's most logical that we send the orc savage because he can function better in the darkness," said Rilivan.

"His name is Nergal," corrected Dalwen coldly.

"Of course. Nergal," Rilivan echoed, raising an eyebrow.

The damn elf is trying to get you killed! Tell them you won't do it!

"Nergal ready," announced the brute. His eyes narrowed as he looked at the wizard, but he didn't say anything else.

"My helmet lets me see in the dark," said Garbor, "and I—"

"Oh shut up," interjected Melvin. "Nergal is going, it's already been decided." The knight seemed to be in a poor mood now.

They waited until nightfall to begin the sneak attack. The king's knights, including Melvin and Garbor, moved as close as they dared without signaling their presence to the garrison. Nergal, Rilivan, and Dalwen prepared in a nearby copse of trees by the light of a half moon.

"Listen carefully, brave one," Rilivan said to Nergal. "I'm going to cast a spell on you that will enable you to fly up to the ramparts. I warn you that it will only last a short time. You'll have to proceed directly to the top of the front gates and find your way down to the gate mechanisms from there."

"Nergal fly? Powerful magic," marveled the half-orc.

"Reasonably so," said Rilivan. The elf handed Nergal a single smooth stone and stepped a pace back to work his magic. He began to speak in a completely different tone and pace, waving his arms about in the darkness. As he incanted, Rilivan took a long feather out of a pouch and snapped it in two. Then his voice rose slightly and he said three more words before abruptly ending his spellcasting. Dalwen watched from nearby, waiting for the spell to be completed.

"Alright now, Nergal, I'm done. When you're ready, just drop that stone and you will take flight."

I got it, Krollon assured Nergal. *Just nod, if you have questions I'll answer them later.*

Nergal nodded.

"Good luck. I must go back up the knight's charge," Rilivan said, and walked off into the night.

"Now my turn," said Dalwen, approaching Nergal. "I'm going to make it so that no sound will come from you or anywhere near you. You will be able to fight and work the mechanism without a sound. You can even yell and there will be no noise."

"No sound?" Nergal asked, amazed. "Nergal trip, no thud?"

Dalwen smiled. "Nergal trip, no thud. Ready?"

Nergal nodded again.

The priestess knelt down in front of Nergal. Her hands worked in the air rapidly as she invoked the name of Alofzin. She slowly rose from her crouch as she spoke several more soft words in a language that Nergal could not understand. Once she stood upright again, Dalwen threw her hands apart and froze, completing the spell.

A blanket of total silence fell upon them, catching Nergal by surprise. Nergal wondered at the sudden cessation of the soft noises of the night. The sound of insects and leaves rustling in the wind had been below his level of awareness until they were removed. Now they seemed blatant in their absence.

"No hear sound?" Nergal said but he could not hear himself. He stuck his finger into his ear and twisted the digit with no effect.

Nergal felt shock again when Dalwen leaned forward briefly and kissed him on the cheek.

"For luck," she mouthed, but Nergal heard nothing.

Dalwen stood back to give Nergal room, and she swept her hand up into the air, indicating to Nergal that he could take flight.

The stone my friend, reminded Krollon.

Nergal held his hand up, feeling the smooth rock in his palm. Then he dropped it and almost immediately began to rise into the air.

Nergal let out a surprised noise similar to a startled waterfowl. Dalwen's magic absorbed the sound, much to Nergal's relief. Already he swooped over a nearby tree, and he began to realize he had but to turn his head to begin moving in any direction.

Quickly, we must fly to the front gate towers.

"Nergal trying," he replied even though he could not be heard. The hulk moved effortlessly through the air and began to gain speed as he flew towards Salthor Castle. The experience of flight was so overwhelming that the half-orc had to struggle to keep his mind on the task at hand. The torches of the castle guided him unerringly to the front gates. Already he had gained enough altitude to look down on the castle, and Nergal reluctantly swooped down towards one of the gate towers.

As he neared, he could see a single soldier watching the front moat from over the ramparts of the tower. Nergal affixed his attention to the guard so single-mindedly that he hurtled down on top of the hapless man with a great deal of force. The soldier smashed down onto the tower as if in a dream, completely without sound. Even the man's helmet and shield made no sound as they hit the planking. Nergal landed on his feet, standing over the stunned guard.

Nergal smiled, exposing his long sharp canines in the dim light on top of the tower. The soldier looked up at Nergal as if he were a demon straight from hell as the half-orc took up his mace and brought it down upon his enemy. Nergal imagined the scream and crack of bones in the utter silence.

The mechanism is down below, Krollon reminded him. *Under that wooden hatch.*

Nergal nodded and began to slink, trying to be sneaky. He hunched over even more than usual and bent his knees, as if he could escape notice by compressing his body. He held his mace low, almost touching the floor, and brought up the hatch, looking for more guards. He made his way down through empty barracks and a storage room until he found a passageway out of the tower. He entered a room illuminated by the flickering light of two torches in sconces on the stone walls. Huge winches and giant wooden gears sat firmly moored to the floor, with chains winding around the equipment and through holes in the floor and ceiling.

A man in a black robe stood in the room, and he took notice of Nergal's arrival immediately despite the lack of footfalls. The man looked frail by Nergal's standards, like a scribe or priest.

Seeing that surprise was impossible, the half-orc rushed up to dispatch his opponent. He gripped his mace at the end of the handle and just under the head, thrusting it at the chest of the man with bone-snapping force.

The mysterious adversary avoided the strike easily, stepping to the side and whirling to kick Nergal in the short ribs, the impact coming hard and fast. The half-orc grunted in surprise and pain. Nergal retaliated with a hard wide swing, but the robed man somersaulted completely over the attack, sending Nergal staggering off balance. The guard took advantage of the orc's clumsiness and tried to punch him in the jaw, but Nergal dipped his head and took the blow on his immensely thick forehead without injury.

He's too fast for me. Just punch him instead, Krollon urged, speaking in Nergal's head rapidly.

Acting on instinctual inspiration, Nergal tossed Krollon straight at the human's head and launched a vicious low punch. His adversary gracefully ducked under the hurtling weapon but Nergal's fist slammed into his face. The man probably never knew what hit him. He crumpled under the force of the blow, and Nergal unhesitatingly followed up his attack by grappling with the guard, grasping him at throat and arm. Krollon slammed to the floor behind the man but Nergal had to imagine the clamor since the utter silence prevailed.

The soft flesh of the man's throat collapsed under Nergal's superior strength, the body going limp almost immediately. The half-orc snapped a few bones to be sure, then casually tossed the corpse aside. Seeing Krollon on the floor in the dimness, Nergal grasped his mace again.

We're over the entrance now, I think, Krollon said. *That latch over there and those chains are for the drawbridge.*

Nergal found the latch that Krollon mentioned and threw the metal clasp. Then he began to pull the chains upward. They resisted at first until the weight of the bridge began to nullify the counterweights, then they began to pick up speed.

That should do it for the drawbridge, Krollon told him. *Now the portcullis. Turn that big wheel over there.*

Nergal stepped up to one of the floor gears and grabbed it by pegs set in its circumference. The huge wheel was designed to be operated by two or three men at a time. He began to apply force to turn the device but it would not budge. Discarding his primitive sandals, Nergal tried again, digging the claws of his huge hairy feet into the planking of the floor. Nothing happened.

Throw the catch first, it locks it in place.

The half-orc looked around until he saw the metal catch Krollon mentioned. He disengaged it and applied himself again. Nergal could feel the rumbling of the chain through the pegs in his hands but the air still carried no hint of sound. His arms and legs bulged with the effort as he plodded around the gear like an ox drawing a plow in a circle. He continued this exertion until he felt that he could not move any further, and then threw the metal catch back to hold the device in place.

I hope that's far enough, Krollon said. *Look out the murder hole over there and see what's going on.*

Nergal staggered over towards the hole, which angled down towards the passageway into the fortress. Nergal peered down and saw dozens of knights milling in the tight space. The portcullis was not raised far enough for them to pass under while mounted. Even as he watched, a knight risked trying to dismount in heavy armor. The man landed off balance on his legs but fell heavily. It looked painful, but there was still no sound. He saw the mounted knights trying to fight off one or two defending warriors who had detected the assault.

Nergal hurried back to the mechanism, inspired to raise the gate further. He braced himself and undid the metal catch again. Nergal moved the heavy apparatus around several more times, but this time he tired quickly and had to stop sooner, lest he release the heavy gate by accident.

That should do it, Krollon told the exhausted half-orc. *Let them do some of the work now. You lucked out again, this would have been impossible with a full garrison.*

The sounds of battle suddenly snapped into existence, making Nergal twitch in surprise. He could hear the sound of horses making their way into the courtyard of the keep.

"Knights fight now. Nergal rest," he agreed.

CHAPTER 11

A Secret Revealed

The group of adventurers looked out over the battlements of Salthor Castle upon the foot legions of King Callowain. The soldiers were forming up for the march on Halfor Bay, where they hoped to recapture the port city and send the Chu Kutall back to their own island continent.

"The wand is leading us straight east," Rilivan commented. "Yet the road to Halfor Bay is northeast."

"We must follow it exactly, I think," Melvin urged, pointing to the east. "Chu Kutall may have a secret base on the coast. If we go with the legions to Halfor Bay, we may give them the time they need to summon another horror from the nether planes, or wherever these awful things come from."

"Yes, I agree. At least I did get to fight one battle with the king's knights. It was glorious," exalted Garbor. The knight had taken more than his fair share of the battle for the castle. "These Chu Kutall warriors fought fiercely, though. I'm surprised none of them offered to surrender once we breached the gate."

"They're a very warlike people," explained Melvin enthusiastically. He ranted on, "Loosely translated, Chu Kutall means 'race of the slavelords', or 'people who take slaves'. Actually their society has ranks of slaves within slaves. The overlords of the whole island continent are a sect of warrior monks, and these men made slaves of the original population of the island, but now the slaves have emulated their masters and the second rank of the society takes slaves of their own in like fashion."

"If you're done educating us, my friend, we should take our leave," Dalwen said gently. Garbor chuckled.

"Yes, I suppose you're right," Melvin conceded. "There'll be plenty of time for me to speak of Chu Kutall on the trail."

Garbor groaned in mock protest and Dalwen laughed.

The group parted from the king's army and made their way over the lightly wooded countryside on horseback. Nergal had worked out an easy relationship with his mount where neither of them tried to discomfit the other. Nergal allowed the horse to simply follow along with the others. Now and again Krollon would direct Nergal to give a command to the horse, but Nergal preferred to simply let it alone.

They followed the pointing wand for a full day, and took an uneventful night's sleep. Late in the second day of their travels, they came to a rocky cliff overlooking the Niyalan Sea.

"We're straight south down the coastline from Halfor Bay," Melvin told them. "Clearly the wizard we seek isn't on the mainland."

"He must be on a war galley," guessed Dalwen.

"Or the continent of Riken, in the lands of Chu Kutall itself," grumbled Garbor.

"That's possible if he's given up his task," Rilivan ventured, "But I think that he'd want to operate closer to his target if he's still summoning monsters to harry us."

"Yes. Even though the Reaver could've flown to the coast, I don't think the Shadow Beast swam all the way from Riken," Melvin said.

"Although the Crawler certainly could have," Rilivan said with a hint of disgust in his voice, recalling the creature. "It had gills, after all."

"Well in any case it's pointless. We can't continue without a ship," Garbor concluded.

"And the most logical place to get a ship is Halfor Bay," Melvin sighed. "I guess we should have gone with Callowain and Morkath after all."

"The army is slowed by the footmen," Garbor pointed out. He fingered the pommel of his war axe unconsciously as he contemplated battle. "That means that we could still ride up the coast and take part in the fight. They might need us."

"Ah Garbor, ever ready to ride into battle," commented Dalwen teasingly. "You're right though. Our way is clear in this."

Nergal listened to the conversation trying to glean what he could.

These guys are really distracting us. We could be killing wizards back in Raktan right now. I'm beginning to tire of the promise of this wizard that could be a continent away for all we know.

Nergal gave no reply. He felt content to stay with the group and help them fight Chu Kutall, wizard or no wizard.

The group rode back away from the cliff and then turned north towards Halfor Bay. They camped that evening just over the heights that overlooked the city. Hot air coming off the bay warmed the night air, so the group gathered a good distance from their small cooking fire.

"We could move west and link up with the king's forces as they arrive tomorrow," Garbor suggested. The man stretched his head one way and then the other, causing his thick neck to crack loudly.

"That would be fine with me," Dalwen said.

As usual, Melvin disagreed. "We'll need a good ship. Imagine the advantage of taking a galley of Chu Kutall. We'd be able to approach the enemy more easily. Some of the warriors may try to flee Callowain's attack and take the galleys back with them."

"So you're saying we should attack behind them at the docks. Interesting," said Rilivan as he mulled the idea over. "It could be dangerous, of course. If the warriors decide to retreat en masse, we could be slaughtered at the docks, overwhelmed by numbers."

"You forget the arrogance of Chu Kutall," Melvin announced, pointing his finger down towards the bay. "They won't yield without a fight. And it may degenerate into a siege of the keep. At least this time, the weakness of that fort will work to our advantage."

Garbor nodded. "I like your plan better, Melvin. We can take a galley or two for our use, and help panic the rear of the enemy. If we could free some slaves, that might be even better. They might take up weapons for our cause as well."

"Nergal, do you like the plan?" Dalwen asked.

Nergal feared becoming a slave again. "Nergal fight with you," he said, hiding his fear from the others.

Garbor took the watch and the others went to sleep. The night passed peacefully and when the morning came they moved over the ridge and down towards the city, keeping to the trees.

They commanded an impressive view from the hills overlooking Halfor Bay. The group could see most of the docks in the east as well as the approach from the west where they expected the legions' attack to originate.

By midday the signs of an army were visible in the west. The group watched as the king's knights arrived and held the flanks of the valley while the footmen marched down the center. The enemy did not come out of the city to meet the army in the open field, but stayed back behind the low wall of the town in a defensive position.

Nergal watched, fascinated, as the situation developed below. Within the hour the king's attack began, and the group observed anxiously as the walls were assaulted. The defensive works were inadequate to defend against an army the size of the king's, as they were only in place to defend against bandits and the like. As soon as the legions had broken into the city, the adventurers went into action. They rode their horses down towards the city, coming to a side gate in the wall. The enemy soldiers had been recalled to defend more vital areas of the city as the king's attack broke through from the west, leaving the gate undefended.

The group reached the first of the docks without meeting any resistance. They dismounted and drew weapons, Melvin and Garbor leading the formation. The sounds of battle could still be heard emanating from the city. Up ahead several of the galleys of Chu Kutall were tethered to the docks.

Garbor waved Nergal forward. "Nergal and I will take that one!" the knight said, indicating a galley fifty paces ahead on their right. The group split up, the others heading for another ship farther down the docks. Nergal could see that the ships were not fully manned, being held only by a handful of sailors. Garbor approached the galley without a hint of fear.

Nergal ran up to the ship that Garbor had indicated. He leaped on a connecting plank and ran up onto the galley's deck. Garbor made his way onto the ship as well, quite a distance from the half-orc's position. Several of the sailors saw Nergal hurtling towards them and jumped into the bay rather than face him. One officer drew his sword and came to oppose Nergal as he headed towards the stern of the vessel.

Nergal could see the arrogance and pride in the man's face as he squared away to fight the orc. The officer wore only leather as did Nergal, armed with a spear in one hand and a rapier in the other.

The sailor cursed at Nergal and hurled the spear at the orc straightaway, trying to impale his enemy at the outset. Nergal dodged his torso aside, avoiding the throw with practiced ease. Spears were a favorite of orc warriors, and Nergal understood how to fight with a spear.

The orc could tell that the dodge surprised the man he faced, and Nergal decided that the mace was too heavy and slow to face a lissome man with a rapier.

What—Krollon demanded before being cut off as Nergal dropped the mace and seized the spear, ripping it from the deck.

"You throw spear like baby grubling," Nergal insulted his opponent. He skipped forward, spear raised to throw. The man's eyes held fear as he crouched to avoid the throw, rapier held up before him. Instead of throwing the spear, Nergal charged and thrust it at the eyes of his enemy. The rapier came up to deflect it, knocking it aside as the half-orc's foot planted itself flat upon the man's chest and sent him reeling back with the crack of broken ribs. The sailor hit the deck hard with a grunt of pain. He struggled to rise, but pain shot through his chest, forcing him back down. Meanwhile Nergal had retrieved his original weapon. The next thing the officer saw was a huge orc raising a giant's mace over his head. The rapier came up to block the blow, but it snapped like a twig under a boulder. Nergal smashed the officer with the strike, feeling very satisfied with his victory.

No one remained to oppose the orc on the upper deck, so Nergal made his way below, searching for Garbor. He found the corpses of two sailors and followed the blood until he found the knight, at the entrance of the slave hold. Garbor had a ring of keys in his hand. The knight glanced approvingly at the gore on Nergal's mace.

"Nergal, I'm going to attempt to free and arm these rowers. Maybe you should go and make sure that the others met with success as well."

Nergal nodded his assent and made his way back out onto the docks. He scanned about trying to see one of the other adventurers. The king's footmen had made it to the docks now, and they were rooting out the last remnants of enemy soldiers. Some of the galleys had managed to flee, and they moved swiftly towards the exit of the bay. Nergal could still hear the distant sounds of fighting in the city, especially in the direction of the baron's tiny keep.

Let's head back to the town. Maybe we could kill a wizard in the confusion.

"No, Nergal want to find friends," he told the mace. He had last seen them heading over to seize another galley somewhere in this direction.

"Look it's an orc!"

The yell came from a group of Callowain's soldiers directly ahead.

"Filthy slave driver!" spat one of the other men.

"Kill him!"

"No! Nergal not..." the orc gave up an attempt at explanation, seeing swords drawn, some of them covered with blood. He turned and ran for his life.

The group of men immediately fell into pursuit, shouting as they clambered after him. Nergal's lack of armor allowed him to make some distance on the men behind him, but then he saw another group of footmen approaching from the front. They caught sight of the pursuit and began running towards him from the other direction. To his right a short span of water stretched to the city. The orc glanced in that direction and saw still more of the footmen. As he watched one of them ran their sword through a sailor, presumably of Chu Kutall.

Nergal had no choice but to head left out onto a pier, running swiftly. The two groups of soldiers became one as they swarmed up the planks behind him. As he fled desperately he looked all around, trying to figure out how to escape. He realized that there was nothing to do but fight the mass of soldiers or swim for it.

There's no way off this pier, the mace shrieked. *I'm too heavy to carry in the water!*

"Shaddap stoopid mace!" he yelled, flinging the weapon from him. He sprinted up to the end of the pier and jumped, legs flailing. He hit the water feet first, and immediately began to swim away as best he could. He felt as if this were his escape from the slave galley all over again, angry soldiers after him as he swam for his life. This time no weapon hampered his retreat.

Nergal swam out into the bay until the docks were far away, and he began to fear that he had gone too far to make it back. He turned onto his back and drifted for a while, kicking more slowly back towards the south side of the bay. Nergal found the strength to swim back to the beach, and he skulked up the hot sands barefoot. He continued to move away from the city for several minutes, afraid that patrols might be sent out after him.

At last he felt safe enough to stop and rest on the beach. He sat down heavily, feeling drained and dejected. The humans would have killed him if he had not fled. Now what would he do? Where were his friends?

The orc waited on the beach for long hours, until at last he spotted a form heading down the beach towards him. Excitement flowed into him, and his heart pounded. After a few minutes he could see that it was Dalwen. She dragged his mace behind her, so Nergal walked up to meet her.

"I saw you get chased off the pier," she said slowly, looking at Nergal fiercely. The half-orc felt something wrong now, as Dalwen stared at him.

"I felt horrible that they mistook you for the enemy. I took up your mace to bring back to you. Imagine my surprise when I found out it's a magical weapon."

"Yes, big surprise," Nergal muttered, uncertain of the problem.

"That was the small surprise. It told me things. It said that you killed Zanithweir," she said, her voice rising in intensity. "Now tell me the truth. Did you Nergal? Did you really kill Zanithweir?"

Nergal cringed. "Elf bad," was all he could utter. The more frantically Nergal tried to say more, the less he could think of. Nergal thought of the death of his father again, an elven arrow through his throat.

Dalwen dropped Krollon in the sand. She stood completely forlorn, her eyes sad.

"We trusted you. I am very disappointed in you, Nergal," she told him quietly. "I should kill you for your foul murder, but I just don't have the stomach for it. Goodbye."

Dalwen turned and walked back the way she had come up the beach. Nergal watched her wretchedly, trying to think of some excuse. He could think of nothing. His eyes fell upon Krollon lying in the sand.

Now as he regarded the weapon, anger flared up to combat the pain he felt in his gut. Why had the weapon betrayed his secret to her?

"Why you tell her?" snarled Nergal, walking up to the mace. He snatched it up from the sand, holding it up to his face. "Why you tell her?" he demanded, spittle flying from the force of his words.

Look, I know you're upset, Krollon explained. *But the fact is that those losers were just getting in our way. We can really kill wizards more effectively without them around.*

"Arrghhh! Stupid mace! Nergal make you pay for this!!!" growled Nergal, his rage rising beyond reason. He strode rapidly up away from the ocean towards the boulders of a nearby escarpment. The orc brought back the mace and slammed it with all his might into the nearest rock, shocking his hands with the impact though Krollon's handle.

This is useless, Krollon told him. *You cannot hurt me by doing this.*

"You ruin everything!" Nergal screamed, bringing the mace back for another swing. Nergal chose a larger boulder this time, and struck it with tremendous force, chipping fragments off the rock.

I promise we will only kill elf wizards, how about that?

Nergal regarded the mace for a moment, and this time a shred of cunning cut through the haze of rage to direct his next swing. He brought the mace down so that the head was aimed just past a sharp ridge in the rock. The ridge struck the handle directly below the metal head of the mace, splintering the haft and sending the head clanging along the rocks. Nergal's hands were shaken brutally but he ignored the pain.

Nergal flung the handle over his shoulder and grabbed the solid metal head of the mace. It felt awkward without its handle, but he held onto it and trudged back down the beach, towards the ocean.

Nergal, listen to me. I'm sorry. Do you know what it's going to be like for me if you do this? Krollon pleaded.

"You be sorry now," Nergal promised the mace, as he walked out into the water.

Nobody's going to find me out here, Krollon wailed, panicking now. *Do you know how long I could be—*

Nergal heaved the mace out over the water with every ounce of his strength. The heavy mace head flew over the waves for a second or two and then plunged into the water, instantly dropping out of sight.

Nergal spent a miserable evening next to the ocean, sleeping fitfully and aware of crawling things that moved about on the rocks in the night.

CHAPTER 12

Vindication

The sun rose in a clear sky but Nergal's spirits stayed low as he contemplated what to do next. He had become so used to simply letting the humans or the mace lead him where they would that he realized he had no goals of his own.

The half-orc thought very poorly on an empty stomach. He wandered along the fine sand of the sun-soaked beach for hours, collecting crabs and other tasty morsels from among the rocky tidal pools he encountered. He sifted through his motives one at a time. There was eating, which Nergal loved to do, but Nergal felt that there must be more important things. He thought of his father and his tribe of orcs, and realized that he could devote his life to avenge the death of his father. After a while he thought about how Chu Kutall had enslaved him, and his desire to get revenge on them as well. All of this thinking just brought Nergal back to the subject of his friends, and gave him a fierce headache besides.

Nergal realized that soon his friends would be sailing from Halfor Bay in search of the evil wizard who had been making the monsters. Gazing out over the choppy blue-green waters, he imagined himself leaving with them as if his secret had not come out. A terrible sense of missing out on something important filled him. He longed to rejoin the group and fight Chu Kutall.

He would help his friends even if they didn't want him to.

With this decision, Nergal began to make his way back towards the cluttered port. He approached as far as he dared in the daylight, waiting amongst rough boulders on the beach until nightfall. Then he entered the warm tropical water again, ignoring his complaining muscles as he started to swim.

Nergal traveled through the water back towards the docks, but this time he took a route closer to the shore, hidden by the darkness. At one point he approached close enough to land to allow himself to touch bottom and rest. Occasionally he heard the distant voices of sailors and soldiers calling out to each other. Sometimes he could make out bobbing torches moving along the wharfs as if marking the paths of patrolling men. Soon he continued, determined to make his way before daylight.

For a while he thought that he would not find the galleys in the dark, but he swam under several piers and persisted until he recognized three of the multi-deck slave galleys of the type used by Chu Kutall. Next to one of the vessels two torches cast light from the pier. The half-orc tried to figure out which of them he had battled the officer on, but he was not sure in the darkness.

Nergal wondered how he would discover which galley the adventurers had chosen for their mission. He headed towards the one with lit torches flickering on the pier next to it.

Nergal heard voices coming closer in the darkness. He hunkered down next to a piling in knee deep water, and watched the planks leading onto the galley. Soon a pair of legionnaires carrying a large crate came into view.

"This thing is heavy," remarked one of the soldiers.

"It belongs to that crazy wizard," said the second man.

"I wonder what's in it?"

"I don't want to know, the way wizards are, it's probably something alive! Let's just put it on the second deck with his other things."

I have the smarts, Nergal told himself. He didn't think of the possibility that they were talking about any other wizard than Rilivan. Once the soldiers had dropped off the crate and headed back down the pier, he grasped a mooring line and pulled himself out of the water, quietly climbing aboard the galley.

For the next hour the half-orc nosed about the ship, finding places to hide. Most of the vessel was dark and gritty, smelling of pitch and wood. The rowing deck was empty, but he supposed that it would be manned by soldiers the next day. For a moment Nergal fantasized about concealing himself in the wizard's crate and throttling the elf when he was discovered, but he decided that he would ignore the elf. Chu Kutall would have to satisfy his need for revenge. He finally decided to hide in a storeroom on the lowest deck. He moved crates and barrels around slightly to form a cubbyhole that he could conceal himself in. Nergal also cached a short wooden spear he had found in his investigations, just in case.

When the morning came, Nergal heard voices approaching and he retreated within his hiding place. His wait soon became boring. Once Nergal thought he could hear the booming voice of Garbor, but he could not be sure. It was hot and miserable in the hold, but Nergal managed to sleep for a large part of the day.

When night came he could tell by the rolling of the deck that they were on the open sea. Nergal could hear that the rowers had ceased their work. The half-orc realized that he would have to find food soon. Sniffing about his hiding hole, he could not detect any foodstuffs nearby. He had been foolish not to think of it earlier, but he seldom planned well. He endured the complaints of his stomach for long hours.

Finally the orc could wait no more. He carefully extricated himself from the tight space and stretched his stiff limbs. Next he retrieved the spear from its hiding place. Then he slinked quietly through the hold, hunched low, clutching the spear before him.

Being quiet, thought the orc.

Nergal explored the creaking deck carefully, sniffing here and there to find a hint of food on the air. Soon he decided to ascend to the next deck and continue his search. Nergal forgot the rumbling of his stomach in an instant as he spotted Rilivan moving stealthily ahead of him. The elf wore a black robe with dark red trim that blended well into the darkness. Nergal waited until the elf had disappeared up a stair, and then he followed quietly.

When Nergal got to the stair he peered upwards but could see no sign of the elf. He took the ascent slowly, and came out on the upper deck. Up ahead, at the bow of the galley, Nergal heard a voice. He approached closer to observe and saw that Rilivan stood at the prow. A few feet in front of the elf, some sort of reptilian creature flapped its wings, darting about. Nergal couldn't see anyone else nearby.

"The fools don't have any clue they're heading right into our trap," Rilivan told the reptilian bat delightedly. "Nor do they suspect that Zanithweir spied upon them for you."

The creature emitted a quiet snarl.

"The priestess told me that the orc killed him. I must say that I thought more highly of Zanithweir than that; he must have been caught by surprise."

The bat hissed and growled again.

"They called the Vak-Nagr the Shadow Beast. They slew it with the help of a magical amulet created at Salthor." Rilivan fished in his robe and brought out some sort of cylindrical object that Nergal could not make out in the darkness. "Here's the rest. We'll arrive at the outpost in three days."

Nergal gripped his spear tightly and brought it back for a throw. With a roar he launched the weapon at the bat and charged at Rilivan.

The flying reptile snarled as it saw Nergal, and then squealed as the heavy spear impaled it in the chest. Half of the weapon went through the avian and then stuck. The creature hurtled backwards, disappearing over the gunwale as it fell to the waters below.

Rilivan backed away from the half-orc in surprise, dropping the cylinder to the deck. Then he started to speak in a low quick voice, motioning with his hands. Nergal grabbed both of the elf's lower arms and wrenched them violently, breaking Rilivan's forearms. The elf screamed.

"You no trap my friends!" growled Nergal, standing very close now.

"They'll kill you for hurting me, you stupid oaf!" Rilivan spat, his voice twisted with pain.

"Rilivan? Where are you?" came Melvin's voice from astern.

"Help!" screamed the wizard. "The orc is trying to kill me!"

Nergal held the wizard firmly with murder in his eyes. He peered out over the dark waters to see if he could see land from the ship. It looked like he might have to swim for it again.

Melvin came up a set of steps and looked at the two, sword in hand. Dalwen followed close behind him.

"Kill him, please!" urged Rilivan.

"Wizard spy on you!" accused Nergal, watching Melvin's sword warily.

"Don't move Nergal!" yelled Dalwen.

"If you kill him I will strike you down, I swear it," said Melvin as Garbor strode up from astern and absorbed the scene.

"Nergal! How could you do it?" the big knight asked, unbelieving. Behind him a tall man in leather and a legion uniform came up to see what was going on.

"How could he do it? He's an orc!" whined Rilivan.

"Shaddup!" yelled Nergal. "He spy on you! Zanithweir spy too. Nergal hear it all!"

"Kill him now!" wailed the elf, trying to sustain a sense of panic. It wasn't difficult with the bones of his forearm grinding together.

"Stay calm," Dalwen commanded. "Nergal, let him go."

Nergal released the wizard's hands and stood back. He remained tense, ready to spring into the water below. The half-orc bent over and scooped up the cylinder, and then rolled it over towards Garbor.

"He give that to bat-thing!"

"Careful with that," Rilivan warned, holding his broken arms out before helplessly. "It's a powerful wand, if you touch it someone could get hurt!"

"That's not like any wand I've ever seen," Dalwen said, her brows coming together.

"I want to hear both of your stories," Dalwen said. Garbor looked hopeful, Melvin surprised. Melvin's sword dropped just a hair, but he stayed alert, watching both Nergal and Rilivan.

"There is no story, priestess," said Rilivan, "except that this brute returned to murder me just like he did to your late friend, Zanithweir!"

"What're you doing up on deck?" shot Dalwen back.

Rilivan actually sputtered. "Well—by Zanthar! I…I just wanted some fresh air! Elves are not at home on the sea, you know." Pain filled his voice.

"Nergal," Dalwen turned to the half-orc. "What is it that you're trying to say about Rilivan?"

"He talk to scaly bat," Nergal told them. "He say you go to trap. He say Zanithweir spy for Chu Kutall!"

Melvin blinked. "And that wand?"

Nergal took a deep breath and formed his words carefully. "He want give thing to bat. Nergal spear bat and catch Rilivan."

Dalwen crouched down and retrieved the cylinder. She tugged on it, and the cylinder opened to reveal a scroll inside. "It's some kind of carrying case for this scroll," Dalwen said, her voice rising. "Rilivan, you said this was a wand!"

"I thought it was my wand!" Rilivan retorted hotly. "My arms are broken, how am I supposed to keep anything straight? So it's not my wand. I wasn't up here trying to kill people!" he finished, exasperated.

"The scroll is in elvish. I can't read it," Dalwen said.

"It's nothing more than some notes I made on my latest project," Rilivan told her.

Garbor looked at the others hopelessly. "How can we tell who's lying?" he asked.

Dalwen began to wave her right hand in intricate circles, speaking in the voice Nergal remembered from outside Salthor castle. Her left hand remained rigid and vertical in front of her as the other hand made its dance through the air. With her spell executed, the priestess faced Nergal calmly.

"Nergal, did you see Rilivan talking to a bat creature?" she asked.

"Yes! Scaly bat-thing," Nergal said.

"Did Rilivan say that he and Zanithweir were spies?" she asked.

"Yes!" Nergal said.

"He's telling the truth!" Dalwen exclaimed. "Rilivan, tell me that you are not in league with Chu Kutall."

The elf stared at Dalwen and glowered.

"Zanithweir was a spy as well?" she asked in a pained voice.

Rilivan said nothing. The wizard's arms trembled slightly as he held them before him, and then the elf threw himself backwards over the low deck wall. Garbor leaped forward to catch him, but he moved too late. A splash emanated from below.

"Alofzin!" Dalwen said, running up to the edge of the deck.

"I will not save him," uttered Garbor solemnly. He turned to Nergal. "Instead, I'll apologize to my friend Nergal, who I treated so unfairly."

"I've been so horrible to you," Dalwen said, looking Nergal in the eyes. She spread her arms out, palms upward. "Please forgive me."

"I'm sorry too, Nergal. Will you join us again?" asked Melvin.

"Nergal come back, help you fight Chu Kutall. Nergal have mighty sword arm," he elucidated, flexing his muscles. The tightness in his gut diminished and he felt a wave of relief.

Garbor laughed his vociferous laugh, and slapped Nergal on the arm, then hugged him. Nergal returned the embrace awkwardly, uncertain of the strange custom.

CHAPTER 13

Battle on the Niyalan Sea

"It occurs to me that we're in a bad situation," Melvin announced to his friends. Nergal, Dalwen, and Garbor had assembled on the high aft deck with the captain of the ship, a short slender woman named Teranae. The captain wore a sword at each hip and the rough tunic of a common sailor, which barely covered her muscular body. Pale scars crisscrossed her otherwise tanned skin. Her long raven hair danced in the wind.

"How so, future Lord of Elniboné?" prompted Garbor, stretching his powerful frame in the light breeze.

"Rilivan was quite sly. We thought we were following the black wand that he made. Now we know the wand was a ruse and he was leading us into a trap. The question is now: How best to proceed?" Melvin elaborated, eyeing his companions.

"First we should think of what options we have, as we always do," Dalwen said. "Then we'll choose together."

"We continue on course, and meet any challenges head on," said Garbor. "We have forty elite legionnaires with us, and twenty experienced sailors. Even Nergal is back on our side. Trust in fate for all else."

"Or we could go back and get more help," said Melvin. "Another wizard, for instance. We've sorely needed a battle mage of some sort for a long time now. Of course, I thought Rilivan would fulfill that function…"

"It's barely worth talking about. We can't just give up and go back. We must continue on this course. What other choices could we possibly have?" asked

Captain Teranae. The woman exuded a sense of harsh strength that allowed her to command without question.

"I could ask for help from others who know more of the universe," Dalwen murmured, touching her silver holy symbol. Nergal noticed that it was the device she obtained as her reward for slaying the Shadow Beast. "But it isn't a thing I can do easily or often."

Melvin nodded. "Alright. That's three possibilities. Do we have any other ideas to choose from? Nergal?"

"Umm..." Nergal gulped. He floundered, for once missing the voice of the mace. Looking out over the sea to avoid the eyes of his patiently waiting friends, Nergal found the answer.

"We run from galleys," he said, indicating the horizon.

"What!" snapped Teranae, glancing out over the waves. She yelled up to her lookout, indicating the direction Nergal had pointed.

"Galleys tacking from the northwest," the man hollered down a moment later, peering out from his high perch on one of the vessel's two masts. "Looks like two squadrons of four or five ships each."

"Damn you Gauradius, are you asleep up there?" the captain berated the lookout. Nergal had a vantage point almost as high as the lookout, on the aft command deck.

"You have sharp eyes, Nergal!" Garbor told him. "I cannot see a thing."

"Friend or foe?" Dalwen voiced the question in everyone's minds. They studied the ocean for long moments in anticipation.

"Galleys of Chu Kutall," the lookout yelled out. "Heading towards us," the sailor added.

"Bugger my dryad!" Garbor spouted, slapping his axe hilt.

"Can we outrun them?" Melvin asked the captain.

"That's our only hope, against such odds," Teranae replied. "We have two sails and my rowers are good, but the long oars may have to be manned by Zeleph's men. We—"

"Slith!" exclaimed the lookout. "Four vessels are Slith, waving the banner of the Matriarch of Slecktar! They run from Chu Kutall!"

"Slith," echoed Teranae. "Not friends of ours, but certainly enemies of Chu Kutall. We're in luck. The smaller group of vessels are fleeing the Chu Kutall, so we may be able to pass without pursuit."

"Although our mission is important, we cannot ignore their plight," Dalwen asserted. "They're the enemies of our enemies..."

"Yes," Melvin agreed, struggling to make out the distant ships. "If we could befriend the Slith they might be able to help us. Nothing like walking into a trap with a little surprise up our sleeves!"

Teranae considered this carefully. "It's an interesting idea, but be warned. The Slith are distrustful of strangers. They may not feel indebted to us in the slightest, even assuming that we could assist them here."

"Go into battle I say," maintained Garbor. "They'll understand that we're their friends, once we have joined together in battle against Chu Kutall!"

The captain accepted this without comment. Nergal found her inscrutable. Apparently she had been instructed to obey the adventurers, for she acted on their decision.

"Trim the foresail and take the mains down," she ordered calmly. One of the sailors on the aft observation deck bolted to enact her command. Teranae summoned a short legionnaire to her side. "Zeleph, we need your men on the top oars."

Nergal examined the man she addressed. He recognized the legionnaire as the man present at the scene of last night's interrogation of Nergal and Rilivan. He was a rugged looking warrior with hints of gray forming on the sides of a thick head of hair. His features were sharp and gaunt, his eyes dark. At his side hung a legionnaire's sword, and a round shield hung loosely over his shoulder.

Zeleph commanded the forty legionnaires that accompanied the adventurers on this mission, on the orders of King Callowain. Teranae had half that number of sailors on the shorter oars of the lower rowing deck. The shorter oars offered less power but were more suitable for long term rowing.

"Man the top oars!" bellowed the legion commander.

The soldiers set aside their shields and swords. They fell upon the rowing benches and took up the longer, more powerful oars of the upper deck, two men per oar. Nergal could immediately sense the difference, as the ship surged forward with greater speed stroke by stroke.

"Your men draw poorly," complained Teranae, commenting on the bad oarsmanship of the soldiers. "I wish we had had more time to train them."

"You won't have any complaints if we grapple with the enemy and they take up their swords," Zeleph replied calmly. Nergal's instincts told him the man had seen battle before.

"These men are a hand picked elite of King Callowain," Garbor boasted to Nergal. "Between Zeleph's men and our own swords, we can probably best any group of sailors in Chu Kutall's entire navy."

"If we ever even get there with these miserable excuses for left handed rowers," countered Teranae.

Nergal simply listened to this exchange while he eyed the ships in the distance. The half-orc had obtained two long spears from a storeroom just this morning, and he examined them again as he thought of impending battle. This time there would be no swimming to shore. He would have to be victorious or die.

Now that their vessel's sails were down and the men had fallen into the rhythm of their rowing, Nergal could make out details of the ships ahead. It seemed that the smaller group of four vessels were trying to disengage the group of five ships, but each of the Slith vessels only had one mast rigged with a square sail. The Chu Kutall ships boasted two large masts and a forward leaning sail at the prow as well, giving them more wind. Nergal didn't know how the Slith were managing to stay ahead at all, but it looked like their lead might be flagging.

"We should fly the banner of his majesty," suggested Garbor, his deep voice carrying well across the windy deck. "We don't want to be mistaken for Chu Kutall in this fight."

"We might as well," said Teranae. "With our sails down it will be clear we mean to attack. Who we attack, however, should be a surprise to both of them." The captain stood back to direct the men controlling the rudders.

Nergal realized she spoke of the fact that they now occupied a captured Chu Kutall ship. The vessel extended longer than fifteen men lying head to foot, and had the double oar set and double mast of most Chu Kutall ships. Most likely the Slith would expect that they were coming to attack them as they fled from the other Chu Kutall vessels.

"The Slith are taking down sails and doubling up on their high oars," called the lookout.

"They think we plan to ram one of them as we pass," the captain said. "I've picked our course carefully to the side of the Slith formation. We shall have to hope that they can see we're too far west to catch them from the side. If the Slith captain is a fool he may try to line up with us, but I think they'll angle eastward to avoid battle," she explained.

"Hopefully both the Slith and Chu Kutall will think us fools until they realize our real intent," Melvin agreed.

"We will be fools if the Slith don't turn to help us," Teranae muttered. "Even with Callowain's best aboard, we cannot fight Chu Kutall from the bottom of the sea."

Soon Teranae's maneuvers proved sound, as the Slith vessels swept farther east, thinking that they were avoiding a Chu Kutall captain intent upon ramming them. Now the Chu Kutall vessels loomed ahead. Their course brought them much closer to these five ships, which were drawn out in a line side by side.

"Their sails are going down!" announced the lookout.

"We caught them by surprise. They won't line up in time," Teranae said, holding back her excitement. "Prepare to ram!" she yelled forward.

The rowmaster started screaming below and Nergal could see that the galley bore down on a vessel rapidly. The ship's oars were out, trying to turn it into the oncoming ship, but the half-orc could see that the target would not come around in time.

At the last moment Nergal had an impression of oarsmen and soldiers scrambling out from in front of their ram before they struck the ship. A shudder went through the entire vessel, slamming Nergal against the railing of the command deck. A ragged cheer came up from below, followed by the sounds of fighting from the bow. Soldiers were moving from the oars to the front, eager to engage the men of the other vessel.

"Let's go to it!" said Garbor, drawing his mighty war axe.

"No! We pull back and let them sink if we can," said Teranae harshly. "Sever that grapple! All oars reverse!" she called out.

Turning back to Garbor, she said, "Don't worry, your blade will see blood before the day is over," she told him.

"Are we going to be able to break free?" asked Dalwen watching the scene at the bow. Warriors from the crippled ship were trying to board them, opposed by half of the legionnaires that Zeleph had pulled from the top oars.

"We'd better, and quickly. The other ships are coming around," said the captain grimly.

Dalwen bolted forward and down the ladder towards the front of the ship. Garbor and Nergal followed her, uncertain of what was going on. They made their way across the top decking, just over the heads of the rowers on the large upper oars. Garbor stopped and Nergal came up beside him. The rowers were pulling back but the ram seemed stuck, or perhaps there were grapples up front that had not been cut. They were not moving back from their embrace with the enemy ship.

"Looks like they're going to die by our swords, not the sharks below," said Garbor.

To the port, Dalwen incanted, her voice carrying on and off in the wind. Her hands clapped together over her head. A loud whoosh sounded from the other vessel. Nergal snapped his head over in time to see a pillar of flame erupt from the center of the enemy galley, tossing men and equipment in all directions.

The noises of the growing flames were joined by the shouts of the beleaguered men and the cheers from their own vessel. Now Nergal could see that the other vessel sat low in the water. He heard a loud snapping and creaking from the bow. Nergal felt the deck move, then he could see that they had broken free of the Chu Kutall galley. Sailors and soldiers ran about the ship, trying to bring the flames under control. The situation did not look good for them.

"They're turning to help!" exclaimed Melvin, calling down to them from the command deck. "The Slith are turning to join the battle!"

They returned excitedly to the command deck to see what events had transpired.

"The Slith are coming?" Dalwen asked the captain.

"They're too late for us," Teranae snapped, and for the first time Nergal heard the strain affecting her voice. The captain indicated a second Chu Kutall galley coming in from their side. "They will cleave us in two," she said with certainty in her voice.

"Port side forward row!" she bellowed.

The captain's orders were repeated by a rowmaster and the legionnaire commander below. Most of the soldiers had abandoned the upper oars in preparation for battle, but now they scrambled back to their positions. Nergal could hear Zeleph yelling below, ordering the men to start rowing. The heavy ship continued back for long moments, then began a slow turning movement. Nergal looked out at the Chu Kutall vessel that headed straight for them, and could see that the captain was right. This time they would be rammed from the side.

"I can help us here as well," Dalwen told the captain quickly. "Get ready for battle, my friends," she said, and then ran back to the ladder leading down from the high aft deck.

Nergal followed the priestess, returning to the highest deck that spanned the length of the ship. He could see Melvin and Garbor watching them and talking excitedly from the command deck above. It seemed he could do nothing but watch as the battle progressed. He remained anxious and ready to fight, but he did not know what to do on a ship. His tribe had never gone to battle on the sea.

Dalwen stood directly before the oncoming vessel fearlessly. She calmly began incanting a spell while Nergal watched, fidgeting nervously as he eyed the incoming ram. Their own ship turned agonizingly slowly. The priestess worked quickly but with great concentration, sweat gleaming on her body in the bright sun that burned down and reflected from the waves below. As she reached completion of her spell her hands grasped the wall of the deck, gripping the smooth wood in front of her.

The priestess ran back from the edge of the ship and braced herself. "I have strengthened the planking. Hang on!" she yelled to Nergal. The half-orc dashed back as well, searching for something to hold onto. At the last moment he simply dropped flat to the deck close to the far side of the ship.

The ships collided with a thunderous smack. Water sprayed over the deck, and the ship shuddered so violently Nergal slid forward, unable to stop himself. Side oars snapped and men screamed down below, crushed by the swinging lengths of wood. With a long, shuddering moan of wood scraping on wood the Chu Kutall vessel came up alongside them, the ram skidding off the side of the ship. Oars continued to shatter, making sounds like a giant smashing through a forest of dead trees. Everyone hunkered on the deck, stunned for a moment, before rising to their feet.

Both sides seemed so astonished by the result of the collision that the battle paused as men stood, blinking, stunned by the shock of the impact and its impossible result. Most of the oars of each ship were broken away or discarded on their common side, creating a mess of mangled wood and men.

Then the Chu Kutall seemed to recover. Dozens of the determined warriors were reacting at last. Grapples started hurtling from the enemy ship, their lines being used to anchor the ships side by side.

Nergal rushed to the side of the ship, eager to spill blood at last. A plank came down across the ships and a lone warrior headed across it before his fellows were ready to charge en masse. The half-orc launched his first spear, striking the man directly in the center of the chest. His victim squawked and fell from the side of his ship into the ocean.

Nergal and Dalwen reached the edge of the railing, joining the other defenders accumulating there.

"Easy fight," Nergal said to Dalwen. "We stand and—"

Nergal felt a stinging impact on his left shoulder and looked down to see a fountain of blood pouring from a hole in his upper arm. Dalwen pulled him back, and an eager legionnaire stepped up to their place at the rail. The sounds of fighting were beginning to intensify as a group of Chu Kutall warriors rushed the galley in a concerted attack.

The priestess examined Nergal's arm hurriedly.

"Crossbow bolt," she said matter-of-factly, her voice barely audible over the din of battle. "We should get you a breastplate. You could have been killed."

The brute shrugged, causing his wound to spill blood faster. Dalwen turned him briefly and remarked, "Went clean through."

She began speaking in a manner that Nergal had learned to associate with her spellcasting. Nergal almost said something, thinking of the long hours his village shaman had spent rattling and singing over a wounded orc. Surely now was not the time!

"There, you will live you stupid orc," she told him with mock harshness. "Try to stand behind something when they start firing crossbows next time."

"Huh?" Nergal said, looking down to see his wound had closed. Just as rapidly he looked back up to see the priestess had left him, loading her sling and running towards the aft command deck.

Then he heard the unmistakable sound of Garbor roaring in full battle mode. He could see the knight crossing over to the enemy galley with Melvin close behind. Nergal blinked. He had thought they were supposed to be killing the enemy as they boarded this ship. He ran over to join the knights, but became separated from them by battling soldiers.

Directly in front of him, a warrior slashed at a legionnaire with a double-handed sword. As the legionnaire took the blow on his shield, Nergal thrust his spearhead at the enemy, running him through his neck, just above his shield. The man fell to the deck, grasping his throat futilely as the blood gouted out.

"Thank you, my friend!" called the legionnaire, looking in surprise.

Nergal grunted in response and headed for the planking that the knights had crossed on. Nergal could see that the battle raged on all sides, men struggling on both ships. He balanced his spear before him and nervously crossed on a plank to the other vessel, looking for an enemy.

To his right he saw a legionnaire backed up against the railing, fending off two attacking swordsmen. Nergal roared a challenge, getting the attention of one of them so as to even the odds. The man held his sword up between his body and Nergal, so that he could block aside any thrust by the spear. Nergal thrust directly into the man's sword hand, deeply slicing a finger and sinking the broad metal head of his spear into his enemy's palm. As quickly as the dropped sword hit the planks Nergal's spear found the man's vitals. The legionnaire sunk his sword into the other warrior at nearly the same time, and they stood regarding each other for an instant, glad to be alive.

Nergal moved farther onto the enemy vessel, and spotted Garbor standing with Melvin ahead, blood dripping from their weapons. The fighting on this ship slowed, and it seemed that they were victorious. Bodies littered the deck, a mass of tangled limbs and armor. Nergal saw faces contorted in death, and blood running on the deck.

"The ship is ours!" announced Garbor grandly. No sooner had he uttered these words than a wounded man rose behind him, sword in hand. Nergal shouted a warning, watching the sword come down. Garbor skipped to the side to avoid the unseen attack, but the weapon cleaved completely through his left forearm. Garbor bellowed in pain and rage, his left hand falling to the deck like a discarded gauntlet.

Nergal lunged, slamming his spear into the assailant's chest. The man fell back dying, but Nergal pursued the man to the deck. The half-orc angrily grabbed the man's head and wrenched it savagely, feeling vertebrae crack and grind inside the warrior's neck.

"Bind the wound, or he will bleed to death," gasped Melvin, still trying to catch his breath from the fighting. Hurriedly Melvin ripped away part of his tunic under his breastplate and put it onto the other knight's arm. Bright red blood pooled under Garbor, slowly turning black in the hot sun.

"What of the battle?" asked Garbor in shock, sitting down on the deck, holding the wrapped stump of his left forearm in his right hand.

Melvin looked out over the water, trying to assess the results of battle elsewhere on the sea. Not far from their position, a Slith ship was grappled to an enemy galley much as they were. Two of the single-sailed Slith ships were pursuing a Chu Kutall galley as it attempted to disengage. There was no sign of the fourth Slith vessel anywhere other than flotsam and bobbing corpses.

"We've won, at least for the moment. Now sit still here with Nergal and I'll find Dalwen."

Nergal guarded the wounded knight, walking around him in circles and poking at bodies with his spear. When Dalwen arrived Nergal saw that she had been hurt as well. Her beautiful hair lay wet with blood, which poured down the left side of her face.

Dalwen seemed unconcerned with her own condition, but she winced in pain when she saw the knight's arm.

"Alofzin," she muttered quietly. "Garbor, I cannot…I have woven too much magic today already…" her voice broke, unable to maintain a detached tone.

"Don't be troubled priestess! You would have been foolish to save anything in a battle such as this," Garbor told her. "I understand...don't worry about me." The big knight fainted, his face pale.

"Is he..." asked Melvin.

"He will live," Dalwen assured him but her voice was sad. "As long as we watch him carefully he will live. But I cannot restore his arm."

They carefully moved Garbor over to the original ship, moving him in with the rest of the wounded on a lower deck. Dalwen stayed to watch over him while Nergal and Melvin went up to the command deck.

As Nergal arrived he saw that one of the Slith ships had approached very close. He examined the inhabitants of the foreign ship carefully.

The Slith had long snakelike bodies of blue and green scales which widened to form erect humanoid torsos, from which very human arms sprouted. They had long, curving necks and their heads were wide and flat like those of giant snakes. Their chests were covered in finely decorated breastplates painted with bright reds and yellows. They were armed with ornate, wickedly curved spears and shields. As Nergal studied them, he could see that the shields had spikes on them, too.

"There're so many of them on that ship," Melvin noted.

"Yes, these ships are more suited as transports than for fighting at sea," Teranae told them. "I don't think the Slith were expecting to get caught on the open ocean. They probably set out for a land raid."

Now the galley moved closer, as several of the Slith began to wave yellow banners at them. Some of the creatures moved to the side of their vessel, holding grappling lines and planks.

"What are they doing?" asked Melvin.

"We're invited aboard," Teranae told them. "To talk with their leader."

CHAPTER 14

Assault on Nov Rosul

"Nergal?" Melvin's voice grabbed Nergal's attention.

"Hmmm?" He looked up from a shield that he had been examining. Dalwen had mentioned a breastplate, and when the half-orc saw a discarded shield left on the deck after the battle, he decided to appropriate it for his own use. The shield was a small round metal buckler, seeming very light on his muscular forearm.

"Do you want to come over to talk to their leader with us?" asked Melvin, glancing at the buckler. The knight stood next to Teranae and Zeleph, but it was not clear exactly who 'us' meant.

"Yes, Nergal go," he replied.

Nergal followed Melvin and Teranae to the edge of the deck, and approached the planking that had been placed between the two galleys. Zeleph did not move to follow but they were accompanied by another of Teranae's sailors, a thin man with a bristly beard of dark hair. The captain led the way, striding across the makeshift path to the other ship. She moved slowly as if being careful not to startle the Slith.

Melvin followed her lead and moved over next. Nergal could see that the snake-men were making room for the newcomers, and they seemed to be leading them farther on board. Nergal wondered if the Slith planned a trap. He grasped his spear tightly in his hand as he considered this.

Nergal moved over quickly, still not comfortable on the thin ramps.

He looked at the strange warriors up close. The first thing that he noticed were the long dark green snake bodies all over the deck. Nergal's eyes grew wide, and his heart beat faster as he stared in horror. The snake-men had no legs, only human arms. Their giant snake bodies extended back far enough to balance them as they held their torsos erect. The things did not seem to mind that their tails writhed and twisted all together like the twisted roots of an ancient tree.

The spears they held were quite different from Nergal's. Instead of a sharp spearhead at the tip, their spears had short, curved sword blades on the end. One of them had blades on both ends, he noticed.

He forced himself to look away as he followed Melvin and Teranae to a ramp set in the deck, leading down. Surrounded by the serpent-things, Nergal barely kept a grip on the fear that thrilled through him. The snake creatures' faces were painted in the same bright reds and yellows as their armor and banners.

They came to a circular hole cut in the deck. Nergal could see that this allowed the snake men to move between the levels of their ship. One of the creatures moved down through it, and others directed them to follow.

Melvin looked back to be sure that the half-orc followed him, and Nergal could see that his friend shared his amazement and fear. Only Teranae seemed unaffected. She carefully dropped down through the hole and landed on the deck below. Melvin and Nergal quickly followed her. The adventurers were brought before a large Slith on the central deck of the crowded vessel.

Nergal understood that this snake-man led the Slith force. Other Slith attended him on all sides. The serpent's head turned to examine each of them in turn. Bright red and yellow paint adorned the head of the creature, and it held a long spear and a large round shield.

Nergal looked at the shield. A curling snake was emblazoned on the face in bright yellow. A large, sharp spike extended from the center of the shield. He looked back at his own buckler, tiny and inadequate on his heavily muscled arm.

"Nergal need bigger shield," he said to himself quietly.

The snake-leader handed his spear to a nearby guard, and hissed to his underling. The guard gave him his round shield, which the leader then held out towards Nergal.

The orc's eyes bulged as he stared at the shield.

"Take it, Nergal," whispered Teranae.

"Er, be thanking you," Nergal told the snake-man, and grasped the shield. Like the others he had seen, the shield bore the image of a colorful serpent on the front, coiling around a sharp central spike protruding from the face.

Nergal handed the leader his spear. "Is good for throwing," he said quietly, embarrassed at the paltry offering.

The leader accepted the gift. He rasped and hissed for a moment, forming alien words that Nergal could not understand.

"I am Rovul, son of emperor Heozex of Matriarch Ulantra," translated the sailor. Nergal realized that Teranae had brought the man along because he could understand the snake language. The half-orc realized that the leader must be able to understand their language, but he wondered if the snake-thing could speak it.

Teranae bowed low before Rovul. "You are a kind and wise leader," she said. Nergal could see that the Slith's eyes had no lids, and that the creature had a forked tongue which flickered out at Melvin. The half-orc suppressed a shudder.

The leader emitted a series of slurred words and snarls.

"Rovul, son of Emperor Heozex offers his respect to powerful warriors," said the translator. "You are invited to feast on the bodies of those slain with him tonight, as we sail for the islands of our enemies."

"Chu Kutall?" Melvin asked.

The leader made his reply in the speech of the snake-men.

"Our target is the outpost of Nov Rosul, two days sail east from here," the sailor spoke for him. "It is a small island base, occupied by Chu Kutall. They attempt to spread their influence too close to the home waters of the Slith. For this, they will be taught a lesson."

"We're headed there as well," Melvin informed the Slith carefully. "The Chu Kutall make war on us. There is a wizard or wizards that we must seek out and slay, so that our soldiers can prevail. We suspect that the wizard may be on this island you speak of."

"Then join with us. You are strong warriors, and the glory will be great. I cannot rule as emperor until my father hears of my battle-prowess," the translator finished.

Melvin, Teranae and Nergal joined the snake-men in a great feast to strengthen the ties of the growing friendship. As the leader had mentioned, the Slith were dining on the roasted flesh of fallen enemies and comrades alike, which they cooked over large flaming braziers on the upper deck.

The group of visitors sat on the deck, since the snake-men had no need of chairs or tables. Melvin and Teranae refused most of the offerings, although they did put some cooked fish onto their plates, nibbling at it from time to time. Nergal greedily partook of the cooked human and Slith flesh, which seemed to please the serpent men. By the end of the meal, the knight and the captain seemed rather wan.

"Fish no good?" Nergal asked.

"Uh, not bad really," Melvin said halfheartedly, staring at a human thigh-bone on the deck before him. Teranae raised her eyebrow and looked at Melvin, wondering if the orc jested.

Nergal nodded knowingly. Clearly the fish had bothered Melvin's stomach, but he was too polite to say this in front of their hosts.

"Try this, it taste better," Nergal offered, holding out a strip of Slith flesh. Melvin covered his mouth with his hand and shook his head, refusing the food.

Nergal shrugged and finished the meat. He burped loudly, leaning back against a railing. "Good eating," he said contentedly.

Over the next days they sailed towards the outpost of their common enemy. Slith soldiers prepared their long, spiked spears and spiked shields for battle. The creatures had a proliferation of colorful banners. Their armor was finely crafted and the shields bore bright symbols of the snake god, Slecktar. Melvin and Garbor were both delighted at the prospect of accompanying this skillful race to war, and Dalwen returned to her high spirits. By agreement Rovul had command of the invasion, and the young reptile seemed extremely anxious to prove his competence at war.

Garbor practiced at strapping a shield onto his partial arm, but met with limited success. The difficulty in controlling the shield without his left hand made the tactic less effective, but the knight took it all in stride. He resolved to keep working until he could manage with his new disadvantage, and even joked about having a hook crafted for his arm when he returned to the kingdom. If anything Dalwen seemed more affected by it than the knight, as if she still held some guilt for her inability to heal him.

The isle of Nov Rosul was sighted late one evening, and they kept their distance from the outpost so that the enemy would have no warning of their arrival. Once night settled in the ships moved to the shallows next to a long beach.

They disembarked under cover of darkness. The Slith were powerful swimmers, able to make it to shore on their own even in heavy armor. Nergal thought their long snake bodies seemed to have certain advantages over the humans. The legionnaires and adventurers made it to the beach in boats, joining the snake men on the island.

Rovul had instructed the legionnaires under Zeleph to attack the enemy barracks. The snake leader maintained that the outpost had no defensive wall, but that guard towers were spread about the tiny base. The Slith warriors would concentrate on the towers, which could be scaled by the snakes easily as they were constructed of wooden timbers. With luck the legionnaires could strike before any counterattack could be organized out of the Chu Kutall barracks.

The attack group set off a few hours after sunrise. It took them hours to march to the site of the base. Slith scouts reported the status of the outpost, and the soldiers moved into position, concealed by the dense island vegetation. As Rovul had described, the base had no wall. There were ten wooden towers scattered about the perimeter, with archers in the cupolas. The buildings were also of wood with roofs of wood or palm fronds. The entire outpost sat next to a sheltered lagoon where two galleys were housed. One of the galleys had been drawn out of the water for repairs.

Rovul gave the order to charge and they were underway. There were three barracks to attack, and so the adventurers headed for the largest one, while the legionnaires had been split into two groups to cover the other two. Nergal and his friends ran out of the jungle into the camp, lost amidst the larger charge of the Slith. The Chu Kutall were clearly taken completely by surprise, as Nergal's group penetrated the camp without being opposed.

Nergal could hear the snap of bowstrings and the angry snarling hisses of the Slith. He followed Zeleph and Garbor with Melvin at his side as they ran through the base. Zeleph had drawn both of his swords, holding one in each hand. Apparently he fought without a shield. The group came to a barracks door and pushed it open.

Immediately a warrior attacked Zeleph in the doorway, but the legionnaire blocked the man's sword with the sword in his left hand and countered with his right. The man went down, fatally wounded in the chest. Zeleph quickly cleared the door allowing the others to follow. The interior of the barracks was lined with beds along the outer walls. The open expanse of the middle was broken only by a few support pillars of stone. The ceiling arched up high above, showing the wooden beams holding up the roof. The building was quite large, with enough room for four soldiers to stand side by side and fight in the middle.

Dozens of Chu Kutall soldiers were milling about inside, rushing to grab their gear and join the battle. Garbor and Melvin stuck several men near the entrance quickly, taking full advantage of their surprise.

Nergal waded in, spearing a man in the calf with his spear and impaling another on his shield spike simultaneously. He growled like an angry wolf, shaking his spear free and attacking again. The Chu Kutall warriors fell back briefly. Some stood atop the bunks to support their fellows in the middle of the room.

The half-orc became aware of their leader, an unarmed man dressed only in a simple black robe in the middle of the room. Nergal thought this man looked very similar to the robed warrior he had battled in the gate room of Salthor.

"What are you waiting for? Kill them!" commanded the robed figure. The group of warriors rallied and moved towards the adventurers, led by the mysterious man in the black robe.

Zeleph faced the leader, and thrust at him savagely as he approached. With amazing speed, the Chu Kutall warrior batted the sword aside by hitting the flat of the sword with his bare hand, and he slid inside of the range of Zeleph's second sword. The enemy leader emitted an explosive yell and struck Zeleph in the chin with a brutal palm strike, dropping the legionnaire instantly.

No sooner had Zeleph fallen than Garbor and Melvin thrust at the robed fighter, but the man was no longer occupying the space they attacked. He jumped completely over their heads, landing behind them. Now the knights were threatened from both sides, as the soldiers rushed to join their leader in the assault.

The orc distracted many of them, screaming in rage and charging the front three from the side. He smashed his shield into the first so hard that the man rebounded from it, throwing his companions off balance. Nergal could still sense the knights battling with the robed figure out of the corner of his eye, so he turned to meet the other warriors.

Somehow Dalwen appeared beside him and her voice spoke in rapid tones that Nergal could not understand. Two men were coming for him, but suddenly the half-orc forgot about them, looking at Dalwen. Her voice was rising and menacing. She held the silver cross before her, and Nergal stepped back. The men in front of Dalwen were staring at her as well, looks of horror forming on their faces.

Nergal knew the female warrior would unleash some terrible magic any second! Nergal's heart pounded in his ears. He dropped his spear, turning to run from her. His only hope was to run away, and maybe her spell wouldn't kill him. He ran up towards one of the beds in panic, dropping to the floor and trying to roll underneath it.

Much to Nergal's surprise, there was a soldier under the bed with a loaded crossbow, pointing out towards the center of the room. The man seemed just as surprised to find the half-orc under the bed with him. He frantically tried to bring the crossbow around, but Nergal grabbed the hapless soldier by the throat, breaking his neck easily.

Nergal looked back out into the room, seeing fleeing soldiers as they tried to fight their way out through the other door to escape Dalwen while Slith tried to force their way in. The orc looked at Dalwen, trying to understand why he had found her so terrifying a moment before. He could not understand it.

His attention was diverted to the robed leader, who was circling Melvin warily. Garbor lay on the floor, moving slowly. Nergal had not seen what happened to him. Realizing he had a loaded crossbow right next to him, Nergal shoved the corpse aside and aimed at the robed man. Nergal let fly, the crossbow jumping in his hands with a loud thwack.

The bolt missed miserably, flying well behind the robed warrior and burying itself into the wood of a wall. The man looked over towards Nergal, his face a mask of rage. Melvin struck in that instant, throwing his sword forward in a long thrust. The warrior dodged and counterattacked with startling speed, trying to kick Melvin in the knee. Melvin retreated, holding his sword before him.

As Nergal rolled out from under the bed, looking for a weapon, a Slith warrior came to help the knight. The snake-man whipped his body around powerfully, throwing his tail around the legs of the Chu Kutall leader. The man was caught by surprise and struggled, but Melvin moved up and put his sword at his enemy's throat.

"A curse upon you!" snarled the leader, and in one motion he drew something from his robe and pounded it down into his own thigh. The man's eyes rolled up into his head and he collapsed, held up only by the snake-man's tail. Nergal had found a sword but he could see the fight was over. He recognized the Slith as Rovul himself.

Dalwen looked at the small spike that the leader had stabbed himself with. "Poison."

"A formidable opponent," Melvin panted. Garbor sat up behind him and nodded, nursing a bleeding nose.

"Unbelievably quick," Garbor added.

"I believe he was one of the ruling caste," said Melvin. "If all of the monks can fight like that, I can see how they enslaved the entire continent," he added, rubbing a bruised arm.

"Nov Rosul issss ours," Rovul told them, his tongue flickering briefly. "Teranae stopped two shipsss trying to escape, but your vessel wassss destroyed in the processss."

The humans considered this news in silence. Nergal blinked in disbelief, surprised that the snake prince could speak in another language.

"I know thissss must worry you. I suggessst that you travel with ussss to Neyala. Then we sssend emissary back to your empire with you."

Melvin nodded gravely. "We accept your generous offer, Prince Rovul," he said simply.

"We're very grateful," Dalwen said.

"Be thanking you," Nergal told him. "Will be good eating," Nergal added.

"We have managed to capture some prisonersss, but there are no wizardsss," the serpent-prince told them.

"Then perhaps this is the wrong island," Dalwen said.

"We know we were going into a trap is all," Melvin said. "Rilivan may have been taking us away from the wizard, for all we know."

"Or Rilivan himself may have created them," Garbor suggested.

"I don't think so," Melvin told him. "I saw his workshop...Rilivan's work was of a completely different type. Unless he had another secret workshop somewhere and it was all a ruse...I just don't think it was him, though."

"Let's talk to a prisoner. Maybe we can get some information out of one of them."

"That's a good idea," Melvin said, helping Garbor up off the floor. Dalwen came up to Nergal.

"I am sorry that you were caught by my spell, Nergal, but I had to scare the warriors back from us," Dalwen explained. "Sometimes if a friend is close to me, they are affected as well."

Nergal listened carefully. "Dalwen use magic to be scary?" he asked.

"It is very useful," she said, nodding to him.

Nergal shook his head. "Magic strange thing, make Nergal confused."

The group spent the next few hours recovering from the battle, until the sun had set. Zeleph had a dislocated jaw, but he assured them that it had happened before, and he put his mandible back into place with a quick shove with his hand.

The victors began to question the prisoners one by one, trying to intimidate them into speaking. The first three men did not have anything to say, and the group was beginning to despair of making any progress. Each man they took to question was brought to a different holding pen when they were finished with him, so that the remaining prisoners would wonder if they were being killed.

The fourth man was on his knees next to the fire, being interrogated by Dalwen.

"Where are your wizards?" demanded Dalwen.

"What wizards? There are only soldiers," the man said. "You are all stupid. My son will have you for his slaves," he told them.

"We know there are wizards on this island, one of the others already told us," lied Garbor. "But he said he didn't know how many. Now tell us before I start breaking your bones too," growled the knight.

The man stood resolutely, although it did seem that he was afraid.

"Tell us now, or we'll give you to the orc," Melvin suggested in a sudden inspiration.

Dalwen caught on immediately. "Yes, we always give him the ones who don't talk," she agreed with a smile.

Nergal's heavy brows came together in confusion. Garbor stepped up to the half-orc. The prisoner watched carefully. Garbor inclined his head briefly towards the Chu Kutall soldier. "If he doesn't talk, you can do what you like with him, Nergal," Garbor said dramatically, winking at his hulking companion.

"Uh? Er, he no talk?" asked Nergal. The orc stood for a second as understanding dawned on him with the swiftness of a glacier melting. "Oh, he no talk!"

Nergal casually walked over to the prisoner, who shrank back in fear. The huge brute leaned forward and sniffed at the soldier loudly.

"Hmmm, I wonder if soldier-boy good eating?"

The man swallowed hard. Nergal grabbed his arm, bringing the soldier's hand up to his mouth. The prisoner resisted with all his strength, but could not break the orc's grip. He whimpered.

"Me taste before cooking," Nergal said, unrolling the man's index finger and placing it between his long yellow fangs.

"By the spirits!" wailed the prisoner. "Stop him! The man you seek lives in the Mountain of the Dead God! It is straight up the path to the southern heights of the island!"

"What is this place you speak of?" demanded Melvin. Nergal tilted his head, hearing an odd smacking noise. He released the man's hand, but the prisoner's eyes bulged, and his mouth formed an 'O' of surprise. A small trickle of blood poured from the side of the man's throat.

"What?" Melvin asked, confused. Suddenly the knight's head snapped back briefly.

"Ach!" he yelped, his hand coming up to his cheek.

"What was that? Are you—"

There was another whirring noise and Nergal brought up his shield instinctually. Just as he did so a sharp impact reverberated through the metal, accompanied by a snapping sound. He looked over his edge of his protection, searching for the source.

Dalwen saw it a split second before him. "Look out!" she cried, stepping back and fumbling with her sling.

A monstrous thing eyed them from the edge of the torchlight. A long exhalation of breath grew louder until it was the snarl of a malevolent beast. Nergal could see it stood at least a head taller than he, and the outline was suggestive of a giant spiked insect of some kind.

Nergal raised his shield higher to protect his throat and brought his spear back, but his throw was blocked as Garbor and Rovul charged the creature with Zeleph on their heels. The half-orc hesitated, then skillfully launched his weapon over their heads.

The target emitted a completely alien hiss and rattle. Nergal knew he had struck the thing but he could not see the results. Nergal brought out his second spear, pulling it over his back.

The three who had charged the creature were now milling about uncertainly in the brush at the edge of the firelight.

The terrible entity was gone.

Garbor came back into view, walking towards the fire. "Everyone get torches, we'll go after it!" he said. Suddenly the anger left his face, replaced with a look of alarm.

"Melvin! Ah my friend, what a horrible end!"

Nergal grunted in confusion, turning to look at Melvin. The knight was still standing…but something was wrong.

"No!" Dalwen cried. She ran up to Melvin, putting her hand on his face.

The knight stood motionless, his entire body, armor and all, turned to solid stone. Every detail of the man remained permanently engraved in the rock, even the dribble of blood running down the left cheek of his surprised face.

The prisoner had suffered a similar fate, the stone mouth frozen open in a grimace of fear and surprise. The rock figure held the finger Nergal had threatened close to its body.

Rovul crawled up to the scene, regarding the statues through his cold, lidless eyes.

"All hope issss not lost," Rovul told him, forming the words with difficulty.

Dalwen nodded. "This magic can be undone," the priestess told Garbor. She sounded as if she were trying to convince herself as much as the other knight. Tears glistened bright on her face in the dancing torchlight.

"Well what do we do then?" Zeleph said, looking at the stone grimly. "How can it be undone?"

"I cannot do it," Dalwen said. "But we must move him somewhere safe, until we can bring someone."

"Our shaman must ssssee," Rovul urged.

The half-orc hid his surprise at hearing that Rovul's band had a mage. He had never heard of a creature that could turn men into solid stone! Only his shield had saved him.

They carefully moved the statue of Melvin deeper into the camp. Rovul led the way, indicating a large tent covered in eye boggling red and yellow designs. The emperor's son and Dalwen moved into the tent while everyone else waited outside. Nergal waited nervously, scanning around for signs of the creature that had attacked them.

In a short time Rovul and Dalwen came out of the tent. The priestess had a determined look on her face.

"We must find that thing that did this to Melvin and kill it," she announced. "If we can bring the shaman some of the poison that did this, he says he can reverse the effects."

Nergal nodded to her. "We kill hissing thing," he assured her. Then he noticed Rovul staring at him, and added, "Er, Nergal mean big hissing monster."

Rovul flickered his tongue. "I understtand," he said.

Nergal looked at his bright Slith shield and remembered the missile that had been deflected. He could see a chip in the paint, very near the edge, where the missile had struck.

"Nergal need bigger shield," he announced.

"Everyone gather together some supplies," Garbor said. "We'll need food and torches, among other things. Meet back here within the hour. We must track that thing down and destroy it."

Nergal nodded. The thought of food or torches did not cross his mind. To him supplies meant a bigger shield. The group dispersed and the orc walked off to find a suitable candidate.

He moved through the three ransacked barracks, finding several smaller shields but none to rival his current one. He picked up four spears, strapping them to his back. Nergal began to realize the problem with spears, in that he tended to throw them all away. Almost as an afterthought he grabbed a normal-sized mace off the floor, a long handled weapon with a smaller, rounder head than Krollon.

"Hello mace. You speak?" he asked, looking expectantly at the weapon. There was no reply.

"You good mace. No be speaking at me," Nergal announced, placing the weapon into his belt. "Last mace talk too much."

He exited the building, searching about the camp for a good place to find more shields. Nergal emitted a grunt of surprise. Over next to a storage shed, next to some bantering legionnaires, Nergal saw several huge metal shields. The shields were rectangular, much taller than wide. They were convex, standing up on the ground without support. The half orc immediately strode over and took up one of the large barriers, setting his Slith shield down on the ground.

One of the legionnaires saw Nergal grasping the tall shield, and walked closer to Nergal.

"Uhhh, why are you taking that siege shield?"

"Nergal need shield. Good big shield. Nergal take," he said, trying to look menacing. The big brute didn't have to try hard. The legionnaire stepped back slightly, obviously intimidated.

"You can have it," he said quickly. "It's just that it's not a normal shield. That's a siege shield. It's used for cover when you approach a fortress. It's too heavy to be…" the man's voice trailed off as he saw that Nergal was casually holding the shield off the ground with one arm.

"Never mind," he said in a small voice, and stepped back amongst his fellows.

Nergal grunted and turned to return to the campfire.

"Nergal have big shield!" he exalted.

CHAPTER 15

Hunting by Starlight

Nergal watched his companions in the light of their torches as they assembled in the dark tropical night.

A priestess of Norngawen, whom Nergal now saw to be beautiful, practiced throwing her shield aside to begin casting a spell. Next to her, a one-handed knight struggled with leather straps to attach a shield to his crippled arm, a determined look set on his wide, red-bearded face. Criss-crossing the scene, a legionnaire commander played with the hilt of his sword and paced around the dead campfire, eager to begin the hunt. Last to come under Nergal's gaze, a serpentine warrior-prince of the Slith flickered his tongue out at the jungle, his thoughts a mystery to the half-orc.

"Five of us against that creature," summarized Garbor, looking the group over. "We owe it to Melvin to find that thing and kill it quickly. It pains me to see him in such a state, nothing more than a pretty statue."

"I hope we can kill the thing and restore him before we have to go after the wizard," Dalwen said. "The mage is undoubtedly powerful, to control these horrible things."

"It may not be wise to stalk the thing in the dark," Zeleph commented.

Garbor looked at Zeleph in surprise. "Actually, you just made me realize something. We should extinguish our torches."

"That would be even worse, wouldn't it?" asked Dalwen.

"Well, Nergal has good night eyes, and my helmet allows me to see clearly at night," Garbor explained. "We could keep a lookout for the thing."

"Are you sure you're not just making an excuse to finally use your helmet?" asked Dalwen.

Garbor shook his head. "Without the torches we'll make a harder target for the creature. We may even catch it by surprise, if it sleeps."

"If we meet it again, I'll cast a spell to make it glow in the dark," Dalwen told them. "Then we should be able to kill it easily enough. But I can't cast the spell on the thing if I can't see it myself."

The group absorbed this idea for a moment, then Zeleph concluded, "I think that we should either wait until morning, or give your helmet to Dalwen. With her wearing the helmet, she could see the thing and then make it glow." The legionnaire stopped pacing to await the answer to his suggestions.

"How is your night vision, Rovul?" asked Garbor.

"I cannot sssee well even in the light of day," Rovul told them. "However, if the creature approachessss I will smell it."

"Very well," Garbor said. He handed his helmet to Dalwen. "I'll stay farther back. Nergal, you have the lead this time."

"Eh?"

"You can see well in the dark. So can Dalwen, but we need her to be in the middle, so that she is protected while she casts her spell," Garbor explained.

Nergal watched, his spirits dropping, as the group formed up behind him. He would have to go first. He looked out into the blackness of the jungle ahead. Somewhere out there, a huge monster awaited them, and he would have to be first in line? Nergal clutched his shield before him and moved forward uncertainly.

"Whatever those projectiles are it uses, we know that a shield will stop them. Keep your shields up," announced Dalwen. putting her left arm through the straps of a shield she had picked up in the encampment. Although the priestess almost never used a shield, the desperation of their situation against the monster demanded it.

"Its trail is clear," Zeleph pointed out. "It was large enough to damage the foliage as it passed." The legionnaire and Dalwen extinguished their torches in the sandy earth. Nergal saw that the moon had retreated below the trees leaving the night darker. Only the dim light of the stars would aid them.

Nergal stood for a moment, letting his eyes adjust. He looked down at the ground, trying to see the thing's tracks. After a moment he resolved the signs of the monster's passage on the ground. It seemed to have many small legs. There were dozens of small circular indentations in the sandy earth leading off into the jungle.

The vegetation grew thick, but as Zeleph had pointed out, the thing had left a swath of damaged plants in its wake. Nergal hunched down slightly and began gently padding along its trail in silence, nervously looking ahead. Rovul followed him slightly to the left, clutching his spiked shield. Dalwen and the other two warriors followed along at a greater distance, since the snake-man's body slithered along behind Nergal for several paces.

They followed the trail first upslope and then back down, winding their way south through the jungle. Even at night the air remained hot and humid. Soon Nergal was covered in sweat. Following along at the rear, Garbor and Zeleph looked especially miserable in their hot armor.

Nergal came to the edge of a small clearing and hesitated. The half-orc hunched behind his shield, his eyes darting left and then right. He looked out over the fronds of lush ferns, glistening ever so slightly in the feeble light. Did the monster lurk just ahead, ready to attack? He scanned the flora carefully, half expecting to see eyes staring back at him.

Rovul came quietly up beside him, testing the air with his tongue. Nergal looked questioningly at the Slith, trying to see if the snake warrior smelled anything. Rovul returned the look, shaking his head.

They continued through the clearing. The hairs on Nergal's back stood up but he ignored his fear, trusting in his companion. He traversed the open area without incident, re-entering the dense growth at a break in the leaves caused by the monster. The trail angled sharply uphill, to the half-orc's right.

He slinked along, followed quietly by the others. Eventually they approached a rocky cliffside. It became darker as they approached the rock face which blocked out part of the sky. Nergal slowed, growing more fearful as the way became darker. He emerged from the underbrush facing the rock. Straight ahead Nergal saw the ragged black mouth of a cave. He turned to Rovul.

"Nergal no be going in there," he whispered to the Slith quietly. Rovul nodded in silent agreement, then moved to the side so the others could join them.

Garbor looked at the cave mouth, his brows coming together in consternation. "Let's lie in wait for it here," the knight whispered to Nergal, his voice barely audible. Garbor turned to the other two. "Let's wait for it here," he repeated. "Spread out."

The orc winced at the noise, as the adventurers fanned out into a concave formation in front of the opening to ambush the monster. They moved behind plants and rocks, feeling their way in the darkness. Nergal settled himself in a concealed niche with his back against a palm trunk, hidden by a large frond.

One of his eyes had a clear path to the mouth of the cave. The hunters began waiting for their prey.

Inexorably, seconds stretched into minutes, minutes into hours. Fear battled with complacency in the half-orc's mind. At last Nergal's eyes became somewhat heavy, as the boredom waxed supreme. At some point he dozed off.

"Attack!" bellowed Garbor, snapping the orc back to consciousness in a single mind-wrenching instant.

Nergal bolted to his feet, feeling cramped leg muscles complain painfully. Realizing he had left his shield on the ground, he ducked down to grasp it and heard the smacking sound of projectiles hitting the tree trunk above him. The half-orc pushed through his leafy cover, holding his shield up before him.

Garbor had charged out from the trees brandishing his axe. Rovul and Zeleph rushed up with him to join the attack. Nergal could hear Dalwen spell-casting to his left. Seeing the huge shape of the monster at the foot of the cliff, he brought his spear back.

The huge thing screeched in anger and ran up to meet Zeleph. Nergal launched his spear and immediately grasped another one off his back. The first weapon sank into the form of the monster but the darkness concealed the severity of the wound from the half-orc. Garbor yelled at the thing, which seemed to overbear Zeleph, its form becoming one with the legionnaire in the night. Rovul released a disconcerting war scream, stabbing at the monster repeatedly from a good distance with his spear.

Dalwen's spell took effect, lighting up the plated integument of the beast as if it were a giant living lantern. The thing resembled a huge spiny centipede, rearing up its foreparts high into the air. It had two long tentacles hanging from the sides of its flat head, covered in long sharp spines.

The sense of horror that Nergal felt in such close proximity to the awful thing deepened as he realized that the monster had almost completely consumed Zeleph. The man's lower body fell from its huge mandibles, which were still working on the upper half of its victim, rending the body into an unrecognizable mass of blood, flesh and bone. Garbor stood with weapon upraised, silhouetted before the glowing beast. The knight hacked down on one of the tentacles in a mighty blow, completely hacking the appendage off. The bundle of spines fell down over his shoulder, and Garbor cursed as some of the points pierced his flesh beyond the edge of his breastplate.

As Nergal ran forward with his second spear, he realized that the knight had been turned to stone. He mastered the fear that rose in his chest and aimed his weapon for a fold between two of the armored plates that covered the thing's back.

The creature hesitated, confused by its strange luminescence. Nergal hurled his second spear into its side, and the monster howled in pain and rage. It turned on its centipede-like legs and clambered back into the cave, harassed by Rovul. The acrid smell of the monster's blood filled the alcove in the jungle next to the cliff.

Nergal came up beside Garbor, looking at the frozen knight. He reached out a hand to touch the rock, not quite able to believe that the warrior had been transformed so quickly. The surface of the statue remained warm to the touch, but as solid as granite.

Rovul came up beside Nergal. Light came from the depths of the cave for a few more moments and then disappeared altogether.

"The priestesssss," he said quietly.

Nergal shot a look at Dalwen. He could see that she stood very still. He abruptly realized that she had met the same fate. Shaking his head in dismay, he moved up to her. Her shield lay nearby, where she had discarded it to cast her spell.

"Despite this turn, we have sssucceeded," Rovul told him.

"What?" Nergal blurted, confused.

"We have a cluster of the spinesssss," Rovul said, indicating the severed tentacle of the monster. Nergal slowly understood that the spines were poisonous, and that they needed to return them to the snake shaman.

He nodded to the Slith. "You take poison back. Nergal guard others," he said.

"You will stay alone?" queried Rovul carefully.

Nergal nodded again. "It poison everyone but us," he said. "It is like orc hunting with poison spear tips," he told the Slith.

The snake-man looked at Nergal strangely, and then gazed about the dense trees and shrubs that surrounded them. Then Rovul turned away, and began to search through the trees. Nergal followed along gloomily. The Slith leader came to a tree holding bunches of odd shaped bulbs in its branches.

"There may be a way," Rovul rasped. "These bulbs are very poisonoussss," the Slith leader told him. Nergal watched with interest as the Slith warrior cut several of the hourglass-shaped bulbs free of the plant. Placing the bulbs in a pile on a flat rock near the cliff, he cut them open and began to mash the substance together with the curved blade on the end of the spear. The snake-man spit into the mush several times as he worked, creating a pulpy green paste.

"Dip your spear," he directed the half-orc. Nergal rolled the iron heads of both of his remaining spears in the concoction. "Don't touch, it is very danger-ousssss," the Slith told him. "I will be back with the knight and some men to carry the otherssss."

Rovul turned in the burgeoning light of early morning, and slithered away down the trail, leaving Nergal utterly alone.

The cries of jungle birds echoed from the cliffside as the half-orc returned to the cave, carrying his two poisoned spears in one hand. He reexamined the statues of his friends in the new light. The jungle blocked most of the low sun, but enough light filtered through to allow him to see much farther into the cave. Nergal spotted a small carved alcove inside the entrance, though most of the tunnel seemed of natural origin.

He looked about the clearing, trying to decide if he should occupy his old hiding spot behind the statues of Dalwen and Garbor, or if he should stick closer to them. Nergal realized that he had once again neglected to pack any food, having focused entirely on the acquisition of his new shield and weapons. He looked at the petrified backpack on Dalwen's smooth stone back, thinking of the rock food that must be inside.

His eyes returned to the opening of the cave. Would the horrible monster return to eat Nergal? Or had it bled out in the back of the cave? The orc looked at the carved niche in the lair. It would be an ideal spot to ambush anything moving out of the cave. The half-orc took a few uncertain steps towards the opening and set his huge shield down on the ground on a flat shelf of stone. He set one of his spears down on the ground, still watching carefully. Then he picked up a fist-sized rock and hurled it into the passageway.

"You be dere, monster?" Nergal called out. He listened carefully as the rock clattered farther into the cave. No other noise came from inside the cliff.

Nergal rushed up to the cliffside, and screamed into the opening wildly. He quickly danced back to his former position, and set his spear facing the cave. Once again, he detected no activity in the tunnel mouth.

"Monster being dead," he told himself. Nergal picked his shield back up and approached closer, now within only a few steps of the opening. His eyes picked out a long, straight crack in the stone backing the alcove that had interested him. Nergal stood a few more moments, listening carefully. Only the sound of the jungle birds and a gentle breeze blowing up the mountainside came to his ears.

He moved up into the tunnel, peering as far inside as he could. Massive stalagmites and a curve in the passageway blocked his view. The orc stepped into the carved hollow in the side of the cavern, coming closer to examine the crack. It formed a square the size of a doorway in the wall, but no handle presented itself. Nergal sat his shield in the corner, and listened again for the beast. There was nothing.

Pressing against the panel, he found that the segment of stone swung open to reveal a square passageway of worked stone. It extended straight into the mountainside, and many paces ahead he could see a spike extending from the wall with a glowing lantern at its tip. The light it emitted barely made the passage traversable.

The big brute sniffed uncertainly, examining the doorway. The opening was too small for the monster to fit into, so he knew that the thing did not await him ahead. He could detect a confusing conglomeration of sulphurous and pungent odors that he could not identify. Grabbing his shield, Nergal entered the clean, smooth walled tunnel and walked towards the lantern.

Behind him, the panel smoothly slid shut without a sound, closing him in the mountain.

CHAPTER 16

Mountain of the Dead God

Nergal walked uncertainly towards the lantern, oblivious to the fact that the door had closed behind him. The meager light revealed a man-made passage. As he approached, he realized the light source differed greatly from the usual. It seemed to be nothing more than a glowing ball of glass or wax. He saw no flame inside it. When the half-orc got next to the wall spike, he observed the ball for a moment, and then looked farther down the corridor. Up ahead, he could see that the passage connected to a room which emitted more light.

Abandoning his inspection of the strange glowing sphere, he moved towards the room. The half-orc came to an open doorway and looked into it.

Four full suits of armor were arrayed against the walls, two on each side. Each clutched a halberd in the metal gauntlet of its right hand, the haft resting against the floor. Two more of the light spheres rested on the ends of spikes coming from the walls between the armor. The room contained little else, like some sort of entranceway. Another corridor exited the room from the opposite side. The half-orc froze in the doorway for a moment, staring at the armor.

"Anybody dere?" he asked uncertainly, his eyes shifting nervously from one side to the other and back, studying the armor. The suits were absolutely still and silent. Nergal's eyes traced the intricate and sinister lines of the metal. He decided that the armor sat too still to be occupied.

Nergal smiled. "Nobody dere."

He stepped forward to make his way through the room. All four guards moved forward in response, startling the half-orc. They moved their halberds to point towards the intruder. He roared in surprise and anger, moving quickly back into the entrance corridor.

"You trick Nergal. Now I hurt you!" he warned them. He stepped back into the corridor, allowing his attackers to follow in after him. He faced all four in a single file since the corridor restricted their formation.

Nergal mercilessly thrust his spear tip into the face of the first man, sliding the spearhead right under the narrow-slitted visor. The tip slipped into the helmet as the orc intended, but the result was most unexpected. His weapon met no fleshy resistance and produced no scream. The tip of his spear clanged against the back of the helmet and knocked it completely off. The helmet contained no head. The suit of armor swung at Nergal with its halberd, and Nergal stepped back out of range, staring at the headless form in surprise.

"Eh?" he grunted uncertainly, retreating a few more steps down the corridor. "Magic!"

Then his face became set in determination, and he dropped the spear, fishing his mace out of his belt. Nergal knocked a halberd thrust aside with his huge shield and swung back in a rapid counterattack on the first enemy. His mace exploded into the arm of the headless armor suit before him, taking the arm completely off with the clang of metal on metal.

His opponent seemed unfazed, and pushed against Nergal's shield. The orc ducked as the next foe in line thrust its halberd at him from the second rank. The orc pushed back, causing the magical guardian to hesitate as it regained its balance.

Seeing this, Nergal had an idea. He took two rapid steps back and then charged back forward with a feral snarl. He put his muscles into it, ducking behind his oversize shield and pushing hard. Nergal caught the automaton off guard, and slammed it back against the ones behind it, still pushing.

The armor suits flew back sprawling, metal pieces flying off everywhere. Nergal could tell that all the suits were hollow, with no real occupants. The orc found he had run completely over the first guard, and so he simply charged on, swinging at the head of the third suit as he ran past. The blow took the helmet off.

A sharp pain erupted in Nergal's left calf and he howled in distress. He turned to face his opponents, three of which were getting back up. He now faced the guards from the other side of the corridor, with the room at his back. The armor closest to him had blood on the end of its halberd.

The half-orc roared and brought his mace back, moving forward. Instead of swinging the mace into the first guard, he brought his leg up and placed the sole of his foot flat against its breastplate, pushing the automaton back off its feet again. Now the mace swung around and connected with the next suit of armor in line, hitting it with a great deal of force but not inflicting any noticeable damage. In fact the strike hurt his hand somewhat.

The half-orc howled in frustration, ignoring the wound on his leg. He threw the mace at his opponents without aiming and grabbed the gauntlet of the suit that faced him. He stepped to the side to avoid a halberd thrust and pulled hard, ripping the arm off another suit. He retrieved the halberd from the severed arm and backed off again.

The three guards facing him were now a motley collection of humanoid shaped armor, each of them missing one or two key components such as a helmet or arm, or both. Nergal breathed heavily, the exertion of combat already starting to wear on him. The suits of armor were gathering for another attack. His only known escape route lay beyond the magical guardians.

Trailing blood from his calf, Nergal moved back into the room. He drew the first set of armor out of the corridor. As soon as it cleared the doorway, he swung the halberd hard and low, holding it only by the end of the wooden shaft. The metal axe head of the weapon slammed into the lower leg of his advancing enemy, sweeping its legs out from underneath it.

The guard behind it had no halberd, but it stepped over the struggling mass of metal and swung at the half-orc with its spiked iron gauntlet. Nergal took the blow across the side of his head, and the spikes ripped into the flesh of his ear and upper cheek. The sound of tearing cartilage carried louder through his own head than the air.

"Rag nok!" he spat in rage, and mindlessly dropped his halberd to strike back with his own fist. Nergal howled again, this time from pain from his fist as it struck the metal. He backpedaled, nursing his bruised hand and hiding behind his shield. He found himself in the corner of the room. Two of the guards moved to attack him.

He set the shield upright on the ground before him, waiting for the attack. One of the guardians thrust its halberd at him, and Nergal blocked it aside and grabbed the haft of the weapon, pulling it out of the grip of his attacker. He tossed it to one side and then ducked, narrowly escaping another mailed fist strike from his other enemy.

The orc toppled his shield towards this attacker, and charged the other guard, who was retrieving the halberd from the ground. He grabbed the armor by its open head aperture and the bottom end of its breastplate, picking the entire thing up and lifting over his head. The orc growled insanely, turning towards the other guardian. He hurtled the armor above him, throwing it like a huge stone to smash a rock lizard. The breastplates smacked together loudly in a tangle of greaves, gauntlets and mail skirts.

The armor scattered about on the ground and lay still.

Nergal growled as the blood ran down the side of his head. Still enraged, the orc growled deeply again, looking about for enemies. The other two suits of armor seemed to be disabled as well. Heaving huge breaths and stalking about the room, dripping blood everywhere, he slowly came back to a more placid state of mind.

As the pain came forward to replace the anger, Nergal realized that he sustained grievous wounds on the head and calf. He remembered his friends outside, and suddenly felt guilt for leaving them unprotected. The tunnel had distracted him. Nergal wished that he had some cloth to tie up his wounds, but the mass of dried blood that covered him would have to suffice.

He staggered back down the corridor he had entered. He came to the entrance, and realized that the door had closed. Nergal pressed against the rock portal, but the slab of stone that sealed him in did not budge. He grunted in sorrow, leaning against the stone. Then he gathered himself and pushed with all his might. The door seemed solidly in place.

Miserably, he turned back towards the tunnel. He had no food or equipment to speak of. He shook his head. Why didn't he ever remember to bring food?

"Nergal not have the smarts today," he told the empty corridor.

He moved towards the guard room again. His calf wound felt like it burned in a fire, causing him to limp. Coming back to the room, he took stock of the carnage. The room looked like a stampede had come through, smashing several men to bits. Although there were no fleshy parts in evidence, Nergal's blood splattered all over made up for it.

The half-orc reclaimed his large shield and his mace. He put the mace back into his belt and grabbed the poisoned spear, deciding that it held more value than the halberds.

He made his way to the far corridor past the guard room, still favoring his injured leg. It was only a short distance to a four corridor intersection. The smooth rock walls had no features other than the spike holding another glowing ball to light the intersection.

Choosing the path to his right, he continued down the corridor. The way darkened slightly as the intersection receded behind him, but Nergal could see another lit doorway ahead. He slowed, thinking of the need for stealth. He had found in his short and brutal life that combat proved much easier when he had the element of surprise.

Nergal took another silent step forward. He discerned another two suits of armor, standing at the walls in the room ahead. Immediately he retreated, thrills of fear running through him. He could not face more guards now! The orc needed food and rest before he could consider any more such painful encounters. He turned back and returned to the intersection. There were only two choices left.

He chose the center corridor, leading straight into the mountain. After perhaps thirty paces he detected a side door ahead. It consisted of wooden planks braced together with brass strips. The portal was recessed into the wall slightly. He approached quietly to listen for activity on the other side.

A wondrous scent reached Nergal's nostrils. Food! The unmistakable odor drifted in from farther down the corridor. The half-orc abandoned his thoughts of investigating the door and made his way down the corridor hastily, already forgetting his need for stealth.

He came to the end of the passageway. There were two doors there, lit by another of the glowing objects attached to the wall. One of the doors waited straight ahead and the other to his left. Like the previous one, they were made of brass and wood. Nergal sniffed steadily and targeted the odor as coming from the left door.

He set his shield down and used that hand to open the latch. Then he pushed the door open, holding his spear ready. The room beyond seemed unguarded. The familiar light of a wall sphere showed him some kind of kitchen. Straight ahead on a wooden counter, he saw a loaf of bread and a large round of cheese. He quickly moved his shield inside the door and shut it behind him.

Nergal ate desperately, shoveling the bread and cheese into his mouth. Oblivious to all else, he made grumbling and smacking noises as he ate. Soon the food on the counter dwindled, but Nergal found a storage cabinet with dried meat in it. He devoured several salted strips of the flesh, almost biting his fingers as he pushed food into his mouth.

Finally he returned to his senses, realizing that he fed in a strange place with no real idea of what he should do. He remembered dimly something about the evil wizard residing inside the mountain. Nergal licked his fingers and sat still for a few moments, trying to detect danger. The area remained quiet and Nergal could only smell the food. He burped loudly, breaking the silence.

He exited the kitchen and tried the latch on the second door. It seemed to be firmly locked. Nergal fished for his mace, thinking to break his way in, but then decided against it. He would try to be quiet first.

Returning to the now familiar intersection, he tried the last corridor. The light faded behind him and the corridor became somewhat darker. He continued for a few moments until he could see new light down the way.

Voices echoed from up ahead.

Nergal immediately dropped lower, bending his knees. He began to slink forward carefully. The strange suits of armor had never spoken. He would sneak up on these men and kill them.

I have the smarts, he told himself.

Nergal hugged the wall as he approached the room ahead. He saw a large natural cavern, with rough stone walls and ceiling. The floor had been carved smooth. He could still hear the voices, so he cautiously peeked in, trying to move slowly.

There were two men standing with their backs to him at a red and gray stone dais. A ball of glass the size of a wine barrel rested before them. White mists shifted lazily within it.

The first man wore a black robe like the kind that Nergal remembered seeing on men at Salthor Castle and the barracks at Nov Rosul.

"It is completely ruined," this man said, holding his hand over his eyes as if they pained him. "Those bastards have crippled my Shok Nogua."

"It might still be of some use to us. We could keep it around to patrol the island…it might be able to neutralize any pirates that come nosing around," suggested the second man. Nergal saw that this one wore leather riding pants and boots. The half-orc imagined him to be a scout of some kind.

Nergal's attention shifted to the large sphere before them on the dais. He could clearly see an image of the centipede monster floating in the glass. One of its tentacles had been removed just like the real monster, but this image was much smaller than the creature that he had fought outside the cave. The shaft of the orc's spear clacked lightly against the hilt of the mace in his belt.

"What was that?"

The two men turned around to see Nergal, looking at them over the top edge of his shield. Immediately the scout drew his sword and attacked Nergal. Just as rapidly as the man attacked, Nergal threw his spear into his attacker's chest. Clutching at the spear that impaled him, the man grunted and died, falling onto the steps of the dais.

"Who are you?" demanded the man in the black robe. The man made no move to defend himself. He had a wide forehead with a pointy chin and a short black beard. The lack of fear in the man made Nergal uneasy.

"I be killing bad wizard," Nergal asserted, bringing up the mace from his belt.

"There seems to be a bug on the end of your mace," the mage pointed at the end of Nergal's weapon, and his fingers curled and danced in a nimble pattern. Nergal looked at his mace and then back at the robed man. The orc's great hairy brows came together in anger as he saw that the wizard had fooled him.

"Zefaele rulan donocktagard," said the mage, "Yulu hanhan brunatick!" As he uttered these words, Nergal rushed forward to crush the skull of...his true friend!

Nergal stopped short, dropping the mace onto the stone steps. He shook his head, blinking in surprise.

"Nergal sorry," the brute told the Chu Kutall wizard. "Confused.."

"That is not a problem, my dear orc friend," said the robed man slowly. He smiled a most pleased smile, and approached closer to the half-orc. "You can call me Kantru, of course, since we're the best of buddies," he explained.

"Kantru," echoed the brute.

"Yes, and just let me test you a moment. You took quite a lump on the head, there, my friend. Do you even remember your name?"

"Lump on head?" Nergal thought for a moment, his hand coming up to probe his skull under the dried blood. "Eh, me Nergal!" he remembered, and smiled back at the wizard grandly.

Kantru's eyes bulged slightly at the sight of the orc's bared fangs, but he recovered swiftly. "Umm, very good! You still remember your name. That is a good sign. Come in here, and tell me more about yourself, just so that we know nothing is permanently damaged. I will remind you of course, if there is anything that you cannot remember."

CHAPTER 17

Nemesis

Nergal looked up as he heard footsteps approaching down the long entrance corridor. He scurried up from his napping spot in the guard room and peered down the hall. Almost immediately he could see his friends approaching. Rovul must have succeeded.

"Nergal!" called Garbor, catching sight of the half-orc. "You're alive! We feared the worst."

"Nergal okay," he assured the group. Garbor, Melvin and Dalwen fell in around him and Rovul watched from the entrance of the chamber.

Garbor patted Nergal on the shoulder and then stared at the carnage all around.

"Quite a fight, my friend!"

"Let me see your head," Dalwen told him, putting her hand on Nergal's forehead and pushing his head to the side, so that the priestess could examine the head wound that had been inflicted by the spiked gauntlet of the automaton.

"This must have bled like crazy. At least all that congealed blood kept the wound protected," she said, grimacing. The priestess began to cast a spell while the others milled about, looking over the remains of the armor.

"There are no bodies left…" Melvin commented.

Nergal did not answer, as a pleasant warmth spreading from the side of his head distracted him. Dalwen whispered a few more unintelligible phrases and then finished. The half-orc blinked, and realized that the pain in his head had completely subsided. His mood lifted considerably, despite the throbbing of his calf wound. He ignored this other pain and did not point it out to Dalwen. The priestess watched him expectantly and the orc realized that human custom demanded an acknowledgement of the assistance.

"Hrm, be thanking you," Nergal told her, nodding his head.

"Nergal, where did you put the bodies?" asked Garbor.

"No men. Empty armor," Nergal explained. "Is magic," he added knowingly.

"Phantom soldiers of some kind?" Melvin looked about at the metal pieces again. "This wizard has no end of tricks. We can expect more of these, I suppose. How did you kill all of them?"

Nergal shrugged.

"Was hard," he told them. The others waited for a more elaborate account until it became obvious that none was forthcoming.

"Well, now that Dalwen has cleaned you up, we can settle our score with this evil wizard," Melvin said.

"Kantru not evil. He good wizard," Nergal explained urgently. The others, even Rovul, looked at him in open surprise.

"His name is Kantru?" asked Melvin.

"He's a good wizard?" Dalwen followed up.

Nergal nodded. "He wait to meet you," he told them. "Come this way."

Melvin and Dalwen exchanged perplexed looks, but Garbor simply shrugged and fell in behind Nergal. The half-orc led them down the hallway further into the underground complex. He turned left at the next room, heading back towards the dais where he had first surprised Kantru.

Nergal led the group into the cavern. They could see twelve of the automatons, lined up against the walls to either side. Nergal continued uncertainly to the center dais, and turned towards the others.

"Kantru say he will meet us here," he informed them.

"Uh, Nergal," croaked Melvin, drawing his sword and looking at the armor, "Are you sure…"

The automatons raised their halberds and moved to encircle the party on the dais steps. Nergal watched the adjoining tunnels expectantly while the other adventurers readied their weapons. Kantru entered the cavern from the far entrance, pale and shimmering.

"See? Kantru here," Nergal told them.

Dalwen gasped. "Is Kantru a ghost?"

The orc raised an eyebrow, then looked at Kantru again. He realized that he could actually see completely through the wizard.

The facsimile of Kantru laughed wickedly.

"It's a trap for sure!" Garbor snarled. "Nergal, draw your mace!"

"Eh?"

The shimmering image of the Chu Kutall wizard spoke, his voice echoing hollowly in the cavern.

"Ah. By now my good friend Nergal has unwittingly led you into my trap, and I am long gone. Glorious!"

The pale image of the mage smiled at them.

"Nergal can attest to the hospitality of my automatons. I'm sure they will show you a good time—and I added a little extra something to them just for you. I won't warn you off since I know you're all so very determined to kill me…I look forward to our next encounter, if any of you survive."

The apparition laughed again and faded away. Garbor roared and charged in, not caring to wait for the armor suits to attack them. He swept his huge axe out level with the head of the nearest enemy to take its head off at the neck. A sharp snap erupted from the impact accompanied by a shower of sparks. Garbor cried out and staggered back, almost falling over.

An automaton swung its halberd at Nergal. The half-orc danced aside, angered. Remembering his overrun attack in his first encounter with the spirit warriors, he retaliated by ducking under his shield and charging the group in front of him.

The impact resulted in a sharp spasm of pain that wrenched his gut. Sparks flew around his shield as energy discharged from the two automatons that Nergal had tackled. The two guards still flew to the ground as Nergal intended, but the half-orc ended up hurtling down with them, stunned. He rolled under his shield and struggled to breathe while lights danced in his eyes.

"Don't touch them!" he heard Dalwen call distantly.

A crackling noise and an anguished screech came from Rovul. Nergal blinked and breathed raggedly, trying to shake off his torpor.

"How am I supposed to do that?" demanded Melvin. Nergal heard another crackling snap and a cry of pain.

Nergal lost the struggle to regain his wits until a sharp pole arm blade thwacked against his left arm, bringing him out of his shocked stupor. He roared and spotted his attacker, one of the armor suits that had fallen to the floor with him. Nergal grabbed his mace and began to counterattack, smashing the suit beneath repeated blows of the mace. The stunning force did not repeat itself. It seemed that once the energy had been discharged, the automatons were identical to the ones he had fought previously.

Nergal regained his feet and saw that Garbor was in trouble, with three of the armor suits assaulting him at once. The burly knight tried to bring his shield up to block an attack, but his leather straps slipped on his crippled arm, allowing the shield to dangle from his elbow strap. The halberd came in just over the edge of his defense and caught the knight in the face, slashing at his flesh. The spear tip of the weapon penetrated Garbor's eye socket until the axe blade of the halberd snapped against his skull. Garbor ducked away and down, cursing and dripping blood. In desperation he swept his axe blade across the leg of the suit in front of him, knocking it off balance and bending the knee joint of the leg guards. The automaton hopped clumsily and fell to the ground, struggling in an eerie mechanical fashion like an insect with several legs cut off.

The half-orc heard Dalwen begin to sing in a strong, sure voice. At first Nergal ignored the sound as he turned from one destroyed automaton and began to smash another. Quickly, though, he began to feel the power of the song in his chest.

The shaking left his arms, and the dazed feeling cleared from his mind as the hymn flowed through the air. To his right Melvin had regained his composure and kicked the chest of another automaton. Nergal winced, and as he feared, Melvin grunted as the energy discharged into him. The armor fell and Melvin staggered. A halberd smacked across his helmet and the knight went down hard.

Nergal rushed to his aid, attacking the armor that had hit Melvin. He smashed its helmet off with one Herculean blow and followed up with a tremendous shield ram. The armor hurtled back under the blow and fell to the ground, thrashing about.

The half-orc glanced around to see how the battle had developed. The remaining automatons besieged the group on all sides of the dais. The battle hymn still sounded in the air and flowed through his veins, urging him to further heroic action. Nergal picked another suit of full plate and attacked. He swung his mace down on an arm of the automaton hard enough to break it away. Once again a bolt of energy clenched his insides, and Nergal half charged, half fell forward onto the enemy.

The suit thrashed beneath his weight, unable to use its long polearm against an enemy at point blank range. Mailed gauntlets began to smash into Nergal's ribs. The orc grunted in pain and responded by grabbing blindly for the helm of his attacker. He grasped the visor opening and ripped the helmet off, hurtling it away. Still the gauntlet pounded at his side, drawing blood. Nergal took hold of the shoulder guard and shook at it fiercely, trying to dislodge the plate from its hinges. When it didn't give way he moved his other arm to intercept the attacking appendage. He tore the gauntlet off the arm and rolled away from the armor.

The sounds of battle had abated. Dalwen's song had stopped with it, and now the priestess flitted about, examining the warriors. Nergal seemed better off than most. Both of the human knights had been stunned to insensibility, and Rovul slumped down so that his arms could help support his torso.

After a few long moments, Melvin blinked and seemed to regain lucidity. He looked dazedly about him, breathing heavily. "Is everyone alive?" he asked.

"Everyone is alive, but Garbor's eye has been hurt," Dalwen told him. The priestess looked at Rovul, and Nergal followed her eyes to the great bloody welts on the side of the Slith's body. The half-orc could tell by Rovul's sluggish writhing that he had been terribly wounded.

Melvin contemplated Nergal as they rested.

"You need to choose your friends more carefully," Melvin told him.

"Kantru good friend of Nergal."

"What? Nergal, he fooled you. It was all a trap, you see?" Melvin pleaded. "It was a trick."

Nergal shook his head vigorously. "Not Kantru's fault. Kantru good friend."

Dalwen looked askance at the half-orc as she prepared to heal Rovul's wounds. "Nergal, how long have you known Kantru?"

"Long time…" Nergal's brows came together as he launched into heavy thought. "Not sure."

Melvin wasn't ready to give up. "Nergal, you know how mages can do some amazing things. Well, Kantru is a wizard. He ensorcelled you."

"Eh?"

"He tricked you into thinking you are his friend, using magic," Garbor spoke up. Nergal saw that one of the knight's eyes was a bloody gash, already swelling shut. Nergal could see that the wound caused pain but Garbor handled it well.

Nergal just shook his head. "Kantru no trick Nergal. He no trick his friend," he maintained. The orc crossed his arms defensively, feeling somewhat uncomfortable.

"Hmmm, well let's discuss the matter later," suggested Melvin. He looked over at the adjoining tunnels on the far side of the cavern. "What's down that way?"

Nergal shook his head, indicating he didn't know. The group gathered themselves together, moving slowly and nursing their injuries. Melvin led the way to the leftmost of two tunnels, holding his sword out carefully before him. The passage led thirty or forty paces up to a strong wooden door, lit by a glowing sphere set into the wall.

"I wonder if we pried the globe out of its socket if it would keep glowing," wondered Melvin out loud.

Dalwen smiled. Turning to Nergal she whispered, "We just about died five minutes ago, and already Melvin is back to himself again."

"Let's just force the door and see what's in there," Garbor told him. Garbor squinted with his remaining eye and tapped the door handle cautiously with his war axe. When nothing untoward happened he tried the handle, and found that the door was not barred.

"Never mind. It's open," Garbor announced, carefully looking inside as the portal swung open. Nergal could see tables filled with strange equipment inside. The group made their way into the new chamber.

"This is certainly his workshop," announced Melvin. Nergal stood in awe of the chamber, which extended for quite some distance. Thick stone pillars supported the ceiling and giant vats of stone were carved into the walls in many places.

The group milled about, keeping close together as they made their way around, examining the laboratory.

"He took his books with him, I'm sure," Melvin announced. "The tables have ink and paper but there are no notes here."

Nergal heard a bubbling sound coming from some of the vats, and for a moment he thought he heard a mumble or a moan.

"What that?" He listened for a moment, trying to catch the sound again.

The others were silent for a moment, and then the groan sounded again, very faint. Dalwen moved over to a large stone vat of some kind built into the floor, and looked into it.

"Alofzin!" she cried out in horror.

Alerted, Nergal and Garbor moved over to the chest-high lip of the vat to examine its contents next to the priestess. A spasm of fear gripped Nergal's gut as he looked down into a green mass of slime to see a humanoid figure struggling there.

Nergal voiced the group's thoughts.

"What that be?" he asked, staring in a mixture of amazed fascination and horror.

"Unholy B'aalzebul," whispered Garbor. "It…he…looks partially…dissolved."

Melvin and Rovul reached the vat and looked in.

"They are," Melvin said. "This is dissolved flesh! It was probably to be used in constructing the next monster. Kantru used slaves as…. building material."

This time a louder moan erupted from the green fleshy putrescence. The corpselike victim writhed briefly again, slopping the slime around slightly.

"We've got to get them out of there!" urged Dalwen, her voice stricken with horror.

"No, it's too late…too late for this one," Melvin told them. A look of nausea covered the knight's face. "I will finish him off."

"You can't…" Dalwen's voice broke.

"We'll be doing him a favor for sure," Garbor said.

Dalwen looked away but she did not argue. Nergal thought she might get sick for a moment, but she seemed to recover. He watched Melvin dispatch the unfortunate with his sword in a somewhat detached manner. Killing the wounded or dying was quite familiar to the orc, who came from a tribe where even the young were put down if they were crippled or chronically sick.

The vats seemed to contain no other still-living victims. The group found no other exits, so they looped back to the second passage leading from the cavern with the large dais.

This second corridor branched out into a maze with several doors set into the walls. Each of the doors had a barred window at head level. Melvin peered into one and then looked back at his friends.

"Prison cells," he told them. "There is a man in there." Melvin looked back through the barred window. "We'll get you out of there, friend," he called. A lock secured the door, so Garbor took his war axe to the door near the latch. Soon the portal had been opened.

The prisoner seemed uncertain at first, until he realized that the group at his door was not of Chu Kutall. He said something in a language Nergal could not understand. He moved outside his cell, still somewhat in shock at his sudden rescue. Nergal could see that starvation had thinned the man. He wore only rags, and a long growth of white beard had formed on his gaunt face.

Then suddenly the man saw Nergal, and he cowered, yelling out in fear. It took the man long moments to absorb that the orc meant him no harm. Melvin reassured the man by motioning for him to rise and join them with friendly gestures.

They dispersed through the prison, each stopping to look in the tiny windows as they passed the cells. Nergal peered into several cells, seeing nothing but bones and filth until he got to the end of the passage and checked the last chamber.

A large man stood bravely in the back of the cell, staring back at Nergal. The half-orc could tell that this one's spirit had not been broken. The spirit of a warrior. The man had long dark hair and a wide, rough face with a flat nose. He looked stout enough for a human, Nergal thought.

"Nother one here," Nergal called. Melvin appeared from another corridor. The half-orc saw that the knight had found some keys, and he watched Melvin unlock the door.

"Thank you for freeing me," the warrior said, and placed his hand on his forehead in a strange manner of greeting. "The Chu Kutall are dead?" he asked immediately.

"The outpost has been taken by Slith," Melvin told him. "The wizard got away though."

The man's face twisted in a grimace of hatred. "I will not rest until I have slain them all."

"I understand your sentiment," Melvin told him. "We'll introduce ourselves as soon as we find out how many of you are left."

Dalwen called out, announcing another prisoner. Nergal walked with the man he had found and they watched Melvin release the third prisoner, a thin man with a graying beard.

"I am Melvin," the knight announced. "This is Garbor, Dalwen, Rovul, and Nergal," he indicated to the newcomers.

The warrior placed his hand to his head again. "I am called Roktan," he said simply.

The other two men talked animatedly in the unfamiliar language for a moment. They seemed to introduce themselves as Yafledr and Jaksehn, but Nergal could not understand anything else of the speech.

"It isss a language from acrossss the sssea," Rovul told them. "It isss not unfamiliar to me."

"Can you tell them they are free? We can all leave this place now."

Rovul spoke a few short words to the men, who simply nodded and bowed. Nergal thought that they looked excited to be out of their prison at last. He remembered his first few moments of freedom from the slave galley, and realized they probably didn't care where they were going as long as they were no longer slaves.

"Where will we be going?" Roktan whispered to Nergal. "You are warriors...do you fight Chu Kutall?"

Nergal nodded. "We fight Chu Kutall. Fight monsters made by wizard," he added.

"Where do you travel now?" he asked. Nergal only shrugged.

Melvin had been listening to the questions. "We have no choice but to travel back with Rovul," he answered for Nergal. "We owe a great debt to the Slith, without whom we would have been sorely outmatched by the garrison here."

Melvin saw that Garbor was having trouble making his way with only one eye.

"Don't worry, my friend. We shall restore you to health soon enough," Melvin assured him.

"No, I am finished," the knight maintained in a sluggish voice. "I almost cost you your lives this time. I can't fight like I used to with one arm and one eye. You'll need to find another to take my place."

"Garbor, there are ways," Dalwen told him. "My Klandur may have the power to restore your eye. Of course, they would only do it for a hero of the land...like you. Don't give up hope."

"I don't think so," he said quietly. Garbor's usual spirit had fled him, leaving him glum.

"It is a long journey back. You will have a good deal of time to think on it, my friend," Melvin said.

"What of that horrible thing that turned us to stone?" asked Dalwen.

Melvin just shook his head. "Look at us. We're near the end of our energies. We should just leave this island and regain our strength. We wounded the thing at least; isn't that enough?"

"It might hunt again," she reminded them. "We cannot leave it alive, so that it might hunt down innocent victims."

Garbor shook his head. "I am sorry, my lady," he told her heavily. "But I agree with Melvin."

Dalwen pursed her lips, clearly sorrowful for the state of Garbor's health as well as his spirit. She looked at Nergal who merely shrugged. Even the powerful half-orc wore the signs of heavy battle, with deep wounds on arm and calf. Dalwen seemed to accept the decision and she did not carry the argument further.

"Very well. But at least we're committed to hunting down Kantru, are we not?"

"Yes. But not today," Melvin said. "We should keep what we have of the monsters he created. Even though Rilivan was faking it, I believe magic could lead us to him with those fragments we have collected. Someday we shall have another chance to put Kantru into an early grave."

CHAPTER 18

Neyala of Slith

The outcry alerted Nergal under the crowded decks of the Slith vessel. He had learned to recognize the strangled hiss that the Slith lookout emitted to announce the presence of land.

In the makeshift wooden rack above Nergal's tiny sleeping area, Roktan stirred. "Land again," he muttered, stretching powerful muscles.

Melvin appeared, hovering animatedly nearby.

"This is it! We near the fortress from which Rovul's father rules over the Slith, called Neyala, I believe," he announced. "I'm told it lies on a peninsula of a large island continent."

Nergal literally pried himself from his cramped bunk. The quarters that the adventurers had taken on the Slith vessel were poor, comparable even to the level of discomfort Nergal had experienced as a slave rower. It was hard to imagine how crowded the initial voyage must have been before the Slith attacked the outpost, with even more warriors on board.

The three made their way onto the open deck. The sun warmed Nergal's skin, and he stretched languorously, breathing in the fresh ocean air. Finally taking the time to look around, he realized that the ships were making their way through dozens of rocky islets, rising great distances out of the sea. Heavy vegetation covered the tops of the rocks, each of which was about the size of a large castle. Nergal looked intently at the unusual formations, and saw Slith peering down at him from the heights. He realized that the broken faces of the cliffs must be relatively easy for the snake-men to negotiate.

Dalwen and Garbor were already on the deck, hoping for their first glimpse of Neyala.

"Each of those rocks themselves must be like a fortress," Melvin noted.

Nergal's eyes broke away from the rocky heights and scanned the waters. Several large Slith were accompanying the ship in the ocean, their long bodies moving swiftly and easily through the water. The half-orc marveled at their speed, watching the long scaly bodies undulating in the water. He tapped Melvin's shoulder to indicate what he saw.

"What? Oh! Amazing! Dalwen, do you see them?"

"Such strong swimmers! Of course they swim just like a snake," Dalwen observed.

"The Slith are at home in the water and the cliffs," Roktan told them. "They can swim great distances. In fact, they can even board enemy ships directly from the water."

"Ah!" Dalwen exclaimed. "I saw a lot of them in the water during the battle, but I thought they had fallen overboard in the combat or something," she told them.

"They're well suited to the water," Melvin agreed. "No doubt it's a factor in their dominance of these far seas. I shall be interested to see—"

"There it is!" exclaimed Dalwen.

Nergal looked in the direction indicated by the priestess. Dominating the horizon, a huge rock formation towered above the sea. Nergal could see a great city carved into the rock. Neyala dwarfed the rocky islets they had been examining.

The half-orc stared at the Slith city for long minutes as they approached. Countless walkways were built into the cliffs, allowing movement among carved cave entrances, stone dwellings and towers. The colors were as bright as the Slith shields and war banners, mostly the vibrant reds and yellows that the snake-men seemed to prefer.

They sailed around the spectacular city to enter a sheltered bay beyond. Once on the far side, Nergal could see that the enormous rocky cliffs of the city were joined to the flatter land that framed the bay by a narrow isthmus of land. On the sheltered side of the rock Nergal saw the intricate, cleverly designed docks that the Slith vessels were heading for. From a distance the docks looked like the remnants of spider webs clinging to the side of an ordinary rock. Long tendrils of walkways made their way up the side of the cliffs. There were also large openings at sea level to accommodate heavier cargoes.

"Most remarkable!" Melvin uttered again, completely absorbed by the scene.

"I'm glad our city pleasessss you," Rovul said somberly, "but the sssituation on the land bridge doesss not look good." The snake-man pointed his clawed finger out across the waves, towards the land that connected the mighty city to the mainland. Nergal squinted to see the figures and shapes moving there, and he saw great war machines and a large number of round objects, boulders or huge shields of some sort.

"What are those things, Rovul?" asked Dalwen softly. "Are those siege engines?

"Those are the Kallox," rasped the prince. "They rule the lands beyond asss we rule the islandsss and the sssea. They ssseek to control Neyala," he told them. "We must talk with my father immediately."

"But what're those round constructs they're hiding behind?" asked Melvin.

"Those are the Kallox themselves," Rovul told them. Nergal looked carefully again. The round things were light brown in color, but he could see no arms or legs of any sort. Here and there they were being rolled into new positions, but Nergal could not fathom how they could be alive.

"I don't understand," Garbor told Rovul. "Are you telling us that these Kallox crawl into rocks when they go to war?" The knight's voice showed the same incredulity that Nergal was feeling.

"They're shellsss. Most Kallox spend their entire livesss in them," Rovul said, and then turned to direct the docking procedures of his fleet.

"Unbelievable!" Melvin burst out. Turning to the others, "We should have traveled across the seas much earlier," he told them. "We need to see the shells up close."

"That's likely to be dangerous," observed Roktan.

"Dangerous," Nergal echoed, nodding his agreement.

"You may get your chance," Dalwen told Melvin. "If the city is in trouble, we'll be obligated to help. After all, we owe a great deal to the Slith."

"Agreed," Garbor said. "We've been keeping in some semblance of shape, at least."

The knight referred to the sparring that the adventurers had done during the trip. The journey of two weeks proved tedious, and the adventurers had practiced with mock battle to pass the time. Melvin had shown Nergal some of the basics of imperial swordplay, and the half-orc had reciprocated by sharing his knowledge of the spear. Garbor and Roktan had worked out a great deal as well.

"As you know, I've been sparring with Roktan during our exercises," Garbor began. "I've decided that Roktan shall take my place in your quest," he told them. He held up his remaining hand at the resulting outpour of voices.

"Wait, and listen. You know I'm not the same fighter I once was. Roktan is an enemy of Chu Kutall. You've seen his fighting ability. It is time for me to make way for a younger man," Garbor told them.

"Garbor, I've told you that my Klandur may restore your eye," Dalwen protested.

"And I've told you that it's foolish to deny the truth," Garbor replied. "I've been wounded severely. In ways that cannot be healed. It's true that I could pretend for a while...I might or might not be slain immediately. But I'm facing the truth. I endanger all of you pretending to be whole. Roktan has agreed to take my place."

Roktan stood forward. "I'm the enemy of Chu Kutall. Garbor has told me that you possess magic to discern if someone speaks the truth. Test me now. I'll take an oath to fight with you."

Nergal listened to this speech, quite surprised. Roktan had not spoken much more than Nergal since the group had freed him. Now it was quite apparent that Roktan wanted to join the group as much as Garbor wanted him to.

Melvin and Dalwen accepted Garbor's wishes as the ship came to rest at the docks of Neyala. While Nergal looked on, Dalwen cast her spell to discern the truth. Roktan gave his oath before her, and she announced that he spoke truly. There could be no doubt that he was a sworn enemy of Chu Kutall, and that he would not betray them as Zanithweir and Rilivan had done.

Rovul returned to urge the group to gather their gear. "I'll introduce you to my father, the king," he told them. "We must learn about the sssituation with the Kallox."

The adventurers took their possessions and clumsily followed Rovul as he disembarked on one of the strong poles that served as ramps for egress. They found that the walkways suspended from the cliffside had no stairs, but were smooth ramps of wood. Nergal struggled with the others to keep up with Rovul as he led the way up the cliff and into the city. He carried only his backpack, the huge tower shield, and a wooden spear.

They moved into the dense city behind Rovul, wondering at the strange sights of the Slith civilization. The first thing that Nergal noted was that the tunnels into the giant rock were round like tubes, even on the bottom where the inhabitants slithered along. There were no completely flat surfaces for horses or wagons. The snake-men didn't seem to mind the curved floor, and they made their way along its sloping sides effortlessly. Nergal and his friends staggered along as best they could, oftentimes simply staying in the lowest part at the center rather than fighting to move farther up the sides.

The Slith watched them curiously, but none addressed them directly. Rovul made contact with several officials as he moved through the tunnels. They didn't stay underground for long, as the twisting passages often reemerged into the open air above. They arrived at a huge barred entrance with metal doors and four large Slith guards. The guards were adorned in bright red metal armor with red crests rising from the center of their helmets. Banners of Slecktar, their snake god, adorned the stone to either side of the entrance.

"These are the royal chambersss. I'll bring you in to show to my father Yurithar, but he doesss not speak your language. I'll translate for you later," Rovul told them. "Best you be sssilent," Rovul added.

"We'll assume a humble demeanor," Melvin assured him. Nergal did not know what they were talking about. The others indicated their understanding with nods and mumbled acceptance.

Rovul turned and approached the guards at the entrance. It was clear that they recognized the king's son, and they scrambled to open the doors for him.

The adventurers entered the giant chamber beyond. Nergal could hardly believe his eyes. The court had the shape of a giant cylinder on its side, with a smooth sloping floor and flat circular walls capping both ends. Passageways led in at random points all over the walls and even the ceiling, many with a Slith or two lounging partially concealed within. The snake-men were packed so densely in the rounded hall that there was not room for him to walk forward. Hundreds of colubrine bodies were intertwined thickly, forming a titanic knot of smoothly scaled muscle.

Somehow, the knot melted before them as they hesitantly began to move forward. The bodies slid around and uncoiled almost magically so that they could make progress. Nergal had always thought it must be simple to be a snake with fewer limbs to control, but now he realized that just trying to keep track of such a long body would be confusing.

Nergal saw the snake king up ahead in a clearing of the serpent bodies. Yurithar was gigantic, exceeding even Rovul's size. The patriarch's giant, dark-scaled body wound randomly around his throne and a nearby stone pillar. His human arms and torso rivaled Nergal's bulging physique. The half-orc imagined that the king was pleased to see his son again, even though he really couldn't read the Slith's emotions very well.

Yurithar spoke in long and sinuous tones, his tongue flickering as he communicated in the Slith's language. His son Rovul dominated the conversation, probably relating the battles and adventures he had experienced. Nergal became bored, listening to the strange sounds and squirming under the gaze of the dozens of Slith in the cylindrical court.

After a while he realized that Rovul was speaking their names to the court, and he came back to full alertness. The other adventurers made obeisance as their names were mentioned, and Nergal copied their movements. The introduction seemed to pass without any accidental insults. Once again the conversation left Nergal's interest, although the two seemed to be discussing a matter of great importance, and the king's volume rose considerably.

Finally Rovul turned to the others and spoke in their language. "What would you do, my friendsss? Yurithar will send you back with a representative of the Slith for your king, if you'd have him."

Melvin spoke for the group. "That would be our honor, Rovul. Of course, we had hoped to fight by your side against the Kallox first, as we owe you a tremendous debt. I'm sure I speak for the legionnaires and Teranae's men as well."

Rovul nodded and spoke with the king again. Nergal imagined the king was pleased at the bravery of the adventurers. Rovul spoke in the kingdom's tongue again.

"Pleassse accept quarters here in the city. I'll sssend a messenger for the other men as well. I must speak with my father at length, ssso I'll return after you've fed and rested to tell you of our plansss. We'll battle with the Kallox sssoon. Of that there can be no question."

Rovul signaled another Slith, which emerged from the tangle of snake bodies. "This is Grelask. He speaks your language asss I do. He'll show you to your chambers."

The adventurers went with their new guide to see where they would be staying while at Neyala. Other guides appeared with Teranae and the legionnaires. The guests were broken up into groups of two. Melvin and Nergal decided to share a chamber, so they left with Grelask after arranging to reunite with the others the next day.

Nergal and Melvin followed their guide into a gloomy room. Carved from stone, the room had a slightly green tint, and the briny smell of the ocean permeated the chamber. There were two alcoves in the wall and a hole in the floor. The half-orc thought the function of these features was clear, but in one corner of the small chamber he saw a bowl-shaped depression in the floor with a tiny hole in the center.

"Hrm. What dat be?" he asked the guide.

"That isss for relieving yourssself," the Slith told them.

"Oh," Melvin uttered, rather surprised. "I thought the hole was for that," he said, echoing Nergal's thoughts. "The alcoves are for sleeping, right?"

"Yes," verified their guide.

Melvin stood staring at the depression in the stone floor. "I'm sorry, but I really must ask…there is only a small hole in the bottom…" For once, Melvin seemed reluctant to speak further.

Grelask hissed thoughtfully.

"Sssome will drain. The rest, the Ssschlenak will clean up," Grelask offered, pointing about to the floor.

Nergal followed the snake-man's pointing claws. For the first time, Nergal saw small scuttling insects or crustaceans of some sort moving about in the darkness.

"Hrm," he grunted in acceptance. The half-orc had seen worse.

But Melvin would not be so easily satisfied. "What will they do with it? Where will it go?" he asked, looking around at the floor with a poorly hidden mask of distaste.

"To their nests in the ocean," the guide explained. He pointed to the hole. "Through there. If you want to go for a ssswim, you go through there too."

"Amazing…" Melvin muttered unhappily.

Grelask nodded, his tongue flickering briefly, and then slithered out.

Nergal placed his shield and spear against the wall. He tossed his backpack into his alcove.

"Did you see the size of Yurithar? Apparently the Slith keep growing throughout their lives just as snakes do," Melvin theorized.

"Rock lizards too," added Nergal. They contemplated the vermin-infested room in silence for long moments.

"This is the price that must be paid for adventure, Nergal. Living in strange, wondrous, exciting filth pits of unspeakable vileness," Melvin stated knowingly. Nergal nodded at his wisdom.

"I'm not feeling well," Melvin told him. "Perhaps you could go and see if there's any other way we could go for a swim and clean up without crawling through that hole?"

"Find ocean," Nergal agreed. Melvin scuffled into an alcove, trying to rest. The half-orc moved slowly towards the exit, listening for the guide. He could hear the snake-man's voice rasping away distantly, probably explaining the rooms to other guests.

Nergal moved away from the voice and down the tunnel. He marked his position carefully so he would not lose his way. Sniffing the air, he tried to determine if there were any scents of interest to him. He could smell the ocean almost everywhere, so he picked a tunnel at random. It seemed to slope downwards slightly, so he decided it might lead to the ocean.

The half-orc moved through the tunnel for several minutes, stopping occasionally to listen. Large patches of glowing lichen on the walls or ceiling lighted his way. Nergal stopped to touch the strange fungus briefly but it did not seem harmful. The walls became rougher and more natural as he proceeded, and at one point he passed a small pool of ocean water.

He came to a much larger cavern partially filled with more seawater. He tested the water with his hands. The water felt cool to Nergal's hot skin. He waded in a little, splashing himself with the water. With a shocking suddenness a hideous horned head appeared out of the water in front of him. Three beady eyes appraised him from a lumpy scaled head at least half again as large as his own. The thing had a wide gaping mouth filled with small pointy teeth.

Nergal faced the terrible monster, his heart racing. Clearly the thing saw him, as it grunted and waved its two long pointed tusks in his direction threateningly. It lumbered forward clumsily, emitting its foul breath into the limited airspace. Its stench almost gagged even Nergal. Despite his nausea, the half-orc acted, seizing the wicked tusks in his hands to prevent the ugsome creature from goring him.

The monstrous thing thrashed about, highly incensed at this turn of events. It bellowed loudly, fighting to free its natural weapons. Nergal threw his weight to one side, desperately trying to hurt the thing. The half-orc's huge muscles overcame its neck muscles, and he could feel the bones breaking as he wrenched its head to the side savagely.

Nergal staggered back in the salt water, gasping for breath. The encounter had been brief but deadly. He smiled in the dim glow of the fungus, appraising his kill. It had been almost as easy as killing an adult rock lizard.

"Monster not so strong," he announced to the empty cavern.

Nergal decided to return to tell Melvin of his adventures and the pools of water he had found to bathe in. He returned up the twisting tunnel, and as he made his way back to the chamber he met a Slith.

"Hello, large one," it greeted him. Nergal realized it was Grelask, their guide.

"What've you been up to?" the snake-man asked.

"Big monster! Nergal kill," he told the Slith, pointing back towards the down sloping cavern entrance.

"Monsssster? Show me," Grelask replied.

Nergal led the Slith guide back down into the dank caverns he had explored. They came to the body of the thing the half-orc had slain.

"See? Big monster," Nergal indicated.

The Slith examined the corpse briefly.

"It's only a meat-beast. It seemsss you've broken itsss neck. Quite an impresssive feat," lauded the Slith. "It's easier to ussse spearsss. Anyway, perhapsss we can move it up to the kitchen?"

Nergal grunted. "Monster good eating?" he asked hopefully.

CHAPTER 19

The Shelled Ones

Nergal and Melvin joined the other adventurers after a night of fitful sleep in the dank stone alcoves. They met Rovul in another chamber of carved rock with a round opening in the ceiling to let in the day's light.

"Usually the Kallox fight more amongst themselvesss than with usss," Rovul explained. "This time, their demon-god Brekku is with them. He hasss organized the assault on Neyala, and he usesss his sssupernatural cleverness to instruct the Kallox in the artsss of sssiege."

"How have you learned this?" asked Garbor.

"Prisonersss we captured in a battle for the land bridge," Rovul replied. Rovul did not comment on the obvious methods of obtaining such information from the unfortunate captives.

"So we must destroy this alien god, if we hope to stop their campaign?" Melvin asked. The knight seemed to have recovered some of his enthusiastic air of discovery after his bad mood of the day before.

"Yessss," Rovul responded.

"The demon must be powerful indeed, if it has united the Kallox tribes," Roktan said. "How will we find this demon?"

"We won't have to. It'll come to usss," Rovul told them. "They prepare to storm the gates at the land bridge. We should gather armsss today, and sleep at the tower barracks tonight. They may attack tomorrow, or perhaps the next day."

"Tell us how these Kallox fight," Dalwen said. "They look like simple round boulders. Do they trample their foes?"

"I'll tell you as we prepare," Rovul said. "Time may be short."

The long, powerful snake-man led them out through a low opening in the chamber and into a network of larger rooms filled with weapons of war.

"These are the royal armoriesss," Rovul told them. "Here are our finest armsss and armoursss."

Nergal wandered into the rooms, looking at the brightly colored collection of Slith weaponry. Melvin pointed to a piece of armor that caught his attention because of its shiny black color. It was obviously crafted for a large Slith. The huge torso covering was constructed of heavy black metal plates resembling snake scales, ingeniously woven together with metal links underneath.

"That must be as heavy as Garbor's breastplate," Melvin commented, "But I don't suppose that would bother you," the knight said to Nergal.

"That isss a special piece that belonged to one of our heroes of ancient timesss," explained Rovul. "Legend holds that it was ssstained black by the blood of the sssea dragon Naikullar. Our warriors, asss you know, wear red and yellow. It is because they believe that the colors of Slecktar will bring them hisss favor in battle. That's why this piece has been shunned. If you fancy the armor, Nergal, you may wear it, since no Slith will."

Nergal grunted and set his tower shield down heavily. He reached up and grasped the scale armor and lifted it from the rack. As Melvin had observed, the protection was quite heavy, noticeable even to the immensely strong half-orc. Nergal pretended not to notice its weight.

Melvin assisted him in getting the armor on, and when they were done, Nergal flexed his muscles and twisted his torso underneath the scale mail. The armor flexed with him, adapting well to the shape underneath. He nodded approvingly. His opinion of armor had improved since his experience with the crossbow bolt. Besides, the half-orc wanted to fit in with his companions, who obviously highly valued their metal armor.

"Is good armor," commented Nergal.

"Hmmm. Perhaps you should leave that here for now," suggested Melvin, indicating the tower shield.

"Is good shield," Nergal maintained, although he secretly realized that perhaps the combination of shield and scales would overburden him. On the spur of the moment, he decided to place the tower shield up on the wall where the black armor had been. "You keep here."

"That ssspear may not be sssufficient," Rovul announced, looking over Nergal's weapon. "There are only a few holesss in the shellsss. You can pierce them but your weapon will stick," the Slith told them. "Melvin, your sword issss mighty, but beware it becoming stuck in the shellssss."

"I don't know much of other weapons," Melvin said grimly. "Although Nergal here handles the mace well, I believe."

"No talking maces," Nergal clarified.

Melvin's right brow jumped at this but Rovul was already leading the half-orc into an adjoining room. The knight followed them to observe the weapons that Rovul pointed out.

Nergal felt a pinching sensation under the scale armor. He slipped a hand under the right edge, feeling the inside weave of metal scales against his rib-cage. He slipped out a small piece of metal and looked at it. It was a carved ring of some kind. The half-orc brought it closer to his eyes, and saw that it had a snake carved around the outside surface. The serpent consumed itself where its head met its tail. He slipped the ring onto the little finger of his right hand, where it fit snugly. Nergal looked around but it seemed that none of the others had observed this occurrence.

"Only an enormousss mace can smash the regular shellsss," Rovul was telling them. "And the leadersss of the Kallox wear metal spheresss into battle that are almost impregnable. I'm certain that the demon Brekku will have a metal shell."

Nergal picked up a large mace to examine it. It seemed quite strong and did not speak to him. He was about to announce his choice when Melvin spoke up.

"Rovul, do you think this could pierce them?" he asked, holding up another mace. The weapon he had found possessed a large crescent shaped spike on one side of the head. Rovul nodded approvingly.

"Nergal, I think you should try this. If you line up the spike just right, I think you might be able to deal a devastating blow."

Roktan entered the room, and Nergal saw that he wore an ornate breast-plate of bronze, carved with the likeness of Slecktar.

"That does look like a formidable weapon, but if these creatures are encased in iron, I'm not sure it will work. When two human knights face each other, they can strike for joints or they can simply bludgeon their opponent into submission without piercing the armor, bruising them severely inside their protection. But how would you bruise something completely surrounded by a metal sphere?" asked Roktan.

"How do your people fight the Kallox knights, Rovul?" asked Melvin.

"We cannot oppossse them on the open land," Rovul said. "Sometimes when they become grouped together too tightly to maneuver, you can skewer one through their own attack holesss. Mostly, though, we simply retire to somewhere they cannot follow. Into the sssea, or up a cliff," the snake-man finished.

"Neyala has many cliffs and towers," observed Garbor.

"True, but the island fortresss is also filled with underground passagewaysss and corridorsss."

"I think the shells will keep them from being able to move well in the fortress corridors," Melvin said.

"There will also be legions of the Kallox lower classs, who have no shellsss," Rovul told them.

"I thought you said Kallox spend their entire lives in shells!" Garbor spurted.

"I sssaid most do," Rovul corrected him. "And I meant most warrior Kallox. But they have a militia of lower-classed Kallox with none. It is a great shame to them. They'll fight savagely to earn the right to wear a shell."

Nergal had attempted to follow this conversation as best he could. Considering the huge mace he asked, "Some Kall-ox wear metal shell?"

"Yesss, their championsss," Rovul verified.

"Nergal take spear too," the orc concluded, indicating his other weapon.

"We have long metal fishing spearsss," offered Rovul. "They're ssstrong enough for Kallox fighting. Wooden spearsss may sssnap off in one of the Kallox shell holessss."

Roktan nodded at this. "Come, Nergal, and we'll find some of these metal spears he speaks of."

Nergal nodded and followed the proud warrior. The two examined the collection of weapons further, finding a section with the brightly painted spiked shields and helmets. Here and there they found long metal tridents and spears.

"These tridents are beautiful, but we had better take a regular spear, so that it'll fit through a Kallox shell-hole," Roktan guessed.

Nergal nodded at this sage wisdom, and copied his friend, taking a six foot metal spear with a thin bladed head as long as his hand.

They looked briefly at the collection of helms but the snake-men's heads were too flat and broad. None of the headgear would fit Nergal or Roktan. Then the two adventurers rejoined the others who were gathered around the snake-prince.

As soon as Dalwen spotted Nergal with his new spear and armor, she smiled. "Nergal, you're quite the chameleon! Every time you gird for battle, you've something new!"

Nergal simply shrugged. "Is good armor," he explained.

"Do you know anything about what they're like inside those shells?" Melvin was asking Rovul. "Or outside of them, for that matter."

"Yesss. They look like a shellfish, with tiny black eyes and many-legged bodies. They're sssmall but amazingly ssstrong. They have no claws but there are ten sssharp legs. The inside of the shells are filled with dimplesss that the ends of their legsss fit into."

"And the shells are covered with holes?" asked Dalwen.

Rovul nodded. "They each have at least ten holes in the ssshells, and they can alwaysss attack out of them without hesitation. Don't make the mistake of thinking you will be sssafe if you run up next to one of them, even if you're not in front of a hole. They each have many sssharp legs like long curved ssspikes, that they have ready to slide out and ssskewer anything nearby with great flexibility and ssskill."

"How quickly can they move?" Roktan asked.

"They roll relatively slowly, but they can change direction asss quickly asss you. The shells are ssstrong but light, and they can actually hop if hard-pressed, by pushing out a leg ssspike beneath them."

"Amazing they don't get dizzy, rolling like that all the time," Dalwen commented.

"I believe that they run along inside of the shells, but only the shell rollsss," Rovul told her. "They have ten of the sharp curved legsss, shorter in front and longer towards the back. I think they use their back legsss to attack through the holes more often. But we must head for the walls now, I'll tell you more there."

As they made their way farther more and more Slith warriors became apparent. The party made it to the courtyard just inside the city-side gates of the bridge, and saw a large group of warriors working quickly to set short spikes of thick wood into the ground of the courtyard.

"The ssspikes will make it more difficult for them to move," Rovul explained briefly. Nergal watched the snake-men's long dark bodies slide easily between the stakes, and realized the defenses hardly hampered the movement of the snake-warriors.

Rovul led them to one side of the courtyard and through an open iron door into one of the stone towers flanking the gates. They moved up to the wall, and took a position to view the Kallox forces as they assembled.

"It ssseems I may have underestimated them. They will attack within minutesss," observed Rovul.

Advancing across the muddy and body-strewn land bridge, a huge bobbing mass of Kallox and slow-moving siege machines approached the lower towers of Neyala.

"That's strange. Most of these banners are alien to me, but I've seen that one before, over there on the left," Melvin said. "Isn't that…?"

"It's the banner of Chu Kutall," Dalwen announced grimly.

CHAPTER 20

The Demon Brekku

"Surely Kantru wouldn't be among them," Garbor said.

"Possible, but unlikely," Melvin agreed.

"Wizards do have ways of speedy travel…it's possible that he beat us here," Dalwen said. "We'll never know what he's doing unless we manage to create a wand like we thought Rilivan had done."

Nergal looked away from the conversation, and examined the land bridge. The scene looked more like a stately procession of possessed rocks than an attack. Kallox warriors rolled forward, their shells taking the uneven terrain with difficulty. Nergal strained to see any hint of the creatures living within the round cases. Every now and then, a shell would fall into a crevice or come up against an obstacle to stop its rolling, and then the half-orc could see a brief glimpse of a leg of some kind poking out through one of the holes to pop the shell over and forward.

"The creatures seem amazingly adept at keeping track of where the holes are, even though they're always rolling." commented Melvin.

Rovul nodded. "I once observed two dueling Kallox. It wasss amazing, maneuvering around each other and trying to impale the other through their holesss. Believe me, they're completely at home in those shellsss, even more ssso than you are in that armor."

The front defenses of Neyala formed a box shape, with towers at each corner and beside the inner and outer gates. Additional towers rose out of the rock of the city beyond the inner gates, although at that point any invader would enjoy the benefit of the protection of the walls and towers of the entrance. The mountain of the city proper loomed up behind this small entrance keep.

Melvin and Garbor stepped back to examine the inner courtyard on the other side of the wall. Nergal walked over to join their discussion.

"We fight Kall-ox in dere?" Nergal pointed down at the courtyard.

"Yes. There will be Slith on the walls to cover us. But if they breach the front gates, there should be defenders down on the ground of the courtyard as well."

"Dalwen should stay up here to cast her spells," Melvin said.

"Ridiculous!" Dalwen spat. "You know I'll go down there too."

Melvin seemed troubled by her reply but he did not respond.

Nergal turned back towards the Kallox. He could see that a huge siege engine advanced on the fortress. It rose as tall as the front wall, and housed a huge spiked ram in its innards.

"It won't take long for that to splinter the gates," said Melvin.

"It may take sssome time," Rovul asserted. "We've filled in the wall behind the wooden gates. It's quite sssolid now."

Slowly the siege tower approached the main gates. As it entered bow range, the Slith loosed a volley of flaming arrows at it. A few of the missiles lodged themselves, but the construct had been smeared in a fireproof coating of some kind, and the flames only burned briefly before guttering out.

Garbor shook his head. "Rovul, if we survive this remind me to talk with your engineers about catapults," he said grimly.

Rovul flickered his tongue briefly. "We did have many heavy weaponsss overlooking thisss position. They were sssabotaged by a dweomer of some kind. The wood turned rotten overnight," he said.

As the Kallox neared, Dalwen began to intone a spell. She lapsed into the unintelligible phrases, and began to point her arms towards the machine. Suddenly she stuttered to a halt, and exhaled loudly.

"Arrrghh! Someone is interfering!"

"It may help if they can't see you," Melvin suggested.

"The only way I can see the engine is over the battlements," she said.

"No, I think there are arrow slits down below," Garbor said.

"Never, mind, I'll save my strength," Dalwen said.

The group watched helplessly as the engine advanced. Slith gathered over the front gate to oppose any force that might gain the wall from the top of the device.

The huge siege engine finally nuzzled up against the great wooden doors. The Kallox, still largely ignoring the missile fire from above, began to stake down the engine so that it would not roll back from the gate.

The first thump sounded, felt more than heard in the stones of the tower. Nergal vaguely understood that the mobile tower represented a threat to their fortress.

"Dey pound on doors?" Nergal asked as the vibration erupted again from below.

Dalwen nodded. "Shall I strengthen the gates?" she asked.

"Sssave your ssstrength, priestessss," Rovul advised.

"Yes, I agree," Melvin said. "You'd only delay them. There are still the inner gates and the city itself."

The pounding continued for a few minutes, while Slith archers skirmished with the Kallox in front of their towers. Nergal saw spears or javelins hurtling up from below. He watched a Slith archer scream in a strangled hiss as he fell from the battlements, impaled by one of the attackers.

A Slith ran up and spoke quietly to Rovul. "They've sssplintered the old gatesss, but the new wall holdssss," Rovul reported.

"The party of Chu Kutall approaches," Melvin pointed out.

A group of humans pushed an armored cart forward across the difficult terrain towards them. Kallox rolled out of the way to make room for their advance. The banner of Chu Kutall waved over the metal-plated vehicle.

Nergal peered at the man standing proudly at the front of the cart.

"Kantru!" Nergal exclaimed. "Is my good friend…?" Nergal's brows knitted in consternation.

"Alofzin!" uttered Dalwen in dismay. "I'd completely forgotten! Nergal, you must listen! Kantru is our enemy!"

"Yes Nergal, he's an evil wizard!" Melvin said.

"Kantru good wizard?" Nergal asked weakly, a sweat breaking out on his forehead.

"Fight it, Nergal," urged Dalwen, taking the half-orc's hand. "Remember, he tried to kill us."

"Head hurt," Nergal said, and stood swaying.

"His cart has stopped within bowshot," Rovul told them, bringing their attention back to the battlefield.

"By all means, shoot!" Melvin said.

Rovul signaled and several shafts darted out towards the wizard. Predictably, the Chu Kutall mage had protected himself. An invisible barrier turned away the arrows, splintering them and sending the remnants tumbling to earth.

"Come no closer, Kantru!" Melvin called out loudly. "Shield or no, we'll kill you if you do not stop this now!"

The wizard laughed wickedly at them. "What a pleasant surprise!" he called out across the tortured landscape. "I trust your other friends survived my little trap?"

"You didn't even get one of us, wizard!" Melvin taunted.

"Quite impressive. As you can see, I've returned to another, more important project," the wizard waved his hand broadly, indicating the Kallox army.

Melvin turned to the others and spoke quietly. "Returned?"

"Perhaps he was here originally, before the island," Dalwen guessed.

Melvin snapped his fingers. "Brekku probably isn't here at all, if he even really exists. Kantru probably just created another monster and duped the Kallox into thinking it was their god."

"Duped?" echoed Nergal faintly.

"He fooled them," Melvin stated flatly.

Finally Nergal seemed to recover, and his eyes focused on the wizard.

"Kantru fool Nergal too," said Nergal, gaining certainty.

"Wizards work the foulest hexes upon the minds of warriors," Roktan stated, slapping Nergal on the back. "But you have a stubborn nature, my friend. Remember that."

"Nergal smash head in!" Nergal growled loudly at Kantru and waved his spiked mace.

Kantru laughed again.

"Such refreshing candor! But now, I suggest you flee, adventurers! Brekku thirsts for your blood!" Kantru threatened them from afar. Then the robed man motioned to his retinue of monks, and they pushed his armored cart farther back from the entrance about forty paces.

Kantru faced the gates at the edge of his cart and began to cast a spell.

"Dalwen!" urged Melvin.

"It's no use! It's too far away," she shook her head. "He's too powerful for me, I fear."

Three or four more arrows arced towards the cart from the battlements, but the defensive spell held, smashing the arrows aside. Kantru reached the climax of his magic, a few of the words reaching the walls of the gates.

"I don't know what he is doing, but we'd better duck," Dalwen advised. Everyone but Nergal huddled behind the thick granite battlements.

"He do magic now?" Nergal asked.

"Get down, you buffoon!" admonished Melvin gently, tugging at Nergal's arm. He might as well have been trying to pull down an old oak, as the huge brute hardly noticed.

Suddenly an unsettling noise erupted from below. Nergal couldn't immediately identify the cause. A thrill of danger ran down his spine as he looked left and right, trying to discern the source. It sounded almost like a large ocean wave washing through the courtyard, accompanied by yells of dismay from the Slith below. It quickly subsided, and Nergal peered downwards.

"Sand," Nergal noted. The sounds of fighting broke out in the gate tunnel.

Melvin and Dalwen bolted up to observe the situation. Rovul moved towards the inner courtyard and looked down.

"The new gate wall hasss been breached!" he announced. "It hasss been turned into sand!"

"To the courtyard!" yelled Roktan, bolting for the stair. The group quickly clambered after him, trying to get down to the yard and help the stricken Slith defenders.

Nergal emerged from the stone stairway into the confines of the courtyard, just behind Roktan. One quick glance was enough to tell him that the Kallox were in the courtyard in force. The creatures rolled against the stakes, sometimes slashing at a Slith defender, other times hopping unexpectedly over the obstacles.

The half-orc forgot the others and snarled a savage war cry. He joined the ranks of defenders and targeted one of the shelled creatures as it struggled to maneuver around a wooden stake in the ground.

A sharp spike darted out of another one of the holes to attack Nergal. He felt the impact on one of the scales on the top of his armor, a few inches below his exposed throat. He targeted the spiked leg, which was drawing back for another strike. His mace scraped along the shell at the hole and cracked the insect-like leg completely off. A squeal sounded from inside, muted by the shell.

Nergal pressed his advantage and struck three more times, slamming the sharp ridge of the mace into the shell each time. Each time he pulled the weapon free, fragments of the smashed shell went flying. The creature tried to roll back, and a leg spike caught Nergal in the little finger, smashing the end of his appendage where it wrapped around his weapon. He snarled and ignored the sudden pain, deep into the lust of battle.

Despite his overpowering attack he was unable to finish off the enemy warrior. It rolled back and hopped over a stake in the ground, merging back into the line. Other Kallox rolled in front of it to either side, and Nergal did not pursue it. There were too many of the sharp leg spikes ready for him.

"Nergal! Help me protect Dalwen!" Melvin yelled over the noise of battle. Nergal looked around and spotted the knight as the words tried to sink into his brain. Then he blinked and nodded, moving back slightly with the human knight and taking up a position in front of the priestess.

Dalwen held up her cross and began an invocation. Nergal stepped back slightly, uncertain of her magic. The priestess had always helped Nergal with her abilities but he did not understand them. They reminded him of the powers possessed by shamans of his civilization, who were orcs to be feared and respected.

This time Dalwen's voice rang out louder than before. Nergal realized something was different as the spell continued well beyond the normal amount of time. Nergal saw that an avian outline on her symbol glowed. Dalwen yelled urgently, almost pleadingly. Then a bright flash of light exploded from the cross and a clap of thunder rumbled in the sky. Dalwen brought her cross down, but Nergal couldn't see anything unusual. He began to wonder if the magic had failed.

A hunting-bird's cry erupted from above, heard even over the din of battle. A shadow flew over the courtyard. Nergal looked up to see a huge flying creature gliding by overhead. It progressed rapidly across the sky, a creature of silver and bronze feathers. The creature was certainly larger than a man but it was difficult to tell its exact size.

The Kallox did not hesitate, and Nergal doubted they had detected the avian. He stopped watching the flying creature and darted forward to smash another of the creatures with his huge mace. The Kallok he had chosen was wary. It counter-thrust a sharp leg at Nergal as he moved in, forcing him back.

Suddenly huge claws slammed down and grasped the shelled creature, lifting it instantly away even as Nergal attempted to swing at it. Nergal saw the flash of a huge hooked beak as it pierced the shell and ripped the naked Kallok out to toss its body across the courtyard. Nergal only got a glance at the shriveled, insect-like creature as it shrieked and fell amidst the other Kallox.

The avian darted back up into the sky, its wings beating powerfully. The other Kallox shifted uncertainly, confused by the sudden attack from above. Nergal took the opportunity to slam his mace into another shell, chipping a buckler-sized fragment out of it. The Kallok he had hurt retreated warily.

An outcry arose at the entrance. Nergal looked towards the sundered gate and saw a group of metal-shelled Kallox rolling into the courtyard. A horde of grotesque insectoids surged directly behind these Kallox knights, a huge mass of spindly arms and legs. The monsters had small beady eyes on stalks and thin pulsing bodies.

A volley of arrows rained down on these naked creatures, taking a fair number of them down. The Kallox line surged forward and Nergal was forced to pay attention to his more immediate adversaries. He took his mace like a battering ram and attacked the same Kallok again, smashing completely through the shell this time and burying the end of his mace into its soft body. Other Kallox stuck out at him, and he felt a spike drive itself partially into his upper left arm. Nergal swung the crushed shell left and right in front of him as he backed away, trying to protect himself while dislodging his weapon from the gore.

One of the metal shelled knights rolled forward to fill the line. Nergal freed his mace from the shell and contemplated this new foe. He decided to test the armor against his weapon, and launched a powerful swing at the knight. The blow fell onto the metal shell and dented it, hurting Nergal's hand in the process with the shock of the strike.

The knight rolled to counterattack as Nergal stepped back behind a stake in the ground. The Kallok hit the stake and ground to a halt. It chittered at the half orc angrily, frustrated at the obstacles between them. Once more Nergal heaved his mace at the creature, delivering another terrible blow to the metal sphere. A long spike struck Nergal in the belly twice, seeking a flaw in the scales protecting his torso. The orc grasped the spike with his left hand to keep the knight in place and struck the metal shell again in the same spot. The spike of his mace pierced the armor but didn't penetrate far enough to hurt the Kallok knight inside. It chittered again and another spike came out and sunk into Nergal's thigh. He screamed in anger and pain, slamming his mace down on the spike he held, hitting it where it came out of the shell. The limb was ripped off in a shower of blood.

Nergal and the knight retreated from each other to recover from their wounds. Blood ran in a bright red stream from Nergal's leg wound, but his leg muscles still obeyed his commands. Reaching down with his left hand, Nergal snatched up the severed limb of his enemy. Charging the Kallok, he slammed his mace into one side of the shell while plunging the leg spike into one of the shell-holes nearest him. There was a muted shriek and Nergal heard a frantic scuffling from within. He pulled the leg spike back out and it withdrew with a fountain of brown blood. The knight's shell quit shifting. Nergal hoped it was dead.

Nergal stepped back a little and looked around again, trying to measure the tide of battle. The naked Kallox fought to enter the stairways and doors of the courtyard, while the knights surged to aid them as best they could in the open ground. Nergal couldn't tell who was winning. As he stood trying to catch his breath, the metal shell next to him slammed forward, almost crushing him.

The half-orc slid to the side and fell down as the knight's shell moved by. At first he thought he was mistaken to assume that the knight was dead. Then he looked up to see another, much larger, metal shell covered with small spikes advancing on a Slith defender. The shell had merely brushed by the dead knight, and pushed the dead knight's armor and Nergal aside easily.

"That's Brekku! We must kill it!" yelled Melvin, pointing to the giant ovoid. The knight was clearly tired as well, and he stood breathing in huge gasps of air.

"Take smarts to kill big Kallok," Nergal grunted.

"That or magic," Melvin shot back. "Maybe we could roll this dead one at him…" the knight said. He was interrupted by the enormous scream of the air creature, which dove into the courtyard again, heading straight for the Kallox god.

At the last moment, the huge metal sphere rose up on its own, propelled by two immensely powerful spikes extending from the lower ports of the armor. The avian's body slammed into the demon's shell, caught by surprise. A keening scream came from its wickedly curved beak, followed by a torrent of blood. The bird tumbled over its target and Nergal glimpsed long skewers withdrawing from its feathery flesh back into Brekku's shell.

The giant bird struggled on the ground as its life drained out onto the packed earth of the courtyard. The metal clad creature rolled forward to finish it off, and the dying avian clasped it in place with its large talons.

"Nergal! It's now or never!" came Melvin's cry.

Nergal snapped out of his paralysis at the sight of the titanic conflict, and dropped his mace as he ran forward to help. He drew his metal spear over his back as he approached at a lope. He seized his weapon in both hands, and as he arrived at Brekku's side he vaulted clear up onto the metal shell. Somehow his feet landed atop the bases of two spikes instead of being impaled by them. Acting on instinct, he switched his grip and plunged the sharp end of his weapon into the first armor hole he could find.

A low growl made the metal Nergal stood on vibrate. Nergal could feel the grinding of bone against the head of his spear. The world bucked mightily as his end of the spear smacked into Nergal's head and shook his entire body around. The orc grasped the shaft tightly and struggled to hang on. Gravity tilted and Nergal slammed into the ground, opening his eyes to see the huge armor ball rolling towards him. For a moment he was sure he would be killed, impaled on the spiked shell as it ran over him. Then the shell jolted to a halt, stopped by Nergal's metal spear sticking out of it.

Melvin arrived at last, slamming his shield over one of the large holes in the shell. He braced his knee against it and released his arm, taking his long sword in both hands. Nergal moved back slightly, realizing that he no longer had a weapon. Melvin found another hole and slid his sword into it, trying to skewer it further.

A terrible scream arose from within the shell. Melvin hurtled back as a spike pressed against his shield and threw him away. The thing screamed again, quieter this time, and it tried to move but the sphere only wobbled. The spear and the sword still stuck out of the ports in the armor, and they rattled around weakly. Behind the giant Kallok the avian creature stilled, its blood running out onto the sand.

Slith archers looking on from above raised a triumphant cry. Emboldened by the apparent victory, several more Slith warriors charged out of a barracks doorway in one of the towers adjoining the courtyard. Nergal scurried back to retrieve his mace, looking cautiously around for enemies. He realized that the Kallox knights in the courtyard were beginning to move back towards the entrance, rolling over the crushed bodies of Slith and the lower class Kallox who had died without their shells.

Nergal pursued them, running up to strike at a metal-shelled Kallok that struggled to get around a crushed shell blocking its path. He dealt the creature a terrible blow, smashing a large hole into the metal sphere that protected it. He could feel the strike in the throbbing palm of his blood covered hand, even through the adrenaline of battle. Spiked legs tried to strike back at Nergal through the rent in its armor, but the orc was ready. He smashed the legs completely off as they shot out of the hole with a swipe of the heavy mace. Foul smelling blood erupted out, covering his right arm. Nergal left the creature to die and ran off after other retreating Kallox. Nergal saw Roktan twenty paces away, finishing off one of the lesser shelled creatures as it tried to run.

"Nergal! What're you doing?" called out Melvin behind him.

"Dey running!" Nergal yelled back, hopping up behind another of the Kallox warriors as it retreated. The half-orc brought his spiked mace up for another kill, but before it could begin to cleave downwards, a mailed hand came up to oppose it. Nergal turned to face Melvin.

"You must give them quarter," Melvin told him. "They're surrendering!"

"The more we leave alive, the more that will attack next time!" exclaimed Roktan, appearing from behind. "We must kill them while we can!"

Nergal grunted his assent and turned from Melvin. He ran to catch up with Roktan as he attacked other retreating Kallox. He didn't look back.

CHAPTER 21

Aftermath

Rovul met Nergal and Roktan as they returned from their pursuit of the routed enemy. Flocks of sea birds were gathering to feast over Neyala, filling the air with their jeering calls.

"Where others?" Nergal asked, examining the aftermath of the battle in the courtyard. Bodies lay thick on the sand, even though the Slith had been working for some time to clear them. Once bright red splatters of blood from the stabbings, slashes and crushings had dried into gory black accoutrements that decorated the corpses as well as the living.

"Dalwen hasss fallen, though she still livesss," Rovul said. "Come with me. I'll show you where they are."

As they followed Rovul, Nergal noticed that his right hand and forearm were heavily splattered with bloodstains from the battle. Nergal scratched at the blood idly, but it resisted his efforts to remove it. He scratched harder, but it didn't come off.

"Blood stuck on," Nergal noted quietly.

Roktan looked down at himself. "Yes, I need to clean up too," he said, and scraped some flakes of blood off. "Scrape it off," he told Nergal, as if he thought the orc had never had to clean off after a battle before. The orc tried again, scraping his hand against the metal scales of his black armor, but his efforts produced no flaking as Roktan's had done. He shrugged and gave up.

Nergal and Roktan followed Rovul into the keep. Nergal slowed for a moment, unable to see once sheltered from the bright light of the sun. The half-orc stumbled through twisting round corridors, leaving the bird cries and the smell of death behind.

When they arrived in some inner chamber, he saw that Melvin and Garbor already attended Dalwen. The priestess lay on a flat slab of stone. She looked dead to the half-orc, utterly still and pale. Yet he could see no wounds on her body.

Rovul exchanged a series of snake-noises with the Slith that attended her. He nodded his serpentine head and turned to the adventurers.

"Her life force was linked with that of the avian she summoned," Rovul said. "Her body still lives—but he cannot awaken her. It is beyond his power."

"I'm taking her back with me," Garbor said. "We'll leave with Teranae tomorrow. Her Klandur will revive her," he said with a deep certainty.

"I'll come with you," Melvin nodded.

"You aren't going to come find the wizard that did this to her?" demanded Roktan, appearing on the scene abruptly as he often did. The tough, dark warrior stepped forward to look at Melvin.

"I should be with her…" Melvin's voice fell off.

"Nergal and Roktan will need your help," Garbor told him. "How will they find Kantru without you? You should work with the Slith mages, and create another wand, a real wand this time, that can lead you to Kantru. You know that's what Dalwen would want."

Melvin looked at the Slith who attended Dalwen. "Will you accompany them, to keep her alive until you reach the Klandur? It's a long journey."

"He will do ssso," Rovul answered for the other Slith. "Our representative will want the company of others of our kind anyway."

Melvin stepped back from the table, a mask of dismay on his face.

"So now there are only three of us," he stated hollowly.

"Four of ussss," Rovul interjected. "I'll go with you. My father has promised me the kingdom if I destroy this wizard."

"Hmmm. I thought you were already next in line for king. Aren't you the king's son?" asked Melvin.

Rovul hissed loudly, startling Nergal. "The king hasss fathered thirty clutchesss. He has over a ssscore of ssscores of young. I must prove myself further if I'm to ascend to the throne!"

Nergal jumped slightly, as he tried to decide if the snake-man had hissed in anger or mirth. Melvin shrugged and looked at Nergal's blood-stained arms.

"You should clean up, Nergal. Perhaps a dip in the ocean," he suggested.

Nergal nodded vigorously. "Yes."

"I'll meet you at our chambers, then," Melvin said. "Rovul and I need to talk with some of the Slith mages, to see if we can make a real wand that can lead us to Kantru."

Nergal turned headed for the door, then realized he was lost. He turned around to ask them for directions, but Roktan had already guessed his dilemma.

"I'll show you the way to our rooms, Nergal," he said, slapping the big brute on the back affectionately. "It was a great battle, and I'm tired."

"Great battle," echoed Nergal.

After they had left the area with the others, Roktan shook his head sadly. "It's a terrible thing about Dalwen. She is brave. But she may never see battle again. And Garbor too, with his injuries."

"In orc tribe, if warrior get hurt bad, den we kill him," Nergal said.

The powerful warrior nodded. "Where I come from, that's considered a mercy," he said. "Only the strong should survive…anything else is a disgrace."

"Where is dat?" said Nergal.

Roktan only shrugged. "Nowhere interesting," he said, avoiding Nergal's question.

The two warriors continued in silence. They made their way into the tunnels of the mountain and found their chambers. Roktan went into his room to sleep, and Nergal followed the path that he had found that led to the ocean, where he had slain the horned monster the Slith called a "meat-beast".

Nergal arrived at the cavern. Keeping a careful eye out for other monsters, he shed his armor and left it with his spear. He didn't want to rust the metal as he had done so many times in the past with various weapons.

He waded into the water, still wary for the presence of dangerous creatures. Nergal began to scrub himself clean, dunking his entire body into the water. Although he removed a great deal of dirt and filth, the dried blood refused to come off his arm. As Nergal scrubbed, he remembered his ring, which was also metal. He thought to take it off and dry it, but he discovered that the ring would not come off his finger. The fit was too tight, although his finger did not fall asleep.

At last he gave up. Nergal exited the pool and reclaimed his armor and spear. He went back to the room that he shared with Melvin, and found that the knight had not yet returned. An overwhelming urge to sleep came over him, so he crawled into his alcove, swatted away a few tiny bug-things, and reclined.

Nergal thought about those who had fallen in battle with him. His father, Zeleph, and Dalwen. Garbor once seemed invincible, and now he had left, a shaken man who didn't feel he could go on fighting. Nergal decided that he preferred outright death to the possibility of being crippled so severely that he couldn't fight. Somewhere amidst these thoughts he fell asleep.

At some point much later Melvin awakened him.

"Nergal, it's time to rise. I have something to show you and the others," Melvin told him. The half-orc arose slowly and followed Melvin out of their room. He realized he had forgotten his equipment and turned around to get it, but Melvin shook his head.

"We'll be back before we leave. Don't worry about it."

They walked a short distance through the worn passageway. Walking into a small chamber with a low meeting table carved from rock, Nergal saw that Rovul and Roktan were already awaiting them. There were no chairs, and so the three humans sat cross-legged at the table and Rovul wrapped his body in a heavy coil.

Melvin produced a wand from his tunic. It was a white bone rod with silver cap pieces. He held it up to show the others.

"With this wand, we'll hunt down Kantru and all who aid him. Hunt them down and kill them," Melvin growled darkly.

"You said we should be merciful earlier," Roktan noted.

"That was before…I knew what happened to Dalwen," Melvin said. "I've decided that this one is not worth wasting mercy on."

"He will be expecting us. Doubtless there will be more traps," Roktan said.

Melvin nodded. "We'll need a plan. We have to figure out how to kill him even if he expects us."

"We need the smarts," Nergal summarized. "Like time de elfs…." Suddenly Nergal fell silent, unsure of how Melvin would react to the mention of war with the elves.

Roktan prompted him. "Well? What were you going to tell us?"

Nergal cautiously continued, slowly relating the tale to his friends.

"One time elfs be waiting when orcs come. Many orcs die, and lose battle. But orc leader be having smarts next time. He make whole orc tribe take bath in river, and put on smelly flowers. Elfs so used to be smelling orcs coming, dat we surprise dem and kill…many elfs dat day."

When Melvin and Roktan nodded their understanding, Nergal relaxed and smiled. He felt a glow of triumph for having related such a complex tale to them in the human tongue.

"Hrm. Not useful in the specifics, but the general idea is that we disguise ourselves in some way," Melvin summarized.

"We could travel in garb that would make us look like Monks of the Kutall. In the black robes of the ruling caste. That might save us from Kantru's wrath for a short time," suggested Roktan.

"If I were not with you," Rovul said. "There are no Slith in the ruling caste."

"No offense, but you could be our slave or guide," Melvin suggested.

"Maybe," Rovul agreed. "Do the monks travel with slaves?"

"I don't know," Melvin said. "The only one I have ever met was at the island compound. He was in the barracks, and not traveling."

Nergal remembered the fierce fighter at the barracks and his black robes. Then he realized that he had killed another in the gate tower of Salthor castle.

"I kilt anudder one at Salthor," Nergal announced, remembering. "Fast. Move fast."

"All right, maybe it's worth trying," said Melvin. "Let's go over what we know about them. They're in absolute control over the two other castes. I know that they're all from the high plateaus in the center of their island continent. They undergo intense training from childhood in their secret arts and lore. It is this strength that allowed them to dominate the other cultures they have enslaved."

Nergal listened to this as best he could. All he understood about the monks was that they were fast and much less frail than they appeared. It seemed that Melvin knew so much about everything. It amazed Nergal, but he was even more amazed when the normally quiet warrior Roktan took his turn to speak.

"They start life as a child of a Chu Kutall warrior and a slave female," Roktan said. "If the infant is female it's killed. If it's male, he's taken into the mountains, where he's raised in a warlike environment of the monasteries and fortresses of the highlands. They join one of several sects of warriors or wizards. They're culled against each other in merciless conflict. By the time they're men, three of every four of them are dead by the hands of another. Then they're sent out in search of glory and conquest. They capture the women they use to breed and treat them as prizes. The most successful of them are given commands of their own or the governorship of conquered nations."

Melvin looked at Roktan in shock. "There must be many of the warrior monks in your land for you to have learned so much," he said.

"There are...." Roktan said. He seemed to make a decision then, and continued. "I'm from Riken itself," Roktan told him.

"You never said anything about that!" Melvin shot back, his voice rising.

"You would never have trusted me. I'm telling you now. I've come from the second class, the Jargatans, who were the first nation to fall under the fist of Chu Kutall. The Jargatans are slaves to the Chu Kutall, but take slaves of their own in turn. I rebelled against this hierarchy that Kutall put upon us, but my band was defeated and I was captured. That's why I was a prisoner."

Everyone remained silent for long moments. At last Melvin spoke. "You're correct that such information makes you suspect. Had you not passed Dalwen's test of truth, I'd still doubt you despite your actions thus far."

Rovul's tongue flickered out, testing the air. "In any cassse, with Roktan's help, we'll learn enough to give the russse a chance of working," he rasped. "You will pose asss our enemy. We'll use the wand to find Kantru and ssslay him."

CHAPTER 22

Trail of the Wizard

The group set out the next day, laden with supplies. Melvin and Roktan wore the harshly cut black robes of the elite class of Chu Kutall. Nergal and Rovul did not don black robes, as they posed as the servants of the other two men.

Melvin led the way, occasionally waving his delicate bone wand in the air. Nergal understood that the fancy stick would somehow lead them to Kantru, the wizard who had caused them such trouble. The spectacular rock cliffs of Neyala lost their detail in the distance and then disappeared as the group of travelers entered the forest of the mainland, following the hard-packed dirt of a Kallox trail.

As Nergal swaggered under the weight of his weapons and a bulging backpack full of food, he noticed that the dimensions of Rovul's snake body had altered somewhat.

"Rovul have lump in side," Nergal observed.

Melvin nodded. "I must admit, I had been wondering about that, myself," the knight said.

"I knew that thisss may be a long journey," Rovul told them. "So I ate a boar to break my hunger."

"Amazing!" Melvin said. Roktan laughed.

Nergal considered this for a moment, and realized that the snake-man must have eaten the boar whole. The half-orc considered the immensely wide mouth of the snake-man, and shrugged his shoulders.

"Pig good eating?" he asked.

"Most sssatisfying," Rovul assured him. Nergal licked his chops at the thought of food, but since no one else slowed to eat, he restrained himself.

"How far out into the mainland have your people explored, Rovul?" asked Melvin.

"Not far," rasped the snake-prince. "We usssed to patrol these flatlandsss up to the hillsss, before the Kallox army arrived. There are native peoples, men like yourselves, who co-exist with the Kallox and other ssstrange creatures. It isss odd, but I know more about far away islands acrosss the sssea than I know about the mainland here."

The group fell into the routine of travel. Nergal kept up with the others even though he would have preferred a slower pace. The leather straps bit deep into the thick skin of his immense shoulders and his belt chafed at his hips, but he ignored these minor annoyances. They left the coastal flats and traveled into hilly terrain. Nergal found the plants and wildlife quite alien to his experience. He found himself wondering at the strange array of shrubs, trees and birds. The land here seemed to be more lush than his homeland of Nod, which was dominated by barren wastelands. The temperature became warmer as they left the sea behind, and Nergal drank deeply from their supplies of water.

The odd blood stains that had dried onto Nergal's skin still held fast. As the days went by the others seemed to get used to it, and they didn't ask him about it again. Nergal had been perplexed at first, but he became so used to it being there that it really didn't bother him either.

Every few hours, Melvin would produce the new wand and let it guide his hand. The direction it indicated stayed fairly constant, pointing northeast, deeper into the mainland.

On the first night as the group prepared for sleep, Roktan took advantage of a moment when Melvin left the campfire. Coming over to the half-orc's side of the fire, he conspired with him in low tones.

"Nergal, when the time comes that we believe we're close to Kantru, we must use this poison on our weapons. It may make the difference between success and failure," Roktan told him quietly.

"Poison work fast?" Nergal asked, looking down into the tiny bowl of black gel that Roktan held.

"Fast enough. Who knows, he may also kill us at the same time, but if we succeed in destroying him we'll be remembered favorably by the Gods of Earth and Sky."

Nergal nodded.

"You must not tell Melvin. He doesn't believe it's right to use poison, even on his enemies. Nergal, do you think for a second that the wizard would hesitate if he could poison us?"

"Eh?"

"If Kantru could poison us, would he?"

"Er, yes," Nergal answered.

"Yes. He would. So why should we not try and use this advantage against him?"

"Why not?" Nergal agreed. "You having de smarts. When time comes, we use poison to kill wizard."

Roktan put his small container away, and the two warriors returned to their repose before Melvin returned. Nergal envisioned poisoning the wizard as he sought sleep, and didn't worry about it further.

In the evening of the third day, Nergal could see they were approaching a rough escarpment, visible as a pale streak across the horizon. They set up camp late, almost in the dark.

When Nergal awakened in the morning, Roktan had already gone scouting and spotted a trail nearby, running along a depression in the land. It headed straight for the escarpment, and the group decided to parallel the road.

Melvin and Roktan did not want to attract the attention of anyone on the road, so they crept along through tall grass on the hillside overlooking the trail. By midmorning they had arrived at the edge of the plateau, and they could see where the wide path met the rock face of the escarpment. They settled down at the crest of the last hill and observed the area from their bellies.

The rock face had been carved with huge but intricate twisting images of hideous beings with large eyes and round mouths. At the foot of the rocks two wooden towers and a surrounding stockade had been erected. The road led straight to the gate of the fort. Nergal saw feather-helmeted figures at the top of the wall and in the towers.

The warriors did not seem particularly vigilant, but their vantage point did not require it. The foliage had been cleared away well in advance of their outpost. The rocky ground afforded little opportunity to approach unobserved. Nergal tried to estimate their numbers. He did not see more than a hand's fingers of them, but he could not tell how many others resided within the small fort.

"Is Kantru allied with these people as well? How else could he have gotten past these guards?"

"He may not have passsed thisss way, even though that is the current direction he liesss," suggested Rovul.

"I suppose wizards have their ways," Roktan said. "He could have cast a spell upon them."

Melvin nodded. "All possible. I guess the more important question is how will we get past them?" He thought for a moment while peering at the wooden towers. "These men may have dealings with Chu Kutall. Perhaps they'll let us by if they see our robes. That may be how Kantru made it."

"I have sssmelled these before. They are the men who pushed Kantru's battle-cart before the gatesss of Neyala. I would not willingly give up the element of sssurprise," countered Rovul.

"We have no ranged weapons," Melvin said.

"I have my sling, but I usually use it only for hunting," Roktan said. "It's hardly the equal of the bows the guards have."

"I can negotiate that cliff," Rovul said. "Its face isss very rough. I'll kill the guard on the far right side, while you creep up along the cliff from that direction. I'll get you up the wall, then we fight them on even termsss."

"We should do this at nightfall, of course," Roktan added. "Otherwise you might be spotted by the rightmost tower."

Nergal nodded his heartfelt agreement. He much preferred battle at night. Somehow the darkness made him feel much less vulnerable.

With a plan in mind, the group set into action. Crawling back from the edge of the hill, they moved out of sight of the towers far to the right of the road.

Melvin examined the flora of the area and ruled out making a rope of some kind. They spent the afternoon searching in the few copses of trees in the area for wood that could be used to fashion poles to scale the wall with. Nergal took a long section of dead tree at Melvin's direction, and he practiced climbing up on the stumps of dead branches they left on it for handholds. Although Nergal's branch did deform somewhat under his weight and that of his armor, he remained confident that he could scale the short barricade wall quickly when the need arose.

As evening fell, the group made their way back to the cliffside. They moved closer to the wooden towers, hugging the cliffside as they approached.

"Wait here for me. As sssignal, I'll lower the rightmost torch on the wall. When that happensss, make your way quickly and join me on the wall."

"And if something goes wrong?" asked Roktan.

"We must decide now if we'll break off if they sssee me, or if we'll just attack anyway."

"Wait," Melvin said suddenly, his voice urgent with an idea. "You might not be able to kill this wall guard without alarming others. Could you attack from the far side, and try to raise the alarm? If you could kill one or two of them and retreat along the cliff, we could use that distraction to climb up from the other side."

Rovul nodded. "That isss clever," he agreed. "I'll do one or the other. Come running if you sssee the sssignal or if you hear them become alarmed."

Nergal watched in fascination as Rovul reared his human torso up onto the rock face and began to slither up the obstacle. He used his human arms and hands to help the grip of his long, sinuous lower body. Soon Rovul's upper body merged into the darkness and his tail hung for a moment, suspended from above. Then he was gone.

The other three would-be assailants began their long wait for a signal from the lone infiltrator. Melvin waited closest to the towers, which were now illuminated by watch-fires on the ground below and torches from above. The knight kept his eyes locked onto the rightmost torches, looking for some kind of signal from Rovul. Roktan watched with him after a while, as he came to expect the signal. Nergal shuffled listlessly behind them, waiting for the time to charge. His spear was slung over his back and he shifted the ladder in his grip as he fidgeted.

Time wore on while Nergal waited behind the other two. It was impossible to judge Rovul's progress in his climb towards the fort. The half-orc waited until it seemed unthinkable that Rovul could not have made it to the barricade walls.

"Rovul no make it?" Nergal demanded. By fortunate happenstance, the half-orc remembered to keep his voice low.

Roktan shrugged, and looked at Melvin. Melvin answered without taking his eyes from the towers. "He may have had to go to the far side after all," the knight said.

"Attack now," Nergal insisted.

"Patience, my friend," Roktan whispered back. "I'm anxious to join battle myself, but we must stick to the plan."

Nergal turned back and leaned his makeshift ladder against the cliff. He sat down, placing his back against the cold stone. *We never be attacking,* he thought. Nergal picked a stone up off the ground and began to idly toss it between his hands.

A few minutes later Nergal stood back up and took a peek at the fort. It seemed that nothing had changed. Still his companions waited, watching closely. Nergal turned away and looked back the way they had come. Several paces back, a large crack in the cliff extended up as far as he could see. Nergal walked idly over to investigate the crevice.

From behind him, a frantic whisper: "Nergal!"

Nergal turned to see Roktan disappear around the bend in the rock, ladder in hand. Melvin was not visible. The half-orc turned to sprint for his own ladder, but tripped over a stray rock and fell flat onto the ground. Recovering rapidly, Nergal seized his ladder and ran after his friends, his nose smarting from its sudden meeting with the stony earth.

Melvin and Roktan had quite a lead, and they were both running as fast as they could manage and still stay close to the cliff wall. Nergal couldn't see any guards clearly as he ran. He was still running as Melvin and Roktan placed their ladders against the wall and began to climb.

The orc arrived at the wall and placed his ladder haphazardly against the timbers of the stockade. Nergal clambered up the ladder as he had during practice earlier in the day. He had made it almost halfway up when he heard the sharp snap of wood cracking. Suddenly he felt the unmistakable sensation of falling as his tree branch shattered beneath him. He managed to land on his feet but immediately fell backwards, landing hard on his back. Nergal lay stunned for a moment, looking straight up from the ground at the forms of his fellows as they disappeared over the wall.

Still no sounds of fighting came as Nergal staggered up and desperately began to climb Melvin's modified branch. He reached the top of the wall and pulled himself over the sharpened ends of the poles that comprised the stockade.

Nergal saw the dead body of a guard at his feet. The man had an elaborate series of bright green and purple symbols painted on his skin, and wore necklaces and rings of colorful stones. Nergal couldn't see a wound on the corpse but blood was pooling under it. To his right the platform ended, twisting down towards the ground behind the stockade wall in a rough series of steps carved into the cliffside. To Nergal's left, Melvin stood on the raised platform behind the wall's top, his sword and shield at the ready.

"Roktan is farther down the wall," Melvin told him rapidly. "Haven't seen Rovul."

An arrow struck and threw sparks from Melvin's shoulder guard. Melvin held his shield up to protect himself from the archer. "Nergal, can you take care of him?" The knight pointed to the nearest wooden tower, and Nergal saw an archer in the dim light of the torches, drawing back another arrow as he yelled out in some language Nergal didn't understand.

Nergal nodded and bolted down the crude steps towards the tower ladder, which came up from the ground inside the barricade. He ran at full speed for the ladder and began to climb. He could hear the answering shouts of other men from the far side of the stockade.

Nergal was over halfway up when the face of the archer appeared at the lip of the wooden tower above him. It was a man with a colorfully painted face and some kind of elaborate armor woven of plant fibers.

The warrior pointed his bow straight down and drew awkwardly, trying to line the arrow up with his assailant. Nergal reached over his shoulder and grabbed the sharp end of his spear, flinging it up with all his might. The spearhead struck the archer in his bow hand the instant before he released, throwing his aim off just enough to send the arrow streaking over Nergal's head and into his backpack. The warrior above desperately tried to regain control of his bow and nock another arrow, dislodging the spear tip from his hand.

When the spear fell Nergal caught it expertly. This time he thrust the weapon up, getting it inside the man's several necklaces and lacerating his neck. One powerful heave of the half-orc's enormous musculature was all it took. The man screamed and fell, landing with a sickening thud. Nergal climbed up and over the tower's side before realizing that the small tower was now empty, and he would have to immediately turn around and climb back out if he were to rejoin the battle.

A stack of wooden spears with stone tips in the corner caught his eye. Nergal walked over towards them and saw several warriors running across the open ground towards the tower from the far side of the stockade. Nergal immediately discarded the idea of vacating the tower and hurled one of the wooden spears down at the first oncoming warrior. Driven by the half-orc's tremendous strength, the spearhead penetrated the twisted fiber armor and brought the man down.

Two of the warriors ignored Nergal and ran up the crude steps to the wall while two others began to climb the tower. Nergal mercilessly taught them the foolishness of the maneuver he himself had just accomplished by skewering them both before either got close to the cupola. Now he had two wooden spears left, and he spotted one of the warriors on the wall platform within range.

The first cast fell low but caught the man in the lower leg. As the victim dropped onto the platform gaping at his leg, Nergal hurtled the second weapon and caught him in the neck. Satisfied with his handiwork, Nergal took up his iron Slith spear and headed back down the tower. He heard the occasional cry of battle or the clash of weapons. Even with the light of the torches, darkness still concealed the true state of the battle around him.

Nergal ran back across the ground covered by the charge of the enemy moments before. He came to a thatch covered building and made his way carefully around it, expecting attack from any direction. Nergal didn't see anyone so he made his way to the next corner. Now he could make out the tower on the other side of the stockade, and saw that there was another plumed archer in it. Melvin and Roktan were back to back on the wall, attempting to hold back a larger number of the lavishly decorated warriors.

As Nergal ran toward the wall he spotted Rovul at the base of the tower. The long snake-warrior shot up the tower supports, wrapping his powerful sinuous body around the timbers. He gained the height with amazing speed and dispatched the plumed archer, who had been concentrating on Melvin and Roktan.

Nergal came to a set of steps carved into the cliff, the mirror image of the other side. He took the ascent in leaps and bounds, trying to make good speed to assist Melvin and Roktan. He came onto the platform on Melvin's side, with four of the enemy between him and the knight. Nergal charged full speed at the backs of the men, who had not yet realized their peril. The long metal Slith spear in Nergal's grip skewered two of the warriors in one mighty strike. Then Nergal realized that his spear would not come back out without a serious amount of work. The two impaled warriors fell to the side, gripping the spear in horror as they staggered down.

One of their comrades turned to see Nergal backing away, grabbing the mace at his belt. The man took up his machete and attacked Nergal, trying to cut him before he could get the mace ready. The half-orc realized that he would be too slow just as an axe buried itself in the side of his attacker's head. Nergal blinked and looked to the tower, where Rovul waved back at him. Apparently the prince had some skill with the thrown axe that Nergal had been unaware of.

He brandished the mace and returned his attention to the fight, but found that it was already over. Melvin had not wasted any time since Nergal had taken two of his foes, and now the last warrior between them fell from the platform trailing a stream of blood. Melvin turned to aid Roktan, but the last two warriors who had been fighting him saw the way of things and broke. Neither Roktan nor Melvin pursued them, as they were both desperately gasping for air. Nergal shrugged and began trying to extricate his spear from the two corpses.

There was a scream from the direction of the gate, and Nergal looked at the tower again. Rovul was nowhere in sight.

"I think Rovul got them," gasped Melvin, watching Nergal as he struggled with the spear. "Thank you, my friend. You got those two just in time, I think."

"They no fight so good," Nergal said. His spear came loose and he began to clean the gore from it.

"No, they were not skilled fighters or I would be dead," Melvin agreed. "Between that archer and their superior numbers, it was all I could do to hold my own. I think perhaps our plan making abilities need some honing."

Now Rovul came down the platform, his human-like chest heaving with deep breaths that hissed through his nostrils.

"Rovul! How serious is it?" asked Roktan, running up to the prince. Nergal looked carefully at his Slith friend, and noticed an arrow protruding from the serpentine body, at least a man-length down from his arms.

"It isss painful, nothing more," the Slith rasped. "Can one of you push it through?"

"Aye," Roktan said. He kneeled down next to Rovul, and grasped the arrow. Nergal watched as the barbed head emerged from under Rovul's scales, sending a fresh rivulet of blood pouring down his side. The Slith made no sound but he seemed to be holding his body stiffly as if in pain.

"Their arrows aren't filthy but they aren't clean either," Melvin said. "We'll have to watch the wound."

"My kind heal well," Rovul told them. "Think nothing more of it."

Melvin didn't seem convinced but he didn't say anything. Rovul held a strip of leather over the wounds for long minutes. Nergal and the others finished cleaning their weapons and made their way down the platform. They looked around the inside of the stockade, examining the four simple shacks and towers inside the walls.

Nergal noticed that fresh blood had splattered onto him from the fight. He scraped at the new spots on his legs and torso, but the dried blood held fast to him. He glanced at the others, but they didn't appear to have noticed. Nergal shrugged and continued poking around.

When Rovul had finished waiting for his wound to stop bleeding, he came down and joined the others in the clearing between the towers. Melvin took out his wand and it drew his hand to the northwest again, not quite straight towards the broken rock of the escarpment.

"Surely this isn't a dead end," Melvin said, looking around. "I thought there would be a path up the cliff or something, at least. It would be a huge waste of time to have to go around."

"The way you seek is in this building," Roktan said, pointing to one of the structures set against the rock face. "It's a large cave opening, going straight into the cliff. Very dark in there, I didn't investigate it long."

The knight looked over the group briefly.

"Not as smooth as I had hoped, but we're all still alive, at least," Melvin said. "Now we can resume our journey. The wand clearly indicates that Kantru is in the direction of the cave, inside or beyond these cliffs."

"Then that'sss where we shall go," said Rovul. "Into the darknesss after our enemy."

CHAPTER 23

Passage through Darkness

The passage wound on and on as if it led into the heart of the earth itself. Sometimes the group came upon carved out areas that looked like deserted guard stations or rest areas. Part of the way were passages carved out of the stone of the earth, and other areas were natural caverns where they had to explore carefully to find the right course.

They found their way with slow burning torches, which gave just enough light to make out the floor and walls. The group had found a stockpile of torches in the small shack built over the cave entrance in the cliffside, and not being certain how many they would need, they took them all. Each of them had nearly a score of torches in their packs and belts. Melvin and Roktan had skins of oil as well.

Nergal often led the way in the underground passages, as his night vision was superior to the others in the group. Occasionally he would lose the way and Rovul would help, using his sense of smell to pick directions through the natural caverns. The snake-prince claimed that there was the faint odor of the men they had battled, as if the men of the stockade or their kith had sometimes traveled this way.

The group stopped for the first "night" on a broad platform of flat stone, fitted with torch sconces and alcoves where they stowed their gear. They set up a rotating watch in case something disturbed them. The air was damp but warm, and Nergal slept with his head on his backpack and his back on solid stone.

When everyone was rested, the group gathered up and prepared to continue. Nergal lit a torch from his pack and led them out. The open area compressed into a narrower corridor, and the group advanced cautiously shoulder to shoulder.

Melvin scuffed up against Rovul's long scaled body in the corridor.

"It must be difficult for you," theorized Rovul, "trying to keep your legsss from getting caught on thingsss all the time."

Melvin blinked. "I was just going to say the same thing about you. Your body takes up half the corridor," he told the snake-prince.

"At least my kind can move over and between othersss of our own," Rovul replied. "you humansss get your legsss all tangled together when packed too closely."

An unfamiliar scent washed over Nergal, and he sampled it deeply. He turned and waved the others silent urgently, pointing forward. Rovul sensed it too, as his long forked tongue flickered out silently to test the air.

The group quietly brandished their weapons and continued in silence. Up ahead, the corridor opened into a natural cavern that extended beyond their sight. It had large branches that broke off to the left and a smaller one leading right. In all directions the flickering lamplight revealed stone formations from the floor and ceiling, large spikes of rock that sent fearsome shadows leaping up behind them.

"Nergal smell dead things," the half-orc grumbled, but Melvin silenced him with a hand signal. The smell was so strong that even Melvin's human nose could detect it. Nergal shrugged and gripped the metal Slith spear in both hands before him.

There was the sound of something scraping against rock and a growl or snarl so deep it was almost a rumble. The scraping sound grew nearer and Nergal saw a huge form shuffling rapidly towards them amongst the stalagmites.

"It's big!" shouted Melvin as he saw the thing. Nergal saw the knight brace himself against a rock pillar, sword raised before him, and then the half-orc had to look to his own defense. A huge reptilian head mounted on a agile snake-like neck darted forth from the shadows above, and tried to close its jaws over him. Nergal ducked, placing the butt of his spear against the ground and leaving the point waving in the air. It pierced the roof of the gaping mouth that snapped at him, causing the thing to wail in pain. The head was the size of a man's torso, and though the wound splattered blood down on Nergal it seemed only a nuisance to the monster.

The half-orc saw that the sinuous neck of their attacker joined a body that was still shuffling awkwardly toward them. He let loose a roar that was half anger and half astonishment. Sprouting from the body, several other necks waved wicked looking heads at his fellows, snapping and roaring. The creature had more heads than Nergal and his friends put together!

Nergal ducked under the hungry jaws again, thrusting his spear at the base of the neck of the head that assailed him. The metal spear sliced deeply into the monster's flesh, and the orc felt it strike bone. The head turned down and suddenly teeth were clamping down on Nergal's right arm. The creature's strength pulled Nergal's hand away from his spear, and the hungry mouth bit down again, consuming Nergal's entire forearm.

The half-orc fell back in shock, trying to snatch his arm back. Dimly he realized that his arm would be destroyed by such a powerful creature. Somehow he pulled his hand out of the huge teeth as the head began to flail in pain from its injury. Nergal looked at his gore-stained arm, and held his hand up before him. Instead of a ragged stump of chewed flesh, his hand seemed intact. Somehow the rows of dagger sharp teeth had failed to damage it.

After pausing to absorb this, Nergal rolled back from the monster. The head still flailed sickly about, the spear protruding from its neck. Melvin had severed one head completely and was hacking with Roktan on another. Rovul was not visible.

Nergal grabbed his mace and swung wide at the damaged head that had bitten him. The metal struck with a sickening crunch. He caused a large dent to appear in the thing's head, showering Nergal with more gore. The blood ran thick down his right arm, but it seemed that it was the monster's blood, not Nergal's.

The entire monster's body convulsed, and its legs thrashed about. Melvin and Roktan stepped back, looking at the remaining heads as they opened their mouths in death rattles. Rovul appeared on the monster's back as it collapsed, his sword buried deep into its back.

"I believe I have ssstruck its vitalssss," Rovul announced. The creature bucked once more and then became still.

"What a horror it was," Roktan said, panting to catch his breath.

"A hydra of some kind," commented Melvin. The knight turned to Nergal. "Is your hand alright, Nergal?" Melvin looked at the half orc with concern. "I could swear I saw it bite you. I was sure it would rip your arm completely off!"

Nergal held up his blood covered right hand and flexed his fingers. "Is fine," he said.

Melvin nodded although he still seemed troubled by the event. He started to sift through the refuse, looking for anything valuable. Roktan and Rovul were cleaning their weapons.

Blood now covered Nergal's arm up to the elbow, forming a flexible dark red crust over his hand. The outline of his ring stood out clearly on his little finger under the gore. This time his left hand had also been covered in blood and a fine spray of it had speckled Nergal all over when he had wounded one of the monster's mouths with the spear.

Nergal scraped at the dried blood, but it quickly became apparent that the blood would not come off. Annoyed at this recurring problem, Nergal tried to pick off a flake of the residue at the edge of the stain, but it resisted his efforts like iron, despite the fact that he could easily move his wrists and fingers under the coating. Nergal had become accustomed to the blood from previous battles, but now he was covered in even more blood that wouldn't come off.

"Let's get going then," Melvin announced in Nergal's direction. The half-orc looked up, seeing that the others had finished cleaning their weapons and searching around. It seemed that they were waiting on him.

Nergal stared at their weapons and armor, looking for similar blood stains on his companions. He couldn't see any residue on his companion's flesh, despite the fact that he knew they had gotten some on them as well. Shrugging, he moved forward and nodded his assent to leaving the horde.

"Nergal ready," he told them.

Melvin glanced briefly at the blood on Nergal's arm. "We'll have to see if we can find a pool or stream for you to clean that off," he said casually. The orc nodded, then fell in behind Melvin and Roktan, silently scratching at the blood covering as he walked.

They tried to make good progress but found that the battle with the hydra had left them drained and tired. When they came to another large carved alcove with sconces, they decided to rest on the area of flat stone. Melvin discovered that this station had a small supply of cut wood stacked in one corner, and he set about making a small fire. As the flames first flickered, Nergal thought that smoke might fill the cavern, but he saw that a small vent hole had been placed above the alcove to carry the smoke away.

"Is good cave," he commented to himself, marveling at the smoke vent. Nergal had slept in a few caves with fires before, and realized how miserable it could be without an outlet for the smoke.

Roktan offered to take the first watch, so Nergal threw down his backpack and collapsed, using it as a makeshift pillow.

Soon Nergal had fallen into slumber. After what seemed like only an instant, a voice brought him to wakefulness.

"Nergal. Nergal, wake up please," Melvin's voice penetrated the half-orc's consciousness.

Nergal opened his eyes and found himself looking up at Melvin, Roktan and Rovul. The three were staring down at him. The human knight's face was a mask of worry, and Roktan seemed to be giving him a slightly bug-eyed look.

"Eh?" Nergal grunted, still waking up. "What wrong?"

"We couldn't help but notice…ummm…." Melvin hesitated. "Your arm is in the fire."

Nergal looked down at himself and saw that Melvin spoke the truth. Apparently he had flung the arm into the fire as he slept. He flinched and pulled his blood-covered arm back from the fire, but he felt no pain. He felt his hand and moved his fingers. Everything seemed normal, other than the dried blood covering that Nergal hadn't been able to scrape off.

"Is ok," Nergal told them.

"Is there something you want to tell us, my friend?" asked Roktan. "The fire does not harm you?"

Nergal stood up and shrugged. "Fire should burn, but does not," he said. "Nergal no understand."

"Is that your blood?" asked Melvin, reaching out and poking the blood stain on Nergal's forearm. "Ah! It might be the hydra's blood, and it protects you from the heat…we should have collected more of it!"

"I try to wash off, it stay on," Nergal explained. He took the opportunity to speak openly about his problem. "Since battle against big shells, blood not wash off," he said.

"What? Ever since the battle at Neyala?" Melvin asked. "There was blood on you before the hydra? Oh yes! I remember that, I thought…I thought you had forgotten to go wash off."

Nergal nodded. Roktan drew a knife from his belt. "Try this," he offered. The orc took the knife and scraped it across the stain. He could feel the pressure of the knife but the blood covering was impervious to it. Nergal clutched the knife dagger style and tapped his arm lightly. The point, obviously dangerously sharp, refused to penetrate.

"Well, it will protect you, at least," hissed Rovul. "It may even sssave your life, if you can live with it."

Nergal shrugged again. “Is like having muddy arm. Nergal not always clean anyway,” he confided. Melvin nodded and Roktan took his knife back, looking at the blood admiringly.

“Any more battles like that hydra, and you will be completely covered in it!” said Roktan. “That is a trick I wouldn’t mind learning. Is it orc magic?” he asked.

“Nergal no know,” Nergal said honestly. He bent over and carefully placed his hand back in the fire again. He could feel a gentle warmth but nothing more.

“Let’s try an experiment,” suggested Melvin. “Nergal, hold out your arm.”

Nergal came back from the fire’s edge and walked up to Melvin. He held out his arm, and Melvin brought out his dagger. Nergal started to withdraw his arm, but then he saw that Melvin was turning the blade in his hand. The knight pricked his own thumb lightly with the shining pointed end of his dagger and replaced the weapon at his belt.

“Let’s see if this comes off,” Melvin said. He rubbed the drop of blood onto Nergal’s upper arm, well above the blood stains that covered his forearm. They waited for a moment, and Melvin actually blew lightly onto the blood to dry it.

“I wonder how long we should wait,” Melvin thought out loud. “Let’s give it a few more moments…” Nergal watched the blood congeal on his upper arm. They waited in silence for a long minute as the blood turned black, and then Melvin nodded.

“Okay, Nergal. See if you can scrape it off.”

Nergal scratched his claw through the middle of the dried blood smear. Flakes of the dried blood came off easily. Nergal scratched it a few more times, and all traces of the drop were gone.

“Ah, so it must be the hydra blood,” said Melvin.

Nergal shook his head. “No! Blood no come off since Kallox,” Nergal insisted.

“He’s right, Melvin,” Roktan said. “I saw it after the battle, but didn’t realize what he meant. I thought you were only making comment about how you were covered in so much blood, I didn’t realize that it really wouldn’t come off.”

“Hrm. Some blood comes off, and some doesn’t,” Melvin puzzled. “I wish Dalwen were here….” Melvin didn’t continue, and he seemed to have been depressed by thinking of her.

“Well, let’s talk of it more after some rest,” Roktan said. “Nergal, can you watch for us while we sleep?”

"Nergal watch," he said, accepting a lazily burning torch from Roktan.

The others went back to their packs, and Nergal decided to walk a short ways and poke about. He wandered around their campsite just off the flat carved stone, looking for anything that might hold his interest. He quickly came to the conclusion that it was a dull cave, and that he was in for hours of intense boredom.

Nergal waited about listlessly, and finally came to rest with his back against a sloping stalagmite. He picked his claw-like nails and scratched idly for a great deal of time, sometimes talking softly to himself in orcish. Nergal had long ago forgotten about remaining alert.

At some point a while later, he remembered to look up and around.

Someone stood only a few feet away. Nergal twitched in surprise. The intruder wore a shiny smooth blue robe, with long baggy sleeves and no hood. The other had no source of light, and Nergal could only see him by the flickering light of his torch, which he had left on the ground several paces away.

"Oh, dear, an orc," the man said. The oddly accented voice seemed to feign fear, but Nergal did not smell fear on the being.

Scrambling to his feet, Nergal realized after a moment that it wasn't a man or an orc. The stranger stood a head taller than Nergal, although he was impossibly thin. His forehead stretched an eerily long distance over his eyebrows. Nergal reached idly for his mace with one hand.

"I wouldn't do that if I were you," warned the stranger.

Nergal froze, watching expectantly.

"You mean you're not going to ignore my warning, and threaten me with your weapon anyway?" asked the enigmatic being, sounding pleasantly surprised.

Nergal shook his head. "Nergal look for bad wizard," he explained. "You not being the wizard."

"I see. That's good, I half expected that you'd bear me ill will, seeing that you're covered in blood, and all...what's your name?"

"Nergal," the half-orc answered easily.

"Nergal, who are you...talking to?" asked Melvin, walking up from behind, his hand on his sword hilt.

"I'm Halgathar, lately of the Temple," explained the newcomer.

"We're pleased to meet you, Halgathar," Melvin said. His voice was friendly although his hand lingered near his sword.

"My apologies, your grace," Halgathar said as he bowed low. "I didn't realize I addressed a man of your status."

Melvin looked perplexed. "No need to bow, as I'm but a simple traveler."

"Oh, you weren't speaking in the royal plural?"

"I just meant Nergal and I, and our fellow travelers Roktan and Rovul," Melvin explained.

"Oh, yes, of course," Halgathar said, and stood back to his full height. "Are Roktan and Rovul…like yourselves?"

"Rovul is Slith," Melvin said uncertainly, hoping he understood the question. "They're over here," the knight indicated a direction. They walked over towards the campfire, and Melvin awakened the others.

Halgathar studied Roktan in his black robe, and his eyes ran over the long serpentine body of Rovul.

"You are of Chu Kutall?" asked Halgathar, in a conversational tone. Melvin hesitated, and looked at Roktan.

"We're just travelers," Roktan said. "Share our fire, and we can trade news," he offered.

"Surely," Halgathar said. "You'll probably ask about the wizard."

"You saw Kantru!" Melvin shot out. He recovered, saying more quietly, "Um, that is you saw him? Do you know him?"

"No, I don't know him. Nergal said you were looking for a bad wizard," Halgathar said matter-of-factly. "I didn't know his name was Kantru…. can't say that it sounds familiar."

"You said you were…. that you came from the Temple? What temple did you mean?"

"The Temple of Ralthashool," Halgathar told them. "I guess I misled you, since I made it sound like I was really there…I mean I was really there, but they didn't know I was there…know what I mean?"

"You mean you snuck through?" Roktan asked.

"Ah yes, exactly," Halgathar said. "Sometimes it's best to keep a low profile."

The man's eyes looked over Nergal's blood spattered form again. "Tell me, Nergal, is it the way of your orc tribe to paint yourselves with blood? It is a very interesting custom. You must be quite fierce in battle!"

"Yes! No! Er, blood no come off!" Nergal objected.

"Oh, I'm so sorry to hear that," Halgathar said in a sincere voice. "A cursed ring, is it?"

Nergal froze again. This smart one had noticed his ring. Melvin looked at Roktan, who shook his head.

"What ring?" asked Melvin.

"Why, the ring your friend Nergal here has on his hand," explained Halgathar. Nergal blinked in surprise. The ring was virtually invisible on his hand under the crusted blood, and none of his companions had noticed it.

Melvin and the others moved closer to examine the ring. "I had no idea," Melvin said. "Nergal, how long have you had that ring? Since the blood started sticking to you?"

Nergal nodded. "Ring inside armor," Nergal tried to explain. "Nergal put ring on, no one notice," he finished in a small voice.

"How did you sssspot that ring?" Rovul asked the tall stranger. The snake-prince brought his head close, looking at Nergal's hand. "I still cannot sssee it," he said.

"I…. I have a talent for such things," Halgathar told them. "I noticed it immediately, like all your other magical things. That Yorithian, for example," he pointed to Melvin.

"My sword? You're familiar with the work?"

"Quite. It is a masterpiece, that sword."

"Yes, Wormstringer has saved me many times over," Melvin agreed, patting the hilt of his weapon.

Nergal leaned back against the wall, losing interest in the conversation. He had just barely understood that they were discussing Melvin's sword, but many of the words meant nothing to him. At least Rovul had not become angry at him for taking the ring. Nergal grasped the ring on his finger and tried to take it off, but like the blood, it would not budge.

"Ring no come off," Nergal announced.

"Oh, I'm terribly sorry," Halgathar said. "You will have to have someone look at that."

"Can you help him?" Melvin asked. "We have some gold…"

The thin man waved his hands in refutation. "Oh! No, I, that is, I don't know how to do that. I would, of course, if I could. But no."

"Are you traveling to the south, then?" asked Roktan. "Can you tell us about the Temple?"

"It seems to be some huge underground fortress," Halgathar said. "The priests and such worship some kind of dark god or something…not a friendly lot, on the whole," Halgathar explained. "As I said, I found it wise to remain unnoticed. Are you missing one of your friends? I'm afraid I have bad news, if you are."

"No, we're all here," Melvin said. "I mean, since we entered the caves anyway. What exactly are you saying?"

"Well, it's how I know they're a mean lot, you see. They captured a man just like you two, in a black robe, and it didn't sound good for him. Not at all. I hope he isn't a friend of yours."

Melvin and Roktan traded looks again. "What did you see?" asked Roktan.

"I saw enough. They swarmed him under, and dragged him away in chains. I couldn't understand their language, but I got the distinct impression that something unpleasant awaited him. If I were you, I would strongly consider heading back the other direction!"

"Ah, that is too bad," Melvin said. "We have had a hard time of it already, yet we must continue. Kantru cannot be allowed to escape without suffering for the misery he has brought our nations."

Halgathar nodded. "Forgive me, but I must continue my journey," he told them. "I also have matters of grave import which require that I travel with speed."

"Please, share our camp," Melvin offered. "It is warm here, and safe enough, as long as one of us has the watch."

Halgathar held up his bony thin hand. "Please do not be offended, but I cannot dally. I must go on immediately."

"May I ask you before you leave, how did you evade the men of the temple?"

"There were no subtle strategies involved, I assure you. When a patrol would come by, I hid in the nooks and crannies of the caverns," he told them. "I had no desire to be dragged away in chains. It was simple enough, all by myself, to slip into a side tunnel when I heard the patrols coming."

Melvin nodded and looked thoughtful.

"I wish you luck, may the gods smile upon your mission," he told them.

"And luck to you, Halgathar," said Melvin. Roktan and Rovul agreed.

Halgathar bowed and turned, making his way through the cavern the way the group had come. After he was gone Nergal shook his head.

"Funny blue one," he said to the others.

"Yes, he was a little odd, but quite fascinating on the whole, and a very friendly man," Melvin agreed. "At least now we have some idea of what we face ahead...I hope that Kantru was the one these men captured. However, the wand still guides me, so I think that he's still alive. We'll have to keep going to be sure."

Rovul offered to take the next watch, so Nergal resumed his rest.

CHAPTER 24

The Temple of Ralthashool

The soft voices of his companions awakened Nergal. His back and feet felt clammy from the damp coolness of the caverns. The half-orc gained his feet and moved about slowly, trying to restore warmth to his limbs. He listened to the others as he donned his black scale armor and gathered his scant possessions.

"It sounded like it was just luck that Halgathar had somewhere to hide when the patrol went by," Melvin was saying. "We already fought a small outpost of men, and I think we got lucky that none of us were seriously hurt or killed. Now we might face a similar fight."

"No one said this would be safe," Roktan said, shrugging.

"We should come up with a plan," Melvin said. "At least we can think of something to improve our chances."

Nergal sighed. Melvin always wanted to think before doing things. Nergal resigned himself to waiting while his friends talked things over.

"If they surprise us, our robes may protect us. These men may be allies of Chu Kutall," suggested Roktan.

"Are there allies of Chu Kutall? Or only thralls?" Melvin replied.

"Sometimes the difference isn't clear."

Nergal thought for a moment. "When enemies come to orc lands, we make ambush for them," he said.

"If we knew where the patrols went, we could set an ambush I suppose," Melvin said.

"That issss easy enough," Rovul told them. The snake-prince's black eyes gleamed with reflected torchlight from the slits of his red helm. "I'll be able to sssmell them, if they patrol an area with any regularity. As soon as we get to sssuch an area, I'll tell you."

"Excellent! Let's get to it," Melvin said.

With the plan resolved, the group set out. The passage returned to a natural state only a few paces beyond the rest area. Nergal had to watch his footing lest he stumble and fall onto a spike of rock.

"On second thought, maybe an ambush is too aggressive," Melvin thought out loud. "If we hide and watch for a patrol, we could just follow them back towards the temple, and then pass it by as Halgathar did."

"At least until we see the size of these patrols," Roktan added.

They moved through the dim caverns. Already a third of their torches had been used up, so they agreed to conserve them, using only one at a time instead of two. Nergal led the way while Roktan bore the torch from the middle of the group.

Now the darkness pressed ever closer, broken only by the variant light of a single torch. Several times Nergal stopped, crouching and freezing next to a stalagmite, thinking that he heard the scraping of another hydra nearby.

It seemed that each noise one of them made became magnified by the rock and bounced back. Melvin seemed to share Nergal's nervousness, and he traveled with his sword before him, looking this way and that.

Nergal saw the smooth surface of a worked passage ahead.

"Shelter," Nergal called back quietly. They walked up to a familiar carved out area, with flat stone and torch sconces. Nergal saw that this particular station had a large alcove on either side of the passage, each large enough for ten men to rest.

"I sssmell them," Rovul announced, cocking his head and flickering his tongue rapidly. "More men like the feathered warriorsss that we fought at the entrance."

"How long ago were they here?" asked Melvin, his voice barely above a whisper now.

Rovul shook his head. "Not long. I think we should wait here if we're going to try out your plan of following a patrol."

Roktan and Melvin agreed. Nergal simply shrugged and looked around for a convenient rock formation to hide behind. The group took positions in the cavern before the carved alcove.

"I suppose we must extinguish our torch," Melvin muttered, looking around. "Will vermin or scorpions or something come out when the darkness returns?"

"Place it in here, and I'll partially block the light with this rock," Roktan suggested, indicating a hole in the wall and a small flat stone. "Nergal can move to the front and watch for the light of their torches. When he sees it, he can make a sign and I'll seal the hole with this rock, and it will keep them from seeing the light."

"How will we see his sign if it's almost dark?" asked Melvin.

Rovul hissed oddly, as if in laughter. "There isss an old Slith trick for thisss," he told Melvin. "I'll move up with Nergal, and leave my tail back here. When the patrol approachesss, I'll flicker my tail rapidly in warning."

"That sounds fine," Melvin said. "No offense, Rovul, but I'm glad that I don't have to crawl along on the floor of these caverns as you do. Do you ever get bitten by spiders, rats or such creatures?"

"That isss what scales are for," Rovul replied. "I would have asked you the same question about your soft puffy feet."

Melvin had no answer, and in fact he looked distinctly unhappy. Rovul twisted himself through the cavern so that his tail remained near Melvin and Roktan in the back with the torch.

They set themselves to waiting. This was the part that Nergal hated the most. It seemed the others had infinite patience for such things, but the half-orc didn't like planning out things that required inaction. Rovul's head was only a few feet away from Nergal, and he watched the prince's tongue flicker out to taste the scent of the air.

Suddenly, curiosity struck him.

"How come Rovul look like snake?" he asked.

Rovul was silent for a long moment and Nergal began to worry that he had said something wrong. Then the snake-prince took a long slow breath and answered him.

"At first, in the early times of the world, the Slith were only large ssserpents, and they had no armsss or shouldersss asss they do now. Our ancestorsss lived in peace with the men of the islandsss, who were sssimple fishermen. Then other men came to our islandsss, and they bore metal weaponsss and armor. They ssslew many of the island men and many of the Slith. Though the Slith were large and powerful, the invadersss used these tools to hunt us down and kill us."

"In desperation, an island shaman Ylatuan and hiss Slith companion Olmgard traveled to the hottest regionsss of the world, and sssought out an ancient god of the Earth, living in a thundering volcano. The god was Slecktar, and he heard the pleasss of Ylatuan and Olmgard. Slecktar told Ylatuan the sssecret of forging metal so that he might make weaponsss like the invadersss had, and transformed Olmgard into a ssserpent with the torso and arms of a man, so that he could take up those weaponsss. Every youngling of every clutch of Olmgard had arms asss well, and eventually all the Slith had them."

"In return for giving usss our armsss so that we might forge metal and stand against men as equalsss, the Slith must forever pay homage to Slecktar, and no other god. All other gods of the islands have been forsaken."

Nergal nodded at the sense of this, and he was silent.

"You do not ask, why are there no men on the islands now?" Rovul said.

Nergal thought for a moment, but he could not figure the answer. So he asked, "Why?"

"Although they worshipped Slecktar as well, they refusssed to destroy their templesss to the old gods. Slecktar became angry and destroyed them, causing the sssea to open up and consume them, leaving behind only the Slith."

Nergal nodded. "Is good having arms," he said.

"Yesss," Rovul agreed, shifting his bright yellow shield. Nergal saw the long spike protruding from the center of the shield. He knew it was quite sharp, and he found himself regretting leaving his behind. It had seemed a good idea at the time.

Nergal looked down to contemplate his scale armor. He had grown accustomed to its weight, but it still slowed him in battle. His attention wandered again, searching for something to do. Within the next few minutes boredom seized Nergal in its agonizing grip. Nergal fidgeted and shifted uncomfortably while Rovul seemed to freeze as solid as a statue.

Some indeterminate time later, Nergal roused from a light nap to a strange rustling sound. Opening his eyes, the half-orc saw the flicker of a torch approaching from beyond the alcoves. The rustling sound halted but now Nergal could hear the sounds of men moving through the caverns ahead. He looked at Rovul, who nodded at him slowly. Nergal grasped his mace more firmly and sat still, watching the light grow from down the passageway. The torchlight behind them grew dimmer as Roktan shifted a stone to block it.

The adventurers watched from the darkness, sitting absolutely still as the strange men came into view. Nergal saw paint on their faces and feathers in their headpieces, confirming Rovul's analysis that these were the same kind of men they had fought at the entrance to the caves. They carried spears and other crude weapons and bore their peculiar woven fiber armor.

One of the men spoke with the hard voice of authority, and the others stopped to rest. This leader remained standing, and his eyes seemed to lock on Nergal and Rovul as he peered out beyond the alcoves. Nergal's heart raced in his chest but the man gave no sign of seeing anything. Their leader turned away and talked to one of the others for a while, and Nergal relaxed.

The entire group seemed less than a dozen men, and the half-orc calculated that they could destroy the patrol with little effort. He looked imploringly at Rovul, but the snake prince was looking at the men in the alcoves, his tongue flickering out to test the air. At first Nergal had thought that the flickering tongue meant that his companion was hungry, but he had since decided that it meant he was excited. The tongue seemed to flicker most when things were about to happen.

They watched the men in silence but it became clear that the others did not want to attack the patrol. Nergal resigned himself to spying on the strangers, and he did his best to stay quiet. At last the men seemed ready to continue, and they gathered together to head back the way they had come. Before the light of their torch had faded Nergal rose to his feet and started after them.

"There isss no need to hurry," Rovul told him in a rough whisper. "I can sss-mell them."

"Good," Melvin whispered from behind. "We can stay far enough back that they won't see our torch."

"Not many. No bows. Dem easy kill," Nergal urged.

"Let's not risk anything. These aren't the people we're hunting. It's Kantru we're after."

"What if they have him at the temple?" Roktan asked. "We would pass him by."

"I'll check with the wand, and we'll know it if we passed him," Melvin said. "Who knows? Maybe they'll kill him for us, if it was him that Halgathar saw."

"Thisss way," Rovul said, breaking up the conversation and leading them out after the patrol. Nergal followed, holding his spear ready and hoping for combat.

Rovul led them through twisting passageways after the patrol. Even in the raw caverns the way was clear because the men had worn a path in the stone of the passages. Nergal thought that the temple must be old, that they had smoothed the way with countless treadings of their feet.

"It has been a long ways. They may turn back," Roktan said.

"If we have passsed the temple," Rovul hissed.

Melvin produced his wand. "Kantru is still ahead. Just be ready to find a hiding place if we have to."

They came to a square opening in the natural cave wall. A man-made passage left the cave, and Nergal anticipated another rest station ahead. He couldn't see the torch of the patrol ahead, though. The group moved into the corridor in single file, still following Rovul.

Suddenly an outcry was raised from above. Nergal could not understand the words, but it was clear some sort of watchman had spotted them. He looked up and realized that there were additional galleries above them, and a guard had seen them.

Nergal leaned against the wall with one hand and launched his spear powerfully with the other. Despite the angle of the attack, his spear pierced the guard's lung and the man sagged forward, but it was too late. Other guards appeared, looking down from above.

"Ware the rear!" shouted Roktan.

Nergal glanced back and saw that several savages in woven and plumed armor had alighted behind them from suspended ropes. A heavy net had been cast from above over Roktan, but he was still standing and swinging at them with his sword arm protruding from the weave.

Several of the primitives appeared from ahead as well, alarmed by the watch call. Nergal left Melvin and Rovul to stand in front, heading towards Roktan. Just as Nergal arrived, Roktan was swept from his feet as ropes to the net were hoisted in from above. Nergal smashed his mace into the head of the nearest warrior, killing the man instantly. The others reacted to his charge and stepped back, forming a cluster of spear points and hide shields in the corridor. Roktan shifted and struggled to cut the ropes, but his arm was pinned. Nergal jumped up and grabbed the net, adding his weight to the assembly. Its ascent halted, but the net did not fall. The men in the corridor moved forward, seeing that Nergal was defenseless, and the half-orc was forced to drop back down and bat away several spear thrusts with his mace.

"Forget me Nergal! Look to yourself!" called Roktan from above.

Nergal waded into the three men before him, crushing a flimsy shield and grabbing the haft of a spear with his left hand. The men attacked him, and Nergal had to tilt his head to avoid a jab at his face. A blow fell against his scale armor harmlessly and another was repelled by the dried blood on his arm. Then he felled another savage with his mace and kicked the next one in the leg, causing him to fall. The man on the floor gazed up over Nergal's shoulder, and something made Nergal grapple with his last standing opponent and swivel with him, causing them to trade places. A net fell from above, landing on them both. Nergal thrust his mace into the man's face, not having room for a good swing. The man buckled under the blow, and Nergal stooped, letting the man take most of the net with him. While he was bent over Nergal finished the last warrior, stepping on his chest and smashing his head with the mace. Then he picked up a weight stone of the net and threw it back over him, freeing himself from the trap.

The bloodied half-orc turned and took stock of the situation with Melvin and Rovul. The snake-prince was nowhere to be seen, and Melvin struggled against several fighters who had netted him. He was being pulled down the corridor, fighting against one of them who was trying to pry the sword out of his fingers.

Nergal rushed towards his friend, but warriors flowed past Melvin to engage him. Nergal lost sight of him amidst his enemies, who seemed to press forward like a wave.

Blood sprayed out onto Nergal as his weapon ruined the shoulder of his nearest opponent. The fibrous armor worn by his foes was not the equal of the metal ridges on his mace. Dimly Nergal realized that the blood would probably not come off again, but he did not allow this to dampen his offensive. The orc warrior roared, snatched up a machete from the floor, and came to meet the others with a weapon in each hand.

He struck at another opponent with his mace. The soldier blocked Nergal's attack by parrying it with a spear. Nergal felt the impact of another spear against the scale armor on his chest, but it did not harm him. Nergal snarled savagely and replied with his mace. The man fell backwards heavily, and Nergal leaped forward to stomp on his enemy's chest as hard as he could while swinging the stolen machete at another warrior. The strike completely severed the arm of his opponent, and still more blood sprayed out onto Nergal.

The half-orc attacked in earnest, encouraged by the safety afforded by his strange blood-armor. He lost count of foes vanquished in that tight space, as he smashed through them and advanced steadily, taking no heed of their attempts to fight back. He saw no sign of Melvin or the others.

Nergal snapped out of this battle fugue when a wall of moving rock appeared ahead, moving steadily forward. The half-orc realized it was a rolling boulder, meant to crush him. He had no choice but to beat a hasty retreat, as the huge rock had enough momentum to intimidate him. He did not want to find out if he had the strength to stop it.

He ran back the way he had come, jumping over the bodies of the defenders. Behind him he could hear the carnage as the rock crushed corpses and snapped weapons underneath it. Nergal made it to the entrance of the enclosed passageway with the natural rock ceiling, and dodged around a couple of rock formations before stopping. Several paces away, the rock slammed into the passage entrance with a loud grinding of stone on stone. Darkness and silence descended on the cave.

When Nergal approached the boulder to investigate, he discovered that the passage was neatly blocked off. Only a slight trickle of light could pass through from the other side. It seemed that the boulder had a defensive purpose, and was shaped perfectly to deny intruders entrance into the open chambers beyond.

Now the magnitude of everything that had happened began to settle onto Nergal. His friends had been subdued and carried away. The wand that could lead him to Kantru was with Melvin, and Nergal didn't know his way in the tunnels. Besides, what hope could he have of defeating the wizard alone? He had already failed once, becoming an ensorcelled puppet of the monk-mage.

Even though Nergal could barely see himself, he could feel the blood all over him. No doubt it was dried on most of his body, and would not come off. He could now defeat another dozen or more of the primitive warriors if he could simply get to them.

What would Melvin do? The answer came almost immediately to Nergal. Melvin would make a plan. Nergal paced in the darkness, trying hard to think.

After a few moments, Nergal adopted this as his plan: he would try to find his friends and kill anything that got in his way.

Embracing the huge rock in his arms, Nergal bent his legs and pushed with all his might. The rock shifted once as if it would move away, but then it resisted solidly. The half-orc got a new grip on the boulder and tried again, but he didn't have the strength to move the barrier out of his way.

Nergal turned from the boulder and blinked uncertainly in the darkness. Surely there would be other passages into the strange temple, but how could he find his way in the dark? Nergal staggered forward cautiously, and he felt the smooth stone under his feet. He realized that he could follow the pathways that had been worn into the stone.

Nergal set out, feeling the path with his feet. He did not realize that he might not find branches in the path, simply going by them in the darkness. Often he would stop and listen, trying to detect if anything alive neared him.

It was there in the black of the caverns that a new scent came to the half-orc. The distinct odor of human urine was faint but unmistakable. It made Nergal remember Skaggs fondly, his friend who had supplied the necessary bones to enable Nergal's escape.

Nergal shuffled along, making his way toward the source of the smell. He took a side path and seemed to move into a smaller cavern, where he could hear the sounds of his movements reflected from closer walls.

The stench of urine smelled stronger here. Nergal felt around, and discovered that a large round tunnel joined with the passage he walked in. The foul liquid flowed out from this new rounded passage. It was not protected by any sort of gate or grille. Nergal shrugged and entered the cramped space, shuffling along the tube as quickly as he could manage. He fell forward on a rough spot and ended up sprawled out on all fours as the smelly water flowed by.

"I have...the smarts," Nergal gasped to himself, crawling further down the sewage tunnel.

Nergal could not gauge how far he traveled down the tunnel. The air was poor and the space was tight and unpleasant even to the half-orc. He ignored his burning nose and aching muscles and continued single-mindedly down the black tunnel.

Suddenly Nergal stopped.

Light. From above.

Nergal blinked, uncertain at first. He stared up and definitely sensed some kind of dull but constant light from somewhere above. He groped about in the gloom and discovered the handholds of a ladder carved directly into the stone.

Having nothing to lose, the half orc ascended. He came to the top of the ladder after the space of ten paces, and felt a hole in the stone at the end of the ladder. He crawled through this into a new chamber.

The light came from an odd glowing stone set into the ceiling. Nergal was reminded of the sconces in Kantru's island redoubt. This time instead of a glowing sphere, a grimy looking stone seemed to glow with some inner light. The feeble rays revealed that Nergal was in a large tube carved in the earth that extended in two directions. He could just touch the ceiling if he dared, but Nergal didn't touch the glowing stone for fear of it.

Nergal chose a direction at random and began to walk. Doubt filled him as he thought of the need to find his friends in the temple. How would he find them? He thought of how they smelled, and tried for their scent but he could detect nothing other than the damp stone and urine below, whose scent was weaker here. He came to an intersection of the tube with another. There was no indication of where to go, and Nergal's sense of direction had been lost several turns ago. He simply walked straight through, his way lit by an occasional glowing ceiling stone. Then he detected something, and stopped.

A faint rush of sound flowed down the tunnel from some distant chamber. It sounded to Nergal like a large crowd of beings cheering or singing. He stopped to listen but the sound faded.

Nergal wandered, stopping and waiting for the sound to recur at each intersection. Slowly he made his way to a spot closer to the noise, guided by the faint light of the glowstones.

Finally he made a turn in the tube and a flood of light was visible at the other end. Nergal could hear the yammering of many men, and the smell of the primitives was unmistakable. He fell into a crouch and began to slink forward. He could see that the tube was capped in metal bars at the end. It opened out into a chamber of some kind, but all he could see was a stone wall at the far side. He crept forward slowly, and realized that the room ahead was quite large. Keeping to the shadows of the tube, Nergal moved to the side to get another angle. Now he could see that there was a pit or arena just ahead. A large number of the primitives of the temple had assembled about the pit.

When Nergal finally moved up closer to the bars, he noticed that the crowd was more than a group of the strangely garbed and painted men. Sprinkled among them, huge lizard-monsters watched silently. The monsters were fearsome looking green scaly things that stood on two legs like the men but towered easily half again their height. Their heads resembled those of crocodiles more than men. Nergal stared at the closest such creature, seeing that it wore only a loincloth with a belt, a mail guard on one arm and a huge metal skull cap with holes for its eyes. An unusual weapon dangled at its belt, some sort of double bladed war axe of unfamiliar design.

There was a particularly large monster seated on a throne on the far side of the room. Piles of bright artifacts of gold and silver were heaped all about this apparent leader.

Nergal crouched behind the bars, and continued to watch the collection of men and monsters. After a few more moments he realized that his friends were there as well, surrounded by a group of guards. Nergal saw Melvin in his breastplate, but he could not see the knight's helmet or sword. It seemed the others had been divested of their weapons as well.

"Nergal save you…" muttered the orc under his breath. He wanted to reassure his friends, and tell them that he was here. But how could he do that without giving himself away? Nergal considered the bars before him. They appeared quite ancient, and he felt that he might be able to break his way through and drop into the arena below. Then he could climb out of the pit and resume the slaughter of the primitives. Nergal had decided on this course of action when he noticed more movement in the crowd.

A group of the men came forward to the edge of the pit. They held a prisoner amongst them, and Nergal realized with a shock that it was none other than Kantru!

The group of warriors tossed Kantru down into the pit at the command of one of the lizard-monsters. The wizard monk fell gracefully, rolling at the impact despite his bound hands, and continued the motion to regain his feet.

Nergal stared at the wizard, who still wore his black robe. Kantru struggled to free his hands, and after a second or two managed to escape the rope. The crowd murmured their approval of these maneuvers, and they watched the monk expectantly.

Now Nergal saw that the lizard-thing on the throne slowly rose to its feet. Human servants presented it with its weapons, two huge, pronged implements of metal. The things looked like very wide two bladed swords, or perhaps double hafted battle axes, which it held with the blades flat out before it in each hand. The creature's eerie red eyes blazed with reflected light as it strode purposefully towards the lip of the pit.

The half-orc spotted Melvin whispering something to Roktan as they watched the scene from their station amongst the temple dwellers. Nergal imagined what was being said: Melvin hoped that the scaled monster would kill Kantru now.

The men above began to cheer for the monster that ruled them. Melvin and the others stood stoically, ignoring the ruckus and watching for the battle to begin.

Down below, the monster advanced upon Kantru. It moved in a slow hulking manner. Kantru and the monster circled each other warily in the stone arena. The lizard swiped at the monk a few times as it neared, testing the reactions of his opponent. Kantru moved away easily and did not strike back.

Suddenly the thing darted at the wizard with surprising speed. It seemed that its slow movement had been a ruse. Kantru reacted instantly, sidestepping at the last moment and spinning behind his opponent, striking under one of its arms and as he passed.

The lizard king seemed to ignore the attack and spun to swing at the wizard again. Kantru ducked under the swing and then rolled to the side to avoid the next attack. The monster pursued Kantru, always attacking swiftly, but the wizard-monk gracefully avoided each assault as it came. The crowd became quite agitated, yelling and screaming at the two as they engaged each other.

Nergal saw that despite Kantru's dodging the lizard-king had begun to herd him into one of the corners of the arena. The crowd sensed the impending danger to Kantru and began to yell louder as they watched. When Kantru retreated he continued on into the corner, but now he was uttering low, rhythmic phrases and moving his hands rapidly. The men above went wild and the monster followed him, preparing to strike the death blow.

This time Kantru did not dart away. Instead he finished his quick, sharp words with a gesture of his right arm, and threw his hand out before him as the monster closed.

A bright flash preceded the roar of thunder by a split second. Nergal blinked, his eyes watering, the afterimage of a bolt of lightning dancing in his eyes. The lizard-king dropped both of its weapons, and clutched at its chest as it staggered backwards. From his vantage point, Nergal could see a gaping blackened hole in its back. It opened its mouth but no noise came out. Then the thing fell onto its side, writhing feebly.

There was a long moment of stunned silence, and then a cacophony erupted from the galleries above. The men muttered and some yelled, while the lizard monsters seemed to struggle to calm them. Kantru's opponent fell still, utterly vanquished by the monk-wizard.

Nergal could wait no more. With the tumult that the death of the king-monster had caused, he felt that he might be able to slay Kantru without interference. Perhaps these primitives would even enjoy seeing Kantru die at his hands.

The half-orc hefted his mace and brought the bottom of his foot against the rusted bars with all of his strength. The jar was impressive but the bars were simply too old. The obstacle fell into the arena below, and Nergal stepped forward through the tube and hopped down into the light of the fighting pit. The uproar from up above continued unabated, and if the monsters or the men saw him it must have simply added to the confusion already present.

Kantru looked at Nergal for a moment in obvious surprise. Perhaps it was the half-orc's impressive muscles rippling beneath his scale mail, the size of his metal-ridged mace, or the fact that the top half of Nergal's body was almost completely covered in the dried blood that would not come off. Then Kantru seemed to recognize him, despite the blood, and gathered himself together. He actually laughed.

"I thought some sort of god had come out of the earth to consume me," Kantru told him. "But it's only an orc."

Nergal answered with a feral growl low in his throat. He advanced and swung the mace at Kantru, who danced to the side as he had with his previous opponent.

"Uh, what is that smell?" Kantru's face screwed up in revulsion.

Nergal answered him by charging. He almost caught the monk unready, but Kantru's reflexes were good. The monk ignored the fetor and darted away out of the range of the mace. Nergal wished he still had his spear.

The monk darted and spun, always avoiding Nergal's mace by mere inches. Sometimes he would counter but Nergal ignored the blows, his adrenaline running high. Kantru tried attacking the half-orc at a more vulnerable spot, kicking out at Nergal's kneecap. The orc raised his knee and met the strike on his shin, and then drove the monk back with swings from his mace.

Seeing that the monk had moved closer to one of the corners, Nergal stepped up the pace of his assault. He wondered if the monk-mage would try and use magic on him as he had with the lizard-monster.

As the thought flew through Nergal's mind, Kantru began to cast a spell. His hands weaved oddly and his mouth moved but Nergal couldn't catch the words. He instinctively held his mace up to protect himself. Once again a flash of light arced from Kantru's extended hand and a mighty clap of thunder smashed through the caverns.

The metal of his weapon blackened and sizzled, then fell apart, but Nergal felt no pain through the layer of dried blood that protected him. Nergal focused on his enemy and punched at him. The monk reacted well, blocking the strike and retreating, but his face betrayed his surprise at Nergal's invulnerability.

Nergal bared his teeth and came at Kantru bare-handed. Kantru leaped head over heels, putting a large distance between himself and the half-orc.

"Let's try that again!" he snarled, and began casting another spell. Nergal ran towards him, weaving side to side as if he were trying to avoid the cast of a spear.

But it was only a trick. Instead of releasing arcane energies, the monk simply leaped into the air, flipping his body in mid-flight, and landed upon the lip of the passage from which Nergal had emerged.

"Next time, stupid orc!" he called back, and darted into the tunnel.

Nergal looked up, searching for his friends. It seemed that the galleries above were still locked in turmoil. The mob of painted men had turned on the lizard monsters, and the ensuing combat still raged. Several of the painted men hurled the body of one of the lizard-monsters into the pit as Nergal watched.

"We're coming, Nergal! Don't lose him!" called Melvin, appearing over the lip of the arena. Nergal saw that the knight had recovered his helmet and his sword, and seemed to be helping the others obtain their possessions as the combat raged around them.

Nergal snatched up one of the odd weapons from the corpse of the lizard-king, and turned back to the round tunnel. He leaped up onto the lip of the entrance. Kantru was nowhere in sight. Nergal cautiously went in after him, ready for the wizard to appear at any moment. Nergal advanced rapidly to the first intersection. The tube split off and went three other directions, and Nergal couldn't tell which way Kantru had fled.

He remembered Melvin's wand and how it would point the way to the wizard. Nergal decided to dash back and get the wand, and perhaps join up with the others before they pursued Kantru. He ran back to the arena and hopped back down, moving towards a ladder carved in stone that led up to the galleries.

Nergal climbed up to find most of the men had dispersed. The sound of battle still echoed in the caverns, but there were none of the lizard monsters left in the chamber. Nergal saw his friends sorting through bags of equipment near a stone altar in the back. He ran up to rejoin them.

"Did he lose you?" asked Melvin.

"Need wand," Nergal indicated. Melvin nodded and searched through his hastily gathered possessions. The knight had donned his armor but everything else seemed to be disorganized. Nergal saw his long Slith spear amongst the pile and reclaimed it.

Melvin stood, holding up the wand he had recovered.

"Don't worry. We'll find him," Melvin stated with certainty.

CHAPTER 25

Into Sunlight

They traveled hard through the caves for hours, fighting off exhaustion and ignoring hunger in an attempt to catch Kantru. Rovul had some difficulty, as he was in pain from several wounds that he received after the fighting had broken out in the Temple. Nergal learned that his friend's reptilian appearance had caused many of the men to attack him during the battle with the lizard monsters. Melvin and Roktan had come to his aid of course, but not until the snake-prince had taken several nasty blows.

After several confusing turns and a long straight tunnel, the bright light of the outer world glowed from an opening ahead. They stood just inside the entrance for a few moments, trying to adjust their eyes to the light.

"Be careful, this would be a good place for a trap, if Kantru is waiting for us," Roktan said.

The others agreed, and everyone drew their weapons. Slowly, the adventurers emerged into the light of midday. A breathtaking vista opened up before them. Nergal saw that they were on a ledge overlooking a fertile valley. The landscape slowly descended, heavily covered in trees, to a large river or lake to the east. There were great wide-spanned mountain birds riding the air currents and searching for food. It reminded Nergal of his own stomach.

"Need food," Nergal stated.

Melvin nodded. "We're in quite a state here. We only have a little bit of food. Yet we're presumably fairly close to Kantru."

"We could go back to the temple and find food there," suggested Roktan.

"Yet the farther ahead Kantru gets, the more time he will have to prepare for us," Melvin said. "I hate it when he leaves nasty traps for us, like the empty suits of armor that were painful to strike."

Rovul looked out over the valley. His tongue flickered in the breeze. "There is food below," he said with certainty. "Kantru will find it there, and ssso can we."

"Maybe boar down there," Nergal said. "Can hunt boar with spear."

Roktan nodded. "Very well. We have no bows, though, so finding our own food will be harder. And if we get meat, we have no salt to cure it."

Nergal raised an eyebrow. "Salt?"

"You know, to keep the meat from spoiling," Roktan said. Nergal stared blankly at him.

"We eat right away. It stay fresh in stomach," Nergal explained, patting his midsection.

"Never mind," Roktan said.

Rovul picked up the scent of Kantru, and everyone followed the prince down the winding rock trail that disappeared into the trees below. Then Melvin led the way for hours, eyeing the woods carefully and following the wand. The trail had died off and they found themselves pushing through the undergrowth. The ground descended rapidly as they approached the river, and several times Nergal almost slipped in rivulets of muck where the rainwater flowed down the hill.

After a while, the forest gave way to a marsh. Melvin skirted the lower, damper ground, leading them along the edge.

"We seem to be veering from the wand's direction," Roktan pointed out.

"The water is that way. We should stay up here on dry land, shouldn't we?" asked Melvin. "I figured we would make better time up here."

"Go closer to water and wait," Nergal told them. "Animals drink at water. We find trail, and wait for food."

Melvin looked at Roktan who nodded. "Very wise, Nergal. We shall do just that." The knight started for the water.

"Big swamp lizards though," Nergal added as an afterthought. "Dey come out of water and drag you in, eat you."

Melvin froze in his tracks. "To get food, we must risk becoming food? How horrible."

"Don't worry, Melvin, the swamp lizards probably don't like to eat armored knights," Roktan said.

Reluctantly Melvin followed them towards the water.

"Of course, they'll probably have to taste you before realizing that," Roktan added. Melvin rolled his eyes but did not complain any further, sensing his companion's amusement.

Nergal took the lead, and they moved through tall grass until they came to a bog. The half-orc turned to the left and they made their way carefully as he looked for a game trail. He turned and led them over a small hill and they came to the water's edge. The water was open for about twenty paces. Beyond that, dark trees grew from the black water, their twisted roots merging together to form a maze of wood. Nergal stopped to consider the best route.

One moment the water's edge seemed empty except for the adventurers and the gnarled trees growing from the swamp water, and the next moment a group of tall gray creatures glided out on a floating log towards the shore. They hadn't made the slightest sound.

"Eh?" Nergal grunted, and groped for his mace with one hand, not taking his eyes off the four newcomers. Instead of his mace his hand found the odd two bladed sword he had taken from the lizard king's corpse.

Each of these swamp denizens stood slightly shorter than a man, and they gripped the log with the three long toes on their feet. Their legs extended a great distance like a pair of thin straight palm trees, and the bodies were much smaller than a man's, with a pot belly and four tiny, knobby stick-like arms. Their heads were balanced on thin delicate necks, and although their faces did somewhat resemble human faces, their eyes were giant and round for their size, and all of these dark orbs were fixed at Nergal and his companions. They seemed to be naked, being covered in nothing but knobby dark grey skin.

The two groups froze for a moment, examining each other in shock. It seemed that both parties were completely surprised by the existence of the other.

"Odd looking creatures," commented Roktan quietly.

"Amazing!" Melvin exclaimed, perhaps a bit too loud. The frail creatures before them seemed to crouch a bit more on their stilt-like legs, and they nervously shifted their long toes on the floating log.

"Quickly! We must make friends with them!" Melvin said, this time managing to restrain his volume to keep from alarming the strangers.

"We do?" asked Nergal. He gripped his sword tightly and looked over the creatures. They looked weak, but somehow they made his hackles rise. They reminded Nergal of spiders or scorpions somehow, because of their long thin limbs.

"How should we do that? What do we have to offer?" asked Roktan. "We have little food, and naught else but weapons and armor."

"Do something!" Melvin urged. He looked at his pack uncertainly. "Get me a stick!"

Rovul slithered over and retrieved a stick. The alien creatures looked on with clear curiosity, but they had started to slowly move their ungainly craft farther away. Nergal saw that the log they used still had branches left on it, on opposite sides of each other so that the log remained stable in the water. Still the things exhibited an uncanny balance, standing tall on the floating log like perched herons.

Melvin snatched his coin purse from his belt and looped its drawstring over the end of the long stick. He held it out over the water, but the stick did not extend that far. It was nowhere near the creatures.

"They probably don't even value gold or silver, so keep thinking," Melvin said. "I don't even know how I'm going to get this to them."

The creatures floated uncertainly. They didn't seem to be retreating or advancing. Melvin stuck the stick in the mud so that it remained upright with the coin purse.

"Move back…move back and they will come see what it is, I hope," Melvin told them.

"Perhaps they value iron," Roktan said. "It must rust easily here though."

"Try anything," Melvin told him. Roktan drew out his dagger and rested the hilt in a fork of the stick. It bowed under the weight but did not break. Then they moved back, reversing their course and heading back into the vines and twisted trees.

After a few moments, the swamp denizens seemed to discuss the matter amongst themselves in bizarre hooting voices, and then began to move their craft towards the offerings. They used long poles to push their log along, guiding it to the shore. Nergal looked at the things again, trying to find any sign of weapons or other protection. He couldn't spot any.

"Swamp lizards no eat them?" he asked.

"They do seem rather fragile," Melvin agreed. "Surely they have some natural defenses?"

"I have no guesss," said Rovul.

The creatures retrieved the collection of gifts that the adventurers had set out for them. Nergal listened to their odd voices as they talked over the coins and the dagger. One of the things placed an object into the leather bag. The things seemed to calm down somewhat, and they placed the bag back on the stick and then moved away. Rovul retrieved the bag and looked inside.

"I do not know what it issss," he said.

The snake-prince held up a small oval shape. It had a smooth surface like an egg or a piece of fruit, and a light greenish color.

Nergal took the thing and felt it in his hands. He sniffed at it carefully. "Is not good eating, I think," he told them.

Melvin took his turn to look it over. He smiled widely, and said "Ahhhhh!"

"What is it?" whispered Roktan.

"I have no idea, I'm just looking pleased to make them happy," Melvin whispered back. "Ahhhh!" he said more loudly, and smiled again, waving at the tiny creatures. They motioned back to him enthusiastically. The creatures' fear seemed to be fading fast, and they moved closer to the edge of the dry ground.

"So what now?" asked Roktan. "They seem friendly enough."

"We need their help to cross the ssswamp after Kantru," Rovul said.

"We can't get on that log," Roktan said.

"You're right. This is ridiculous. We can't follow them anyway, not without drowning or being gutted by some monster in those dark waters," Melvin said dejectedly. "My sword won't rust, but this armor will. It is already wet from the mist of the falls and the climb down here."

Nergal examined the black plates of his own armor, and the mail underneath them. There was no sign of rust or wear that he could detect. The scales still held their original shiny black appearance.

Melvin noted his examination. "I imagine your armor is proof against such things, Nergal," he said. "After all, the Slith are at home in the sea, and this armor is of their making."

"Ssstained black by the blood of the sssea dragon," rasped Rovul. "I doubt it will ever rust."

Roktan looked out at the swamp. "The wand points in this direction. Somehow Kantru made his way."

"We don't even really have enough food," Melvin complained. "I can take off my armor but how will I carry it over the water? Should I leave it behind? Perhaps we should just face that we're not going to catch the wizard anytime soon."

Nergal looked at Melvin, and then he placed his hand on the knight's shoulder. "We must. For fallen ones. Dalwen, too."

Rovul flickered his tongue. "Yes. How will you tell your comradesss that you let him get away? Just because of a little water? Asss for me, I must continue sssince I cannot be king without hisss head."

Melvin looked at Nergal, and at the swamp. He nodded and rose. "Help me take this off, then," he said. His voice still sounded dull but he looked determined to continue. They took Melvin's armor off and he placed the pieces into some oiled rags. Melvin tied everything together into a pack, with his backpack nestled inside the curve of his breastplate. Hefting this, he stood up again and regarded the water.

The odd creatures watched all this with open curiosity.

"Well, we might wade through some spots but it may be deep in others," he said. "Of course now that I'm devoid of my armor, I'll probably be eaten by one of those giant reptilians."

"We could make a raft," Roktan offered. "It may be hard to maneuver through those trees. It looks like their log could go most places."

"Of course we're not going to be balancing on a log like that," Melvin said. "At least not with our armor and weapons and a few days of practice besides."

One of the creatures hooted at that moment, and Nergal looked at it. He saw that it was beckoning for them to follow it. He skirted the edge of the water, stepping carefully to avoid the slides of mud. The others followed his lead, and they walked for several minutes.

"I hope you know what you're doing, Nergal," Melvin said dejectedly.

"They're leading us somewhere," Roktan said.

The group advanced into a small cove filled with shallow water. The creatures hooted and tittered, indicating a small group of the swamp trees. Nergal waded out into the shallow water and peered past the serpentine roots.

A massive creature had met its end here. The huge skeleton of a giant turtle was wedged between two great trees. The shell was covered in moss and sticks, and the eye hollows of the skull seemed to stare back at Nergal.

The others joined Nergal in the shallow water to take a look.

"What could kill that thing?" asked Roktan.

"Kantru?" suggested Rovul.

"It might have died of old age," Melvin offered hopefully, approaching closer to examine the corpse. "Uhhh," he groaned. "The stench of it…it smells worse than Nergal after he crawled from that sewer!"

"We can use it," Roktan asserted suddenly. "We can use it as a boat. That is why they led us to it."

"Well if it's such a brilliant contrivance then why aren't they using it?" Melvin looked at it again, mulling the idea over. "It might hold the three of us. I don't know about Rovul, though."

"Use it. I'll push you," Rovul offered. "The water does not affect my scales. It must be miserable, to have your skin that is not friendly to the water."

They moved the huge smelly shell to the edge of the water and tried to clean the remnants of flesh from it with their weapons. Nergal clambered in first, since the smell didn't bother him that much. Roktan made a face, but he entered the craft without complaint.

Of course Melvin was last. He coughed and spat from the shore, then finally clambered into the shell. Nergal thought he looked a little pale.

"This is insane," was his only comment.

The tittering of the odd creatures increased as they beckoned to the group in their new contrivance. Rovul slowly launched the overturned shell towards the stranger's log, and the unusual caravan set off through the waters of the swamp. The shell bobbed and weaved in an unpredictable manner, causing Nergal to think that he would be upended into the water at any time. Somehow Rovul stabilized them enough to prevent any accidents.

They moved for hours through the swamp, bobbing in the huge shell through the murky water. Occasionally the odd swamp inhabitants led them over patches of land, so the shell had to be carried short distances. After a time the group arrived at a small village. Two or three score of the thin swamp denizens came out of their mud huts to stare at the newcomers.

The adventurers slowly waded through the curious swamp denizens, following the group they had encountered in the swamp. They were led under a large open-sided shelter made of wood and fern leaves. The entire village gathered around the structure while several of the creatures beckoned the adventurers to sit.

One of the creatures came forward and began to speak loudly in some other language. It didn't resemble the odd hooting noises that the others were making.

"Thisss one ssspeaks in a trade language I know," rasped Rovul. "This tribe of creaturesss calls themselves Gooshlan."

"Fantastic! I have many questions to ask them," Melvin said.

"Let's stick to questions that will help us find Kantru," suggested Roktan.

"But think of all we could learn. Think of all we have learned from our friend Rovul, here."

Roktan shrugged. "You have one night, I suppose, since it seems we're staying here that long at least."

"Are there really giant swamp lizards here?" asked Melvin.

Rovul related the question.

"Yesss," Rovul said. "They're Yagmi."

"How do they defend themselves against the things?" Melvin asked.

Rovul asked the swamp native. The creature made further hooting noises.

"He says that young Yagmi always eat someone before they learn how bad the Gooshlan taste, but then it won't eat one of them again."

"Oh. How reassuring," Melvin said. "They only lose one tribe member for each new Yagmi."

Nergal nodded at this, missing Melvin's sarcasm. He lost interest in the knight's line of questioning when several younger swamp creatures came in offering food items in small wooden bowls.

Nergal dined on raw salamanders and mud-covered crustaceans with the Gooshlan. For some reason the other adventurers didn't seem hungry, even though Nergal assured them it was all good eating. The half-orc consumed about as much as all the other Gooshlan combined, and this seemed to amuse the thin creatures, as they watched the large warrior eating bowl after bowl of food and eagerly offered more.

After Nergal finished, he sat with the others while Melvin asked an endless series of questions about the Gooshlan and their lives in the swamp. Nergal didn't listen, but instead he found himself dozing off. Occasionally Roktan would poke him in the ribs to try and keep him alert.

At last Rovul bid farewell to the Gooshlan he could speak with, and the visitors were led into a large mud hut. It became obvious through a few moments of hand waving and hooting that this was to be their shelter for the night. The adventurers thanked their hosts as best they could and piled into the hut.

Nergal sat on the dirt floor, tired out from the day's exertions and the recent meal. He watched idly as Melvin removed his footgear. The knight looked at his feet, and the off-color growths that lurked between his toes.

"I have never been so miserable in all my life," Melvin announced. "I would gleefully go back to the cave shelters, or our room in Neyala. We have to get through this accursed swamp quickly."

Nergal made a neutral grunt. Actually he did not favor the swamp either, but at least the inexplicable dried blood had kept his hands and arms warm and dry. He rolled over and prepared for sleep.

"Who wants first watch?" asked Roktan.

Nergal looked back up. He hadn't considered setting a watch once inside the village.

"I suppose it isn't wise to trust them, even though they seem benevolent," Melvin said. "I'll take the first watch."

Nergal grunted and turned back over. He found sleep within seconds.

The night brought odd dreams. Nergal awakened several times, aware of the cramped living space within the mud hut. When it was his turn on watch, Nergal sat with his back against the tree and listened to the night sounds of the swamp. There was the rustling of the wind and an occasional watery disturbance. The cold, damp air seemed to carry sounds well, but Nergal could not tell what was moving in the waters.

Boredom came to the fore again. Nergal twiddled his thumbs for a while, and then he found himself softly singing in orcish:

One orc one elf
This is bad
The orc dies the elf is glad

Two orcs one elf
Is better for sure
One orc kills the other a lure

Three orcs one elf
Is the best of all
The elf dies and no orcs fall

"Nergal?" Melvin asked, prying himself up to a sitting position.

"What?"

"Do you mind?"

"Eh?"

"Could you quit singing?"

"Oh, yes. Me stop now," Nergal said.

Melvin rolled over and went back to sleep. Nergal entertained himself more quietly for the rest of the watch.

In the morning the group moved carefully out of the small hut and made their goodbyes. Rovul explained that they had to keep moving if they hoped to accomplish their goal. They managed to make good time leaving despite the curiosity of their hosts, and soon everyone was piled into the ungainly shell, floating through the swamp far from the little village.

Occasionally the group would stop and Melvin would climb one of the twisted trees that spotted the area. Towards the end of the day, Melvin clambered up one such tree, and suddenly he became excited.

"What is that?" demanded Melvin, pointing forward.

Nergal looked from his spot in the shell but he saw nothing. Roktan climbed up the tree after Melvin. He peered for long moments and then seemed to spot it.

"Civilization?" he offered uncertainly.

CHAPTER 26

The Tower

The tower, constructed of solid gray stones, stood out clearly against the hillside. Nergal could see tall, thin arrow slits in the walls in the light of late afternoon. As the air began to cool down, insects started calling to each other in long buzzing calls.

"At last! Real shelter, on solid land!" said Melvin.

"But who does it belong to?" asked Roktan. "Kind of odd, to see such a thing out here all by itself."

"We're going to find out," Melvin answered. They made their way towards the lone tower. The bogs of the swamp were behind them at last, and Melvin's mood was picking up rapidly. Nergal fell behind and Melvin took up the lead as they made their way into the gently forested hillsides towards the lone tower.

As they approached within a few hundred paces, suddenly Melvin came to a stop. The others caught up to him, wondering at his quick change of attitude.

"Why have you stopped? A moment ago you were charging ahead," Roktan said.

Melvin took out the wand. "I just thought, maybe he's in there," he said. The knight held the wand out and let it move, aligning itself with Kantru's direction. The device pointed slightly to the right of the tower before them. Melvin began walking around the tower to his right, and the wand continued to indicate a different direction.

"Okay, he's somewhere beyond," Melvin announced. "It's safe...well, maybe it isn't safe, but he's not in there."

"That makesss me think, maybe he put a trap here," Rovul rasped. "We should be cautious."

"Or bypass it altogether," Roktan said.

Melvin thought it over. Ever since the group had spotted the tower from down in the swamp, he had been eager to arrive. Now he scratched his chin and considered it further.

"There might be supplies inside, and we're almost out of food," Melvin said.

"Food!" Nergal trumpeted. "Me go inside, look for food!"

"Alright, let's all go in. We'll have to be careful, though," Melvin said. He unlimbered his backpack and took his armor out, carefully strapping it back onto his chest. The armor looked worse than Nergal remembered it, with small rashes of rust forming in spots. Nergal realized that Melvin hadn't been stopping to care for the armor as often as he used to. Once Melvin was ready, they moved closer to the structure.

Nergal saw that a low stone building of some kind adjoined the base of the tower. The ground had been built up on the far side of the building so that it sloped up to the roof.

"The ground slopes up to the roof of this," Melvin said.

"It's so the building affords no protection from archers in the tower," Roktan explained. "With the ground like this, you can't hide behind the building for cover."

Only a single massive door was visible. Heavy plates of metal had been hammered onto the surface of the door to protect it. Nergal advanced to the portal and pushed with all his might, but the door did not budge.

Melvin stepped up and grasped a handle, and pulled the door open.

"Odd architecture," Melvin noted as he walked inside. Nergal grunted and followed the knight into the building.

Nergal stopped just inside and let his eyes adjust to the light. They were in a large room with four beds against the walls. Each bed had a locker at its foot. There was a large table and chairs in the far corner. The place seemed to be a living quarters of some sort. There was another door, presumably opening into the tower, on the far side of the room.

"Ah, glorious! Real beds for us!" Melvin cried.

"For you," Rovul corrected, eyeing the human beds as he slithered about the chamber.

"Oh yes. Sorry about that. But it's almost evening, and we should take advantage of the shelter before we go on," said Melvin.

"Nergal, if you would bar the door," Roktan said, "Then we can check the tower, and if it's empty then I see no reason not to stay here tonight."

Nergal threw the huge timber down into the holders on the inside of the metal-clad door. No one would gain entrance without some considerable effort, he thought. Then he turned and followed Roktan through the other door.

The tower base formed a semi-circular chamber, with a wooden door facing them. Stairs led down on the right and up on the left. The room had only a couple of worn tables and chairs. There were pegs and alcoves on the walls, covered with spider webs.

When everyone was in the room, Nergal tried the door. As soon as it opened, he noticed a wonderful scent on the air.

"Food!" Nergal exclaimed. He peered into the room, and saw that it was a stocked larder. Meat hung from one wall, and he saw bread and beans on a table inside. The half-orc marched happily inside, and began to scavenge for a meal.

"Someone must live here. There is meat," Roktan observed.

"Mmmm, food," Nergal agreed. He grabbed a huge piece of meat from one of the hooks and bit into it eagerly.

"Wait. It's not ours," Melvin objected weakly. The knight's eyes betrayed his words, as he stared at the glorious food. Nergal ignored him, and tore another chunk of salted meat off the haunch.

"Hrm, perhaps we can leave payment here," said Roktan.

"No! We must search the tower and find the owners first," Melvin said.

Roktan looked to Rovul for help, but the snake-prince simply shrugged and pointed to his serpentine underside. "The boar..." was all he had to say. Roktan would not get any help from this quarter.

"Very well. Nergal, bring that food and come with us, in case we need you."

Nergal grunted and followed after, paying little attention to anything but the food before him. Everyone moved up the stairs to the second level of the tower. The second level was one large room, filled with heavy oak shelving that held hundreds of books.

"Amazing!" Melvin said. He began to flit about, reveling in the unexpected library. Nergal found a chair and finished his meat.

"I can't read this language," Roktan said, examining a book he had taken from the shelves.

"There are many different languages here," Melvin told him. "Some of this is Imperial script, but there is also old Jagartan and even some Karpol."

"I cannot read human ssscript," Rovul said.

Nergal got up to take a look for himself. "Looks like ants smashed inside," he noted, peering over Roktan's shoulder at the intricate black symbols.

"Yes it does! And about as readable," Roktan chuckled. "Let's leave this to Melvin and check out the rest of the tower."

Nergal agreed and he accompanied Roktan and Rovul up the stairs. The highest room of the tower was the smallest, and it formed a simple archer's nest with benches and arrow slits. They took this in quickly and headed back down the stairs, to check the cellar.

"It's dark down there," Roktan said. The warrior took a torch out of his backpack and began to light it with flint and steel. Nergal moved down a few more stairs and waited for him. When the torch was lit, they continued down. They came to a dusty chamber, the smell of water thick on the cool air. In the center of the room, a low stone wall surrounded a cistern full of clear, cool water.

"Just a cistern," said Roktan.

"What dis?" Nergal asked, pointing towards an iron door set in the wall. Its surface was ancient and rusted, but it still fit perfectly into the stones set around its edges.

Rovul slithered up beside the half-orc. "That is a most unusual door," he said. "There are no handles on it..."

Nergal and the snake-prince attempted to push the door open, but it solidly resisted all their efforts. Roktan retrieved Melvin from the library and he came down to take a look at the mysterious portal.

"Whatever is behind that door, it must be important," he said. "Treasure? Armory? I wonder what it could be."

"We could make some kind of a battering ram," suggested Roktan.

"I don't know if it's worth the time," Melvin said. "Right now, what could be more important than catching Kantru?"

"Ssso we should leave?" asked Rovul.

"Well, we have tarried too long," Melvin said. "The daylight is almost gone."

"Let me guess, you want to stay the night here," Roktan said.

"Well..."

"And read more of the books," Roktan continued.

"Now that you mention it..."

Roktan sighed. "Very well. At least there is food, and the barracks will be warmer than the ground outside."

"Let usss hope that the true owner doesss not arrive," Rovul said. "We might have sssome explaining to do."

Nergal nodded vigorously, thinking of all the food he had consumed from the larder.

"We could leave some gold behind," said Melvin. "That is, if we didn't give all we had to the Gooshlan."

"I have some small amount," said Roktan.

"I also have sssome," added Rovul. "But now I grow tired, and it's late."

"I have a bad feeling about that door," Melvin said.

"As do I," Roktan agreed. "The front door is strong, and couldn't be opened without waking us up. Therefore I suggest we take our watches at the stair over the cistern, so that if someone, or something, should emerge from the iron door while we sleep, we won't be caught by surprise."

"I take watch," Nergal offered, thinking about the larder. It was mere steps away from the top of the stairs, and there was a door between that and the barracks.

Nergal eat much good food, he thought.

"Okay, you take the first watch, then," Melvin said. The others nodded and moved into the barracks. "I'll be in later," Melvin told them. "I want to take a closer look at some of those books in the library."

Nergal turned and tramped back to the stair. He selected a spot about three steps down from the top, just slightly along the curve of the passage, and sat down. At first he was comfortable, since his legs needed rest from the march up from the bogs. Soon, though, the stone started to bite into his back, and so he rotated so that he could lay flat across one of the stone steps. The stairway grew very dark as the sun set, and so Nergal felt comfortably hidden by the darkness.

"If someone come up stairs, they trip on Nergal," the half-orc reasoned to himself quietly, "So okay if I take nap." He closed his eyes and relaxed on his narrow perch.

At some point much later, Nergal opened his eyes. He blinked several times, uncertain where he was. He lay near the top of a stone stair, but instead of the darkness he remembered, there was a soft light emanating from below. Nergal peered down towards the cistern, his heart beating hard in his chest.

From the door, he thought. Nergal scrabbled for his mace, his hand finding instead the hilt of the large two bladed sword of the lizard king. He gently came up onto his feet on the steps. There was no sound from below.

He brandished the weapon before him and advanced silently. He could only hear his own breathing and the shifting of his armor. The half-orc came to the end of the stairs and peered around the corner towards the iron door. Somehow the portal had opened, and the way beyond was illuminated.

Nergal stepped closer to the opened door. He saw now that it was the frame of the portal itself that was glowing. He walked right up to the edge of the door and looked through. The light from the frame showed that the far side was another cistern room that looked just like the one he was in. He stepped carefully through the door. An odd sensation caused the long hair on Nergal's neck to stand up, and the half-orc crouched in anticipation of an attack.

As soon as Nergal had moved through the door, the strange glow flickered out. Nergal froze, listening for threats in the darkness. Slowly his eyes adjusted. A feeble light poured down a stone stairway leading back up at the other side of the room. He turned and examined the door that he had made his way through. Somehow it had closed, the rusted iron blocking his way back seamlessly. Nergal pushed against it and searched for a handle on this side, but he found nothing.

He turned and realized that the room he was in was an exact duplicate of the one he had come from. For a moment he was uncertain; had he simply been dreaming? Perhaps he was in the same room, and he had imagined the rest.

Nergal could see from the faint light coming down the stone stairway that the cistern here was half full of clear water. He decided that he had been dreaming. He would simply make his way up and check on the others briefly, and then resume his position at the stairwell.

Nergal moved carefully up the stone stairway. The dust was thick here, and it seemed that no one had walked this way for quite some time. Now he became uncertain again. Shouldn't the steps be free of dust at the spot he had been sitting just moments ago?

At the top of the stairs a wooden door adjoined the tower wall. The half-orc slowly opened the wooden door and looked through into the barracks beyond.

Even though the room looked very much the same as the barracks that he was familiar with, Nergal's friends were not sleeping here.

"Mel-veen?" called Nergal. There was no answer. He walked through the barracks and opened the outer door. It was dark outside, and a cool wind blew over the bluff.

"Mel-veen!" he called out into the darkness. Once again, nothing. Where were his friends?

Nergal decided to investigate the rest of the rooms in the tower. He made his way quietly up the stairs and into the library room. At first glance the room seemed an exact duplicate of the one he was familiar with. Then he saw that something was very different.

Sitting just ahead at a reading table with two lit candles, a man sat calmly as if expecting Nergal. The stranger was thin and older looking, with a long beard of fine gray hair. The man wore a dark robe. He held himself with an air of authority and confidence.

"An orc…" the stranger whispered to himself, examining Nergal. A look of concern crossed the man's face.

Nergal approached the table and stood for a moment, uncertain what to do. He looked down at his arms and saw the dried blood, which made his appearance even more intimidating than usual. Why didn't the thin man run?

"Greetings. Can you understand me?" the man asked. He stood up slowly, and then Nergal saw that the robe was the ornate and cryptic robe of a wizard. It was richly decorated in nitid emblems that bent the feeble light in odd patterns.

"Yes," Nergal nodded.

"Who are you, then?" the man asked simply. It seemed that the wizard was sizing Nergal up, looking him over from head to toe.

"Nergal," the orc said. "Am being adven-choo-rer."

"An adventurer?"

Nergal nodded enthusiastically.

"And what kind of an adventure were you on last?"

"We kill evil wizard."

"Oh, that's very interesting. What kind of a wizard? Besides evil, I mean."

Nergal thought about this for a moment. Weren't all wizards alike? Then he remembered the monsters.

"Wizard make monsters," Nergal explained. "Big monsters, dey eat people."

"Hrmm, a Summoner, perhaps." The man laughed at some private joke. "Then it's good that you are a strong fighter, to put down what he brings up, yes?"

Nergal nodded, slightly confused about some of the other's words. "Strong," he echoed, having at least understood that.

"What is that strange crust that covers you, friend?" he asked.

"Eh?"

"That covering," said the wizard, pointing to the dried blood on Nergal's arms.

The half-orc shrugged. "Is protection. From sword, spear, fire," he tried to explain.

"And from fire?" the old man became thoughtful. "That explains why I got you," he said cryptically. "I can offer you much, Nergal. I can take you back to your home, and there may be more rewards as well. But I must task you with something, first."

"Eh?"

"There is a drake that I need to slay. It is most…fortunate for me that you've arrived. I need someone to help me kill it. Together, you and I may destroy this creature, which has something that I need. There will be other things too, weapons and gold, which you may want. Once I have what I need, I'll open the door for you so you can go back."

"Take Nergal back now. Friends need help," Nergal growled. He advanced a step on the small wizard, but the man did not react with fear as the half-orc expected.

"I cannot, not until we have destroyed the drake."

Nergal blinked. Was this clever one trying to fool him?

"No trust wizard. Take Nergal back," he said, but his doubt showed in his voice. He was uncertain.

The small man smiled thinly and spread his hands. "Alas, I cannot. I need the item from the drake to effect your return."

Nergal was silent.

"Allow me to tell you more. I'm Varanius. Please, sit down."

Nergal found his way to a chair at the table. He sniffed around briefly, scanning for food, but couldn't detect any.

"The drake is held in the Palace of Twin Spires as a guardian of the treasure room. I'll take care of the guards at the gate, and distract the others while you make your way into the treasure room and defeat the drake. I would do this myself, of course, but the drake has certain…properties which make it resistant to my powers."

Nergal blinked. The old man certainly seemed to have this all planned out.

"You have quick smarts," Nergal observed.

"Oh, I have been planning this for some time. Of course I needed an accomplice. Fate has provided one for me, it seems," the sorcerer smiled slyly. "You will help me, won't you? That is the only way I can get you back to your friends."

Nergal scowled. "I kill…dray-eek. Then you take Nergal back?"

"Yes."

"You being promising?"

"Yes. You don't know what a drake is, do you?" asked the man in sudden insight.

Nergal shook his head.

"A drake is a kind of...big swamp lizard. You do know what a swamp lizard is?"

Nergal nodded. "Lizard," he said, to prove his understanding.

"Yes, it's a big lizard, with wings like a bat. And it breathes fire," he finished.

Nergal looked skeptical. Perhaps the wizard was making fun of him?

"Yes, I can see that you realize the magnitude of this task. It is a very dangerous creature. But I know that you are its equal. I can feel your power," the old man assured him.

"The king is off on a long campaign against Lorinthia. There are only a few palace guards left behind, eunuchs who watch his wives and treasure. We'll travel immediately to the eastern bridge. Once in the palace, we will split up—"

"Eat first. Then kill," Nergal interrupted.

"Of course," said the sorcerer.

Half an hour later, after Nergal had dined on an enormous amount of dried meat and cheese, the sorcerer led Nergal to the barracks. The old man had provisions already prepared, and he handed the bulk of these to Nergal to carry. It seemed strange that the wizard had everything ready ahead of time, but Nergal had always thought that the ways of sorcerers were strange and inexplicable.

The two made their way out of the tower. Nergal noticed that the landscape bore striking similarities to the tower where he had been with his friends.

"Where friends go?" asked Nergal, looking out over the rocky terrain. "Nergal walk through door, now dey gone?"

"Your friends are still there, Nergal. It is you who have traveled to this place. And you will travel back with my help, but only after the drake is destroyed!"

The pair walked down the adjoining valley to the south. Nergal carried the strange man's heavy provisions without complaint, although he was impatient to kill the drake. He already missed Melvin and the others, and he feared that they would leave the tower once they discovered he was gone.

Soon Nergal spotted stone spires in the distance. He wondered if the fortresslike structure was where the sorcerer was leading him. They came to a gorge with trees clinging to the steep sides most of the way down to a small stream at the bottom. The old man led Nergal along the side of the ravine until they came to a road and a large stone span bridging the river.

"The eastern bridge," explained the old man. "We're close now. We'll have to stick to the trees once on the other side, so that we're not seen."

Nergal simply nodded. This old wizard had the smarts, and Nergal was content to follow his lead for the time being.

The pair moved across the bridge rapidly. Nergal got the impression that their quick walk was the fastest the old man could manage. No one seemed to be about, though, and they made it to the other side without incident. Then the man led Nergal off the road and through a lightly wooded area, until they came to the edge of a huge clearing. Nergal could see from the stumps sticking out of the ground at regular intervals that the forest had been cut back to this point.

"Quiet now," instructed the elder one. Nergal nodded. He moved carefully behind the man, and they approached in the shadow of one of the trees at the edge of the cleared land.

Across the open grass Nergal saw a fortress of stone. The same spires he had spotted earlier rose from behind a formidable looking wall. The place nestled up against a rocky outcropping, and a huge gate stood at the entrance where the road from the eastern bridge met the wall. Nergal could see several armed men at the gate and a few others walking the walls.

"Is city?" Nergal asked.

"No city, just the palace," the old man told him. "As I said earlier, the king is gone and there are not many guards. Now I'll take care of them," he said.

The sorcerer began to speak in a low, urgent voice. Nergal listened to him speak but the words made no sense. The half-orc suspected that the old man was casting a spell. He stood alert, ready for anything to happen.

The old man finished, turning to Nergal.

"It is safe to approach now," he said.

"Guards?"

"They're asleep now."

"You magic dem to sleep?"

"Yes. Quickly, we must make our way through the gate."

The odd looking pair moved across the open ground before the gate. Nergal saw that the soldiers ahead were indeed asleep, and no others looked over the walls to note the intruder's presence. They came up directly to the gate, next to the sleeping men.

"You may need this," said the old man quietly, pointing out the shield of a sleeping soldier.

"Eh?"

"When the drake breathes fire on you, hide behind the shield," the old wizard instructed him.

"Oh," Nergal said. He grabbed the shield and slipped his left arm into it with some difficulty. The strap was sized for a smaller arm, and Nergal could only get his hand through it. He held the strap clumsily in his fist. It seemed like a very light shield to the half-orc, but at least it was metal and would not catch on fire.

The old man raised his staff and began to incant. Nergal watched nervously, waiting for the magic to be over. The gate began to rise with heavy clanking sounds. Nergal leaped back, ready for an attack, but there was no one behind the rising barrier. When the gate was completely open, the old man lowered his device and turned to look at Nergal.

"The way is clear for us, now," he said. "Remember the plan?"

Nergal looked at him blankly.

"You kill the drake. There are other guards I must distract!" the man told him intensely.

"Yes," Nergal agreed, nodding. "Kill swamp lizard with wings," he said, to show the man that he remembered. It all seemed a little farfetched to Nergal, the idea of a swamp lizard with wings that could breathe fire.

"Remember, in the center of the palace," said Varanius.

"Center of place," Nergal echoed.

"Palace. Center of the palace," the man repeated. "If you get lost, just search for the big lizard."

Nergal nodded. The two moved through the gate.

The courtyard beyond was lush and spectacular. Giant plants grew within round red pots, and massive white columns ringed the perimeter of the area. Two large fountains ran, their sparkling water coming from sculptures of a muscular armored man and a beautiful robed woman. Tall stone buildings loomed ahead and to both sides within the wall. Bright red banners flew from pennants above, but Nergal saw no other guards.

There were three large arched exits to the left and right. Straight ahead, a pair of ornate double doors led further towards the central palace.

"Luck to you," the wizard said, and then rapidly walked along a paved road around a fountain, leaving through the exit to Nergal's left.

Nergal moved out through the small courtyard. He looked at the large potted plants arrayed about the area, and luxurious carved furniture in the center. He hunkered low and bounded to the far side, next to the double doors. The doors were locked, but it took only a few seconds to pry the metal handles with his Slith spear until the showy lock failed.

He pushed one of the doors open, and stepped inside, looking for the swamp lizard. He saw a large room, supported by ornate pillars and filled with giant pillows. There were several doorways to other areas of the palace.

There was a scream to his right. Nergal looked and saw that a handful of gaudily clad women were cowering in the corner of the room.

"Where dray-eek?" demanded the half-orc.

Screams were his only reply. Somehow these human women seemed less resilient than Dalwen. Several of them fainted. Only two found the strength to stand and run from him. It struck Nergal that this must be a human breeding area. Oftentimes the orc chieftains would keep several of the most desirable females in a breeding chamber. But some sort of famine must have befallen this palace, as the human women were all skinny and smooth skinned, with hair only on their heads, like Dalwen. Hardly prime breeding material, Nergal thought.

The half-orc shrugged and turned his back on them, and wandered through one of the doorways. Suddenly there was an unmistakable odor. Somewhere juicy flesh was roasting over a fire. Food! Nergal turned immediately in the direction of this new discovery. All thoughts of drakes and wizards were banished from Nergal's mind as saliva began to flow into his mouth.

"Mmmmm. Good eating!" Nergal promised himself, picking up his pace a little. He moved down a marble-floored corridor with a large tapestry at its far end. Nergal noticed briefly that the hanging depicted a roast boar before darting through a doorway on his right, following his nostrils.

A man in an odd white and red outfit turned from a large table and cried out at Nergal's arrival. The man held a ridiculously small knife towards the half-orc. Nergal strode forward, ignoring the puny man and his weapon, instead locking onto the platters of cooked meat sitting on the table. A girl walked into the room from the far side, saw Nergal, and screamed. Both the man and the girl retreated out the far side as Nergal began to consume the bounty he had discovered.

Nergal looked around idly as he feasted, and saw that there were large roasting pits and cooking areas along the side of the room. He walked over and grabbed a drumstick. He almost decided to drop the shield so he could hold food in both hands, but thought better of it. He would eat with one hand…just in case.

The impromptu meal was interrupted by a small serving boy, who walked calmly into the kitchen from another door to deposit a food tray. The child seemed to be daydreaming, and didn't even notice the huge orc warrior feeding nearby. Nergal whirled on the intruder, and snatched him up by the scruff of his tunic.

The boy cried out in alarm, and flailed his arms and legs for a moment, easily suspended by Nergal's right arm. Then he seemed to calm down.

"I—I—I'm not afraid of you," stuttered the lad, putting up a brave front.

"Where dray-eek?" demanded Nergal in a low growl, shaking the tiny waif.

"Ah! Uh, the what?"

"Dray-eek. In center of place," demanded Nergal.

"Oh! The treasure room, with the drake?"

"Yes. You show me," Nergal demanded, dropping the young man back onto his feet. Nergal nudged him with the shield, and the boy started uncertainly forward. The half-orc didn't see fit to draw his sword, but instead grabbed another drumstick to gnaw on.

"This way…." he said.

The serving boy led Nergal out of the kitchen and down two ornate halls decorated with tapestries of gardens and human women. Large plants grew from pottery vases in every corner. They turned through a large meeting hall with more chairs than Nergal could count, and headed across another corridor that bent and twisted. Finally the boy came to a halt in front of two large double doors.

"Here it is," the serving boy said.

"Good, you run away now," Nergal instructed the boy. The young lad took several steps back, but before leaving the room, he turned and looked at Nergal.

"Are you an orcish raider?" asked the boy in open curiosity. "Are—are you going to kill us all?"

"Just Dray-eek," Nergal told him. "Then I go back."

"Zakaraban will cook you like a goose," declared the boy, then he turned and ran out before Nergal could retaliate.

Nergal forgot about the child and regarded the ornate doors before him. They were gilded in solid gold and seemed even more ridiculously decorated than the ones in the outer palace. There were two ivory handles, and the way didn't seem barred.

He grasped one of the handles and pulled one of the great doors open. Beyond was a large vaulted room covered in blue tile, with a large pool of water in the center. It was quiet, and no one seemed to be inside.

Being quiet, thought Nergal. He carefully traipsed into the room, looking for any sign of danger. Nergal held the shield ready in one hand and the strange two bladed sword in the other.

The tiles were slippery with moisture, and Nergal made his way gingerly around the pool of water. There were two archways leading out of the room, and Nergal moved towards the first arch.

The room beyond was a wreck of damaged wood, marble, and pottery. It looked like this room had once been decorated to the level of grandeur exhibited by the rest of the palace, until it had been destroyed. Huge pillars supported a tall vaulted ceiling, as high as the ceiling back in the City of Spires. A glitter caught Nergal's eye, and he stopped in awe. Thirty paces away, beyond a tall archway, he could see piles of gold and silver littering the floor. Chests, busts, armor, weapons, all manner of treasure lay strewn about.

Then Nergal saw the winged lizard bearing down on him.

CHAPTER 27

A Hoard of Trouble

The thing stood easily three times as tall as the biggest swamp lizard Nergal had ever seen. Instead of a mottled black or brown, its scales were the brightest red and yellow, scintillating rhythmically as the beast approached. A puff of flame emerged from the creature's many-toothed maw as it opened and closed, as if in anticipation of a meal.

It took a second for Nergal to realize that he was that meal, and then he dived behind a pillar. Dagger-long claws scraped over the marble floor where he had stood, but the sinuous neck already had the monster's head lined back up on Nergal's new position.

As the mouth opened, Nergal ducked behind an overturned table of marble.

A wall of flame bore down on his meagerly fortified position. Nergal ducked under the shield and closed his eyes. A wave of heat flowed over him, burning his back despite his protection. Some substance flowed under the gap between the table and the floor, and Nergal realized as he crouched there that it was liquid gold, melted by the blast of flame.

Then something more pressing grabbed his attention. He was on fire. His long mane and hairy flanks still smoked. He howled and ran, fanning the flames, heading for the exit that led to the bathhouse.

The drake darted forward with startling speed and threw a claw at Nergal as he tried to make his retreat. Nergal swerved and threw his shield at the thing. His next glance back revealed that the drake remained in pursuit, scrambling rapidly after him. The half-orc sprinted onto the tiles of the adjoining room without slowing down.

Nergal leaped over the shallow water, and fell into the pool with a resounding splash. He tumbled forward in the water, disoriented for a moment, then regained his footing. Now he turned to face the giant lizard again, freshly anointed with the cool water.

The creature bellowed and hesitated, puffing foul sulphurous gases from its heaving nostrils. Then it screeched again, opening its mouth wide and sending searing jets of flame down onto the pool. Nergal ducked almost completely underwater, staggering back to the pool's far edge. He waited for the flame's light to die off, but when it didn't he had to come up for breath anyway.

Now the surface of the pool was on fire. Nergal saw that pools of the thing's saliva had been scattered about and continued to burn on the water and the tiled floor around the pool. The drake itself seemed to be drawing in a huge lungful of air, as if it might try to burn Nergal again.

Nergal slogged forward in the pool and grabbed his sword with both hands. The monster raised its claw to swipe at him, so Nergal thrust his sword into the strike, impaling the drake's appendage with the weapon. The creature screamed out and flipped its claw back, ripping the sword from Nergal's grip and sending it hurtling end over end.

The half-orc took the opportunity to leave the pool. He darted around his enemy and ran back towards the treasure room, drawing his spear from his back. Droplets of water sprayed about as he darted left and then right, searching for a spot to turn and fight. He found no cover but there was a long kite shield on the ground, its strap side facing up. Nergal turned and crouched just in time to avoid having his head snapped off in the drake's slavering jaws.

Seeing that the drake was so near, he ignored the shield and drew back his spear. The monster screamed again and its mouth opened, already spraying fire. Nergal stepped closer to the beast, trying to slip in under its chin to avoid the flame. He ducked his face under his left arm and threw the spear at the creature's face with all the strength in his right.

Nergal felt the pain return to his upper back, where there was no blood covering to protect him. He screamed at the drake in rage, falling onto the ground. All he could do was slap at the flames and writhe in agony.

When Nergal finally extinguished the flames and the pain subsided to a terrible sting across his back, he looked up and saw that the drake lay dead, half of the Slith spear buried in its brain beyond the messy ruin of an eyeball.

Nergal struggled to his feet, still racked by pain. He stumbled up to the corpse of the monster and gave it a swift kick in the mouth. His foot caught the lip of the drake, and a drop of incendiary saliva leaked out, causing a puff of flame. Nergal yelped and fell backwards onto a pile of gold.

"Swamp lizard that breath fire," he said in wonderment. "Nergal seen everything."

He rolled forward off the gold, grimacing as several gold pieces stuck to the raw flesh on his neck above the scale armor. Nergal pried one off and winced in pain.

The half-orc staggered around for a moment, uncertain what to do. As his battle ardor faded, the pain seemed to get worse.

"This stupid wizard's fault," Nergal growled.

Nergal looked at one pile for a moment and grabbed two bright swords from the collection of weapons. Then he ambled over to the next mound and discarded one sword, trading it for another larger one from the new area. He slowly realized that there were too many swords to hold easily.

The half-orc clambered about and located a chest full of gold. He grabbed a couple of handfuls of coins and threw them into his backpack, then upended the chest to empty it out.

"Too much treasure. Be taking smarts to figure it all out," Nergal told himself in frustration. He was not in a good mood despite the treasure. The discomfort in his back rose again, distracting him from the golconda. The raw burns caused a constant agonizing flow of pain.

Suddenly Nergal was aware of others in the room.

"The drake has been slain! Find them!" someone called out.

Nergal saw the four guards just before the closest one spotted him.

"You there! Hold! Throw down your weapons!" commanded the guard.

Nergal stood his ground, holding the scavenged short sword in his left hand and an oversized bastard sword in his right. The pain in his back had put him into a foul mood, and he simply bared his teeth in response, growling like an angry lion. He paced forward, closing the distance between himself and the soldiers, completely fearless.

The front man realized his plight and concern crossed his face. He backed up, raising his sword.

"Uh, need some help here…"

Nergal batted the man's sword aside with the shorter weapon and beheaded his enemy with the other.

He was upon the next without hesitation. The man parried two blows and then slipped on a pile of gold, falling back. Nergal stuck the short sword down into him and left it there, turning to face the other two with his huge bastard sword.

The two men facing Nergal realized they were outmatched. They backed up side by side with their defenses ready.

Nergal advanced to just outside their range and launched a long, looping swipe with his longer sword. A gauntleted hand fell to the floor, severed, releasing its hold on the man's weapon. Its owner turned and bolted, a spray of blood accentuating the sweep of his wounded arm. The other man turned and fled almost simultaneously. Nergal pursued them only a few paces, then moaned as the pain from his neck ignited anew from the movement.

There was a rustle of coins from behind Nergal. He turned and saw that the man he had stabbed was still alive. He walked slowly towards the downed opponent. The man had drawn the short sword out of his side. It lay next to him, dripping blood over the gold.

"Wait!" gasped the soldier. He shifted feebly, clearly in a great deal of pain. "Spare me, and I'll tell you how to heal that," he said, flopping his arm up towards Nergal.

"Heal?"

"Those wounds on your back," the soldier said. "Let me live, and I'll help you."

Nergal considered this for a moment, and as he paused his adrenaline mask of the pain in his back started to subside again. It was a tempting offer.

"Nergal let you live," he said. "No tricking!"

"No trick. The captain, Gaurus, that you killed over there, has a flask of healing elixir on his belt."

"Eh?"

"The captain over there. Get the flask on his belt. Drink it." Blood seeped from between the wounded man's fingers as he breathed. "And, I pray, leave some for me as well."

Nergal narrowed his eyes in suspicion, but he walked over to the fallen man and looked. There were two flasks attached to his belt, and the half-orc retrieved one.

Nergal stood back in front of the wounded man. He took the cork out of the flask and sniffed gingerly.

"Magic water heal Nergal?" he asked.

"Yes. It will heal both of us," the man urged.

Nergal thrust the flask out. "You drink first," he commanded.

The soldier eagerly grabbed the flask and took a long draught. Then he held it back out for Nergal. As the half-orc watched, some color returned to the wounded man's face. The man relaxed, letting his head rest back against the remnants of a giant vase buried in the gold.

Nergal watched a few moments longer, and then he took a slight sip of the drink. It tasted sweet like the juice of a fruit, and Nergal didn't find anything amiss. He dared another sip while watching the man.

"Thank you," the soldier said. "I won't bother you, take whatever you want."

"Nergal just want go home, see friends again," he said, and then he drank the rest of the liquid. Now he felt truly better, and an odd tingling sensation began across his burned back.

"You aren't going to steal the gold?" asked the man.

Nergal shrugged. "Take some stuff," he said. "Is good swords and maces. Be needing good weapons."

The half-orc went and grabbed the second flask from the captain's headless corpse and drank it down.

Nergal looked at his huge sword appreciatively, feeling its balance and power. He then began to walk about, picking up other weapons. He grabbed three more swords and put them into his belt, which fell to pieces under the load.

Nergal shrugged and kicked around until he found another belt, a strong wide sash of bright green serpent scales. He tucked the swords back in, and grabbed several more weapons, holding them in his arms. He had at least seven more swords, maces, and an axe when he saw something out of the corner of his eye.

The old wizard was cautiously entering the far side of the great chamber, staring at the drake's body.

Nergal slowly walked back to the wounded man.

"Play dead now. Wizard coming," he said softly, and turned to approach the mage.

"Fantastic! And you look only slightly singed!" the wizard said as he caught sight of the orcish warrior.

Nergal's eyes narrowed, but he said nothing. The old man's eyes swept the floor, and came to rest on a particularly large jeweled chest. The man smiled and moved over to it as quickly as his advanced years would allow.

"You take Nergal back now!" Nergal growled.

The sorcerer hardly looked up from his kneeling position over the iron chest. He opened the chest and rubbed his hands together, clearly pleased at the shiny baubles within. Nergal paid them no attention.

"You not be taking Nergal back now, Nergal be killing you," he said.

"I have opened the iron door. You may go back now," the wizard replied absentmindedly, looking at a large tome he had lifted from the chest.

"How get through door?"

The sorcerer looked up. "Travel back to the Tower of…to the tower, and you will be able to get back to your friends," he said impatiently.

Nergal stood uncertainly. Was the wizard lying to him?

"Abala shuzala, karamandoo!" exclaimed the wizard, waving his hand wildly in the air. "There, the iron door is open! Go! Hurry!"

Nergal's eyes became large for a moment, and then he lumbered off, gaining speed. He ran through the palace grounds, back the way he had come.

"Better not be fooling," he mumbled under his breath.

CHAPTER 28

Orc Bearing Gifts

Nergal staggered forward to the foot of the stairs, then released the load. Weapons fell to the floor in an explosion of noise. The cacophony echoed back at Nergal in the tight confines of the cistern room. He winced at the sound but he was pleased that the burning in his arms immediately began to subside.

"Nergal! What was that noise?" Melvin demanded, hopping down the stairs. "What's all this?" he asked, indicating the pile of loot.

"Kill dray-eek. Bring back good stuff."

"A drake? All by yourself? Where is it?" But already Melvin's eyes left Nergal and began to examine the many items the half-orc had discarded. "Amazing! Some of this is very, very valuable!"

Melvin kneeled and grabbed one of the swords. Roktan and Rovul were moving down the stair and staring at the cache of weapons themselves.

"You must've opened the iron door," Rovul said. "Isss that where thisss came from?"

Roktan noticed Nergal's new anointment of blood. He pointed.

"The drake's blood?"

"And guards," Nergal said.

"Nergal's going to be completely covered in it. This could be a great advantage. He's going to end up nearly indestructible."

Melvin looked up from a sword he was holding and glanced at Nergal.

"I'm just glad he's on our side," he said. "Is it uncomfortable, Nergal?"

Nergal shrugged. "Is fine."

It felt kind of like the times he got covered in mud and let it dry in the sun. Once used to it, there was little irritation.

Rovul took up one of the throwing axes that Nergal had carried back. "Thisss isss a fine weapon, Nergal."

Nergal picked out the other one, and handed it to the snake-prince. "Is yours, for time you save Nergal, by throwing axe."

Melvin blinked. "Rovul can throw axes?"

Nergal looked at Melvin and Roktan, and held his hands out over the trove. "Pick," he told them.

"Did you take one?" asked Melvin.

Nergal slapped his new belt with both hands, and an instant later he held two large maces.

"Good maces," he asserted. "Dey no talk, either."

Melvin nodded and smiled.

"The belt isss rather tastelesss, though," hissed Rovul, looking at the sash of green serpent scales.

"Eh?" Nergal grunted. "Belt not good eating, is for holding maces."

"Never mind," Rovul said.

Nergal replaced the weapons in his belt and sat down on the stone stair.

Melvin muttered to himself oddly, waving his hand over the sword he had first picked up. He repeated himself, saying something that Nergal couldn't understand.

"What are you doing?" asked Roktan, looking at Melvin.

"I'm trying to detect dweomers on these items," Melvin said.

"I didn't know you could do that."

"Yessss, isss Melvin of Elniboné also a mage?" added Rovul.

"I dabble," Melvin said, a little defensively. "Hey, I didn't know you could throw axes! Now give me a few minutes, this is difficult, and I can't remember all the words."

Roktan shrugged and looked at Nergal and Rovul. The half-orc didn't seem shocked at all, but the snake-prince seemed as interested as he. To Nergal, Melvin had always known an amazing amount of things, and it came as no surprise that the knight also knew something about magic.

Roktan examined various pieces when Melvin wasn't mumbling over them, and he selected a sword in a long black scabbard and put it over his back.

"Two swords are better than one, I suspect," he said, winking to Nergal. "Thank you for the gift."

Nergal nodded enthusiastically. In the meantime, Rovul had slithered over to examine the iron door, once again closed and dark.

"The drake wasss through here?" he asked. "How did you force the door, Nergal? I would like to sssee thisss creature."

"Door closed now. Wizard opened it, but it shut now."

Melvin looked up at this. "I sense there is more to this story than I suspected. What wizard are you talking about?"

"Wizard who opened door. Wizard say kill drake, take Nergal back," Nergal said.

"And he gave you all these weapons?" asked Roktan.

"Nergal take weapons from place...place...pa-la-ce."

"Palace? Uh, let's start at the beginning," Melvin said.

Slowly, agonizingly, Nergal's comrades extracted the whole story from the half-orc. They all believed it, since the proof of Nergal's new belt and weapons was self-evident, not to mention the new blood patterns sprayed onto his skin.

"So if this is the same tower, maybe there is a bridge and a palace close to us, too," said Melvin.

"Perhaps that is where Kantru headed," said Roktan. "Let's go find out."

Everyone stood up, ready to go search for the palace Nergal had described.

"I think this one is the only one that isn't magical," Melvin said, holding up a curved saber, "but it's worth a lot of money. That's real gold and silver on the hilt."

"We need the real weapons more than the money," Roktan said. Everyone agreed with him, so Melvin chose another good longsword similar to Wormstringer at his belt, and strapped it on the opposite side of his hip. He started to discard the ornate saber on the steps, then thought better of it.

"We could leave this as payment for the food we ate," Melvin said, his face lighting up with the idea. "I wonder where the owner is, though. The food was fairly fresh when we arrived."

Nergal stomped up the stair behind his friends, feeling happy to be back. On the way out of the tower, he resolved to check for any food the others might have left behind. He came up behind Melvin, who was setting the sword in the larder. He was happy to see that there was still good meat hanging in the small room.

"Mrm, good eating," Nergal mumbled, taking some meat down from a hook.

Melvin looked at Nergal oddly for a moment, and the half-orc was afraid that he would complain about Nergal's thievery. Then the knight's eyes bulged, and he called the others urgently.

"There's fresh meat in here!" he said, his voice rising with excitement.

"Yes, you saw it yesterday," Roktan said.

"No! I mean there is more meat in here now than last night! The bread has been replenished, as well!"

Everyone stood and stared at the food for a moment.

"The owners came back last night to restock the larder, and we didn't see them? They didn't see us?" Roktan asked.

"It seems unlikely," Melvin said.

Rovul moved up and his tongue flickered in the dim light of the small chamber. He examined the stores of food, and moved back into the outer room.

"I sssmell no one elsss," the snake prince told them. After another moment, he seemed to get an idea and continued.

"Thisss tower has a library in it, and there isss a room that fillsss with food every night. I believe we have found a wizardsss tower."

Melvin snapped his fingers. "Of course! The room is enchanted. It fills itself with food every night!"

Nergal's brows furrowed. "Magic do dat?"

"Yes, it's possible," Melvin asserted. "In the City of Spires, the king has a fountain in the courtyard that fills eternally. Yet no well feeds it. It is one of the greatest works of the court wizards who serve him."

Nergal looked at the food he held, amazed. The food would never end. Nergal could eat endlessly, sleep it off, and return for more food in the morning.

"Nergal remember dis place," he vowed, grabbing fresh food in each hand.

The group moved out with Nergal in the lead. The half-orc showed them the path that he had taken with the wizard, heading towards the palace. As Nergal tramped along, he began to feel that something was wrong. At first he couldn't put his finger on it, but as they moved closer he realized what it was.

"No towers," Nergal said.

"Should there be other towers?" asked Melvin.

Nergal nodded. He pointed over the tops of the trees ahead. "Should be towers dere."

They came to the great gorge, an open crack in the earth hundreds of paces wide. Trees still spotted the sides of the chasm, but the bridge was absent.

"Bridge here," Nergal said.

"Where?" asked Melvin.

"Was here," Nergal corrected, looking left and right. "Don't see it."

"Maybe we aren't at the right spot," suggested Roktan.

Nergal shook his head. "Right spot," he insisted.

"Could it be destroyed so completely?" asked Roktan.

"I think maybe…it hasn't been built yet," Melvin said. "There is some odd magic at work here."

"How could it not be…" Roktan said.

"The portal Nergal describes could have brought him to another plane of existence altogether, or it could have taken him to a different time in our own," explained Melvin.

"Then what are we to do?" asked the snake-prince.

"Let's just follow the wand, then, and keep with our real goal," Roktan suggested.

"Yesss, the wizard," agreed Rovul. "I hope he isss not acrosss the gorge."

Melvin took out the wand and sought the sorcerer's bearing. The wand pointed north, at an angle slightly towards the rift.

"I can't tell. But going left will bring us closer," Melvin said.

They walked for several days, wending their way through the hills after Kantru. They camped cautiously, always aware of the danger that the wizard might be nearby, ready to strike.

In the afternoon of the fourth day, they came to some kind of village in lightly forested land. As Nergal approached he saw that the huts had been torched, as they were scorched black, with no roofs left on the structures.

"Kantru?" Melvin voiced everyone's suspicions.

"Yesss," Rovul hissed. He readied his magical axes, testing the air with his tongue.

They moved forward in silence, entering the primitive village. There were no signs of life, only the remains of small huts and buildings. The clay shells of the burnt out huts were left standing, reduced to empty husks. Nergal sniffed the air, but there was only the scent of burnt vegetation.

"I wonder what happened," Rovul rasped.

"They did something to anger him," Melvin said. "I wouldn't care to guess what…the wand is pointing this way."

They walked through the eerily silent village ruins. Nergal peered into the destroyed huts but he saw no one. As they came out the other side of the houses, he saw that a wide, slow moving river blocked their way. A crude pier had been erected, extending thirty paces out into the water.

"Did he go across the river, perhaps?" asked Roktan.

"Down the river makes more sense," Melvin announced. "The wand points across the river at an angle, but the river probably turns."

"He must have taken the last boat," Roktan said. The warrior looked along the pier and the bank, searching for watercraft.

"All sunk," corrected Nergal, and pointed out over the edge of the little pier. Barely visible under the sluggishly moving water, several dark shapes rested in the mud below them.

"Holed by Kantru?" speculated Melvin. "We'll have to find another."

"Where?" asked Rovul.

"Doubtless there will be a few tucked away along the bank," Roktan said.

The group broke in half. Nergal and Melvin went to search in one direction down the bank while Roktan and Rovul searched the other. Melvin and Nergal moved around a group of trees next to a steep, muddy bank, and came to a well worn path along the river. They walked cautiously for a minute or two, until a dark structure took shape ahead, seen through the filter of dozens of trees.

"Some sort of boathouse, maybe," Melvin said. "We should check and see if there is anything we can use."

As they approached Nergal could see that the structure was dark and decrepit. The pair made their way around the entire thing, finding only a tiny one person canoe on the river's edge.

"I suppose we should look inside, too," Melvin said.

Nergal shrugged. He walked back around to the front and stepped onto the wooden entryway.

Nergal felt the boards give slightly under his feet, causing the walkway to moan and creak as he approached the door. Drawing a mace out into his right hand, Nergal nudged the weathered door with his weapon. The door flexed and fell open. The odor of wood rot assailed his nose.

Melvin followed Nergal in, carefully testing the floor as he went. Nergal's weight and that of his armor caused the floor to creak as he moved, but it held him. Nergal moved into the back of the empty structure, and he was about ready to leave when he saw an old trap door.

Nergal moved over and gently lifted the door up. Wooden planks suspended between two support beams formed crude steps down into the cellar. The half-orc sniffed again, thinking that he caught the scent of death, ever so faintly, in his nostrils.

He stepped down the planks, causing more creaking noises. Halfway down, he looked at the chamber below.

A huge chest sat in the middle of the darkened cellar.

"Found something," he said, surprise in his voice.

"What was that, Nergal?" called Melvin from above.

Nergal made his way down the rest of the rotting wooden steps. One of them started to give under his weight, so he simply hopped down over the last three to the dirt floor.

"Did you say you found something, Nergal?" Melvin called from above, the sound of his voice muffled by the timbers.

"Down in bottom," Nergal called back up, and then walked over to the huge chest. It stood up to his waist. The stout looking wood of its sides showed no signs of the rot the structure did. Its broad wooden planks were held fast with wide metal bands. A large metal lock was attached to the front, but the mechanism was not closed.

"Is unlocked," Nergal said to himself.

Nergal reached out to open the chest.

"WAIT!" Melvin shouted from the top of the stairs. Nergal flinched and turned to look up at the knight.

"What?"

"That looks kind of odd doesn't it? What if there's a trap in it?" demanded Melvin, walking down the old steps.

"Look out," Nergal called just as Melvin stepped on the weak board, crashed through it and fell flat onto the dark soil of the cellar floor. His armor rattled and the visor snapped shut loudly. Nergal could hear a curse from within the helmet.

"Mel-veen should be careful," Nergal told him.

"Uhhh. Ow. Just a minute," the knight grunted, trying to recover his wits. Nergal waited impatiently, leaning against the huge chest as he watched Melvin fumble around.

Nergal noticed that his hand stuck fast to the surface of the chest.

"Mel-veen," Nergal said, becoming alarmed at his stuck hand. He pulled harder, but his hand wouldn't budge. "Help!" he called in growing alarm.

"Uh? What?" Melvin stumbled over, trying to gather himself.

Nergal watched in horror as the wood of the top of the chest deformed into a flexible bulbous-ended appendage.

"Eh?" he grunted.

The arm slammed out and struck Nergal in the face. Caught completely by surprise, the half-orc fell back to the ground, twisting at the end to dangle by his stuck hand. Nergal groaned feebly, water coming to his eyes from the smarting in his clubbed nose.

"By the powers!" exclaimed Melvin, stepping back and drawing Wormstringer. "I'll save you, Nergal!" he yelled.

The knight tried to slash down onto the thing attacking Nergal, but the ceiling was lower than he realized. His overhead slash became stuck in the wood above. The chest deformed further, beginning to ooze over Nergal's left side.

"Argh!" yelped Melvin. Without further hesitation, the knight drew his second sword, from the drake hoard, and stabbed it deep into the monster above Nergal's prone form.

The result was immediate. The creature reversed its attack, forming another pseudopod and clubbing Melvin across the legs. Melvin fell to the ground, grunting in pain and surprise. He lost his grip on the sword, but he rolled away towards the rotting stair boards.

The amorphous mass now held almost no likeness to a chest. The surface of its body had lost the texture and color of wood, and now it oscillated in hues of an angry reddish brown. Once again it bore down on Nergal. The half-orc, still stunned, struggled weakly to regain control of his left arm. The monster was strong, though. It rolled over most of Nergal's body and pressed down, squeezing the life from him.

Then Nergal realized that Rovul was there too. The snake-prince dangled from above, his snake body still mostly in the level above the trap door. With an axe in each hand, he attacked. Rovul sunk both weapons neatly into the monster.

Nergal felt the pressure abate somewhat. His arm still stuck to the thing, but at least he could breathe now. He gasped for air and moaned again, blinking the tears from his eyes. As if it had a mind of its own, his right hand began groping lazily for one of the maces in his belt.

"Smash thing dead," Nergal mumbled, taking hold of a weapon.

Nergal smashed down mercilessly with the mace, hitting the creature where it had molded itself over his hand. The blow was muted by the thing's flesh but Nergal still managed to hurt his own hand with the strike. He howled and struck again, aiming lower this time. The creature flowed back, abandoning its grip on the half-orc's hand.

Meanwhile Melvin had managed to dislodge his favorite sword from the ceiling. He slashed again, this time avoiding wedging his weapon in the cramped quarters. The creature was sliced completely in half, and it rumbled oddly as if in distress. The three stepped back to watch it writhe in its death throes.

"Thanks Rovul! I don't know why you're here but I'm glad you came when you did."

"We found a sssuitable vessel and came back to get you," explained the snake-prince.

Rovul helped Melvin up out of the cellar, but Nergal had begun to dig around in the loose soil, favoring his throbbing hand. He found a few bones buried here and there, and began to search in earnest.

"Be up soon," Nergal told Rovul, who nodded and accompanied Melvin outside. Five minutes later Nergal emerged from the rickety structure. He showed them a rusty dagger he had uncovered.

"Maybe magic dagger?" asked Nergal.

Melvin frowned and stared at the weapon. It seemed nothing but a lump of rust. It was barely recognizable as a human tool at all.

"I don't think that one is enchanted, Nergal," Melvin stated flatly. "Probably best to just throw it aside."

Nergal nodded. He tossed the dagger away and then brought out his other finds.

"Found money," he said, displaying the coins in his palm.

"Ugh! All that work for a few coppers? Ugh!" Melvin groaned. "Well, wash your hands in the river, at least!"

Nergal nodded and walked over to wash his hands off. He was not surprised to see that the blood remained. He removed the dirt and filth from his new coins as well, then they were ready to return to the boat that Roktan and Rovul had discovered.

The two led Melvin and Nergal back to the other side of the primitive pier. Nergal saw that they had found a long narrow riverboat with two old oars in it. Everyone except Rovul clambered into the boat. Nergal grabbed the side firmly with his hands, feeling uncertain in the lazily churning river.

Rovul gracefully slid into the water without making a sound. He appeared at the back of the boat and started to push. The long riverboat moved rapidly downstream, Rovul's long waving body churning water behind it.

CHAPTER 29

Bay of Brislava

From the top of a hill overlooking the river, the group examined a collection of shacks and huts in the distance. The buildings nestled around a small harbor like mushrooms growing in the hole of a pulled tree. Melvin's wand had indicated that Kantru was in this direction, either in the town or the open sea beyond.

"It doesn't look like any settlement of Chu Kutall," Roktan observed. "I don't see any town guards or patrols. It looks like refugees from a shipwreck, or a pirate hideout."

"Pirates would probably just kill Kantru," Melvin said. "Don't they hate Chu Kutall as much as the Kingdom does?"

"He can defend himself well," Rovul noted.

Roktan nodded. "Or he may have some way of disguising himself, magical or otherwise. If he died, would the wand still work?"

"I don't think so," Melvin said. "But I wouldn't mind finding his grave instead of him. We can always hope."

"Well, these buildings aren't huts like the savages use," Roktan said. "Let's simply go in and see who these people are. If they give us any trouble, then we'll set Nergal on them!"

Nergal couldn't tell from Roktan's tone if he was being serious or not. He guessed that the warrior was half joking, and returned Roktan's grim smile.

"Give us trouble, dey be sorry."

No one disagreed with the sentiments and they headed closer to the settlement. There was only one hill between the travelers and their destination when Melvin turned and regarded Nergal.

"Hrm, we have a problem," he said.

"What's that?" asked Roktan.

"Look at Nergal. We're used to this blood covering of his, but to any ordinary townsfolk, or for that matter, even to bandits and brigands, he looks like…well, he looks frightening. With him looking like that, we might not have a chance to parley."

Nergal looked down at the blood covering his arms. The dark, crusty material on his skin made him look like a rotting corpse.

"Fright-ing," Nergal echoed.

Roktan shrugged. He took off his black robe and handed it to Nergal. "Can you fit in this?" he asked.

Nergal tried the robe on. His massive shoulders stretched the robe tight, and his hands protruded way out of the sleeves, which were too short for him.

"He'll attract even more attention looking like that," Roktan said.

"Hrm, next idea," Melvin said.

Roktan took his robe back from Nergal.

"If thisss issssssome kind of pirate haven, then hisssssstrength may be ressspected," Rovul said.

"Yes. We could leave him back at first, but if we get into trouble, then we'll need him at our side."

"Go when dark," Nergal suggested. The half-orc had some experience with this, and he had learned that some people couldn't discern his heritage if the light was bad. "Maybe dark hide blood."

Melvin and Roktan exchanged glances. Melvin sighed.

"It's the best idea we have," said Melvin. "Good thinking, Nergal," he added.

Nergal nodded. He stood a little straighter, pleased that one as smart as Melvin had liked his plan.

"Stay in the back of the group," Roktan said. The Jagartan warrior turned to Rovul. "Are there any Slith pirates?"

Rovul nodded. "Many Slith who fall into disfavor or are exiled become piratesss. I should not attract too much attention if this doesss indeed turn out to be a pirate ssstronghold."

They settled down to await nightfall. Nergal napped lightly and awakened shortly after sunset. When it was time to go he took up the rear of the group and tried to slink along to avoid notice.

No alarm call came as they approached the town. The buildings and streets seemed deserted.

"Did Kantru clear it out like the last village?" Melvin asked.

Nergal examined the dwellings. Unlike the last village, no damage seemed visible anywhere, other than a general state of disarray. He sniffed deeply, but he couldn't smell burning wood or flesh.

The group came to a wide stone street and turned to follow it between rows of shacks. They followed the main street of cracked stone that meandered through the tiny town. Still no one else was visible, and Nergal felt rather odd as they made their way through the town. Then sounds of loud talking and laughing reached his ears.

"I daresay we approach the local tavern," announced Melvin. "Shall we?"

Roktan shrugged. "Why not? If we're going to get into trouble, we might as well go all the way."

Nergal followed them up to a larger building. He saw light streaming from the cracks and joints of the place, and Nergal smelled tobacco and ale. Once again Melvin was correct, he thought. Melvin had the quick smarts, to be sure.

Roktan and Melvin visibly mustered their courage. Roktan pulled up his belt slightly and Melvin adjusted his helm. Then Roktan opened the door and they walked right in.

The inside looked much like the taverns that Nergal had seen in the human cities of Woldwall and Raktan. The air swirled thick with smoke and the smells of drunk people. The group elicited a large number of odd stares, but for the most part the conversations kept going at a loud volume. They made their way to the bar through a throng of smelly men dressed in all varieties of clothing.

"Uh, four drinks, whatever you have," Melvin ordered.

The bartender didn't look happy at the new business, but he produced the requested flagons of ale and held up two fingers to indicate some sort of payment.

"I'm sorry to bother you with questions," Melvin said as he pushed a single silver coin towards the bartender, "But what is this place?"

"Bay of Brislava," the man said. He didn't offer any elucidations.

"Do you know of any ship captains that we might have a word with?"

The man stared at Melvin for a moment with a frown on his face. Then he pointed to the corner of the crowded room, scooped up the coin and returned to his business.

"Thank you," Melvin called back, even though the man had already turned away.

"I think perhaps you're too courteous for this group," Roktan told Melvin. "Let me try next." Roktan took the lead and they walked back into the corner that the barman had indicated.

One large table dominated the corner and five rough looking men sat, busy drinking and dicing with bones. They looked up to regard Roktan as he arrived.

"We seek a captain," Roktan said.

At first there was no answer. The men scowled at Roktan, and then looked over Melvin beside him.

"I know one of you is a captain. Who?" Roktan said, unperturbed.

"I am. What of it?" snapped the man on the far side.

"We need to purchase passage on a ship," Roktan announced. "We're good fighters and we've sailed before."

"You're strangers. I don't take on strangers."

"We can pay as well as provide extra protection," Roktan argued.

"No ships here for you. Leave this place," the surly captain commanded.

Melvin leaned onto the table. "You don't understand. We're on a critical life or death mission against the forces of Chu Kutall! We must have passage on a ship," the knight pleaded.

"How do you intend to do that, given that I've just said no, there's only two of you, and a whole camp full of us?" demanded the captain.

The snickers of sailors who were listening came from the nearby tables.

"Uh, actually there's four of us, sir," Melvin muttered, but his voice was lost in the throng.

From the rear of the group, Nergal came forward. There were mutterings in the back of the room as the half-orc came into the full light of the lantern in the corner. The huge muscles of his arms rippled beneath the crusty black coating of blood that covered him.

"Be showing you how," Nergal growled. Suddenly the half-orc's foot overturned the table towards the captain, and a mace was in each of his hands. Nergal hopped to the side and sent his weapons swinging.

Melvin looked briefly at Roktan, who simply shrugged and drew his weapon.

Nergal worked his way quickly around the table, smashing skulls and kicking downed men in the ribs. When he made it all the way around the table he saw that his three companions had set up a perimeter in the corner, fighting for their lives against an angry mob of sailors. Nergal dashed past his friends and out into the morass of people. Quickly a void opened around him as he swung his weapons wildly. Two or three knives were turned from his flesh by the blood armor, and Nergal smashed a rapier aside and kicked its owner in the groin in the next several instants.

Then he was on a rampage, working his way through the bar and taking no prisoners. Nergal roared, swung, kicked, and bit his way along for what seemed like quite a while.

He chased a fleeing man to a wall, intent on smiting his opponent before he could get away. Someone kicked him in the back, adding to his momentum at just the right moment. Nergal hurtled through the side of the building in an explosion of shattered wood and debris. He shook his head and tried to look around.

Nergal saw blades raised against him out on the dark street. He growled and regained his feet, still attacking with both maces. Some resisted him and others fled, but Nergal kept killing, his weapons describing deadly arcs about him as he advanced.

A couple of times someone managed to nick him in spots where the blood armor didn't protect. He ignored these small wounds, one on the back of his leg, another on his ear, and continued to fight. Two more opponents went down, and Nergal moved free of the corpses around him. He was beginning to learn, if he stood in the same spot the bodies built up, but if he kept moving, the debris were left conveniently behind.

Soon the only opponents remaining were a handful of wiser (or more sober) men who had sabers and rapiers. These ones knew enough to keep their distance. They surrounded him like a pack of wolves, retreating as necessary but always harrowing him, waiting for the huge hulk to tire as he continued swinging wildly.

Nergal saw this and decided to direct his attacks more shrewdly. He picked one man and charged him, ignoring the threat of the man's small blade. The man saw the charge and darted to Nergal's left, but the half-orc was ready. He had a mace trailing to either side, and his long arm swept out and clipped the man on the side of the head, bringing him down easily. At least one of the other men turned and ran. Nergal selected the next target and rushed up.

This man was wearing heavy armor. Nergal realized it was Melvin.

"Nergal, stop!" cried Melvin. "Nergal!"

Nergal stopped and looked around. The last two men broke and ran, headed for a nearby alley.

Nergal paused and looked over to Melvin. It seemed that there were no opponents left for the half-orc to engage. He looked about further, taking stock of the carnage around him. The entire street was strewn with bodies. Roktan and Rovul walked slowly out of the tavern and gawked at the remains.

"Unbelievable! Did you destroy the entire town?" Melvin asked, looking back on the trail of blood and devastation, leading back to the hole in the tavern wall.

"Dey started it," Nergal insisted.

"They were rather rude," Melvin said. "But paying with their lives is a little steep, I think. Well, let's talk about it later. We need to get to a ship and get out of here."

Roktan winked at Nergal as they turned for the docks. He slapped the huge half-orc on the back. "Werlog protect anyone who gets in your way, my friend!" he chuckled. "With that blood on you, we may just have a chance against Kantru! You can hardly be stopped!"

"Careful Roktan, you'll make it go to his head," Melvin said.

Nergal followed the others as he tried to decrypt this last statement. What did his head have to do with anything? The half-orc gave up and looked ahead to the docks.

For such a small community, the docks were well developed. In the darkness of late evening it was hard to tell how many ships were there, but Nergal saw at least three vessels in the water, lit by the dancing light of torches. He thought he spotted at least one guard on the ship nearest them.

Melvin led them up to the first ship. Nergal saw that there was a ramp leading up to the deck, and this area fell under the light of a large torch burning atop a post on the dock. A sailor stepped forward to meet them, a suspicious look on his face.

"Who are you?" he demanded.

"We need this vessel," Melvin said.

"I'm sorry, I can't let anyone—"

Nergal lifted the unfortunate man completely off the ramp. The half-orc growled and propelled the sailor into the air. A splash sounded from below, accompanied by a great deal of thrashing and sputtering.

"Nergal, we should be more diplomatic," Melvin said.

The half-orc stared. "Deeplo-?"

On the deck of the ship a second guard accosted the group.

"Why are you here? Where is Garek?" demanded the guard, drawing his saber.

"We need this ship," Roktan stated harshly. Nergal and Roktan started for the guard.

"If you would hear us out—" Melvin began, trying to head off the confrontation.

"Alarum!" called the guard. "To arms!"

Melvin sighed and freed his own weapon, preparing for another melee. "That's two in one night," he muttered.

Nergal moved forward along the deck towards a torch at the prow. He met an armed man in the low light, blocked the swing of a club with his forearm before it could gain enough momentum to hurt him, and struck back with a mace. The man fell and Nergal dropped him over the side.

There weren't many more guards on the ship. It seemed that most of the men had been back in the town where the previous fight took place. He heard the sounds of a brief fight as Roktan, Melvin and Rovul engaged a small group of men as they emerged from below the deck. Nergal doubled back to the center of the ship to rejoin his friends.

Nergal saw Roktan pull the ramp back up onto the deck.

"Melvin went below," Rovul said, coming up beside him.

"Other men cannot get us," Nergal hoped out loud. Then the harsh snap of crossbow strings sounded in the air, and the sound of a bolt hitting the guard rail startled him.

Nergal crouched low and then hit the deck as he realized what was happening. Beside him, Rovul fell to the deck as well.

Suddenly Nergal realized that the snake-prince was writhing in pain. Blood flowed out onto the deck, looking like a pool of inky blackness in the light of the stars.

"Rovul!" Nergal yelled, bounding over to his friend and peering down, trying to see where the wound was.

Roktan extinguished the torches on the deck, trying to avoid drawing more bolts.

"Where hurt?" Nergal asked, but the only answer was an unrecognizable hiss. Whatever the damage it certainly wasn't a clean kill, as the Slith continued to writhe and spit.

Roktan came over and joined them farther from the side. "Where is he hurt?"

Nergal looked again, trying to figure out where the blood was coming from. His eyes had adjusted slightly, and he could see Rovul cradling his head in his arms. Blood ran down his arms and the side of his neck.

"In head, I think," Nergal said, his voice grim.

"Damn! If only there was light, but if we relight the torch they'll hit us!"

Rovul tried to say something again, but the sound was unrecognizable. The snake-prince clasped Nergal on the shoulder, and then patted him. Rovul did the same to Roktan.

"He's hanging on okay for now," Roktan said. "The best thing we could do for him is take care of our attackers."

At that point Melvin reappeared, coming up from below decks.

"Ware the docks," called Roktan. "Crossbows!"

Melvin crawled over to them.

"Rovul is hurt, hit in the head I think," Roktan told him. "We will have to look at him as soon as we can. Did you secure the rest of the ship?"

"Well, five of them have agreed to join us," Melvin said.

"Five?"

"Yes. They appear to be men such as we encountered at the Temple, or a similar tribe. It seems that the pirates had er, recruited them to service. In any case they seem to have no problems with sailing with us!"

Roktan shook his head. "What are we going to do?"

"We're going ahead. We have no other choice."

Nergal clapped Roktan on the back. "Nergal sail good. Roktan no worry."

"You don't even know which way the open sea is," Roktan challenged.

Nergal shrugged. "Move ship forward, it find sea."

"Five rowers and this puny square sail isn't enough to make it across the harbor," Roktan said. "We're total idiots! We need more slaves."

Melvin crossed his arms. "I have no stomach for enslaving anyone."

"We wouldn't be enslaving them. They are already enslaved. Besides, when we get where we're going, we can set them free. That's better than leaving them here, isn't it?"

Melvin pondered that for a moment. Before he could reply Roktan continued.

"It's our only hope. Maybe Nergal has already killed most of the pirates anyway. We'll go back and find where they keep the slaves, and free them."

They heard shouting in the distance as the privateers still struggled with the sudden events shoved upon them. Nergal saw Melvin nod in the dim light.

"What about the other ships? I'll stay here and care for Rovul, while you two go see if the other ships have any slaves on them. Just free them from their chains, and tell them you have a ship they can take out of here!"

"We'll be back," Roktan said. He tapped Rovul's circular shield lightly. "Can we borrow this?"

Rovul gave no answer but handed the shield over to Roktan. Melvin helped Rovul down below decks where they could have light without exposure to attack. Roktan and Nergal crept towards the side of the ship, next to the ramp.

"Okay Nergal. This is going to be dangerous. You have the best protection, though. Take Rovul's shield, too," he directed, handing Nergal the circular spiked shield in the darkness. "I'm going to push the ramp back out, then you charge down it and draw their fire. You turn right at the bottom and I'll run behind you and turn left."

Nergal nodded, tightly gripping a mace in his right hand and securing his left in the shield strap.

Roktan called "Go!" and pushed the ramp forward. The noise was unmistakable, and Nergal knew that anyone out on the dock was surely alerted. Nevertheless he gripped the shield tightly and came to his feet. Holding the protection high to cover his face, he ran down the ramp. He realized he had forgotten which direction Roktan told him to turn at the bottom, so he hopped off and darted to the right, hoping for the best.

The snap of a crossbow sounded again. Nergal felt a bolt strike his Slith armor, but the magic of the garment was strong, diverting the bolt from one of its shiny black scales. At first Nergal ran on blindly, but then he spotted a form crouching beside a stack of nearby barrels. As soon as Nergal altered his course for this opponent, the shadowy figure turned and ran, tossing a crossbow to the planks.

Rather than pursue the man back towards the center of town, Nergal picked up the crossbow and heaved it over the side of the platform into the water. Then he turned and headed back for the ramp to rejoin Roktan.

The warrior trotted up to him as he circled around a torch sconce trying to avoid going through the light.

"Good! You're unhurt?"

"Fine."

"Okay, follow me! We'll hit the next ship."

The two warriors were cautious as they approached the next ramp but no guards called out to challenge them. They moved up onto the deck. There was no apparent resistance.

"Some of them probably heard what happened back at the tavern and went to investigate," Roktan said. He began to move towards a narrow stair leading down. Nergal turned to follow him.

Someone darted out from behind a rail and slashed a blade at Nergal. He reacted by raising his arm, and the weapon struck the limb but could not harm it through its black covering. Nergal readied himself to strike back. Roktan was slightly quicker, lunging in from the side and dispatching the sailor with his sword.

"A sneaky one," commented Roktan. "I'll free the slaves." The Jagartan warrior turned and went down the steps.

Nergal nodded and paced about the deck, keeping an eye out for more guards. The half-orc listened carefully but he only heard the water slapping against the hull. Nergal began to run out of patience. He had just resolved to go looking below when Roktan emerged onto the gloomy deck leading a column of slaves.

Nergal blinked in the darkness...something was very wrong about these slaves...

"Change of plan," Roktan called to him softly. "We're leaving them in their chains."

Nergal approached cautiously, the hairs on his neck standing up. The slaves stood only as high as Roktan's belly, and they moved oddly. Nergal growled deep in his throat. They were kobolds!

The short little humanoids peered back at Nergal with their tiny, closely set eyes. Even though they appeared calm the half-orc could glimpse the ends of their sharp teeth protruding from their mouths.

"Better not make trouble," Nergal snarled at them, his hand convulsively squeezing the handle of his mace. The leading slaves cowered, momentarily halting the column.

"It's alright, Nergal. They won't dare rebel against the likes of Garhand the Cannibal!"

"Eh?"

"Our captain, Garhand the Cannibal," Roktan said loudly again. He yanked the chain savagely. "Get moving!"

Nergal glowered at the creatures as they shuffled by. He was familiar with the kobolds, as the race was fairly common in his homeland of Nod. Orcs often enslaved or simply slaughtered the Kobolds. To Nergal's race they were contemptible cowards who hardly deserved notice. Apparently humans treated them the same way.

Nergal followed the end of the column, watching closely. The weak creatures probably wouldn't attack unless they somehow broke free and charged in overwhelming numbers. They marched along the dock without trouble, and met Melvin back on the original ship.

Roktan started the column moving below decks and stopped to talk with Melvin. Nergal looked for Rovul but he didn't see him.

"Kobolds! Are you insane!" yelled Melvin. The knight hopped up from Rovul's side, putting his hand on the hilt of his sword.

"Quiet down, Melvin," Roktan said in a low voice. "They are cowards that will do the job."

"They are weak little conniving monsters that will turn on us as soon as they get the chance!"

"They won't get the chance. We told them that you're Captain Garhand, a cannibalistic death worshipper who sometimes raids these waters."

"You what?"

"Make some angry noises, slap me around a little," Roktan told him.

"What?"

"C'mon, they're watching," whispered Roktan.

Melvin lightly slapped Roktan across the face.

"You're right, they're going to turn on us, if you don't make it more convincing!" Roktan said. It took Melvin a second to make up his mind.

"Is this all you could get?" screamed Melvin at the top of his lungs. "A bunch of useless, foul-tasting kobolds! Do you know how stringy their meat is?"

"Sorry, Cap'n it was the best we could find," Roktan replied loudly.

"Well, maybe if I cook them longer they'll soften up," Melvin said, rubbing his chin thoughtfully and eyeing the last of the slaves as they marched below decks. The kobolds were clearly worried despite the fact that Nergal doubted all of them could understand Melvin's words.

Nergal and Roktan went below to secure the new rowers. "Don't let me see one of those filthy things above decks again!" screamed Melvin after them.

CHAPTER 30

Back to the Sea

Nergal examined Rovul's powerful serpentine jaw in the bright noon sun of the upper deck. The flesh still looked swollen near the perforation of the snake-prince's dark scales.

"You were right when you said your kind heals well," Melvin observed. "The wound looks bad but it's draining and healing from the inside out."

Nergal watched from a few feet away. The jaw wound had troubled Rovul greatly for a few days, but it was now a week since the fight had taken place, and he was starting to move more easily. The snake-prince still could not talk, though, and the others wondered if the bone would mend properly.

Rovul's tongue obviously had not suffered damage, as it still flickered out on occasion to sample the ocean air.

Roktan spoke up from his position behind the rudder bar. "I hope these are calm seas. I don't think this craft could survive a storm."

"It was our only choice," Melvin said.

"Yes, I suppose…things did not go well at Brislava."

"That was a total disaster. It's because we used brute force instead of our heads, that we ended up fighting the whole town. It's our fault that Rovul is hurt. We should have just figured out a way to hire one of the ships."

"I doubt if we could have offered them enough," Roktan said. "The booty they get from trade ships is probably more than we have. I must get back to the rowers, watch our heading."

Melvin took over and Roktan headed below. Nergal watched Melvin at the rudder and relaxed. Each of the adventurers except for Melvin took turns watching the slaves below to make sure that they kept out of trouble. They were a week out of the Bay of Brislava, and they had no idea how long they would be at sea.

Luckily the kobolds ate less than men and with a skeleton crew, there was plenty of food on board. Nergal ate his fill and more every day, enjoying the time off his feet at last.

The next day, Roktan came up, dragging a kobold with him. He grasped the little creature firmly by its arm, holding it warily. The kobold stared at Melvin through beady eyes. Its face was an angular parody of the humans', although its snout protruded more and the teeth were quite sharp.

"Why is that kobold with you?" Melvin asked.

"This one refuses to row."

"Does he speak common?"

"No. Only four or five of them do," Roktan said. "We need to punish him. If we don't, we'll lose what rowing power we do have soon."

"It's not right. We're monsters to force them to this."

"The others call this one Ur Gammon," Roktan told them. "It means half-hand."

Nergal saw that the creature had only half of its left hand, the rest chopped off in some old accident. The creature stood nervously, restrained by Roktan's powerful arm.

"I still don't feel right about using any creature as a slave," Melvin said. "What do you think, Nergal?"

Nergal thought back to when he was a rower for Chu Kutall. He remembered the smelly hold, the tight cramped benches and the endless labor.

"Nergal glad he not rowing," Nergal said.

Roktan yelled, startling Nergal. He looked to see Roktan clutching his hand and Ur Gammon scurrying away from his grasp.

"He bit me!" Roktan snarled.

Nergal bolted to his feet, already in pursuit of the kobold. Ur Gammon, seeing that there was nowhere else to go, jumped onto a rope and climbed up to a corner of the square sail.

Nergal tugged on the rope and shook it, but he could not dislodge the little creature.

"Now slow down! There's no hurry, he's not going anywhere," Melvin said.

"We need to set an example, and it bit me anyway. I'm going to kill it," Roktan countered. The warrior did not reach for one of his swords, rather he took out his hunting sling and loaded a stone into the leather tab. Blood dripped down from his hand onto the deck but the wound was not slowing Roktan down.

"We could set him adrift in one of the landing boats," Melvin suggested.

"A waste of a good boat!"

Melvin looked to Rovul for help. The snake-prince shrugged and said nothing, still without a voice while his jaw healed.

"Nergal? Shouldn't we show the kobolds some compassion?"

But it was too late. Roktan released his stone and sent it straight into the kobold, which yelped and fell. Ur Gammon hit the rail on the ship's edge, grabbed at it weakly, then fell over the side and down into the waters.

"Nergal think for while," Nergal said, oblivious to the kobold's death. "Say answer to Mel-veen's question later."

Nergal thought on the subject for a minute, but he came to no conclusion. The others dispersed after the incident. Nergal walked up to the rail to contemplate the fate of the kobold further. He was shocked to see the small creature below him, clutching desperately onto a rope that trailed overboard.

Nergal looked back. Roktan had returned below and Melvin manned the rudder. He stared down at the kobold. It clutched the rope and returned the stare. Nergal could not read kobold faces, and he wondered if he was looking at terror or defiance.

· The half-orc reached over and began to slowly haul the rope in. The kobold seemed frightened at first, but it seemed to gain confidence from Nergal's calm.

"Glef dejarg hekton blugg," Nergal said in orcish.

I give you one more chance.

Nergal saw understanding in the kobold's eyes. It nodded.

He led the creature into a storeroom and gave it a strip of dried meat. The creature accepted eagerly, seeming taken aback by the kindness but too hungry to reject it.

"Bregletz, kar yumgar u kropf!"

Eat now, then row or die.

The kobold finished quickly, and then Nergal led it back up onto the top deck. Melvin spotted the two this time, and he gaped, then ran over.

"Is that...?"

"Yes," Nergal responded. "Take him back down, he row now."

"Yes! Thank you, Nergal. Wait for a moment, I'll distract Roktan and you put him back...in a different spot, though, in the back."

Nergal nodded. "In back is clever. Quick smarts," he marveled.

Melvin's plan worked well enough. Roktan was drawn out and Nergal took the kobold back in. He went to the aft of the rowing area and put Ur Gammon in a row that only had two kobolds on an oar. Three of them easily fit on a two man bench.

Nergal chained the kobold and then looked at him one more time.

"Yumgar u kropf!" he growled, and then returned. The adventurers returned to their routine.

The days at sea began to add up and Nergal adopted the same gloomy state of existence he remembered from the journey to Neyala. There was not enough food to occupy his time with eating it, and sleep was the only escape from the boredom which ate at him.

The others seemed quite busy with the operation of the ship, which although small for an oceangoing vessel was still a lot to handle for three adventurers. Sometimes they would call on Nergal's tremendous strength to pull on ropes or to hammer metal rings into different shapes. The half-orc was so tired of doing nothing all day long that he didn't mind the occasional call to work.

One day Nergal was wandering around on deck, seeking any release from boredom when he came upon Melvin in front of the single mast of the ship. Melvin was sitting on the deck with an array of weapons placed around him. Nergal recognized Melvin's sword Wormstringer as well as the magical axes that he had given to Rovul.

"Sulay Virith Natex," Melvin uttered, holding an axe out flat with his left hand. "Sulay Virith Natex."

"Eh?"

"Hello, Nergal," Melvin leaned back against the mast, sighing deeply. "I'm still trying to figure these weapons out."

"Is axe," Nergal offered helpfully.

"Ah, I mean, I'm trying to figure out if there is anything particularly spectacular about it, or if it just hits its mark a little better than most axes."

Nergal grunted in pseudo-understanding.

Melvin took out a weathered looking book and began to study the strange markings inside it. Nergal idly walked up and took up one of the axes that he had retrieved from the drake's hoard.

"Hits mark better," he mumbled to himself, mimicking Melvin's phrase. Nergal flipped the axe end over end, trying to catch it again. He caught the weapon's head in his hand, and tossed it again. Once again he caught the axe's blade instead of its handle.

Nergal grunted in frustration. He walked slowly around the mast and tossed the axe again, carefully timing its spin. Nergal grabbed at the handle, already smiling in victory, but he was foiled again. His hand caught the blade end.

"Mel-veen," Nergal called.

"Uh?"

"Mel-veen."

"What is it Nergal? I'm trying to study here. This is kind of important you know. These weapons might have powers we don't know about."

"End moves to other end."

Melvin looked up. "Huh?"

"Watch Mel-veen," Nergal instructed carefully. "End moves to other end!"

Nergal tossed the axe gently, imparting a slow spin. Nergal's hand reached out to catch the handle, and in a brief almost undetectable flash of reflected sunlight, the axe head appeared on the other side. Nergal's hand closed around the axe head.

"Uh, what, er," Melvin struggled. "Oh, the axe head moves to the other end," Melvin's voice rose. "Ah, so you can't screw up and hit the target with the wrong end!"

Nergal shrugged. "Is good axe."

"I'll go tell Rovul that I figured his axe out!" Melvin walked quickly back, clearly excited.

"Mel-veen very smart," Nergal agreed.

More days went by. Nergal ate his fill, slept long hours, and did his part to maintain the ship and watch the slaves. Sometimes he and Roktan would spar on the deck, trading false blows and running about to keep their wind.

One day Melvin caught Nergal alone by the rudder bar and spoke to him quietly.

"Nergal, I've been meaning to talk with you."

"Mel-veen thinks we bad because hurt kobold," Nergal guessed.

"Sort of. We should think of how we can help them. You know that Dalwen would not approve of our use of them. And she would be right. Do you remember what it was like to be a slave?

"Yes."

"We shouldn't do it to other creatures. Even kobolds. You have to promise me that when we arrive, you'll help me protect them from Roktan. We have to let them go, so that they'll be better off than when we found them."

Nergal shrugged. “Okay,” he said, meaning it. If Melvin thought it best to let the kobolds go, he had no objections. The creatures didn’t interest him either way.

Days went by beyond Nergal’s counting, more than two hand’s fingers and two feet’s toes worth at the least. The half-orc was in the oar chamber glaring at kobolds as they struggled to row when he heard a cry from above that could only mean land.

“Better be keep rowing,” Nergal growled at them, and then moved to take a look.

CHAPTER 31

Riken

"I know that port," Roktan told them. "Helenix. We find ourselves approaching Riken itself."

"This is crazy," Melvin said. "We're going to die in some far-off enemy land, or worse. We may end up slaves, forgotten by the Kingdom."

"You think we should go back?"

No…of course not. It's just crazy, that's all. I should have expected that Kantru would be heading here."

"Where we be?" asked Nergal.

"This is Kantru's homeland," Melvin explained. "We'll have to hunt him in his own home, perhaps."

Nergal nodded. "We kill bad wizard."

"You forget, this is my land too. Kantru's kind has conquered it, but it was originally Jagarta. I know this area as well as he does. And my old personal estate is not far."

"Your estate?"

"I was a second tier citizen of Riken. Master of many slaves. The monk-wizards are the masters of the masters."

"Very well, how do we get to your estate?"

"The harbor is large, we should be able to slip in without causing a disturbance. If we can make it in then we could get horses and ride there in a few days."

Melvin exchanged looks with Nergal.

"We'll come close to land and take a landing boat. The kobolds can have the ship."

"They'll be caught and enslaved anyway."

"Maybe. Or maybe they'll make it. We have no reason to take the ship into harbor. It'll raise suspicion anyway, and you might be noticed."

Rovul slid forward. "I have no illusionsss about getting on a horssse." Rovul's first words since his jaw injury surprised Nergal, but he was glad to hear the snake-prince talk again.

Roktan nodded at this. "Very well, we'll do as you say. But once ashore, you must trust me. I have some loyal servants that we may be able to find. They could help us hide while we locate Kantru."

"Agreed, once we're ashore you take charge," Melvin said.

Roktan veered away from the port, seeking to find another spot to launch the smaller boat. Nergal and Melvin gathered everyone's equipment and some food supplies while Rovul prepared to free the kobolds.

Rovul came to the deck. A couple of particularly bold rowers followed him up, guarding their eyes against the bright sun. The adventurers hoisted their landing boat and lowered it into the water while the anxious kobolds watched and talked amongst themselves.

They abandoned the ship to the slaves. Rovul slipped directly into the water and pushed the boat from behind while the other three rowed. As the boat headed towards the shore, kobolds looked over the rail at them, as if the creatures couldn't believe that they were being let free. Melvin actually waved at them, and smiled.

"We're doing the right thing, Nergal. They have a chance now, at least."

"Actually you might be killing them," Roktan said. "If a Chu Kutall ship comes across them, they might assume the kobolds mutinied and slaughtered the crew. Then they would kill the kobolds to punish them."

Melvin looked crestfallen. "I hope that doesn't happen," was all he said. After a few minutes he seemed to shrug it off and put his mind on the task at hand. They rowed up onto the rocky shore and pulled the boat into dense green vegetation that grew beyond the rocks.

"Very well. Hard to believe we now stand on Riken soil," Melvin said. "I guess the next step is your old home?"

"I had friends there, when I left. If we're not seen by an outside visitor, the authorities would not be notified."

Melvin took out the wand. It pointed inland. "Well he's still in that direction."

Roktan led the group towards the city they had avoided, then as they neared it he directed them straight inland. They came to a road, and began to walk along it away from the city.

Nergal felt the solid earth under his feet again, and struggled to regain his land legs. Once again he found himself surrounded by alien flora and fauna. The trees were fat and round, with branches splitting off in all directions. Colorful birds roosted in rows along the branches. Instead of calling and flitting about as Nergal was used to, the avians sat quietly and stared at the adventurers as they passed.

After only a few hours of marching he complained to the others.

"Feet feel bad," he announced. "Need sit down."

Roktan acceded to the request, and they found a tree to stop under. The stop to rest became a campsite. The next morning they revived their old marching habits and began to travel in earnest.

After three days Roktan led them carefully off the trail. They traveled a short distance through the woods, coming around a rise and finding a gully near a small stream.

Roktan indicated a clearing and they formed a makeshift camp.

"We're close to the estate now," Roktan told them. "I'll go ahead and see who's there. I need to make sure there are no outsiders who will note our arrival." Roktan paused for a moment, as if considering whether to go on. "For all I know, there may be entirely new people there. That would be bad, but there might be new owners, with all new slaves."

Nergal and the others accepted this explanation and agreed to wait. The half-orc first slept, then ate, and then began to walk idly around the camp as he awaited Roktan's return. The hours wore by and it became clear to Nergal that the wait could extend longer. He decided to take a look around a little further from the camp in an attempt to entertain himself.

He moved out through a screen of underbrush and skirted a line of trees, keeping to the shadows by instinct. At first Nergal moved in a relaxed way, meandering through the foliage. As he moved he slowly became aware of other noises around him.

Nergal's thoughts moved back in time to another place, in a woods filled with elves holding nocked arrows, waiting to pick off fleeing orcs after a raid. The woods dwellers were almost invisible when on their home ground, darting from limb to limb and striking from above without warning. Nergal imagined the elves surrounding him and the others, preparing to strike.

Then he saw a bush move slightly along with a rustling sound from beyond. The plant settled. Nergal watched the foliage carefully but nothing else seemed to happen. Was an elf in there?

He turned around and encountered a slim female, regarding him from behind a rapier.

"What are you doing here?" she demanded.

Nergal automatically looked at her ears to see what race she was. He saw that she was human, and relaxed a little.

"Hrm? Er, looking for ess-tate," Nergal grumbled. "Who you?"

"I'm the Lady of Elkenshire," announced the girl proudly, and raised the rapier to point between Nergal's eyes to accentuate her statement. Nergal realized as he examined his assailant more carefully that she was younger than he had first estimated. Barely an adult at all, in fact.

"Dat no hurt me," Nergal said.

"I assure you, I'm quite skilled with the sword," she replied. "I could kill you instantly, so make no move, you monster!"

Nergal heard a quaver in the girl's voice. He realized that he was quite repulsive looking, covered in the dried blood armor. The human was afraid.

"You poke me, it no hurt," Nergal persisted, holding out his arm. "Is covered in magical stuff."

"You don't have any magic. You are just a—a raider or something."

"Look for wizard," Nergal said. "You go now."

"I'll give the orders here. We're going that way. Now march!"

Nergal shook his head.

"I'm not fooling around!" she threatened, waving her sword briefly.

"Go away."

The girl set her jaw and lightly jabbed Nergal in the arm. The half-orc felt nothing, being protected from the blade by his skin coating. Now his assailant frowned and thrust again to no effect.

"Told you. Be going now," Nergal smiled.

"What—what are you?" she howled.

"Orc."

"You look like…a monster."

Nergal shrugged. "Blood look funny. Come with me, meet Mel-veen."

"Who is that? Another one like you?"

"Mel-veen be having quick smarts. He tell you anything."

"I won't come with you!" she snapped.

"Bye," Nergal said, and turned to leave.

"Wait a minute! I have not released you!"

Nergal ignored her as he walked back to camp. The young woman followed behind, bellowing commands in her most imperious voice. Nergal paid her no heed, and went straight back to Melvin.

The knight met Nergal, sword in hand and ready for action.

"What's the matter?"

"Found girl," Nergal said.

The girl tromped up and regarded Melvin. Nergal saw her start to open her mouth, then she fell silent as Melvin took off his helmet and greeted her.

"Welcome to our camp. I am Melvin of Elniboné," he said, bowing to her.

Apparently this behavior was more to her liking. Or perhaps she thought Melvin was an orc as well until she saw his face. She smiled and lowered her weapon, trying to regain her dignity and her breath at the same time.

"Well met, Melvin. I'm the Lady of Elkenshire. Is this ruffian your…squire?"

Melvin laughed. "Nergal is my friend. He's a mighty warrior," Melvin added as he saw the doubt in her face.

"Well, he is rather large…but there's more to combat prowess than sheer strength!"

"True. You're wise beyond your years. Still, I assure you Nergal possesses many aspects of combat prowess."

Nergal puffed his chest out and smiled. The girl ignored him.

"Why have you come here? These are our lands."

"We're on a mission of tremendous import," Melvin told her. "I'm afraid I cannot tell you more at this time."

"But I demand to know! You must come to Elkenshire."

"Well, Lady, we beg your pardon, but we'll have to detain you for a short time, until our friend Roktan returns."

"Roktan! Roktan of Elkenshire?" she blurted.

"You know of him?" Melvin winced, afraid that he had given away too much.

"He was…he is," the girl seemed flustered, "He used to be the lord of the estate. Until…. he was removed."

"Are you surprised he is back?" Melvin asked.

"Is this a test?" she demanded.

"No. Let's just wait until he returns."

The girl seemed to brighten at that. Then her face contorted in terror.

"Ware! Behind you!" she yelled, whipping her sword back out.

Melvin danced to the side, reaching for his weapon. Nergal looked behind the knight, but he only saw Rovul emerging from the vegetation. Melvin saw the snake-prince and relaxed, greatly relieved.

"He's on our side," Melvin said.

Rovul had frozen at the reaction he elicited, but now he resumed his slither out into the clearing. The girl retreated until Nergal reached out and grabbed her by the arm.

"Release me!" she snapped.

"Cannot go," Nergal said.

"Let me go!"

"Do you promise to wait until Roktan returns?" Melvin asked.

She frowned. "Very well."

Nergal released her arm. Rovul, sensing her fear of him, kept his distance.

"What isss your name?"

"Ah! Uh, I am the Lady of Elkenshire."

"And I am the sssixty-ssseventh heir to the throne of Neyala," Rovul told her. "But my name isss Rovul."

"My name is…Caytha."

"I'm glad to meet you, Caytha."

Rovul's straightforward manner seemed to relax Caytha somewhat. Nergal moved over to a flat rock and sat down next to a pile of firewood they had collected. Melvin and Caytha followed his lead and sat to await Roktan's return.

The hours passed quickly, as Melvin inquired further about the lands surrounding Elkenshire. Caytha seemed to lose her standoffishness when speaking with Melvin, so Nergal just listened. They spoke of the plants and creatures of the woods, and the history of the estate. Nergal picked up that the land had belonged to nobles of Jagarta before Chu Kutall defeated them and enslaved the entire people.

Roktan returned to find them arrayed about the campfire.

"Who is this?" he asked.

"She is the Lady of Elkenshire," Melvin said.

"Hardly the lady of the estate," Roktan snorted. "More likely an errant servant girl."

The young lady's eyes betrayed another hint of fear. She managed to snort again disdainfully, but she said nothing this time.

"What did you find?" Melvin asked.

"Bad news. The estate is very different now. The Lattar family is no longer in charge there."

"But we should be!"

"You are a Lattar?"

"I told you! I'm the rightful Lady of Elkenshire!"

"Back at the estate I saw—"

"Our usurpers, put there by Chu Kutall to ensure that we remain under their control."

Roktan considered this for a moment. Then he asked, "And the Enir?"

"He rules from hiding. How do I know you're really Roktan Lattar?"

Roktan reached into his pouch and brought out a large coin. He flipped it to the girl, who sat and examined it by the fire.

"So you have returned. Everyone thinks you were killed."

"It's safer for me that way."

"Why have you returned?"

"We hunt Kantru, one of Chu Kutall. We hope to slay him. If I can speak to the Enir, it might help us a great deal."

"It can be arranged."

"How long?"

"Two nights, perhaps three."

"Very well then. We will trust you, and wait here."

The girl nodded, a very serious look on her face. "I am the rightful Lady of Elkenshire. I'll do what I can to resist the invaders for Jagarta."

The young girl flitted off with a spring in her step. When she was gone Roktan simply shrugged and sat down with everyone else.

"Does anyone have a problem with trusting her? We could leave at this point and resume our hunt. But there are advantages to be gained by linking up with secret factions in my country who still resist Chu Kutall. I think it's worth the risk."

"I'm willing to trust her. But thank you for asking," Melvin said.

Roktan and Nergal nodded.

"Silly girl. We wait anyway." Nergal added.

The wait was not long. One and a half days later, Caytha returned with two older male scouts dressed in leather. The men were slender, almost elfin, but Nergal thought they could not be more than half elf. They paid him no special notice, instead content to let Caytha do the talking.

"This is Ulek and Nexex. We will take you to meet the Enir now."

The group gathered their equipment and fell in with their new guides. They moved through the forest away from Elkenshire. They traveled for days along seldom-used paths that only the guides could have followed.

Nergal began to wonder if the scouts would lead them to a city in the trees like elves made, but they led the way up a heavily wooded mountainside and stopped at a rocky cliffside with two or three small cave entrances. Ulek beckoned to the group, indicating the first cave opening, and he walked inside. Nergal followed him.

As soon as Nergal entered he realized that it was no ordinary cave. The rough, naturally formed walls quickly became square and smooth within ten paces of the entrance. Alcoves had been carved into the walls on either side. Guards stood in each alcove, crossbows leveled at the newcomers.

Nergal ignored them as Ulek did and followed the scout down the corridor, his friends close behind. They came to a large square chamber filled with men and women. Some of the men were armed and armored but others were robed like merchants or priests. The cave had been transformed to look like the hall of a wealthy merchant or king. Nergal felt smooth marble stones beneath his feet, and saw intricately carved furniture and tapestries.

An old man with short gray hair stepped forward. He looked briefly at Nergal with concern on his face, then his eyes alighted upon Roktan and he smiled.

"I did not know you were still alive," he said.

"I'm honored to see you again, Enir," Roktan replied. "These are fellows of mine, enemies of Chu Kutall. This is Melvin of Elniboné, Rovul, Prince of Neyala, and Nergal of…"

"Nod," Nergal finished for him. Nergal smiled broadly, then clamped his lips down after remembering the effect seeing his teeth had on people.

"So the girl was not telling us tall tales."

"Caytha. Is she the Lady of Elkenshire?" Melvin asked.

"In our eyes she is," the old sage said. "But not officially anymore. The old families were killed or dispersed three generations ago. The new ruling order was given slaves and a higher status as long as they took orders from the warrior monks of Chu Kutall."

"Can we trust this man?" asked a large warrior standing nearby. He walked up boldly to continue his inquiry. "How do we know he is with Jagarta?"

"I recognize him, that's how," the old man said harshly. "He has fought Chu Kutall long and hard, unlike others of us."

That seemed to cow the fighter somewhat. He still wore an angry look on his face as if he resented Roktan's presence.

"What of the others? Surely we cannot let them go, they might give us away to our enemies."

"I speak for them," Roktan said. "They have fought by my side. Who are you?"

The warrior started to answer but the Enir interrupted him. "This is Kel. He is the war leader of our forces, what forces we have anyway."

Roktan bowed his head briefly to Kel but kept talking to the old Enir.

"I have come to claim the Shakkran. I go to do battle with a monk-wizard of Chu Kutall, the one named Kantru."

Silence descended. Nergal could tell these people were impressed by Roktan's statement.

The sage nodded and motioned to a nearby man with his hand. The man nodded and left. "We have heard of Kantru," the Enir said.

"You are taking him seriously?" Kel demanded, his astonishment plain.

The old man nodded. "This one is strong. Experienced. I can feel his power."

"You will bestow the Shakkran based on a feeling? It is the only hope we have of—"

"Silence!" hissed the old man. "If you insist on being this foolish, then you will get what you deserve. You may fight Roktan for the Shakkran."

Kel inflated his chest. Nergal saw anticipation written on every feature of the young warrior.

"Thank you, Enir," was all he said. "It is only right since I have been training to use it for years."

Roktan frowned. "I'm in a hurry. We will fight tonight," he told Kel.

"That is fine with me," Kel said. "Anytime you're ready." He turned and strode away.

"This is Yorenat, he will help you prepare," the Enir told them. "Luck to you, Roktan."

Yorenat bowed to Roktan briefly. "Is there anything that you require?"

Roktan took a long draught from his waterskin. "Show me the place," he said.

"Follow me to the circle," Yorenat told them.

Yorenat moved through a side tunnel and the group followed him. Melvin fell in behind Roktan, eager for information.

"What is this Shakkran? Why must you fight for it?" Melvin demanded.

"The Shakkran," Roktan said. His eyes focused on some point far away. "It is a legendary focus of power. The Shakkran is not just one weapon, many different swords have borne it. The weapon that our priests bless with the power of our god of war is Shakkran. Once per day at midday and once per night at midnight, the priests gather and make obeisance to the war god."

"This weapon is a focus of their power?" asked Melvin, clearly fascinated. "Tell me more."

"At midday and midnight, the wielder of the Shakkran harvests the mana of the priests. He becomes stronger, the weapon becomes more powerful. Long ago, there were many thousands of priests and the wielder of a Shakkran became nearly invincible."

"But Chu Kutall defeated these men?"

"As I said…nearly invincible. When we lost to Chu Kutall, the king left behind him a battlefield strewn with the dead monks…but it was not enough. In the end, their warriors, their wizards, their horrible Shok Nogua…it was all too much. They truly were stronger."

"And so Chu Kutall became your masters?"

"The old temple was destroyed by Chu Kutall, in the war where we were enslaved. That was generations ago. Now the priests of the old ways meet in secret places, new temples that are kept from…our Lords."

"So the Shakkran are still produced, and you want one of them."

"There are not as many priests to the old Jagartan ways as there once were. There is no doubt the Shakkran will be weaker. But I believe it will be enough to destroy Kantru. Maybe even several of his kind."

Melvin was silent. Yorenat led them through an intersection and into another man made tunnel.

Rovul let out a long breath. "Then you must do thisss," he said. "We need that kind of power on our ssside."

"He must be a good fighter. And Kel said he has been training—"

"He has been coddled," interrupted Roktan. "He has not learned as I have, from real combat in real life or death situations. I'll defeat him and then we'll be on our way."

Melvin let his objections drop. They arrived in an underground amphitheater, with steps carved from stone surrounding a central flat area twenty paces wide. A circle was engraved in the floor of the chamber, about five paces in diameter. The stones inside the circle were bright red.

They awaited Kel. A few minutes later he appeared, sword in hand. He walked into the circle on the stones and motioned for Roktan to join him.

Nergal walked away and stood next to the entrance with Melvin and Rovul. He thought that perhaps the old man would tell them when to begin, but Kel simply attacked Roktan as soon as he set foot in the circle.

Roktan met him at the center of the circle, at first simply deflecting Kel's attacks then replying with his own. The men circled each other warily, and to Nergal it did not seem that either had the upper hand. They exchanged long series of blows, each riposte leading to a counter smoothly. It seemed that both men were in superb shape and were familiar with the ways of the Jagartan battle circle. Nergal noticed that the style Roktan had fallen into was circular, causing the two to spiral around as they fought.

Then Roktan changed tactics and charged straight at Kel. The younger warrior retreated to the side, so Roktan continued around him, walking out of the circle and attacking him from the far side. Kel became clearly agitated but he thwarted Roktan's assault. Roktan then skipped up the first few steps of the amphitheater and looked down at Kel, his sword ready.

"What are you doing?" Kel asked angrily, looking up at Roktan.

"You think Kantru will fight you in that little circle, boy?" demanded Roktan. "You think he will fight fair?" Sweat beaded on his forehead, and he stole great breaths between the statements.

"Can he do that?" Kel cried, looking at the priests. None of them made to answer, except for the ancient one.

"He is right," the Enir admonished Kel. "Fight on, if you dare."

Kel stepped out of the circle and pursued Roktan up the stone steps. Roktan turned back on his younger adversary, attacking him with a series of overhead strikes that whipped down from above and then returned in smooth circular motions. Kel warded the blows off, still standing lower than Roktan.

Then Kel tried to counterattack by thrusting at Roktan's belly. The opening was there but Roktan had expected it, Nergal thought. As soon as the thrust came, the older warrior moved his torso aside and then stamped down on Kel's weapon, pinning it to the ground. In the same instant Roktan's own sword was at Kel's throat.

"Surrender to me." Roktan's words were easily heard across the amphitheater.

Kel's jaw clenched in humiliation. Still, he nodded and released his sword.

The sage rose to his feet and ambled towards the fighters.

"The wielder of the Shakkran has been decided," he announced.

Another robed man walked into the center of the fighting ring, holding an object swathed in cloth. Unfolding the covering, he took out a sheathed broadsword and handed it carefully to Roktan.

"Use it well," he told Roktan. "Remember, it makes you powerful, but not invincible. We learned that at the battle of Yuri's pass. And there are less priests now than there once were, so the weapon's power has waned since those days."

"I'll always remember," Roktan said sincerely. He turned to his companions. "Now, we're ready to face Kantru."

CHAPTER 32

Reunion

Although Melvin complained, the barn suited Nergal well enough. Sleeping on the soft hay was a welcome change from the cave floors and ship barracks that he had experienced since becoming an adventurer.

A week had passed since the group had left the secret stronghold of the Enir and his warriors. They traveled through the countryside, avoiding notice. The Enir had arranged for them to stay in various places along their route, with the help of peasants and innkeepers who were sympathetic to the cause of Jagarta.

Having to take a turn on watch was a constant annoyance to Nergal. It seemed that just as he got warm and settled in Roktan jostled him to wakefulness and told him to take the watch. Nergal moved to the edge of the loft where he could see most of the barn.

Nergal considered their situation as he sat in the darkness. It seemed that he had lived an entire lifetime with these new friends. He could hardly remember his life before. He began to think about all the things that had happened to him and his companions. Somewhere along the line his thoughts turned to darker things. In the back of his mind he realized that sooner or later they would be killed. It always happened to those that Nergal knew. Battle was a dangerous thing to participate in even once. Every time they diced with death, there was a chance that death would win. Nergal wondered how long they could go before one of them got killed.

Nergal found that he had managed to thoroughly depress himself. Best not to think too much, he determined. Better to leave such things to those with the quick smarts like Melvin.

Suddenly the hair on his neck rose. Nergal scrambled to his feet, alert to danger. He realized a faint glow was emanating from below the loft, and the air vibrated with some unknown energy. Perhaps Kantru was down below, casting a spell even now!

Nergal decided he would surprise whoever it was that caused the disturbance. His breaths came quickly and his heart pounded as adrenaline hit his system like a hammer. Familiar with this reaction, he smoothly moved to the edge of the loft and dropped down gracefully, his massive legs absorbing the shock of his fall easily.

Nergal had to take a moment to absorb the scene before him. Someone or something had definitely entered the barn. An armed and armored man or woman of some kind. The thing wore a helmet with a thin cross-shaped visor slit, concealing its face. The shimmering being was bathed in a cool blue light, and bore a silver shield and a drawn sword which crackled in blue flame.

Nergal's eyes bulged in shock, and then he cried out. Seizing a mace in one large hand he charged the being that had come to assassinate them.

Nergal swung the mace at the warrior's sword side, hoping to smash the weapon back with the force of his blow. His glowing opponent reacted swiftly. The blue sword sizzled and shifted, striking out and hitting the haft of Nergal's mace above his hand, disarming him neatly. Nergal was so surprised that he stood staring at his enemy and did not attack again even though he had another weapon. The creature froze unmoving in front of him, and did not counter.

"That is not the way, warrior of Nod," the being told him calmly in orcish. "I'm here to return your friend to you."

Nergal blinked. It was very odd to see such a delicate and graceful creature emitting his harsh language.

Meanwhile Melvin had begun to clamber down the ladder. There was a curse and a thud as the knight finally found the earth, but soon he stood at Nergal's side, holding his sword out to confront the stranger.

"Who are you?" asked Melvin. There was no answer, but Nergal noticed a female warrior, floating in thin air flat on her back behind the blue intruder.

When Melvin looked behind the newcomer he cried out, "Dalwen!"

Dalwen glided over to the center of the barn and settled on the ground.

"Alofzin watches over you," the creature crooned, dipping its sword slightly with the announcement. Melvin and Roktan were briefly bathed in the blue light of the creature. Then the being turned to Nergal and Rovul.

"You two are not of a temperament to receive the blessing of Alofzin," the creature stated. "However, I'll bestow it despite this, if you take an oath to protect the priestess with your lives for one year."

"Must promise?" Nergal asked.

"Correct."

"Is promise," Nergal agreed. The strange light covered him as well, and Nergal's eyes bulged as he looked down at his glowing arms. Then he returned to normal, and nothing felt different.

Rovul came forward. "I must refussse. I ssstrive only for Slecktar, and would not lose my armsss," he said.

The being nodded gravely, and then said, "Then you would be wise to seek the boon of Slecktar in the cavern behind the fires."

Without further explanation the creature began to fade out of existence. Nergal squinted as the last vestiges of the thing disappeared.

"Magic," Nergal grumbled. Then he saw that Dalwen stirred, slowly rising to sit on the packed earth.

"Dalwen, I'm so glad to see you!" Melvin cried, coming up and hugging the priestess.

Dalwen smiled and returned Melvin's affections. They even kissed briefly, until Melvin's irrepressible curiosity overcame his desire to be close to Dalwen.

"It's good to see that you're still alive," Dalwen said. "Since you've not returned to the Empire I assume that you still hunt Kantru."

"Yes, we do. Why didn't that creature help us? It seemed very powerful," Melvin asked.

"Alofzin's aid is needed elsewhere," Dalwen said. "Tell me of your travels..."

The priestess cut short as she saw Nergal's new state. "Oh Nergal! What is that stuff?"

"Is blood," Nergal told her. "Ever since ring, blood not come off," he tried to explain, pointing at the ring on his finger.

"It actually turns out to have some history behind it," Melvin began. "The artifact was held by an ancient Slith hero who slew a sea dragon of some sort. It has the effect—"

"I can see its effect," Dalwen interrupted. She had a look of concern on her face. The priestess took Nergal's hand with the ring in her own. She closed her eyes and spoke a few words softly, while moving her hand over Nergal's. Nothing seemed to happen.

"Hmmm. It is powerful," she noted, and tried again. This time there was a warm sensation in Nergal's hand, and he felt the ring slip free as Dalwen quickly tugged it off.

Nergal felt the blood crack and peel on his skin. He brushed his forearm with a hand, and a cascade of shavings sprinkled to the ground. His skin was revealed. He began to thoroughly clean himself, wiping the old blood off with both hands.

Rovul hissed loudly. Heads turned to regard the snake-prince.

"The blood of the sssea dragon isss coming off!" Rovul exclaimed.

Nergal looked down. His hand had brushed along his scale mail, and a bright strip of red was now visible. Nergal rubbed the armor vigorously, peeling off still more of the blood. Unlike the blood on his skin, the black blood of the dragon had been smooth and shiny. It came off slowly, revealing the bright red metal scales beneath. In the center of Nergal's chest, some of the scales were yellow, and they formed a long winding pattern.

"The mark of Slecktar," Rovul observed approvingly.

"Amazing," Melvin smiled. He looked for a moment, then returned to his examination of the ring with Dalwen.

"An inscription," he noted.

"Ternakridon," she read slowly. "The key to the ring's power."

"But some kinds of blood wouldn't stick to him," Melvin said.

"Only the blood of enemies," Dalwen said. She turned to Nergal. "Here you are," she told him. "It is safe to wear, now, as long as you don't forget…say Ternakridon to get it off."

"Ternu—" Nergal said. "Ternukridden?"

"Ternakridon."

Nergal scratched his head. "Dalwen remind Nergal later?"

Dalwen smiled. "Yes, I'll help you remember it."

Nergal felt the naked skin of his arms and hands. It was a strange feeling at first, but a good one. He felt lighter and airier.

"Is good," he nodded.

"But now he is vulnerable again," Roktan said. "You wouldn't believe what he's been through. If it weren't for that ring, we'd all be dead now."

"He can hardly walk around his whole life looking like a blood monster," Dalwen said. "I barely recognized him." Dalwen took a moment to hug Nergal.

Nergal accepted this gladly, and smiled hugely back at Dalwen. Then he saw Roktan's look of concern and remembered the usefulness of the blood armor.

"Still have good armor," Nergal said, patting his scale mail.

Roktan shrugged. "I'll feel better when he's covered again. You should have seen him at the Bay of Brislava, killing pirates like some kind of unstoppable war golem. We need that kind of advantage against Kantru."

"He has the blessing of Alofzin, now," Melvin said.

Dalwen turned to Rovul, a smile on her face. She opened her mouth as if to speak, then frowned as she looked upon him.

"You have injuries," she stated quietly. Moving forward, she reached out to touch Rovul's jaw and then looked along his serpentine body.

"A broken jaw and five broken ribs," she said.

"Five broken ribs!" bellowed Roktan. "Friend, I knew you were hurt, but—"

"I still have dozens of intact ribs," Rovul said haltingly through his injured mouth. "I can still fight."

Dalwen ignored the brave denial and began to speak in another language. Nergal felt a powerful urge to step behind Roktan in fear but he stoically remained where he was, awaiting the outcome of the magic. He didn't like spellcasting but he trusted Dalwen completely. His eyes shifted left and right but nothing seemed to be happening. Then Dalwen was done and he relaxed.

"Nothing happen," Nergal commented.

"She mended my broken bonessss," Rovul explained to Nergal. "Priestessss, I thank you."

"You have kept my friends safe, and now I count you as my friend as well," Dalwen told him.

Roktan rolled his eyes. Rovul nodded in agreement. Melvin stared at Dalwen. Nergal observed all of this, in the warm glow of his freshly cleaned skin. He felt very good, he felt...hungry!

"Need food now," he announced.

Everyone laughed. Dalwen's return had truly breathed life back into the party. They sat down and ate together, for once dropping their grim thoughts and simply enjoying each other's company.

"We need Garbor here too," Melvin said.

Nergal thought of the trusting knight with the deep booming voice. If it hadn't been for Garbor's easy acceptance of Nergal, he might still be wandering the countryside, cold and starving.

"Where Garbor?" Nergal asked, stimulated by Melvin's mention of the knight.

Dalwen smiled at Nergal. "He elected to stay back in the Kingdom, and help to protect the King against further threats. He would be pleased to see how well you have served in his stead, Roktan."

The stoic warrior actually blushed at this. He shifted uncomfortably. "How do you know how I have served? Perhaps I've been a coward."

"I know you haven't been," Dalwen said. "Tell me what I have missed, though."

Melvin and Roktan related their adventures since Neyala to Dalwen. She seemed quite interested in the tale, and at several spots she smiled at Nergal as his deeds were recalled. She asked to see their new weapons, and she was especially admiring of Rovul's magical axes and the Shakkran.

"That sounds like quite a bit more excitement than I had," Dalwen said. "I spent most of the sea trip unconscious and then very weak while Garbor took me back to the Kingdom. My Klandur restored me and arranged my passage here with the avatar."

"Somehow I think it must have been a little more involved than that," Melvin said.

"Well, we were attacked by bandits once ashore, but Garbor and the Slith ambassador fought them off. You'll have to ask them about it someday."

"I shall do that. But for now I suppose we should take our sleep. We have long days ahead of us," said Melvin.

"And one of those days we'll meet Kantru," Roktan added.

Dalwen sighed. "I knew there would be a bad side to coming back."

CHAPTER 33

Plateau of Darkness

Nergal contemplated the mountain before them. The trees thinned out as the rock rose towards the sky. Snow was visible at the top. Already the air was cooler, and Nergal was contemplating putting on the wool cloak Roktan had secured for him at the last farm.

"We go up mountain?" he asked, fearing the answer.

"Actually, it's the edge of a large plateau that spans the center of the Riken continent," Roktan explained.

"It doesn't look pleasant," said Dalwen.

"The plateau before us is a harsh place indeed," Roktan said. "The monks of Chu Kutall originate from there, it was never part of Jagarta. They began as a small sect living in a mountain monastery, striving constantly in the harsh conditions."

"In a way that must be what forged them into what they are today," Melvin pondered. "To live like that probably required supreme self discipline. The monk warriors certainly possess that."

"So what is up there, besides monasteries?" Dalwen asked.

"No one knows but the monks," Roktan said. "I don't think anyone not of the order has ever returned to tell about it. The only things we know are the hints dropped by those of Chu Kutall, on the rare occasions that the Master feels like talking with one of his slaves about home."

They ceased talking and resumed their climb. Everyone had more to carry than before, since Roktan's allies had bestowed cold weather provisions upon them at the last hiding place on their journey towards the plateau.

Nergal, being the strongest member except for perhaps the heavily muscled coils of Rovul, had to carry a lot of the load. There was food, oil, heavy furs, and even a supply of bear fat to rub on faces and hides to protect them from moisture.

Nergal's homeland of Nod was a barren, mountainous place, so he was no stranger to climbing the heights. Rovul, too, was an accomplished rock climber, as his race was well adapted to the rocky islets that rose from the sea near their home. The snake-prince often moved ahead, working out routes for his four-limbed companions.

Nergal began to spot patches of snow and ice, hidden in the nooks of the rocks safe from the sunlight. The next time they stopped to rest, Nergal donned his new cloak, even though the work of climbing warmed him.

When Rovul returned to redirect their course, Nergal noticed a marked difference in his friend. The Slith's arms moved stiffly as if he had fallen prey to the cold. It seemed that Melvin noticed too.

"I hate to say this, but you might have to turn back. Surely your kind is vulnerable to the cold?" Melvin asked.

"Sssssslooooow," Rovul rasped. "Veeeery coooold."

Dalwen saw Rovul's predicament and frowned. Nergal knew that look. It wouldn't do to have one of her friends suffering.

"Mel-veen stand back, Dalwen do magic now," announced Nergal.

Melvin gave Nergal an odd look. It rapidly turned to a look of surprise as he turned to see that the priestess had already begun a spell.

Her voice was soft and rapid as always when she invoked her power. The only word that Nergal caught was "Alofzin". Dalwen dropped to one knee and touched Rovul's bright yellow breastplate at the end of her incantation.

Nergal eyed Rovul warily, searching for the change that Dalwen's magic must have caused. He could see no difference. He even sniffed the air briefly, trying to sense any discrepancy.

"Magic no work?" he finally asked.

Dalwen smiled and grasped Nergal's hand. She brought it to Rovul's armor and held his palm against it. The metal was quite warm to the touch. Nergal's eyebrows jumped.

"Is clever magic, be keeping Rovul warm."

"Cleeeeever," Rovul agreed. The snake-prince still moved slowly, but his tongue flickered several times. "Warm in…. a moment," he hissed.

"Excellent!" burst Melvin, beaming happily at Dalwen. "Let's continue then." He drew the wand out of his pocket and allowed it to point the way. It still indicated that Kantru lurked in the direction they traveled.

They moved out over the lip of the mountain, and then Nergal could see clearly that they had scaled the edge of a large plateau. Rocky, snow covered land stretched out before him.

The march dragged on. Nergal trudged through the snow. He had wrapped his primitive sandals in fat-soaked fur to keep his feet dry, but the cold ate at his hairy legs. He ignored the discomfort, as did the others and they made their way slowly.

When night threatened, they broke camp early, forming a depression in the snow against a large boulder. Melvin and Roktan built the walls of the shelter up as high as they could.

"Insanity," Melvin muttered to himself. "We'll freeze. There is no wood up here. What can we burn?"

"Burn the oil for a while," Roktan suggested. "It will get warmer in here. It's too bad there is not a snowstorm, then we would be buried in the snow and that would be warmer."

They broke out the heavy furs and huddled together, desperately trying to stay warm. Dalwen renewed her warmth spell on Rovul's armor before they went to sleep. No one kept watch.

As harsh as that first day was, and the night that followed, they continued the same way for another three days before they found anything but rocks and snow under a cloudy sky, swept by an icy wind.

They came up to an outcropping of bare rock and stopped for a moment, sheltered from the north wind. Melvin's face looked even more pale than usual, and his lips were dry and cracked. He fished the wand out and let it lead his hand.

"It's pointing beyond the stone…but also it dips down rather sharply."

Roktan stepped up and looked at the device. "Beyond this formation, or under it?"

Melvin nodded. "Yes, you're right. Unless the plateau drops again already, which it shouldn't, the wand is indicating that he is nearby, under the ground."

They slowly began to examine the perimeter of the rock formation. Nergal peered into cracks in the rock while Melvin tapped the stone with the pommel of his dagger as he walked along. Dalwen walked a few steps ahead and looked at the wall. Then she interrupted their operation.

"Ahem."

Melvin looked up. "What's wrong?"

"There's a big rectangular hole the shape of a doorway right over there," she told them.

"Ah, er, yes of course," Melvin stuttered. "Let's check that out first."

Nergal moved with the others over to regard the opening that Dalwen had found. He saw a smooth portal carved straight into the rock. A roughly man-sized passage extended straight into darkness.

"Looks easy enough…too easy, actually."

"Yessss, beware trapssss," hissed Rovul.

Nergal leaned forward and squinted slightly. He thought he saw something just at the edge of his vision. He stepped forward to stand directly in front of the door.

"Bars," he said.

"Where?" asked Melvin, walking up beside him. "You mean there are bars blocking the way?"

Nergal nodded and pointed. "Bars like castle gate."

"Ah. A portcullis makes sense. That's more like what I'd expect from Kantru, a portcullis at the least, probably trapped as well."

"Magical traps would be his style," Dalwen said. "Lethal magical traps."

"Can you…" Melvin said, then broke off as he saw that Dalwen was already casting a spell. The priestess waved her hands in front of her body and stepped slowly into the passageway.

Nergal waited impatiently as Dalwen finished her examination of the portcullis. He stood at the entrance, wanting to go in with her, but unwilling to approach while magic was being used. Finally she turned and strode back out onto the snow-covered ground.

"It doesn't seem to be a trap. I think its purpose is to notify Kantru when it's opened. He will know when it's lifted, I suspect," she said.

"Can you dispel it?" asked Melvin.

The priestess nodded. "I could try. But I think Kantru is smart enough to have thought of that. He is a very powerful sorcerer. I don't think that would do any good."

"Giving up surprise will be dangerous," Melvin said.

"Realistically, though, he knows we're after him. He has to have defenses prepared in his own holdfast."

"I don't see any way around it," Dalwen said. "In fact, how are we going to get by the portcullis at all?"

"Nergal can lift it," Roktan said.

"It has a lock, though," Dalwen persisted. "Can anyone pick it? Can we break it?"

Melvin looked thoughtful. "I may be able to assist there," he said.

The others looked at him. "How?"

"As I have said, I have some knowledge of magic. It should be a relatively simple matter—"

"Oh, no," moaned Roktan. "Like you identified our weapons? You said you could do that, and you tried the whole voyage here and barely got anywhere."

"I figured out Rovul's axes, didn't I?"

"Yes, with Nergal's help," Roktan said.

Melvin bristled. "He may well have had a helpful suggestion or two but—"

"It doesn't matter," interrupted Dalwen. "Just go try."

"I'll do my best," Melvin said.

The knight walked slowly into the cavern and knelt before the portcullis.

Nergal waited expectantly at first, then with a growing boredom as he listened to Melvin's voice echoing outwards from the entranceway. The knight seemed uncertain and experimental at first, then he became more insistent.

"Do you think you will be able to get it?" Roktan finally asked.

"I haven't got it yet. But I'm still trying," Melvin called back.

"With Melvin, magic is no quick thing," Roktan whispered to Nergal.

"Well, I'm going to wait out of the cold," Dalwen said, walking into the tunnel. Nergal thought he detected a bit of irritation in her voice. He wondered if it was because Roktan was making fun of Melvin.

Roktan quickly danced to Nergal's side of the entrance. Nergal raised his eyebrows in surprise at the sudden movement. Roktan took out his small container of poison and motioned towards the spear on Nergal's back.

"Eh?" Nergal grunted.

Roktan motioned desperately to the spear on his back, but still said nothing. Now Nergal remembered their plan regarding the poison. He pulled the spear off his back and handed it to Roktan. The Jagartan warrior dipped the tip deep into the black substance, and then gave the spear back to Nergal.

"Remember, it's a secret. And don't accidentally stick yourself with it!" Roktan whispered urgently.

Nergal winked and nodded. "Secret," he confirmed.

Roktan slowly returned to his side of the entrance. Then Nergal leaned against the rock outside and idly awaited some result from Melvin. The knight's voice was still audible.

"Mulgamma prensar...mulgamma pronsar, mul—Ah!"

There was a discernable metal clank from the entrance. Nergal peered into the tunnel.

"It's unlocked! Nergal, if you can lift the gate, then we can head in."

Nergal looked back to scan the horizon one last time before entering the passageway. The sky was still overcast over the barren plain. He couldn't detect any sign of life.

Once in the tunnel, he felt the temperature rise slightly. He walked by the others until coming up to the portcullis, seeing it up close for the first time. A large metal locking mechanism was attached to the iron at the bottom, with a metal hook that had retracted from its port in the floor.

Nergal began to grab the gate but Dalwen stopped him.

"Wait," she instructed, and unstrapped the shield from her back. Widening the strap, she affixed it to Nergal's head, facing forward. Nergal couldn't see the slightest thing.

"What are you doing? Have you gone mad?" demanded Melvin. Nergal was grateful to Melvin for protesting for him, since he couldn't speak well with the back of a shield smashed against his face.

"It's just in case there's a trap," Dalwen said.

"I thought you said there weren't any traps," Roktan pointed out, joining Melvin's protests.

"I don't think there are, but Kantru is a powerful wizard and a crafty enemy. This is just in case," Dalwen said.

"Great," Roktan said, his voice dripping with enough sarcasm that even Nergal detected some of it. "Good luck, Nergal," he added ominously.

Nergal stood for a moment as he considered his situation. As soon as he became aware of the others waiting on him, he overcame his fear and set to the task of opening the gate.

Nergal grasped the lowest crossbar and began to lift. His first attempt brought the gate slightly up, then it fell back with a heavy clank. Roktan appeared next to him, rolling a large rock up to the gate.

"If you can lift it this high, I'll put the rock under it," he offered.

Nergal nodded and tried again. Roktan's assurance gave him greater confidence in his ability to get out from under the gate once he succeeded. The gate lifted, slowly at first, then moving more rapidly as Nergal straightened. He stood holding the gate, his arms shuddering under the strain while his huge muscles bulged.

Roktan pushed the rock into place under the portcullis and darted back. Nergal began to lower the gate. He attempted to set it down slowly but it clanged hard on the rock despite his efforts.

"Thank you, Nergal," Dalwen said sincerely. She retrieved her shield from his head and replaced it on her back. Nergal nodded and smiled. He was glad that nothing had happened.

They quickly scrabbled under the heavy gate one by one. Melvin had trouble in his heavy armor but Nergal grabbed his arms and helped him through. Soon they were all on the far side of the obstacle.

"Very good, we're in," Melvin announced.

"And Kantru knows it. Let's move," Roktan said.

Everyone readied their weapons. Nergal slipped a mace into each hand and swept his cloak back behind each arm to allow his upper body a clear range of motion.

Roktan lead the way, holding the Shakkran before him. Nergal followed immediately behind him, and the darker interior of the corridor gave way to some light source ahead.

"Large room ahead," whispered Roktan. The warrior moved another few paces and entered a large chamber. Nergal kept close, ready for anything. A surreal sight awaited him.

The entrance chamber was vaulted, with graceful curves of stone supporting the ceiling above. Alcoves lined the walls in three pairs, their contents hidden behind bright red curtains with gold trim. The room was lit by four glowing orbs held in metal sconces that were formed like the talons of a bird of prey. The orbs looked exactly like the glowing spheres that Nergal had encountered inside the so-called Mountain of the Dead God.

At the end of the arched room, a single arched doorway led deeper into the stronghold. Flanking the opening, two warriors clad in gray armor stood rock still. Nergal saw a weird light dancing on their faces. Slowly he realized that the warriors wore some kind of masks, flowing abstracts of the human face. The flames flickered on the masks as if they were windows into another place.

A place of fire.

"I think those are statues," Melvin said, holding his sword before him and lowering his visor. "But I get the feeling that they may somehow guard the entrance."

"Yes, beware. They may be animated," Dalwen agreed.

Nergal peered at the warriors again. Were they statues? The gray armor didn't seem to have any seams or joints. The half-orc began to think that maybe they were entirely sculpted from metal.

"I see fire on their masks…in their masks," Roktan noted.

"They might use fire as a weapon. Dalwen, can you protect us from fire?"

Dalwen nodded. She brought out her symbol of Alofzin and muttered to it rapidly. The symbol flickered into life. A ghostly image of white fire glowed from it.

"The avatar has already bestowed this upon you," she said. "Everyone but Rovul."

Melvin nodded. He looked at the snake-prince and indicated the statues. "Let us take care of these things, in case they try to burn us," Melvin asked.

"Very well, I'll ssstay back and throw my axesss," Rovul agreed.

They advanced into the room with Dalwen and Nergal on the left and Melvin and Roktan paired up on the right. Each pair kept close watch on the mysterious statues as they advanced across the stone floor.

Nergal's eyes flickered to the nearest alcove, hidden behind the thick draperies. Dalwen saw his look and nodded, motioning to the half-orc. They carefully approached the tapestry hanging over the entrance of the alcove. Nergal risked a glimpse around the room, and saw that the statues remained in place and Melvin and Roktan were preparing a similar action on their side of the room.

Dalwen nodded and pulled the drapery aside from a split in the middle. Nergal hulked before the opening, ready to strike.

A hideous insectoid, half again taller than Nergal, leered out from the alcove. Nergal snarled and struck, slamming his mace into the side of the thing. As his mace hit, Nergal realized something was wrong. One of the beast's wicked horns fell to the ground and shattered, spreading fragments of stone about on the floor.

"Hold! It is only a statue," Dalwen told him. "I don't think this one is magical," she added, pulling the curtain farther back to reveal the entire alcove. Then Dalwen made a sign with her left hand and uttered a few sharp syllables.

"There is no danger here," she told Nergal. Looking to the other side of the room, they saw that a similar statue was behind the opposite curtain. Dalwen repeated her incantation and examined the other alcove.

"Nor there," she said.

Nergal looked at the rest of the alcove. Maroon candles littered a small ledge around the base of the statue that he had vandalized. The stone wall had been intricately carved here to frame the statue, covered in images of small humanoids that seemed to writhe around one another as if their bodies were half made of mist or smoke. The statue itself seemed to stare down malignantly at Nergal with its huge compound eyes.

"An image of Kantru's god," Dalwen told him. "Alofzin protect us," she said, tracing the sign of Alofzin across her chest.

Nergal grunted and turned from the alcove. "Check other holes now," he said, indicating the next two alcoves. Dalwen nodded.

Both pairs of warriors moved forward towards the next alcoves. Behind them Rovul moved up to look at the alcove behind Dalwen and Nergal.

They repeated the procedure to unmask the next alcove. This time, Nergal managed to restrain himself when another figure was revealed behind the tapestry. It was an image of a man, robed like Kantru, standing with a pole arm lifted over his head. A look of rage was frozen on the face of the statue. It was surrounded by the same disturbing carvings of masses of creatures milling around each other.

Roktan's voice came from across the room. "Talok, Lord of Chu Kutall. He is their necromancer-king," he said.

A large spider scuttled out from behind the statue, clinging to the carved wall. Nergal snorted in disgust and put his right mace away. He reached over his head and took the spear off his back and stabbed the arachnid with it savagely, killing it.

"What is that on your spear, Nergal?" asked Dalwen.

"Is poison, er, uh…" Nergal winced. He had remembered the poison was supposed to be a secret. "Spider is poison if bite."

"I mean the black stuff on your spear, not the spider," Dalwen said.

"Um, got spider blood on spear," Nergal said, hastily replacing the spear on his back. Dalwen made an odd face.

"Well, whatever. We should check out the last alcove. But keep your eye on those statues at the doorway, there is definitely something special about them!"

Nergal released his breath in relief. Warrior monks, monsters and living statues he could deal with, but the half-orc feared accidentally letting Roktan's secret out. He didn't want to make any of his friends mad at him.

They walked carefully up towards the last alcove. Nergal watched the things flanking the far doorway as they neared that end of the room. As Nergal approached closer, he became more certain that the figures were made of metal. They gleamed slightly as if covered in silver, but there were still no seams or joints visible. The adventurers slowed as they approached within several paces of the works. The central archway between them ended in a large double door.

When they stood before the last pair of curtains, Dalwen opened them while Nergal waited to respond to any danger. Once again there was a statue of a figure in the alcove surrounded by candles and ornately carved patterns. This time Nergal instantly recognized the figure.

"Is Kantru," he announced.

"Hrm, you must be right. I guess we have the right place."

Kantru's statue stood erect and dignified. The man's face was twisted with a slight smirk, as if thinking about his next evil plot. Nergal turned from it and faced the two statues with flaming masks. On the other side of the room, Melvin and Roktan had finished inspecting their alcove, which contained the mirror image of Nergal's side. The adventurers moved cautiously towards the double doorway flanked by the metal figures.

Suddenly a small creature charged forth from the doorway between the statues. The speed of the thing startled Nergal and the others, it seemed that his brain had hardly registered the creature's presence by the time it bolted up to Melvin's leg and clamped its wide mouth down on the knight's ankle. Melvin yelped and swiped clumsily down at the creature. The stroke proved too slow to hit the lightning fast enemy. The creature dodged the attack by releasing Melvin's ankle and then scurried back behind the statues.

Somehow the thing's attack seemed to stir the weird guardians into action. They both strode forward, almost as one. The left statue came straight towards Nergal.

Unintimidated, Nergal stood toe to toe with this new attacker and swung his mace even as the statue's sword threatened him. Stepping inside his enemy's swing, Nergal whacked the opponent across its fiery face. The creature seemed unaffected by his blow except for some small cracks that formed in the mask. The half-orc felt a wave of heat emanating from behind the mask as the statue gazed at him.

The figure pushed him away with tremendous strength, and tried to thrust the longsword it wielded through his belly. Nergal slapped the blade aside with one of his maces and skipped back to prepare for another exchange.

Nergal glimpsed the situation across the room from the corner of his eye. Somehow Roktan had fallen onto the floor. The tall metal statue was striking down at Roktan as Melvin worked his way behind it. Roktan rolled away at the last instant, avoiding being cleaved in half by the falling sword. The weapon clanged and raised sparks against the stone floor. Then Nergal had to return his attention fully to his own opponent to avoid a similar danger.

The statue attacked him again, swinging its sword in a deadly arc towards his neck. Nergal ducked swiftly and skipped back.

When Nergal returned to an upright position after his maneuver, he saw a robed man standing beyond the statues. He immediately thought of Kantru, but despite his desperate desire to attack the monk directly, he dared not leave the deadly statue at his back for even a second.

Once again his opponent attacked with the sword. Nergal batted the sword aside with one mace and hit the statue's hand with his other mace, trying to get it to drop its sword. Metal clanged on metal with enough force to numb his hand, but the sword did not drop. Nergal's frustration bubbled out in a howl and he attacked the statue back, swinging first one mace and then the other.

The statue ignored Nergal's attacks, trying to counter rather than defend itself. Nergal took advantage of the opening and ran in to strike the creature's face again. He struck the cracked mask with his mace. In an explosion of bright flame, the mask shattered and fire engulfed him. Nergal yelped in surprise, expecting to feel his flesh burning as it had when the drake breathed on him. Instead he felt nothing.

He stood and blinked in surprise as the statue dropped to the floor and dropped its sword. It clasped its face as if in pain, the flames licking out over its hands and melting them.

Nergal backed away from the melting guardian and took in the situation with Roktan and Melvin. They still fought the other statue, circling it at opposite ends. Whenever the thing seemed to go after one of them, they parried its attacks while the other attacked from behind. But their weapons were not having much effect. There was no sign of the tiny-scaled monster that had tried to bite Melvin.

The monk who had run in was just standing there, oddly still, as if he were trying to become a statue himself. As Nergal watched, Dalwen called out to him, "I'll take care of the robed one, go smash the other flaming mask!"

Nergal needed no further urging. Turning towards the second metal warrior, he saw that it was still fighting against Melvin and Roktan. The two fighters seemed unable to harm the magical creature, even though their swordsmanship was superior enough to allow them to ward off its blows.

The half-orc charged in from the side, running up and wrapping his arms around the statue in a full speed tackle. Nergal came to a solid halt upon striking the heavy metal, and for a long moment it seemed that his ram had been ineffective. Then the figure in his grasp began to topple back, writhing against the orc.

Nergal snatched his arms back at the last instant. His opponent smashed into the floor, sundering several stone insets beneath it. Nergal sat astride the prone guardian, drew his mace way back, and whacked it across the flaming mask beneath him. The device shattered spectacularly, sending light and flame streaming outwards. Nergal twisted away and fell back instinctually even though he felt little heat. He rolled back to his feet and regarded the destruction.

When the flames cleared, Nergal saw that the original statue had degenerated into a bubbling pool on the floor, reduced by its own magical fire into a pool of bright slag. Several paces behind it were two robed bodies, one with an axe buried in his head. The other lay at Dalwen's feet, presumably brought down by the priestess.

Nergal and the others walked up to her position next to the double doors, one of which was ajar. Melvin began to examine the corpses.

"Dat one no move, like statue," Nergal said.

"That's probably because I paralyzed him," Dalwen said smiling.

Nergal didn't know the word. His puzzlement must have been obvious, because Dalwen added, "I used magic on him."

Nergal grunted and nodded his understanding.

"Did anyone see where that…thing ran to?" asked Roktan.

Everyone shook their heads. Nergal had been too distracted by the statue to keep track of it. Melvin finished searching the bodies and stood back up.

"This one isn't Kantru," Melvin noted. "The other one…well, his face is pretty mangled."

"Neither of them were," Dalwen said. "These were probably just his ordinary defenses. By now I'm sure he's had plenty of time to prepare for us."

Melvin nodded and raised his longsword. "Then let's not disappoint him."

CHAPTER 34

Stronghold

Roktan led the way through the double doors. Nergal followed him, watching for the fast creature that had attacked Melvin. The corridor beyond had a high ceiling that harbored many shadows. Light came from a pair of glowing orbs set into sconces just past the doors. Nergal saw more light in the distance but it was somehow muted.

Nergal thought he heard something, a kind of snarl or scrape of claw on bone. He stopped to listen, but Roktan continued unaware.

"What is it?" whispered Melvin from behind. Roktan stopped and looked back at Nergal questioningly.

"Is…" Nergal began. The skittering noise came again. Nergal's eyes darted upwards, and he saw two tiny pinpricks of light. Instantly he launched his spear at the thing, hurling it towards the ceiling with all his might.

The spear emitted sparks on its impact with cold gray stone. There was a hiss and a scurrying sound, as the unknown lurker retreated. Nergal caught his spear as it fell and ran forward, trying to track the elusive creature's progress along the ceiling.

"Nergal!" hissed Melvin behind him. Nergal ignored the plea and concentrated on the presence. The experience reminded him somewhat of hunting small rock lizards at night. One had to rely heavily on both sight and sound to locate and spear the creatures.

Nergal realized that the corridor ended up ahead, branching to the left and right. He stayed to the right, certain that he had seen a shadow move in that direction. He came to a corner in the passage, and saw light emanating from up ahead. He thought he heard scratching noises again, but he couldn't tell if it was his imagination.

Nergal continued rapidly down this new corridor, scanning the ceiling, and then suddenly the ground fell out from underneath him. He hurtled through space for a split second, and then he hit the edge of a pit that he had run over. Dangling precariously, Nergal held onto the floor with his arms, his legs in the pit.

The quick little creature that he had been pursuing seemed to sense his predicament. It appeared from up ahead, slinking along the floor towards Nergal as he clung to the edge of the pit. The creature looked like a short reptilian humanoid, with severely bestial features. A high-pitched growl gurgled from its wide, toothy mouth.

Nergal replied with a loud roar. The tiny creature was startled by the noise and took a quick set of steps back.

"Coward," spat Nergal.

"Nergal? Nergal!" Melvin's voice echoed down the corridor, still quite a distance behind.

The creature scurried up to Nergal's hands. Nergal spent a second caught between killing the thing and hanging onto the lip of the pit. The creature attacked with amazing speed, biting Nergal on one of his hands. He swiped at it, his grip on the ledge sliding away. The creature darted back, ever cautious, and circled him warily.

"Nergal!"

Melvin's voice rang out much closer this time. Nergal scrabbled at the edge of the pit, and now his imminent fall drove him to look away from the monster assailing him to peer down into the pit. He couldn't see the bottom of the opening, but the tips of long spikes were visible jutting up from below. To fall would mean serious injury, at the very least.

The creature bit his hand again, trying to dislodge his grip. Nergal slipped further away, now holding on with only his fingers. The creature gnawed away at his right hand until Nergal could ignore it no longer. He put all his weight onto his left hand, risking a fall, and snatched the creature by an arm with his right. Grunting in fear and exertion, he tossed the beast over his shoulder and slapped his bleeding hand back onto the ledge.

The tiny thing shrieked as it fell behind him, then Nergal heard more scrabbling. It was still alive! He looked down and saw the awful thing scaling the wall of the pit easily, moving up and climbing back out on the right side of the pit.

How do that? thought Nergal frantically. His feet scraped against the wall of the pit, but he could find no foothold.

Suddenly the creature bolted off. A sling bullet smacked the floor where the creature had been a second ago. It ran up the wall effortlessly, disappearing in the shadows of the ceiling.

"Hold on Nergal! We'll save you!" howled Melvin. Then, more quietly, "We can save him, right?"

Strong arms lifted Nergal from behind. Nergal helped to push himself up, his instinct to survive more powerful than his curiosity. As soon as he was safely lying onto the stone floor, he rolled over, panting from his ordeal. He saw the torso of Roktan hovering over him. The snake-prince's body extended clear over the pit. As Nergal watched the Slith slowly slithered the rest of the way over to Nergal's side.

"That wasss close, friend," Rovul said.

"Be thanking you," Nergal said, holding his bleeding appendage. "Stoopid fairy-kin bit Nergal."

"Dalwen should look at that, when she getsss over here."

On the other side of the pit, Melvin was beginning to inch his way over to the far side by scooting along a ledge next to the wall. Rovul moved out over the pit again, to safeguard the knight lest he fall into the deadly pit. Dalwen and Roktan crossed behind Melvin without incident.

Dalwen immediately came up to Nergal. Nergal held out his hand for her to examine, but she ignored it and struck him on the shoulder.

"Don't run away like that, are you trying to get yourself killed?" she scolded him. "Now, let me see your hand."

Nergal hunched lower in shame and held out his hand for Dalwen. The priestess spoke rapidly and waved her hand over his wounds. Nergal felt warmth spread through his hand, and then his flesh was whole again, the nasty gashes closing up and disappearing.

"Be thanking you too," he said.

Dalwen nodded and looked ahead.

"There's a staircase ahead. Did anyone see if that foul little creature ran up it?"

"I think it did," Melvin said. "What is that thing, anyway? It looks vaguely impish, or like a runt troglodyte."

"It must be a servant of Kantru. Perhaps even his familiar," Dalwen said.

Roktan moved towards the stairs, checking the floor before him with his weapon and his foot. "Let's waste no more time," he said.

Nergal wondered why he was in such a hurry, but he fell in behind him as before. They began to trudge up the wide stone stairs, which were straight at first but eventually began to spiral as they made their way further up them.

Nergal saw more light from above. As they neared the end of the stairs, the light continued to grow. They emerged outside, on a flat stone platform under an overcast sky.

They were at the top of the rock formation they had entered, far above the plateau. The platform was roughly circular, with a waist-high wall of stone enclosing the perimeter. Four squat stone benches or altars were arrayed along the outside edge.

Stones placed around the perimeter of the aerie were carved with perplexing symbols. The runes were filled with gold and silver. Nergal thought that whoever made them must be rich indeed.

"Quite an odd lookout post," Roktan said. "Do you think it's for casting spells at anyone besieging the place?"

"Maybe it's for weather control spells," Dalwen suggested.

"I think it's an observatory," Melvin said. "I recognize this symbol here. It often represents our sun Quan. Notice how the lines with this symbol have a range that varies across the edge here? I think that is the seasonal variation."

Nergal lost track of Melvin after the big 'O' word. He tramped about the perimeter while the knight talked, looking for the tiny creature that had been harassing them. There was no sign of it. As he walked by one of the altars, he noticed a small piece of blue crystal lying on the stone. Walking over, he snatched it up and saw that it was on the end of a slim gold necklace.

"It is nearly noon," Roktan was saying. "The Shakkran will begin to harvest power from the priests. We must find Kantru within a couple of hours if I'm to use its power against him."

"If you don't fight shortly after noon or midnight, then the Shakkran is no use?" asked Dalwen.

"The mana of the priests will slowly drain away. The Shakkran will be no different than a normal sword again two hours after noon."

Nergal put the necklace on. Rovul saw him slip it over his head and came over, his tongue flickering.

"Careful, my friend," he warned. "It may be dangerousss." The snake-prince's warning attracted the attention of the others.

Nergal immediately felt that something was wrong. The ambient light dropped dramatically as soon as he put the crystal around his neck. Nergal looked up and cringed, almost dropping into a squat, as he saw that the clouds were completely gone. He was standing under a clear night sky, the stars twinkling brightly.

"Uh oh," Nergal said.

"What's wrong?" asked Melvin.

"What is that crystal?" demanded Dalwen.

"Uh oh," Nergal repeated. What had he done now? "Nergal didn't mean to make night."

"Make knight what?" asked Dalwen.

"He didn't mean to make me mad," Melvin guessed.

Nergal pointed up at the sky. "Make night. Make night. Sorry."

The others just stared at him, confused.

"Explain more," Melvin said.

Nergal pointed up again insistently. Suspecting the truth, Dalwen reached over and removed the necklace. Once again the clouds obscured the heavens and the muted light of the sun returned.

"Magic," Nergal said matter-of-factly.

"May I try it?" asked Melvin. Dalwen handed the necklace to him, and the knight removed his helm and gently put the pendant on.

"Fantastic! Most remarkable! What an invaluable item!" burst Melvin, spinning around and gazing at the sky.

"Looks like night?" Roktan asked.

"I see the entire night sky, as if on the clearest and darkest of nights!"

"That is truly amazing, I admit," Roktan said. "But please let me remind you, we should try and find Kantru soon. Remember the time. I suggest that we can return to try this out later after we have dealt with the sorcerer."

"Er, yes, of course," Melvin said. He reluctantly took the necklace off. "Well, this is yours, Nergal, you discovered it."

Nergal took a step back. "No want! Keep away," he said.

"You don't want it?" The hopeful tone of Melvin's voice was undisguised. "Can I keep it?"

Nergal nodded. "Melvin keep. Keep," he insisted.

Roktan stood impatiently at the top of the stairs, so Nergal took his place in line and they walked back down into the earth. They returned to the corridor intersection where Nergal had turned right pursuing the agile creature that could walk on walls.

They moved slowly down the remaining corridor. Roktan tested his footing carefully, trying to detect pits in the floor. They approached another large door, made of thick planks and bands of metal.

Roktan listened for a moment and then he flung the door open by its brass handle. The room beyond the door was illuminated by two of the glowing orbs that Kantru seemed to prefer.

There were four simple wooden beds against the far wall and another door leading out from an adjoining wall. Wooden lockers were at the foot of each bed. No one was visible.

"Barracks for the guards," said Roktan, slowly walking through the room.

Nergal followed the Jagartan, Dalwen behind him. His path took him close to one of the glowing orbs, and the light shone briefly over him and the spear strapped to his back.

"Nergal, what is that on your spear?" Dalwen asked quietly. "It can't be spider blood, there is something else there."

Nergal inwardly cursed. He should have avoided the light of the orb.

"Is poison," Nergal answered simply.

"Alofzin! What are you doing with that?"

"What isss wrong with poison?" Rovul said.

"It is an orc's way, Dalwen," Melvin said quietly. "To his people, poison is a useful tool just like the spear itself."

"Actually it was my idea," admitted Roktan.

"You!" exclaimed Dalwen. Her voice started to rise. "Just when Nergal was getting—"

"Not now, you must be quiet," hissed Melvin. "I know that Kantru is expecting us but let's not let him know exactly how far along we are."

Dalwen dropped the subject, although she was clearly not pleased.

Roktan opened the next door. Another lit room was beyond and the adventurers slowly walked in.

Two large tables dominated the center of the chamber. There was an open doorway on the far side and a closed doorway to the right. Nergal could smell food. He moved around a table and into the kitchen to find something to eat.

A single glowing orb lit the larder, but the food was not immediately apparent other than some long loaves of bread on a counter.

"Let's move along. This appears to be nothing more than a mess room for the guards," said Roktan.

"It would seem so," agreed Melvin.

Nergal grabbed some bread and stuffed it into his mouth before falling back into line. Roktan opened the door carefully, and stepped through, followed closely by the others.

Stacks of supplies crowded each corner of this chamber. Despite its considerable size, most of the space was taken up by a confusing array of items. Nergal's first glance gave him the impression of an armory, with shields hanging on the walls, and rack upon rack of weapons. A single man sized opening led away to another corridor.

Nergal moved forward and grabbed a pole arm, picking it up and trying a test swipe.

"I doubt if any of these are as valuable as what you already have," Melvin told him. Nergal grunted neutrally, setting the weapon down and picking up a curved scimitar.

"Looks like it's mostly food in this corner," Dalwen called from Nergal's left. The priestess was searching through sacks and barrels in her corner of the room.

Once again Roktan was the first to lose patience. "We can search this more thoroughly later. Let's continue," he said, indicating the opening they hadn't yet explored.

Roktan slowly checked the floor as they moved along the next corridor. It was dimly lit but the ceiling was low, and Nergal felt that he would see the tiny creature that had harassed them before if it approached. The corridor turned and Nergal could see more light ahead.

The light level increased as they approached the end of the passage. Roktan gasped and faltered. Nergal peered over his shoulder to see what the problem was. Then his eyebrows knitted in consternation.

Up ahead, Nergal could see heavy foliage in the next chamber. Bright light came down from above, and a myriad of plant smells came to his nose. It was as if they were in a cave about to exit onto a tropical island.

"How this be?" Nergal asked. Roktan shook his head and slowly walked forward. Melvin and Dalwen emitted more sounds of surprise as the vista opened up before them.

Nergal walked out into a huge underground chamber. Larger, brighter versions of the glowing spheres shone down from above, providing a magnificent garden with nourishing light. Nergal saw flowers and leaves of every color in the rainbow. Many of the plants stood as tall as a human, their branches and leaves striving upward towards the spheres.

"I must admit, this surprises me greatly. It's hard to believe that Kantru could create such a beautiful place," Dalwen said.

The others seemed as taken with the unexpected environment as well. They moved more slowly, Melvin and Dalwen stopping to examine the fronds of a fern or the flower of a squat bush. It was Roktan who gave a quick word of warning, pointing straight ahead. Nergal looked and saw that in the center of the huge garden, a circular slab of stone sat amidst the plants, serving as a nexus of several small paths like the one they were on. In the center of the little clearing, a robed man stood watching their approach.

It was Kantru. He stood calmly on the circular dais of stone.

"This foolish campaign against me will have to stop," Kantru stated almost playfully. His voice betrayed no hint of strain and his posture was erect but relaxed.

"We would not give up," Roktan called back. "We have come to repay you for your nefarious deeds in Jagarta and lands beyond." He carefully resumed his advance, slowly nearing Kantru as they talked.

"You will only help my cause in the end," Kantru said.

"Ha! Never," swore Dalwen.

"I didn't say you would do it willingly," Kantru countered. He certainly must have been aware of the advance on his position, but he clearly did not care. Nergal scanned the vegetation to either side of the group, expecting some kind of ambush, but he didn't spot any potential supporters of Kantru.

Roktan seemed to gain confidence, holding the Shakkran before him.

"It is shortly after noon. You must realize what that means," Roktan growled.

"Then you're probably wondering why you don't feel any power from your Shakkran," Kantru prodded, smiling again.

"The priests will see to that," Roktan said.

"Ah, yes," Kantru smiled. "The priests of Kuotek. I'm afraid they won't be lending you any power this day. Or any other. I had them ground up for a Khla Klivek!"

Roktan stopped his slow advance in utter shock.

"Kla Kli-ek?" muttered Nergal.

"Yes! A little stew I cooked up. Of course Khla doesn't last long—it spoils if you leave it. So I had to make something out of it…"

Kantru waved his hand over his shoulder in a graceful twist.

From behind Kantru, the plants began to rustle. Several large stems, almost the size of tree trunks, waved rapidly. Then Nergal realized that they were legs.

An abomination of nature scuttled out onto the stone of the clearing. The chitinous monster was pentagonal, having five stout crab like legs, five eye stocks, and five long tentacles whipping rapidly over each of five gaping mouths. The creature stood taller than Nergal, and looked to be ten times his weight. Its green armor had hidden it well in the garden, the mottled brown of its legs aiding in the subterfuge.

"Convenient design, don't you think?" Kantru asked. "Five meddlers, and five mouths to eat them!"

The giant monster scuttled forward towards the group and Kantru rolled backwards through its legs and came back up on the far side of it.

Nergal battled his fear for one second, overcoming his urge to turn and flee from the awful monster. Then he was running to meet it, mace in hand. He swung at one of the armored legs, putting all his strength behind the strike. His mace struck with a loud crack, damaging the exoskeleton of the leg. The leg lifted off the ground and flicked outwards, trying to skewer Nergal on its long pointed end. Nergal skipped back but the leg struck his scale mail, failing to penetrate but bruising the half-orc on his stomach.

With a whip-like motion one of the long tentacles descended upon Nergal. He struggled with the limb for a moment as it tangled his arm and tried to wrap itself around him. Only a few feet away he watched Melvin cleave one of the tentacles with a broad sweep of his longsword.

Nergal had no such recourse with his own club-like weapon, and he considered this difficulty for a split second before he felt the weight leave his feet. He now dangled off the ground, lifted by the powerful tentacle. Below him, one of the hideous many-toothed mouths gaped and snapped, preparing to consume him.

The desperate need for a solution in the face of such an awful fate galvanized Nergal to action. He flung the mace in his right hand at one of the eyestalks, then grabbed his spear without waiting to see the results. Meanwhile his feet were dangling above one of the five mouths. He tried to brace his feet against the top carapace to either side of the mouth while wrestling his spear free. He almost lost a foot in the jaws below, but recovered and managed to get control of the poisoned spear.

Nergal realized dimly that he was screaming in rage and fear, but the sounds were lost in the general melee. He thrust the spear deep into the base of the tentacle that held him, the huge muscles in his arms bulging in the convulsive exertion. Immediately he heard a noxious squeal from below and the tentacle suspending him weakened. He fell back towards the floor, saved from a serious fall only by the waning strength of the tentacle as it struggled to retain its hold on him.

He saw that Dalwen and Roktan were held in tentacles as he had been a moment ago. Melvin was avoiding his tentacle warily, trying desperately to stab his weapon into chinks of the creature's armor.

Nergal wanted to get up onto the thing but he couldn't as long as its legs suspended it. He resumed his attack on a leg, uncertain if he was swinging at the same one he had already damaged. He swung his mace into it, smashing in a section of the outer armor on the leg, and then darted under the creature, crouching low. The underside of the thing dropped like a cave-in, slamming Nergal in the head. The half-orc's consciousness collapsed like a house of cards, blackness consuming him in a single thunderclap.

CHAPTER 35

Prisoners

Nergal awakened. His head hurt terribly, but his curiosity to see what god had taken him into service for the afterlife drove him to open his eyes and look around. He sat on an iron seat with shackles on his arms and legs in a dark room lit only by a hot blacksmith's pit. He had no armor or weapons on his person. To his left he saw Melvin, Dalwen, and Roktan restrained the same way, wearing only shoddy brown robes.

It must be Alofzin, Nergal thought, since these others were here as well. Rovul had mentioned a snake-god…

"Alof-zeen keep us chained?" asked Nergal, uncertain of his surroundings. Somehow he had envisioned Dalwen's deity as somewhat more benign.

"Kantru does," said Melvin. "We're still alive…for the moment."

Nergal saw that the knight had a bloody ear and bruises on his arms. Roktan and Dalwen looked beaten as well, although he saw no tooth marks from the huge monster.

Nergal grunted. If they were still alive, where was Rovul? Dead?

Nergal tried to scan the room while he recovered. He saw that there were black robed guards in the room now. There was a dark substance that could only be blood on the floor. Quickly Nergal scanned his friends who were shackled to the racks next to him, but he couldn't see any openly bleeding wounds.

Then he saw that Kantru himself had entered the room and was regarding the adventurers coolly.

"And now, for a little trick I learned in the Empire of Blue Sands," Kantru said, obviously relishing what was to come.

"The woman! Bring her to the altar!"

"No!" shouted Melvin.

There was a commotion as the adventurers tried to struggle free, fearing the worst. The iron binding them was too strong. The guards were alert. Everyone but Melvin gave up struggling and watched helplessly as four of the younger men released Dalwen and dragged her forward.

Melvin said something in a language Nergal didn't understand. Dalwen looked back at him, a look of sorrow on her face.

"Don't worry knight, you will still have a short time left together," Kantru laughed. "A spell shaper can be difficult to keep in confines. But I found out that a Norngawen can't invoke her powers if she doesn't possess the least finger of each hand."

Kantru turned to command his minion. "Zalef, remove the fingers," he told him. Zalef drew a slender blade from his robe and brought Dalwen's left hand forward.

"Alofzin curse you, wizard!" Dalwen snarled.

Nergal railed against his bonds again as he heard Dalwen's scream. Blood fell across the altar, and Zalef continued to the priestess's other hand. Nergal was helpless and had no choice but to watch the cruel procedure. The other little finger was removed, and then one of the other monk warriors handed Zalef a hot branding iron to cauterize the wounds. Dalwen's screams echoed through the small hot chamber again.

"Why don't you just kill us?" spat Roktan.

Kantru walked a little closer to the prisoners. He swept his hand gracefully, indicating the entire group. "The better the Khla, the better the Shok Nogua!"

"Eh?" grunted Nergal.

"I'll melt your flesh down and use it to construct my most powerful servant-monster ever! The better my raw materials, the more skilled and heroic my sources, the more powerful the result! I fully expect that this creature will be capable of destroying the entire kingdom by itself."

Kantru walked to the end of the line where Roktan was shackled. "You have already seen this principle in action. The monster that captured you, with my aid, was the product of the priests of Kuotek. It was quite powerful. Contrast it to the so called Terror of Halfor Bay, which was simply an average batch of slaves."

"And the Shadow Monster?" asked Dalwen, pain in her voice.

"The Castellan of Salthor, quite an experienced fighter, put a lot of kick into that one. But he was only one man, and not as powerful as any of you. Don't be impatient, my preparations are almost ready. You are actually quite lucky, to be living on in a better form instead of the waste of just burying or burning your bodies."

Kantru signaled to his guards and Nergal felt strong hands grabbing his arms. He snarled and bit at them, but he could not do anything with his arms and legs shackled.

"Don't fight them Nergal, there are too many," Melvin told him quietly.

"Yes, listen to him," Kantru soothed. Nergal fought harder, then one of the guards hit him hard on the side of the neck, stunning him somewhat. They released him from the chair, leaving his arms and legs in manacles. As he recovered he realized that they were carrying him down a corridor, and past a guard station occupied by men in full plate.

They came to a gloomy room lit with a single glowing orb. Nergal saw that Rovul was in a small prison, a section of the room isolated by thick iron bars. There was another man in with him, a stranger Nergal did not recognize.

The monks tossed him into the cage and locked the door. Nergal felt only relief that Rovul was alive. He staggered over to his friend, who steadied Nergal and regarded him.

"The othersss?" he asked.

"Dey chained. Kantru hurt Dalwen, cut her fingers," he said.

Rovul was silent. Nergal regarded the stranger for a moment, seeing that it was a young muscular man, with the beginnings of a beard.

One by one the others were brought in. Dalwen was last, a sad sight, her hands shaking but with her head held high. Melvin embraced her and they said nothing for long moments. Then they released each other and Melvin looked at the stranger.

"Who are you?"

"I'm Bahar. I was caught exploring the plateau a month ago, and the monks caught me, brought me here."

"You know Kantru?" Roktan asked.

"I know of him. He interrogated me when I got here. But I don't know much about him."

"We have a short time to get out of here, or else we'll be cooked up for his next monster," Dalwen said. "Melvin, can you release our shackles, and unlock the door?"

"Perhaps…" he said, somewhat distantly. "Wait a minute."

"What is it?" asked Dalwen.

"You must test this man, first," Melvin said. "See if he is telling us the truth."

"He is a prisoner just like we are—"

"Then it won't hurt to check. Just check that he is telling the truth," Melvin said.

Dalwen looked angry at first, as if she could not believe her ears. She held her wounded hands to her chest as she tried to find words.

Nergal remembered that Kantru said Dalwen would not be able to do any magic with her little fingers removed. What was Melvin thinking?

"We have another way to check," Melvin quickly clarified. "Another way to find out who's our enemy. Or at least, an enemy of Nergal." Melvin took up Nergal's hand and held it up for the others to see. The ring was still on his finger.

"Oh," Dalwen said, relief in her voice. She gave a weak smile, and nodded. "That is a good idea. Bahar, we must test your story."

Bahar burst into motion, clubbing Roktan across the jaw with his fist. In the same smooth motion he spun and his leg arced up to whip across Dalwen's face in a spinning kick. Melvin grappled with the stranger, trying to bring him under control.

Nergal jumped the man from behind, wrapping his arm around Bahar's neck. Then he savagely pried the man away from Melvin. It seemed that he underestimated his own strength, as there was a muted snap and crack that he felt through his arms.

The man fell away, dead. Everyone stood and regarded him while they caught their breath. Blood ran down Dalwen's chin and she looked truly miserable. Nergal found that he did not regret killing this man.

"How did you know?" Dalwen asked Melvin.

"He had only the beginnings of a beard, and he looked muscular and fit. If he had been a prisoner for a month he would have a long beard. He would be suffering from near-starvation. Besides, his accent was fake," Melvin said. Now the knight seemed to regard the body for a moment, and then he became quite excited.

"Nergal!" exclaimed Melvin. "This man was an enemy to us, the blood will stick on you. Rub it all over you! Quickly, in case the guards come by and see that the spy is dead!"

"Yes, that's true!" said Dalwen. "When Kantru finds out that his man has been killed, the guards might come to get us."

Nergal nodded, and twisted the man's head completely off. Dalwen made a noise and turned away, faltering slightly. Melvin caught her and took her over to the corner, averting his own eyes as well. Nergal splattered the warm blood onto his skin, spreading it around. Roktan ignored the gore and helped the half-orc cover himself.

When they were done, Melvin came back and looked over their gruesome handiwork. He scraped at the blood on Nergal's shoulder and saw that even though it had dried, it would not flake off.

"Good! I'll unlock the door."

Roktan held his criticism this time, perhaps aware of the magnitude of their peril. Melvin walked up to the barred door and stood before its iron lock.

He whispered a few words and motioned with his hand.

The lock immediately cycled, and the door opened.

"Melvin! That was fantastic!" Dalwen said. "Now our shackles!"

Melvin walked around Dalwen, ignoring her outstretched arms. "Nergal first," he said.

"Quit treating me like I'm fragile!" she told him.

"It just makes more sense to free Nergal first," Melvin said. "I treat you just like the others."

"That's not what you said when you thought I was going to be sacrificed," Dalwen said. Melvin simply shrugged.

"Although I do appreciate that," Dalwen added, and smiled. She put her hand on Melvin's shoulder, and said more quietly, "And I feel the same way about you."

Nergal ruined the moment. "What you saying?" he demanded loudly. "We have plan now?"

Dalwen and Melvin laughed. Then Melvin coughed. Nergal noticed that the knight had dark circles under his eyes, besides the many bruises that he had taken in the fight.

"No, same plan Nergal," Melvin told him.

Melvin muttered over Nergal's hand shackles. Nothing happened. Melvin tried three more times, finally coaxing the lock to release the half-orc's hands.

Melvin faltered. "It's making me dizzy," he said.

"Be steady," Dalwen told him. "You have already taken quite a beating. The magic will drain you further, even a minor one such as this."

"It's no minor magic to me," Roktan said, shuffling impatiently.

"I didn't mean it that way," Dalwen said.

Melvin began to work on the shackles binding Nergal's feet. He tried several times, waited a minute and tried again.

The center lock opened, and Nergal's feet were freed. Melvin fell forward, unconscious.

"Mel-veen?"

"He has overtaxed himself," Dalwen said. "The fight, the stress, now the magic, is too much. He needs to rest."

"He can't rest, we're all going to die soon! Kantru could be ready in hours or days. We have no idea."

"I kill Kantru," Nergal said. "You wait here."

"I'm not sure…" Roktan started, but he was talking to air. Nergal had turned and tromped out of the prison, towards the exit corridor. Dalwen moved after him, dragging her foot chains.

"Remember, Nergal. If I don't make it, the word is Ternakridon," Dalwen called after him.

Nergal turned to face her. "Terna—" Nergal started.

Dalwen slapped her hand over Nergal's mouth. "You mustn't say it now! It will cause the blood to come off. Just remember, Ternakridon."

"Dalwen must live. Must remind Nergal," Nergal said, and slapped her on the back. Dalwen stumbled forward and coughed from the force of the blow, but she smiled.

"Very well, I'll survive for you," she said.

"Good. Nergal be coming back," he said.

Nergal moved back through the corridor. It darkened in the middle, and then more illuminating spheres lit the way up ahead. The corridor came to a chamber, and there were figures inside. Nergal approached until he could see four guards in full armor, standing rock still in the room. His pace slowed as he considered this obstacle.

Only now, Nergal realized that these guards were not like the monks. They were the hollow suits of armor that fought as if occupied, the automatons that Kantru created to trap them at his last stronghold. Nergal remembered the painful shocks that touching them had caused, but he felt the blood armor encasing him. It might provide some protection.

Nergal strode into the room, and immediately grabbed the nearest guard's weapon, a long pole arm with metal spikes and axe blades on each end.

This sudden assault spurred the supernatural guards into action. The one whose weapon he had grabbed fought him briefly until the half-orc twisted savagely and freed the weapon with such force that one of the gauntlets of the armor flew off, revealing that the armor was indeed hollow as he had guessed.

Nergal had no time to celebrate this victory, as armored hands grasped him from behind, sending a shower of sparks flying. The shock was muted, the blood covering absorbing most of the energy. But the hands pulled him back off balance and Nergal found himself hurtling towards the floor. He landed hard on his back and another pole arm slammed down into his stomach.

The blood armor protected him from the worst of this otherwise fatal blow, but he noted that although the blood could not be cut through, the force of the blow still bruised him through the covering. The blow enraged him, and he struck back, swinging his own pole arm up at the helmet of the automaton standing above him. The armor blocked his attack with its arm, causing a clamor and sending the arm flying away across the room.

Nergal rolled away and regained his feet. He saw a huge object approach and then realized it was the flat of an axe blade smashing into his face. He fell back against the wall, stunned for a moment until other blows began to rain down on him. All four of his opponents were trying to engage him although there wasn't enough room for all of them to attack at once.

Now the adrenaline poured through his system and Nergal forgot himself. No longer thinking, he acted on pure instinct, swiping at the first guard's waist with a powerful sweep of the pole arm. He struck with enough force to split the automaton in half, sending its pieces raining to the floor. He ignored a hard fist slammed into the side of his head, then impaled a helmet on the end spike of his weapon, shoving it like a spear. The helmet stayed on the end of the pole arm so Nergal swung it like a long mace, hitting another suit of armor in the side and smashing an arm off.

Now there was only one opponent more or less undamaged, and Nergal tossed aside the pole arm and grappled with this guard. Its weapon struck him in the side, but Nergal shrugged this blow off and grabbed the armor by both arms. He realized for the first time that this armor was taller than the others, and he found himself staring directly into the dark visor. A set of beady red orbs glared back at him. For some reason this caused a stark fear to grab at his heart. Nergal channeled his fear into strength, and with a startled snarl he ripped both arms off his enemy, then stepped back, uncertain.

The suit was hollow like the others. It staggered briefly, then Nergal snatched up another pole arm and finished the crippled suits off, smashing their components apart until all movement stopped.

Then Nergal stood catching his breath, shaking at the unpleasant revelation that the automatons had scary red eyes. He had thought that there was no sign of anything inside of them, and the discovery had shaken him somewhat. Nevertheless, these things were dead and he convinced himself that he had nothing to fear.

Nergal held up an empty gauntlet from the largest suit, marveling at the armor that moved as if someone were inside when it was hollow. Powerful magic, indeed. The half-orc idly put his hand into the gauntlet, and saw that it just fit. The suit must have been made for a large warrior.

Nergal's eyebrows lifted, and he muttered under his breath. He began to separate out the armor from the larger suit. Donning the leggings, he started to put the armor on. The leggings and arm pieces were easy enough, as would be the helmet, but the thick breastplate and shoulder guards were not only heavy, but also too complicated for him to don himself. He put the breastplate on but he could not secure it. The leather straps that held the pieces in place required another person to help fasten.

Nergal grabbed all the pieces he had yet to wear, and walked back towards the prison where his friends were waiting.

When he returned, he saw that Melvin was still lying prone, Dalwen watching over him. Roktan came up to meet him.

"Nergal! What is going on? Why are you wearing that?"

"Mel-veen okay?" he asked.

"He is still resting. What's going on?"

"Help Nergal put armor on," he said, turning his back to reveal the straps that he could not fasten.

"What for? It will just slow you down," Roktan complained. "You already have the blood armor, doesn't it work?"

"Put on, put on," the half-orc repeated urgently. Then he lowered his voice, as if sharing the darkest conspiracy, "Kantru no be knowing, it Nergal inside."

Roktan stared, and then laughed. "Yes, yes that's good. Take him by surprise." They struggled to fasten his armor with their shackled wrists. They tightened the leather straps that Nergal could not reach, and a few hurried minutes later, Nergal was concealed by the enclosing plates of armor.

"Good. I go now," he said, and turned away.

"Nergal! Walk like they do," Roktan urged.

Nergal realized that his stride was different than the automatons that he had seen. He shortened his stride, slowing down, moving in a stiff, unnatural way.

"Good luck!" called Dalwen.

CHAPTER 36

The Blood of Enemies

Nergal's armor clanked steadily as he shambled back down the corridor and past the scene of his recent battle. He continued on to a split in the tunnel lit by an orb. He didn't remember this split from when he had been dragged away from the room where Dalwen had been mutilated so he simply decided to go left and see where it led.

Slowly the corridor widened and Nergal could see through the visor that he was coming up to a large, high-ceilinged chamber.

The first thing that caught his attention was the huge statue at the far end, straddling an arched exit. It stood three or four times as tall as a man, a giant heavily muscled demon with insectoid eyes and curved horns. Sharp teeth filled its mouth, split in a wicked smile.

There were long narrow fountains along the walls to the left and right, and a dais in the center. Elegant candelabra held maroon candles and Nergal could see a dazzling array of images carved on the walls. He hesitated, seeing that there were robed men in the great chamber. He solidified his resolve and continued, moving stiffly.

They never know it being Nergal inside, he assured himself.

He marched steadily forward, moving through the chamber by the most direct route he could discern. He veered right around the dais in the center, ignoring two monks that were working over some powders and bronze goblets stacked on it. Nergal looked away and concentrated his attention forward as he shambled past.

"Kor-hal! Yalla berratz!" one of the monks barked.

Nergal outwardly ignored the interruption, but his heart began to pound in his chest. He had to check his breathing and continue. He wasn't even sure if the utterance had been directed at him, but he feared it had been.

"Yalla berratz!" the same voice commanded, and Nergal heard feet padding behind him.

Then another voice, "Harna, ketz. Eel varna kuol suffernachi."

This second voice was calm and soothing. Nergal had made his way around the altar by now, and straightened out, heading for the arched exit he had selected as his goal when he entered. He spotted another robed man who was squatting before the redly glowing statue at the end. He watched Nergal for a moment, then he turned and resumed his mantra.

Nergal exited the temple without any further interruptions. He was sweating profusely inside the armor. Now he took deep breaths and tried to calm down. He still didn't understand what the words had been about but somehow his disguise had held.

"I have the smarts," Nergal insisted to himself.

He continued slowly, grumbling in impatience, until he reached the next area. This time he came to a much humbler room, with low ceilings of rock and several spheres emitting light attached to the walls. Tables filled the room, and a set of stone vats were lined against a long wall. All manner of odd devices were strewn about, inexplicable metal tools, weirdly shaped pots with several openings, and containers of every imaginable shape and size.

In the center of the room, working feverishly, was the sorcerer Kantru.

Nergal was so surprised to find his prey so soon that he almost stumbled. Somehow he continued on, moving closer to the monk step by step. Kantru ignored him as he approached, completely absorbed with the tools before him. Nergal walked within striking distance, gripping the haft of his pole arm tightly in anticipation.

Kantru hardly looked up from his work. "Kual naterru anara hesee," he said in the tone of an order.

Nergal didn't understand the words. He stood rock still.

Irritation entered Kantru's voice. "Kual naterru—"

Kantru's snarl was cut short as Nergal's weapon swiped out at the monk-mage. The monk was quick, and he managed to start moving just as the end of the pole arm closed on his head. The metal grazed his jaw instead of smashing his head wide open. Nergal heard the crack of bone and Kantru fell back.

Murderous rage flared in Kantru's eyes as the mage rolled away and regained his feet. Blood poured out of his mouth, and Nergal could see that the mage's jaw was broken.

Kantru struggled to utter words to invoke his magic, but they were slurred and muted. More blood poured from the wizard-monk's mouth. He seemed to abandon the attempt, and his features set in concentration as he faced the half-orc. A curved sword had found its way into the wizard-monk's hand, and he stood on guard.

Too late, Nergal realized that the monk was playing for time. He felt something scrabbling at his leg, and he shook the limb in irritation. The squeal of the small green bat-like creature came from somewhere around his feet, but Nergal kept Kantru in the sight zone through his visor. The creature had probably tried to bite his leg but had been foiled by the blood armor.

The blood armor. Nergal had forgotten. He realized that he was over-armored and swept his helmet off and hurled it at Kantru, who dodged aside.

Then Nergal swept his pole arm at the monk's feet. Kantru leaped into the air, slicing his sword down on Nergal's head at the same moment. The blade glanced off the dried blood in Nergal's hair, having no effect on the half-orc. Nergal swiped the weapon back the other way, surprising Kantru with his counter after what should have been a fatal blow. He knocked the monk back against a table.

Then Nergal thrust the sharp end of his weapon, trying to impale Kantru. The monk dodged to the side, falling onto the ground and rolling under a table.

As Nergal threw the table aside, the warrior monk scrambled clumsily to his feet and ran away, rebounding off a nearby wall and darting around a corner. Nergal started to give chase, but he quickly realized that pursuit in the heavy armor was next to impossible. Kantru, even in his weakened state, could run much faster in his light robe. The odd little creature had disappeared again, perhaps hiding under a nearby table or clinging to a corner of the ceiling. Nergal paid it no heed, content to concentrate only on Kantru.

Nergal slipped the forearm pieces and elbow guards off his arms. Then he unstrapped his footgear and greaves. He ran to the corner of the room, trying out his new weight. It was still too heavy. He risked long seconds to take off the rest of the heavy armor. He had to drop to the floor to work his way out of the heavy breastplate, and finally he was free of it.

Kantru way ahead, he thought to himself. *Where he go?*

He noticed something on a table at the far side of the room. He moved quickly over to a table by the wall. All of the adventurer's weapons were arrayed here sitting out in plain view. His hands played over Melvin's great longsword, the Shakkran, his own maces, and Rovul's axes.

Now a terrible uncertainty came over Nergal. Should he take these items back to the others and see if they could be freed? Or quickly pursue Kantru and try to kill him now that he was wounded?

Nergal decided that he could waste no more time. He snatched up his maces, placing them into his belt, and then took Melvin's longsword in his hands. Then he ran out the exit that Kantru had used, hoping that he hadn't already lost the mage.

He came to a split in the corridor and hesitated. Which way should he go? Nergal examined both corridors for a second, and then spotted some blood on the floor, heading off to his right. He ran off down the right corridor, seeing more blood straight ahead. As he passed the last drops of blood, the floor gave out from underneath him and he fell.

There was a moment of blackness and falling, then something struck Nergal in the back. He bounced off it painfully, tossing to his side and something struck his head and his arm. Then finally he settled between some kind of cold metal bars on an ancient stone floor. It was utterly dark.

Nergal snarled in frustration. Kantru had the quick smarts, to fool Nergal like that. He had led Nergal right into the pit with his own blood!

He felt around in the darkness, feeling several long metal spikes arrayed on the floor of the pit, augmented by many smaller spikes between them. Nergal felt a painful bruising on his back where he had struck one of the larger spikes. Only the magical blood armor had prevented fatal injury.

Nergal felt the walls. They seemed to be very old, some kind of ancient masonry in disrepair. Nergal found a spot where the brick had chipped away, and he tried to put his foot in the depression and claw his way up the wall. He managed to take one step up, but his hold on the wall was precarious. He didn't feel that he could make it any further up the wall.

Nergal stepped back down, feeling despair start to envelop him. He stumbled against a small spike on the floor, and leaned against a larger spike to steady himself in the darkness. The tall spike gave way ever so slightly, rocking in its setting in the stone floor.

Nergal smiled in the darkness.

"I have the smarts," he reveled, overcome by the brilliance of his idea.

Nergal carefully set Melvin's sword on the ground. Then he grabbed the spike and began to push it back and forth, grinding away at its emplacement. Less than a minute later he had freed the spike from the floor. Taking out one of his maces, he began to drive the spike into a crack in the masonry, wedging it deep into the wall so that it formed the first step of his makeshift ladder.

The half-orc continued by feel in the darkness, freeing the large spikes and driving them into the wall until he had access to the roof of the pit. Then he grabbed Melvin's sword from the floor and began to attack the wooden cover of the pit. It was hard going, and Nergal was getting hot inside his blood covering. He ignored the heat and smashed the obdurate pit cover into shattered pieces of old wood. He scrabbled through his opening and found himself standing back in the corridor.

His sense of achievement was only somewhat dampened by the knowledge that Kantru now had more of a head start. He decided to continue down this corridor looking for the wizard, even though it wasn't at all clear which way he had gone anymore.

Nergal resumed the search in the direction he had been going when he fell into the pit. He moved more carefully this time, afraid that he might encounter another trap of some kind. He made his way up a small group of stairs and came to a stout wooden door at the end of the corridor.

Nergal slowed down to a creep as he approached the door, listening intently. He couldn't hear anything on the other side. Bracing himself, he pulled it open by the handle and looked inside.

Light filtered to him through high rows of books placed in solid wooden cases arrayed through the chamber. Even the outer walls were filled with tomes, placed on shelves carved into the stone. Stone gargoyles sprouted from the corners and the ends of the cases, leering down at him.

Nergal hesitantly stepped into the room. The door shut behind him, and the half-orc stood for a moment, trying to sense any other presence in the library. He had just about decided that it was empty when he heard a noise, the scratch of claws on wood or leather, coming from a large bookcase to his left. He looked just as the scaly creature attacked him again, flying through the air to rake its claws across his face.

Nergal swiped at the thing with his free hand, but it had already retreated by bounding off his head and alighting upon the top of another bookcase to the right.

Nergal slashed the longsword down on the creature's position atop the adjacent bookcase. He struck the wood, the small monster having darted away at the last instant. Now it was out of sight.

Pacing slowly forward, Nergal began to stalk the tiny thing. He hadn't taken ten paces before he felt the thing alight upon his back. If it bit him, the blood protected him, as there was no pain. Nergal reached over his shoulder to dislodge the creature. It jumped down and scampered around him. Nergal followed it with his eyes. It rapidly climbed a nearby shelf and regarded him, as if consternated at his universal protection.

Nergal slowly brought his sword back, as if to strike downwards and cleave the creature in half. His sword came down, and the creature darted out of the way, skipping slightly to the left.

This time Nergal expected the move. His other hand had thrust out at the same moment beside his weapon, and snatched up the foul creature by one of its legs. Without hesitation Nergal whipped the small beast around in an arc and smashed its head against the wall. Blood and brains splattered out, and the thing gave one last awful shriek.

"Like fixing frog," Nergal growled. "Smash head in, den you eat." Nergal looked at the lean scaly creature, leaking gore from its rent head and shrugged. "Maybe skip eat dis time."

Realizing that he had been distracted from his purpose, Nergal saw that there was another exit to the room, also blocked by a wooden door. He kicked the small creature's corpse aside and headed for this egress.

The exit was more of a tunnel than a worked corridor. He moved along a packed earth floor until he saw bright light ahead. There were green plants growing near the end.

Then he realized that he was coming back to the garden again. Nergal slowed, fearful of the monster that had knocked him out earlier. He still wasn't sure that Kantru had even gone this way. It made sense, though, that the wounded monk would run and hide behind his monster. Nergal considered his blood coating and the longsword in his hand. He decided that he could defeat the thing given another chance.

He moved out into the huge chamber and down a path in the vegetation. He couldn't tell which direction he was going, but he remembered that all of the paths led to the center where the battle had occurred.

Sure enough, when the center clearing became visible, Nergal spotted the monster, waiting patiently on the dark stone dais. Nergal tried to tell which way it was looking, but the pentagonal monster had eyes facing each direction.

Nergal thought that some of the eyes might be hurt, but he couldn't tell from where he was.

He thought about moving around it by moving through the garden, but as soon as he took a step to the side he knew it was no use. An elf might be able to make it through the dense foliage without making noise, but Nergal couldn't. It would hear him and then he would have to fight in the dense undergrowth. He stepped back out onto the path.

Nergal hesitated, fighting a deep sense of fear at facing the monster again. Then he saw that it had not come through the last battle unscathed. Two of its tentacles were chopped off to varying lengths, and it walked with a severe limp, having lost one of its legs and damaged another.

He broke into a light run, charging towards the monster with Melvin's unnaturally light sword ready. The monster saw him as he approached within ten paces, and its tentacles whipped into motion, agitated by his sudden appearance.

Nergal targeted the nearest leg and prepared a sweeping slash to lop it completely off. But as he got within range, the leg shot out towards him, trying to impale him on its sharp end. Nergal grunted as the leg hit him in the side, causing him to spin. He went with it, slashing the sword around as he faltered, and managed to drive the edge of his weapon halfway through the leg. He fully expected to fall after that, but a tentacle looped down from above and encircled his chest.

The limb may have prevented his fall, but now it began to squeeze him, pinning his arms oddly so he couldn't make good use of his weapon. Yet another tentacle appeared to wrap itself around Nergal's left arm and throat. He now staggered, barely in control of his own body. He fought to get Melvin's sword into a striking position but it was no use.

Suddenly there was a smacking sound and screams erupted from the mouths of the creature bearing down upon him. Roktan appeared standing on the top of the monster. He wore a breastplate Nergal didn't recognize and held the Shakkran in one hand. He struck downwards with the Shakkran, severing the first tentacle that held Nergal's arms.

"Fight it Nergal! Kill it!" Roktan yelled, then hacked off one of the eyestalks of the monster. Nergal's arm overcame the severed tentacle and hacked at the other one entangling his legs. But the tentacles holding him had already retracted to counter the more immediate threat of Roktan.

Nergal swung Melvin's sword way back to chop off another of its legs. Then, as he stood gasping for breath and targeting the leg, he saw a vulnerability.

There was a soft flap of skin behind the leg that allowed it to flex that was not itself part of the shell. Nergal reversed the weapon and dived in point-first, driving the entire length of the sword deep into the monster's innards.

This time when the thing collapsed Nergal stepped out from underneath it. He continued fighting, thinking that it was trying to smash him again, and chopped off another leg with a huge overhead strike. Then he stepped back to find another target, and saw that the thing was dying. The Shakkran stood upright on its back, having penetrated the base of one of its eyestalks. Nergal couldn't see his friend. He walked around the thing so he could see past the bony crest of its back, trying to find Roktan.

Then he found him. Roktan was half consumed by one of the mouths of the dead creature. The warrior's face was the worst, still constricted into an awful grimace of death.

A sick feeling filled Nergal, settling in his gut like a block of masonry. Roktan had died saving him. It was because of Nergal's inability to destroy the monster that Roktan had come to this fate.

There was nothing Nergal could do. He staggered under an intense sorrow for a moment, then he realized that there was something.

He could kill Kantru for him.

No sooner had Nergal thought of the monk-mage than he heard footsteps. Looking sharply to his right, he saw a black-robed figure scrabbling away down one of the paths. Nergal instinctively bolted after the fleeing figure. Was it Kantru?

There was a single door at the end of the path. It had not been closed. Nergal carefully walked up to it, ready for a sneak attack. He stepped through the doorway and saw Kantru waiting for him.

The monk stood calmly in the center of a round chamber with a smooth stone floor. He now held a sword before him, a long slender single-sided sword like those Nergal saw displayed on the wall. A single table holding scrolls and an inkpot stood by the entrance. There were no other exits.

Watching Kantru carefully, Nergal closed the door. He toppled the table and flung it on its side against the exit.

"Only one of us get out," he growled.

Kantru looked as if he were trying to sneer but his ruined jaw hampered even this simple expression of malice. He whipped the sword around before him impressively, making it twist in intricate circles before him faster than the eye could see.

Nergal smiled. "Dat no hurt me," he said simply, and attacked. Kantru deftly deflected the thrust and countered straight into Nergal's chest, but the sword tip, no doubt very sharp, simply bounced off the half-orc's blood covered muscles as if it were the frond of a fern.

Nergal kicked out and struck Kantru's leg, forcing the monk back slightly but failing to damage him. Kantru's sword came in, slashing down towards Nergal's sword arm. Nergal blocked the strike with Melvin's weapon. The longsword felt light and agile in Nergal's hand, its magic augmenting his skill and speed. Nergal thrust at Kantru's midsection but the monk danced aside.

Kantru backed up against the wall and waited. Nergal hesitated, uncertain what this new game was. Then Kantru stepped back out of sight, straight through the wall! Nergal bolted forward, and caught the secret hatch just before it closed. He pushed his way through recklessly, desperate to ensure that Kantru did not evade him again.

He emerged in a smaller chamber. Nergal had time to register a bed, a table, and bookcases full of books and scrolls before he heard the snap of a crossbow and felt a painful wound inflicted in his shoulder. Kantru threw aside the crossbow and looked at the fresh blood coming from the half-orc's left side.

Nergal realized that the bolt had penetrated his defense, and saw the projectile was still half sticking out of his chest. The wound was severe, but it had missed his heart.

Nergal snarled in renewed rage. Oblivious to Kantru's weapon, he swept the table aside with his left arm and started swinging with his right. The warrior monk seemed to sense the change of strategy and took advantage of Nergal's negligent blocking, stabbing at his eyes with the sword. Nergal brought his chin down at the last instant, causing the blow to slide off his forehead.

The half-orc countered with his own weapon, even though he was too close to use the longsword to best effect. Kantru blocked directly, and they stood side by side for a moment, swords braced against each other. Nergal felt Kantru drop slightly and brace his foot behind Nergal's own. The monk was about to throw him.

Nergal clenched his left hand and delivered a punch across Kantru's broken jaw. The monk dropped to his knees, stunned, as a fresh river of blood erupted from his mouth. Then Nergal kicked him over onto the ground and sliced down with his sword, cutting Kantru's chest open. Kantru writhed weakly and died. A river of blood crested the wound and ran down to pool on the ground.

Nergal stood panting over the monk's body. He looked briefly around the small chamber.

"What do now?" he asked himself. Realizing that he still had a bolt stuck in his chest, he grabbed the projectile and yanked it out. He screamed out in pain as he felt the barbs rip his flesh.

"Perhaps that not be so smart," he groaned, looking at the blood pouring out of the gaping wound in his chest. He slapped a hand over it and tried to stop the blood. Then he noticed something about the bolt he had removed.

There was more than blood on it. The tip had been coated in some black substance. It reminded Nergal of the tip of his spear. Poison? He stashed the bolt away and scanned around the room.

He saw a bust in the corner. Swords were crossed on the wall.

He strode over to a cabinet and opened it. There were several vials and flasks of liquid, just what he was looking for. He sniffed each in turn, looking them over. One was full of red liquid, another slightly green, and there were vials of blue and black liquid. Nergal decided the black liquid looked too much like the poison, and so he simply drank all the other liquids one after the other.

"Nergal hope dat is good medicine," he said to himself. He waited for a second, taking stock of his health, but he felt only a pain in his chest where he had been hurt.

Then a strong scent of smoke tickled his nose, and Nergal sneezed. A huge fan of flame erupted from his mouth, roaring and crackling. Nergal stood completely dazed for a moment, and then realized he had ignited some of the scrolls nearby. He slapped at them and knocked some to the floor, stamping on them until the flames were extinguished.

"Very good medicine," he said.

He was tempted to immediately go back to the prison and check on his friends, but then he felt shame that he had allowed Roktan to die. Would they blame him? How could he tell them that Roktan had saved his life, but he had failed to do the same for the Jagartan warrior?

Nergal thought of Dalwen and Melvin. Surely they would forgive him…wouldn't they? He decided he would have to tell them and risk it.

As he was considering this issue, Nergal saw that the wizard's corpse had a necklace of some sort. Nergal searched the body, taking the necklace which held a pendant of some unknown symbol. He also found a large greenish gem that looked valuable.

The inside of Kantru's robe was filled with pockets. Nergal searched further, finding that they were full of all manner of inexplicable things: black pearls, feathers, two small containers of a white and green powder, and other small knickknacks that puzzled Nergal. He decided to only take the necklace and the large gem.

Then he quit dallying and headed back to the prison. On the way through, Nergal picked up their weapons and as much of the armor as he could carry.

When he approached the temple, he realized that he had no disguise this time. Nergal shrugged and just readied Melvin's sword in his right hand and took one of his own maces in his left. He carefully came into the temple, watching for the monks. This time, though, there were no others in the room.

As he came to the dais, he saw a body on the ground. It was a warrior monk, in a black robe, with a ragged hole ripped in the chest. Blood pooled out onto the floor. Nergal felt a sneeze coming on. Wishing to avoid another conflagration, he fought it for a moment to no avail. He sneezed again, sending flames billowing out to a great distance. The smoke lazily wafted up in the large room.

"Oops," he said.

Nergal ran through, looking for other enemies but seeing none. He headed for the prison as quickly as he could, slowing only when turned the corner and entered the holding chamber.

Nergal was relieved to see that Dalwen, Melvin, and Rovul were still alive, gathered just outside the cage.

"Did you find Kantru? Roktan went after you as soon as Melvin found the strength to free another of us."

Nergal hung his head. "Kantru dead. Roktan dead, too."

The others were silent for a moment. Rovul said, "He did not die in vain. Our purposss is accomplished."

Nergal looked away and sneezed. He engulfed the empty cage in bright yellow flames, causing the others great fright.

"What was that?" demanded Melvin and Dalwen simultaneously.

"Is nothing…"

"That's hardly nothing!" Melvin said.

Dalwen put her hand on Nergal's shoulder. "Tell us what happened," she said.

Nergal handed Melvin his sword, and related his story. The others listened without any accusations. When he was done, Melvin also tried to reassure his friend.

"Roktan knew the danger. I know you did your best to save him. But that is the way of these things. You are a hero, Nergal. You and Roktan both."

"We have lost Roktan, but our quest is over," Dalwen said. "Kantru has been stopped. Roktan's people will be proud of the way he died, fighting against Chu Kutall. Now, let me see that bolt that was stuck in you."

Nergal produced the bolt. Dalwen looked it over carefully, examining the black end of the quarrel.

"That isn't poison Nergal, they just do that to keep the head from rusting," she told him.

"Oh," he said. "Well, maybe Nergal should not have taken medicine, then." He accentuated the statement with a mighty sneeze, shooting flame out and causing the others to duck in fear.

"Maybe it will wear off," Melvin said.

Nergal nodded and moved over to rest, sitting with his back against the wall. Melvin managed to use his spell to release a heavy iron manacle from Rovul's neck, freeing the snake-prince. All three of the ex-prisoners worked to sort their gear and put on their armor.

Nergal sat and thought about Roktan and Kantru. He didn't know how to feel about the death of his enemy. Had it been worth the life of his friend?

Dalwen noticed Nergal's thoughtful mood.

"You are staring off to someplace else, Nergal."

"Eh?"

"What are you thinking about?"

"Kantru."

"How did it feel, to vanquish him at last?" she asked.

"Should feel good. But felt…like empty," Nergal said.

"Why should you feel good?" Dalwen asked gently.

"Kantru my enemy, kill enemy should feel good."

"You just killed a man. It was necessary but there was no pleasure in it. That is good that you only felt empty, it shows that you are a good being, deserving of the favor of Alofzin," Dalwen told him.

"Maybe," Nergal admitted. "Or maybe Nergal just hungry."

978-0-595-37854-8
0-595-37854-4